**Raves f**

"As a reviewer who is accustomed to reading t[...]ld, and commercialized offerings, it always come[...]azing and sweet delight to run across a new author who can knock these bad boys/girls off the shelves. Dewey does this and more . . . (She) offers up a tale of a connection between woman and child that will break your heart, a mystery that will challenge your intellect, and the promise of redemption that will remind you to hope. A beautiful and deeply satisfying novel . . ."

—*New Mystery Reader Magazine*

"Hang on for a fast-paced thriller that will grip you first page to last! *Protector* is an extremely fast-paced, page-turning, jaw-clenching story. The reader is pulled into living the story with the characters. If you like suspenseful thrillers, you will love this one."

—*Fresh Fiction*

"Laurel Dewey makes an impressive debut with *Protector,* a gripping thriller that goes far beyond the requirements of the suspense/crime genre to provide penetrating psychological insight into the human condition. She combines her riveting tale with emotionally probing psychological analysis that resonates in the reader long after the case is solved. Dewey's heroine, Detective Jane Perry, is as real as a fictional character can get. Action filled, spellbinding and even spine-tingling, the plot will seize and hold the attention of any thrill seeker."

—Janet Hamilton, *Myshelf.com*

# Protector

## Laurel Dewey

THE
STORY PLANT

The Story Plant
The Aronica-Miller Publishing Project, LLC
P.O. Box 4331
Stamford, CT 06907

Cover and Interior design by Barbara Aronica Buck

ISBN-13: 978-0-9816087-4-7
ISBN-10: 0-9816087-4-4

Visit our website at www.thestoryplant.com

First Story Plant Printing: February 2010

Printed in the United States of America

First Edition
10 9 8 7 6 5 4 3 2 1

To my parents, who encouraged me
to pursue a writing career . . .
To Granny, who continues to provide me
with support, guidance & love . . .
And to David—my best friend, lover & husband . . .
With you, I am calm. With you, I am home.
*With you, I am finally free.*

# Acknowledgments

My gratitude goes out to the many patrol officers, Sergeants and Sheriff's Homicide Detectives throughout Colorado who helped with the research and development of the story. A special thanks to Lieutenant Wayne Weyler of the Mesa County Sheriff's Department in Grand Junction, Colorado.

Kudos to Carol Craven for the photo.

Thanks to Peter Miller for believing in this book,

Many thanks to Lou Aronica for his insight and unwavering support throughout this project.

We cannot live only for ourselves.
A thousand fibers connect us with our
fellow men; and among those fibers,
as sympathetic threads,
our actions run as causes,
and they come back to us as effects.

—Herman Melville

# Chapter 1

The stars were not particularly bright on that May evening. Emily Lawrence craned her neck as she looked outside her open upstairs bedroom window, hoping she could see a pinpoint glimmer of Pluto in the stark night sky. Unfortunately, the large sycamore tree just outside the window prevented a clear view. Discouraged, she pulled herself back into the house and slid down onto the ever-so-pink carpeting that almost matched her night-gown.

Emily took another look at the star chart that plotted the constellations and diagramed the location of her favorite stellar objects. Satisfied, she flicked off the bedroom light and clicked on the overhead Starlight Starbright projector she received on her ninth birthday, six months before. It was the only gift she wanted and once it was hers, it became her constant companion. She would lie on her bed at night after the house was quiet, her shoulder-length brown hair curled around her pillow, and stare in wonder at the myriad twinkling stars and constellations that projected across her bedroom ceiling and walls. By turning one knob, the constellations slowly moved clockwise around the room, melting into the carpeting and resurfacing on the opposite wall. With the turn of another knob, the room filled with the hushed sounds of soft wind and the distant euphony of Puccini's "Nessun Dorma." She stared transfixed by this celestial ballet, engulfed in its embrace, and felt safe.

Outside, a sothing whisper of wind rustled the sycamore leaves. Emily felt herself drifting off to sleep when she was jolted awake by the sound of her mother's angry voice downstairs. Her body tightened as she tried to ignore the escalating volume. Her parents' arguments had grown in intensity over the past few weeks. What began as a disagreement in the kitchen would spread into the living room and then the hallway where the nearby staircase led a straight path to Emily's bedroom door. The only respite Emily had from her parents' constant discord was a peaceful nine-day camping trip in Moab, Utah with her mother. They'd returned the night before, but it didn't take long for her parents to resume their loud disputes. However, on this night, the combative sounds from downstairs were the worst ever. The anger in her mother's voice was now etched with fear. Emily resisted, then gave in and walked toward her bedroom door. She turned the knob, inching the door open.

The upstairs hallway was dark, as was the downstairs entry hall near the front door. Emily and her mother's sleeping bags from their camping trip were still stacked at the bottom of the stairs. The child peeked through the opening of her bedroom door and watched as her mother, Patricia, paced back and forth. Out of Emily's view, her father, David, sat on the living room couch, his hand cupped tightly against his forehead. His terrified eyes focused intently on the circular patterns of the living room carpeting. Patricia clutched a sheet of notepaper. She looked at it, silently read it and then flared into another tirade.

"Exactly *when* were you going to tell me about this, David?" Patricia Lawrence screamed at her husband, jerking the paper toward him.

"I . . . I didn't know how to tell you," David responded, his voice shaking.

"Look at me!" She moved her slender body close to David.

David buried his face in both hands. "I'm sorry," he uttered.

"The hell you're sorry!" Patricia yelled. "How could you keep this letter from me? Goddamnit, didn't you think I would eventually find out? All those nights . . . all those goddamn nights of you calling me and telling me you had to work late . . ."

"I was working," David weakly interjected.

"I don't think they call it 'work' after the second or third cocktail!"

David pulled his hands from his flushed face. "Patty, please! We've got to talk about this rationally."

"Rationally? Oh, that's rich! Suddenly you want to be *rational*? Why wasn't that thought going through your head when the relationship became clear? Why didn't you just walk away?"

"I don't know—"

"*You don't know?*" Patricia's voice was quickly becoming hysterical. "You know what your problem is? *You're weak!* Ever since you were young, you always wanted to play with the big boys, but you *never* fit in."

"No. That's not true," David responded unconvincingly.

"It *is* true! You fantasized about what it would feel like to be accepted by people who lived on the edge. You got off on that fantasy. And then, that fantasy became real."

David covered his face again. "Maybe. Maybe I did."

"Well, you picked a helluva time to live out your fantasy!" Patricia lunged toward her husband, leaned down and forcefully pulled his hands away from his face. "*When the connection was made,*" she continued with a slow, angry cadence, "between the two of you and they saw the kind of close relationship you had, did you ever *once* consider the implications of what could happen? How it would affect us? Or Emily?" At the sound of her name, Emily crawled onto the stairway landing, staying in the darkness so her parents could not see her. Patricia spoke quietly, but there was a penetrating punctuation to each syllable. "*The minute you found out what was going on, you should have walked away.*"

"I know . . ." David replied in a weak voice. "But, I couldn't."

"Jesus!" Patricia pulled away from her husband. "How fucked up were you?"

"Oh, shit, Patty!" David's voice raised several octaves as he nervously got up and walked across the room. "I may have been a little drunk, but I wasn't fucked up!" David brushed back his thick brown hair with his hand. It was then that he realized his hand was shaking. His eyes fell to the floor and he spoke in a hushed voice, holding back tears. "Things were said and the more we talked, the more the trust began to build between the two of us. And then . . . I just wanted to help."

"David, how could you throw everything away that you know is right and true and decent for a relationship that could destroy us?"

"I would never consciously do anything to hurt you or Emily!"

"You don't think you hurt us when drink a fifth and have to stay in bed all day because you can't cope? Because you can't be the man you're supposed to be?"

"That's a low blow, Patty."

"No, David. That's the truth," Patricia said tersely.

David searched for the right words. "We're going to be okay—"

"*Are you crazy?*" Patricia exploded. "Didn't you read this?" She shoved the letter in David's face.

David slid away toward the staircase. "I don't want to read it again!"

"No, you don't want to see what you've done to us! Let's pretend it doesn't exist and maybe it'll go away! Well, *this* is not going to go away! But *I* am and I'm taking Emily with me!"

Emily's throat tightened. She watched her mother

angrily shove the letter into an open wooden slot that protruded from the rear of the hallway desk. Patricia slammed the slot shut, leaving a slim corner of the notepaper exposed.

"Oh, Jesus, Patty," David begged. "Don't do this."

"No more, David! Emily and I should have never come back from Moab! I should have kept driving and put as much distance between us as possible! I will not put my daughter through hell because you wanted your fifteen minutes of fame! I'm packing our bags and taking Emily to my sister in Cheyenne."

"You can't take her away from me! She's my daughter, too! I love her!"

"Maybe you should have thought about that months ago."

"For God's sake—" David stopped in his tracks as he looked up the staircase and saw Emily hiding in the shadows. "Oh, God, sweetheart. Go back to bed."

Emily stepped from the shadows. "Why are we going away again, Mommy?"

Patricia moved toward the staircase. "Emily, go back to your bedroom." Her tone was precise and laced with agitation. "I'll be up to talk to you."

Emily started to turn when she stopped and looked down at her parents. "I love you, Mommy."

"I love you, too. Go on!" Patricia said.

Emily looked at her father's eyes; they were sad and pitiful. It was the same look she saw when he drank himself into a stupor and stared into nothingness. A sense of helplessness welled up inside the child. "I love you, Daddy," she whispered.

David put his fingers to his lips, kissed them and blew the kiss toward Emily. "I love you too, sweet pea."

Emily paused, freezing the moment in her memory, then walked back into her bedroom, closing the door behind her. The sound of her parents' voices were muffled, but still peppered with rage. Her head was filled with the dreaded thought of leaving the only home she had ever known. She nervously paced around her room as the Starlight Starbright projector light cast celestial shapes across her face and body. Emily wanted desperately to feel safe from the world and all the awful possibilities. She quickly grabbed the projector along with the navy blue vinyl carrying case and toted it into her tiny bedroom closet. Closing the door, she situated herself on the floor of the closet, partially covered by the hanging clothes. She tried to get comfortable, and then remembered the mass of oversized pillows on her bed. Wriggling out from under the clothing, she opened the door and made her way in the semi-darkness. Emily dragged two large pillows off the bed and started back when she heard the front 10:00 p.m. in bright red neon. Pressing her ear to her bedroom door, she heard the sound of another male voice—a voice she didn't recognize.

Although she couldn't make out any specific words, the tone sounded like a friendly conversation between her mother and father and the unknown voice. Emily thought she heard the word "accident," coming from the mysterious guest. She hadn't heard any crash of metal echoing from Franklin Street. But then again, her parents' fervent voices could have drowned out the collision.

For a brief second, she wondered if it was A.J.'s dad. Ten long days ago, A.J. had suddenly moved away with her parents with no warning. The only explanation her mother offered was that A.J.'s father got a job offer in California and had to leave quickly or he would lose the opportunity. As her mother told her this story, Emily could tell it was a lie and wondered to herself why A.J. didn't want to be her friend anymore. It seemed odd to her; less than one month before, the two families enjoyed a Sunday picnic in Washington Park. One of the photos from that day of Emily and her parents was proudly propped up against her clock. It was a beaming portrait of family bliss that belied the truth.

The conversation downstairs sputtered out as Emily

plotted the sound of single footsteps walking across the living room floor, heading toward the kitchen. She heard the kitchen door close—a familiar reverberation that always echoed up into her bedroom. She waited, hugging the two large pillows close to her chest. Less than a minute later, Emily heard the sound of the kitchen door opening and an abrupt raised pitch of voices. If that was A.J.'s father, he suddenly didn't sound very happy. Emily pulled away from the door. She figured that whatever was happening downstairs was better left to her parents and that her mother would tell her a dressed up version of the truth the next morning.

She plopped the oversized pillows on the closet floor, closed the door and buried her body under the cushioned mass. It was like a soft cocoon that cradled and hid her from the outside world. She turned on the Starlight Starbright projector and the glimmering stars began their orbital ballet. Every crevice of her closet was painted with twinkling lights and murky galaxies. Emily peered out from between the pillows, captivated by the celestial dance. With another flick of a switch, the soft, melodic tones of "Nessun Dorma," interwoven with the sounds of crashing waves and a gentle wind, drifted into the air.

The voices downstairs became louder. But Emily stayed focused on the brilliant constellations that rotated across the closet walls and ceiling. She could feel her heart pounding harder and harder.

That's the last thing Emily remembered.

# Chapter 2

Detective Jane Perry woke up with a start. For a second, she had no idea where she was. Her breathing was fast and labored, as though she'd just run a marathon. Jane closed her eyes and let out a loud grunt. Catching her breath, she stared at the ceiling in a slight daze. "Fuck," was all she could utter in a raspy whisper.

She'd had the same bloody nightmare again. But it was different this time. There was something else; something incongruous to the usual pattern of violence. But that *something else* was ominously intangible to Jane. It was as though she could damn near taste it and smell the scent of danger but her rational mind couldn't define it. Whatever this was, it felt patently real, as if it had already happened. She'd always accepted her sixth sense—gut intuitiveness that some cops coined "The Blue Sense." But that only came into play after exhaustive logical reasoning. Now it appeared that her intuitive mind was morphing into a chaotic, precognitive monster that hid between the shadows of her conscious mind. Jane tried to chalk up this tender sense of doom to her five-day booze binge. But she'd hit the bottle hard many times and never felt the queasy uneasiness that was beginning to take on a life of its own. The thought crossed her mind that she was finally losing it. After 35 years of barely holding it together, she feared she might be unraveling. That fear alone jolted her back to her senses as she lay alone in her bed staring into the void.

Jane coughed deeply—the kind of gut cough that comes from over 20 years of chain smoking. She reached over to the bedside table feeling for a pack of cigarettes. The table, just like the rest of the house, was a mess—the tactile consequence of her binge. A dozen empty cigarette packs, three drained bottles of Jack Daniels and a thick coating of ashes from the overturned ashtray littered the small table. Coming up empty-handed, she leaned over to the other side of the bed where another table sat askew from the wall. Opening the drawer, Jane found a full pack of Marlboros and a lighter. Her gut-wrenching cough continued as she peeled off the wrapping, jerked a cigarette out of the pack and lit up. She sucked the nicotine into her lungs like a seasoned pro. As the smoke peeled out of her mouth, she examined her bandaged left hand.

The emergency room doctor said the burn could have been worse and told her to apply the silver ointment twice a day to speed the healing. That was ten days ago and she'd plastered her hand with four coatings of the stuff before she gave up on it. Jane would be hard pressed to find the ointment underneath the debris that cluttered her bedroom. Dirty clothes intertwined with empty take-out cartons. A neat stack of beer stained yellow legal pads covered with writing sat on a pile of *The Denver Post* and *Rocky Mountain News* newspapers. In the ten days since "the incident," as it became known at Denver Headquarters, she and her partner, Detective Chris Crawley, made the front page of both papers seven times. One photo of her in the *Rocky* was the same mug on her ID badge. There she was with that sullen, pissed off expression. In contrast, Chris' adjacent front-page photo with his sweep of blond hair and narrow, ruddy cheeks, made him look like an altar boy. Subsequent stories on the pair featured a large photo from the disastrous press conference that left more questions unanswered about the explosion.

It also left the public wondering if Denver Homicide was as inept as the media portrayed them.

To say the incident haunted Jane Perry was putting it mildly. It was one thing for her to replay the whole thing in her mind second by second and ask herself what she could have done differently. But it was quite another to relive the disjointed images over and over again every night in her dreams. Sitting in the patrol car with Chris. Checking her watch. Chris calling the undercover cops on his cell phone and getting Stover's ETA. Seeing the Range Rover coming down the street. Observing Bill Stover, his wife Yvonne and their ten-year-old daughter Amy wave toward Jane as they pulled into their driveway. Feeling that instant between the silence and the chaos. Seeing the hood of the SUV explode in a burst of flames amidst the yellow smoke of the C-4 explosive. And then racing toward the burning car and finding Bill and Yvonne slumped across the dashboard and Amy with her hands pressed against the glass, screaming. Trying to open the back door and finding it locked. Then punching her fist against the glass to try and break it as the flames shot around the SUV from the hood. Feeling the icy burn across her left hand as Chris held her back from the car and smelling the melting paint and metal and flesh. Then staring at Amy's fixated eyes as the life drained out of them. It was that last moment that always shot Jane out of the nightmare and back into her life of hell. And it was just another reason to get loaded.

Jane took a long drag on her cigarette and coughed hard enough to pop a lung. She reached for the empty Jack Daniels bottle in hopes of finding a trickle of liquid relief. No luck. She tossed the bottle across the room and looked at the clock. *8:15.* "Shit!" Jane exclaimed as she threw back the covers and struggled to her feet. Clenching the cigarette between her lips, she pressed the palm of her good hand to her forehead in hopes of pushing back the pounding pressure. *A helluva way to start her first day back.* She had 45 minutes to get dressed, collect her paperwork, fight the morning traffic to DH and be seated in Sergeant Weyler's office.

As Jane made her way across the bedroom to the bathroom, she tripped over the answering machine with its flashing message light flickering like a warning beacon. Kicking it aside, she peeled off her sweat-soaked undershirt and panties and started the water in the shower. She plopped down on the toilet seat and caught her reflection in the bathroom mirror. The term "rode hard and put away wet," crossed her mind. There she was, cigarette dangling precipitously from her mouth, her brown, shoulder length hair falling across her sallow face and those bloodshot, brown eyes staring back with dark circles and bags underneath them. "What would Weyler think?" she wondered.

A million thoughts raced through her head as she showered and toweled off. She may have taken medical leave for five days but that didn't mean she hadn't organized a few scenarios that could have led to the car bombing. Sure, some of them were pretty wild and the result of a fifth of Jack but Jane still thought they were worth pitching to Weyler. That was the crazy thing about Jane—she could have the biggest load on and still pitch a rational series of probabilities for a crime that would prompt further investigation. Her fellow homicide detectives might call her a "rebel," "an outsider" or a "bitch," but no one could deny her intelligence, diligence and that palpable intuition that played a role in solving many of Denver's most baffling homicides.

Jane settled on a pair of brown slacks and a plain light blue oxford cloth shirt. She found one rough out western boot and uncovered its mate after overturning several discarded pizza cartons. *8:35.* She was cutting it close as she walked down the dimly lit hallway and into the kitchen. After adjusting her shoulder holster and securing her Glock pistol, Jane lit a new cigarette on the dying ember of the last one before tossing the butt into the sink, amidst more discarded bottles of Jack Daniels, Corona and dirty dishes. Checking around the corner into the living room, she found the TV on with the sound muted. The bedding was still tucked into the couch where her brother, Mike, had slept the night before. No sign of him. Jane turned to the kitchen counter and found a note stuffed into the mouth of an empty Corona bottle. It read: "Tried to wake you up but you wouldn't buge." Jane's eyes lingered on Mike's version of the word "budge," wondering when he was going to learn to spell. "Gotta work the early shift today. See you at his house tonight. 6 o'clock, right? Good luck at work! Mike." At the bottom of the page, there was one more sentence, written in caps. "DON'T FORGIT THE BEER!"

Jane opened the refrigerator. A quick check resulted in the discovery of five-day-old milk, expired bacon and an assortment of decaying fruit—a get-well gift Mike delivered a couple days after the incident. Slamming the refrigerator door shut, Jane spun around and poured what was left in the coffee maker into a mug. She knocked back the cold, black liquid. The caffeine cut through her foggy head as an unexpected scene flashed in front of her. There was a little girl and the brief swath of navy blue. There was a gun—a Glock outstretched and the blitz of reflected light that blinded.

And there was unmitigated terror—the kind that chokes and paralyzes.

The images lasted only a second but burned like lye into Jane's head. She felt as if she'd already experienced what she saw but there was no link to reality. There was a sense of merging . . . yes, fusion into another reality . . . or someone else's reality. Jane leaned across the sink as a disturbing disconnection took hold. If this was what it felt like to go insane, she wasn't up for it today. Gathering every last bit of mental reserve, Jane forced herself back into her body. "*Not today,*" she whispered, more as an order. Once settled, she collected several legal pads and scraps of paper. Stuffing them into her worn leather satchel, she grabbed her keys, opened her front door and faced the world.

Half a dozen plastic wrapped newspapers sat in a heap outside her doorway. She had given up on them after reading too many stories about the car bombing. The pathway that led from the front door of her drab, dirty brick house to her car was about 30 feet—a distance that should ensure an uneventful journey. However, Hazel Owens, her 65-year-old next-door neighbor on Milwaukee Street was perched on her front porch, dressed in a chenille robe and sipping juice.

"Mornin', Detective!" Hazel exclaimed in her over-the-top chirpy voice. "Happy first day back!" Jane stole a quick glance in Hazel's direction, her dangling cigarette dropping ashes on her shirtsleeve. Hazel held up the front section of *The Denver Post* and pointed her arthritic finger toward the story featured above the fold. "You find the awful people who did this to that poor little child!"

Jane had no idea what the old woman was talking about. Sometimes she would respond to Hazel's regular morning send-offs with a simple "Uh-huh" or "Yeah." But the only acknowledgment the old broad would get this morning was a slight raise of the head and a quick turn as Jane tossed her satchel into her '66 ice blue Mustang. If she drove like a demon, she might be able to make the two-mile trip to Headquarters in Denver rush hour traffic in less than ten minutes.

Jane peeled away from the curb as if the flag had been dropped at the Indy 500. Barreling down Milwaukee Street, past the neat rows of two-story brick houses, she shoved Bob Seger's *Against the Wind* CD into the player and turned up the volume on "Betty Lou's Gettin' Out Tonight." She sped up to 13th Street and turned left onto the one-way, four lane thoroughfare. From there, it was a straight shot to the corner of 13th and Cherokee where the six-story, barrack-like structure, better known as Denver Headquarters, stood. After weaving in and out of traffic like a skilled racecar driver, she squealed into the underground parking garage. Seger sung the chorus of "Fire Lake" as she swung into a spot near the elevator. She downed another swig of cold coffee, grabbed her satchel, slammed the door shut and raced toward the elevator.

*8:58.* Jane slapped the button and shoved the heel of her boot into the closed elevator doors. "Come on, goddamnit!" she shouted. The elevator doors opened, as if in response to her barking order. Jane lunged in, punching the third floor button with her fist.

The elevator stopped on the main floor and a young Mexican woman in her late twenties got on, hand in hand with a terrified looking child who Jane figured was around eight years old. A front desk officer accompanied them. Without looking at the buttons, the woman quietly said "Third floor," in broken English. Jane gave the button another hard whack. The doors closed and the officer stole a glance at Jane and her cigarette, tapping his finger on the "No smoking" emblem. Jane threw the cigarette on the elevator floor, crushing it with the toe of her boot.

The officer looked straight ahead. "You can't leave that butt in here."

Jane would have ripped him a new one if the woman and kid hadn't been there. Instead, she picked up the crushed cigarette and threw it in her satchel.

The little girl turned her body to face her mother, burying her face in her mother's stomach. "*Tengo miedo,*" the little girl muttered.

"Is okay," the mother said, patting her daughter's head and leaning down to kiss her. "Momma gonna make it okay."

Jane suddenly felt that same disjointed sense of reality hit again. She tried to quash the mounting tension that bled across her shoulder blades but it was no use. "Tengo miedo," meant "I'm frightened." Those were two words Jane heard on a daily basis from children when she did her four-year stint in assault during the late 1980s and early 1990s. She hated every second of it but she made it through by maintaining emotional distance with the children and never getting close to the victims. She figured if she busted her ass and nailed some of Denver's worst violators of women and children, she'd have a better chance of getting into homicide—the top of the heap, as far as she was concerned. *Tengo miedo.* So why was the little girl frightened? Jane noticed that the slim woman was a bundle of nerves. Her facial muscles twitched and she continually licked her lips as she fixed her eyes on the elevator door. A lifelong student of human behavior, Jane concluded that if this woman wasn't a criminal, she was certainly planning to become one.

The elevator doors opened onto the third floor. The woman and child got off with the officer as he motioned to the left, "Assault's this way, ma'am," he said. Jane stopped for a second and watched how the kid clung to her mother. If Jane weren't already late to Weyler's office, she would have followed them down to assault to get the skinny on the story. But instead, she took a sharp right and another left into the homicide department.

# Chapter 3

Jane forgot to prepare herself for the intense sunlight that filled the homicide department, radiating from the wall of windows that faced 13th Street. Between the piercing brightness and banks of fluorescent lights, Jane likened it to walking into the eye of a comet. To dodge the blinding light, she directed her attention down to the drab purple carpeting that ran the length of the cramped room. Ten desks, separated by wobbly partitions, filled the space. On this morning, they were empty.

Sergeant Hank Weiting, who was in charge of half of the ten detectives, was out of his office. Weiting, two months from retirement, was spending more time away. Several yards up from Weiting's station was Sergeant Morgan Weyler's corner office. The door was closed but through the slender window, Jane could see her partner Chris seated across from Weyler, engaged in conversation. Jane knocked before entering.

Weyler looked up at Jane. "9:05," he said with an off-hand tone. "Well, I lost that bet. I told Chris you wouldn't make it before 9:15."

Jane slid into the empty chair, stashing the leather satchel underneath it. "That just proves you shouldn't bet against me," Jane said to Weyler, never once acknowledging

Chris. Thankfully, her sense of reality was slowly creeping back.

Weyler leaned back in his chair, a mischievous smile across his face. "Welcome back, Jane. It hasn't been the same around here without you." Weyler's manner was always one of quiet confidence and a strange calm that had always intrigued Jane. Their paths had crossed over the past ten years while she worked her way through assault, burglary and finally into the homicide division. Weyler, a tall, graceful black man in his mid-fifties, wore tailored suits and narrow ties no matter what the fashion trends dictated. He was an enigma to many at DH—partly because he spoke like an eloquent statesman and partly because he listened more than he talked. When he did speak, he could say more in five words than others could say in twenty. His listening posture was classic to Jane; Weyler would tilt back in his leather chair, pressing the tips of his long, slender fingers together to form a steeple. An observant student of body language, Jane saw this posture as one of self-confidence and self-control. "How's that hand of yours?" Weyler inquired.

"It's fine," Jane quickly replied, pulling out her notes from the satchel. "Look, I've got some other angles to consider on the incident."

Chris let out a sigh and shook his head. "Jane, come on, there's no mystery," he said in a patronizing tone.

Jane looked straight ahead at Weyler, ignoring Chris' flippant comment. "It's a no-brainer that the Texas mafia did this so Stover couldn't testify but why take out his wife and daughter . . ."

"Jane, it's the goddamn mob!" said Chris with a mean twist to his voice. "They don't give a fuck who they kill!"

"They still have a code of ethics!" Jane said, her voice tightening. "You take out the witness, but you leave the wife and kid alone."

"Maybe that's the Italian mob's code but we're dealing with a whole new beast," Chris countered. "Christ, Jane, the Texas mafia is an unknown entity. Nobody knows their MO. They traffic in meth, heroine, you name it! If you rat 'em out, they kill you. That's what we know." Chris turned to Weyler. "Am I right?"

Weyler had watched this back and forth contentious exchange between Chris and Jane on numerous occasions. But this morning's repertoire had an edge to it that seemed personal. He wasn't about to take sides or make assumptions about what the Texas mob would or would not do. Chris was correct when he said the group was a mystery to law enforcement. It would take two pages to outline their known criminal involvement. The mob was made up of whites and Mexicans who shared a love for money and methamphetamine, along with cocaine and any other number of hard-core drugs. It was meth, however, that was really making the mob rich and infamous.

Meth, crank or blow as it was commonly called, was known as a "kitchen sink" drug because the average person could buy the ingredients at the supermarket and cook the stuff in their home. Anyone with access to the Internet could download the recipe and make a new batch every eight hours. A meager investment of $150.00 yielded a meth dealer over $10,000 on the street. With that kind of profit margin, it was only a matter of time before the mob figured a way to cut into it. Sales weren't hurt by the fact that meth was one of the most addictive drugs. Between mob involvement and independent kitchen sink producers, meth was quickly becoming one of Colorado's biggest headaches for law enforcement.

As was their pattern, the mob successfully worked their way into various Denver businesses—especially targeting those owned and operated by Asians who were used to paying protection money back in their home country. The mob would approach the business owner and alert him to the fact that drug trafficking was going on nearby and that the gang bangers and druggies would quickly destroy his ability to do business. If the owner agreed to pay the mob a set percentage of his gross, the mob would make sure there'd be no drug trafficking at his storefront.

Very few businesses refused the offer. And if they did refuse, the mob made sure that the drug dealers—the same drug dealers who were selling the mob's goods—would harass, vandalize, rob and assault the business owner until they came back to the mob, begging for protection.

With their sudden and extreme financial windfall, the Texas mafia needed to find the perfect fronts for laundering their money. That's where Bill Stover came into the picture. The 42-year-old business wizard owned a chain of successful Denver convenience stores. He was featured on the cover of local business magazines and newspapers as "Entrepreneur of the Year," a major contributor to local charities and the annual host of Denver's Drug Awareness Police Benefit. Stover had always been the quintessential muscular, chiseled-chinned, man's man. But his physique and temperament were quickly whittling away thanks to his secret addiction to meth. His 210 pound build shrunk to a spindly 175 pounds. A persistent rash covered his body, a result of the vicious toxins let loose through the skin of many meth addicts.

His life may have ended in the front seat of his Range Rover ten days before, but it technically came to an abrupt stop with his first hit of meth in the fall of the previous year. The mob's lackeys who had been supplying him with the occasional "gift" of Columbian cocaine turned him onto crank. He was hooked from the first high. But like all meth addicts, Stover got sloppy and made a lot of mistakes. The stats tell you that serious addiction to meth can occur after a couple months of use. But Stover experienced a powerhouse, line drive addiction after only a few weeks. Already a talkative guy, meth encouraged that tendency. His constant restlessness, anxiousness and frequent insomnia only fueled his garrulous streak. Between the acute paranoia and false sense of confidence—two more effects of meth addiction—Stover was on a roller coaster that quickly careened into a train wreck. After he was busted in an undercover Denver narcotics sting, his life imploded. He knew that his reputation would be destroyed if word got out that this upstanding, anti-drug, "Entrepreneur of the Year" was a closet meth freak who fraternized with the Texas mob. Stover was the perfect insider who understood how the mob operated; he knew names of the powerful in Denver who danced with the mob and he knew the fronts for drugs and corruption.

So the Denver cops gave him a choice: tell us everything you know about the mob and their inside connections and we'll keep your good reputation intact; clam up and we'll make sure you are the daily headline of every Colorado newspaper. Stover knew it was a choice between the lesser of two evils. Unfortunately, he didn't fully comprehend that by siding with the cops, he was signing his own death certificate. He and his family were killed less than 12 hours before he was scheduled to tell everything he knew to the District Attorney.

It could have been so simple. Stover was told to stay with his family in his house; around-the-clock patrol cars were assigned to watch and protect his residence. But after five days of being housebound, he was "tweaking," a term meth addicts use for coming down off the drug. Tweaking, which can last for weeks after stopping the drug, causes irrational behavior and periods of violent rage. In this state of mind, Stover announced to the detectives that he was taking his family out to get ice cream on that May evening. They tried to dissuade him from leaving but it was clear that this was a man who always got his way. It was a classic example of Stover's false sense of bravado reigning over his intense paranoia.

Two undercover cars followed him when he left, leaving Chris and Jane in their car across from the house on Gilpin—a wide, upscale street that skirts Cherry Creek and features two-story brick estates. The Stovers' long driveway, edged with manicured cedars and a single thick, dark green hedge was the perfect entrance to this grand house. It was also the perfect place to hide a small bomb amidst the greenery. Denver PD had searched every inch of that property, but somehow a crude, homemade bomb with one-third pound of C-4 plastic explosives and a remote detonator cord was covertly placed onto the driveway and arranged so that the front wheels of Stover's Range Rover tripped the wires. Whoever did it snuck onto the property in the darkness between the time Stover and his family left for ice cream and the time he returned less than 30 minutes later. And the whole thing happened on Chris and Jane's watch.

Neither of them saw much on that dark, cloudy night. Most of their time was spent sitting in the car, drinking coffee and talking about their future together. After two years of being partners, getting loaded after hours and sharing some of their darkest moments from their past, Chris and Jane found themselves sharing a bed. It wasn't love for either of them. It was more of a way to not be lonely. But lately, Jane was tiring of the relationship. Chris had always been a control freak, but his behavior was becoming unbearable. His desire for sex had gone from reasonable to insatiable. The fact that he was developing a penchant for rougher and rougher sex disturbed Jane. She could easily meet and sometimes top Chris' aggressive nature in bed. But the physical and emotional pain began to gnaw at her psyche. When their violent dance couldn't be numbed by any amount of booze, Jane decided to break off their intimate relationship. She also planned to put in for a new partner at DH. That night in the car waiting for the Stovers to return home, Chris was discussing the possibility of moving in with Jane. If all hell hadn't broken loose, Jane would have told him it was over.

And so, there they sat in Weyler's office. Chris with his cocky, know-it-all attitude and Jane with her stubborn, get-the-last-word-in demeanor. Weyler looked at the two of them, not knowing quite what to think.

"Am I right about the mob, boss?" Chris asked Weyler again.

"Chris, I refuse to walk on that land mine right now,"

Weyler responded in a surefooted, diplomatic manner. "What they may or may not be capable of is unknown. We lost our opportunity for any inside info when Stover died. Right now, I'm more interested in both of your psychological profiles." The comment jarred Jane, given her precarious start to the day. Weyler opened a folder. "I see here, Chris, that you completed your psych counsel and they feel that you have come to terms with the incident and are not experiencing any post-traumatic stress episodes. Is that correct?"

"No episodes at all, sir," Chris said with a shrug of his shoulders. "It was an unfortunate incident but it's in the past and I'm moving forward. My only concern right now is how this may or may not affect my record with the Department."

"That has yet to be determined." Weyler scanned the form. "It says here that you expressed a certain amount of anger regarding the incident."

"Yes, sir," Chris said as his eyes scanned the floor. "I felt that we didn't consider all the angles of what could go down and I'm angry at myself for that. That was one of the first things they taught us in the Marines: figure out everything that can go wrong and have an end run in place." Chris focused his gaze to his left, away from Jane. "As harsh as it sounds, sir, Stover knew the rules but chose to color outside the lines. Going to get ice cream was just stupid on his part! A window of opportunity opened up and some bastard took advantage of it. The more I've thought about it—and *believe me*, I've thought about it—the more I feel that if anyone is to blame for this mess, it's Stover."

"Yeah, blame the dead," Jane said under her breath. Chris shot her a look.

The silence in the room was deafening. Weyler considered Chris' remarks, closed his folder and pushed it aside. A piercing beep cut into the quiet. Chris jerked forward, snapped his beeper off his waistband and checked the message.

"Sorry, sir," Chris said in a strong voice. "I told Marshall to beep me if he needed any assistance at that double murder from last night." Chris slightly hesitated as a vibrating anxiousness buzzed off his body. "Are we okay here?"

"For now, yes. Call Marshall and find out what he needs."

"Yes, sir," Chris said as he quickly popped up and maneuvered his wiry body between the chairs.

"Oh, Chris," Weyler said, "are you working outside duty tonight?"

"There's a possibility of a security gig at a downtown club. Why?"

"The press is going to be all over last night's double homicide. I'd like you to be the media point person."

"Thank you, sir," Chris responded, bloated with new-found confidence.

"Keep it low-key about the kid. Until she's willing to talk to us, it's anybody's guess where this thing's going to go."

"Consider it done," Chris affirmed as he left the office.

Weyler leaned back in his chair, carefully eyeing Jane. She had a good idea of what was coming and could feel her gut tightening. From the outside, however, she sat stone-faced, arms crossed over her chest and looked Weyler straight in the eye. "Well, Detective Perry, I do not seem to have a psych counsel assessment for you. Now, I know I asked you . . . let me rephrase that, I know that I *told* you to make an appointment with psych. And yet, you failed to do as I requested—"

"I don't need to see a fu—" Jane caught herself. "I don't need to see a psychologist. I'm not weak. Trust me, I've experienced a lot worse. What *I* need is to figure out what happened ten days ago. So, if you'll excuse me, that's exactly what I plan to do." Jane dropped her paperwork into her satchel and stood up.

"Sit down, Detective Perry," Weyler said with a strict tenor. Jane stood firm. "Sit down . . . Jane," Weyler said, this time with more equanimity. Jane reluctantly obliged. "You've got a lot on your plate right now. I understand from the boys downstairs that your father won't be able to return to his home."

Jane was caught off guard by Weyler's remark. Between the nightmares and booze binge, she'd conveniently forgotten about her ailing father. "Yeah, that's right. How did you . . . What? Is there a direct line from that hospital to Headquarters?"

"You can blame his old detective buddies for that direct line."

"Well, he's not recovering from the heart attack and stroke as they had hoped." Jane tried to act like she cared. "And the whole failing liver thing, that's not helping matters. So, he's pretty much . . . screwed. I'm meeting Mike tonight at his house to figure out what to do with all the furniture and the other shit."

"I'm sorry," Weyler said.

"Hey, it is what it is," Jane said with a shrug of her shoulders. "Look, I—"

"Is he able to get around?" Weyler questioned, pressing further.

Jane was growing uncomfortable with Weyler's interest in her father.

She rested her right elbow on the arm of the chair and pressed her fingers against her right temple, next to a scar—just one of her many battle wounds—that was partially hidden under her hairline. "To be honest with you, I don't know. I went to see him once and he was asleep so I left." Jane let out a deep breath.

Weyler scrutinized Jane's demeanor. "Are you alright, Jane?"

She knew she wasn't but she figured she could fake it. "I'm fine, boss." The words echoed with a disingenuous tenor.

Weyler leaned forward, seriously concerned. "What's going on?"

Jane regarded Weyler with a forthright look but it fell like a glass curtain across her face. "Nothing's going on that'll prevent me from moving forward with solving the Stover case."

Weyler's penetrating stare was relentless. "Part of my job is to watch over you people, make sure you represent DH with intelligence and mental coherence. You have the intelligence part down in spades. It's the mental coherence part that concerns me."

Jane fell back into the chair, her eyes now meeting Weyler's glance with conviction. If she could get out of his office and start focusing on the case, she was sure everything would resolve itself. "Look, I'm under some stress, okay?" she said, her voice shaking. "First day back and all. It's to be expected, right?" Jane was trying to convince herself more than Weyler. "But once I get back in the swing of it—"

"You get the job done better than anyone. But it seems that lately, you are displaying actions that create some questions by other officers."

Jane couldn't hold back any longer. "When that car blew up on my watch, I did everything possible to get Stover's kid out. If trying to break a fucking window to rescue a little girl is considered insane or whatever those pricks want to say, then so be it! *I'm your best detective!* You just admitted it! So don't talk to me about sanity! Fucking *sanity* is overrated!" Jane leaned back in her chair, teetering on the two back legs. There was dead silence. That's when she could hear the sound of her shallow breathing fill the room. She wasn't about to back down or take her eyes off of Weyler, no matter how much she wanted to look away.

"Are you finished?" Weyler said calmly.

"Yes . . . sir," was all Jane could manage.

"Then I must inform you that, until further notice, you are on suspension."

Jane's mouth went dry. Weyler's declaration was like a

hard center punch. "I've never been suspended in my life! There's gotta be a way to work this out!"

"I might be willing to reconsider if you agree to that psych counsel."

"That's blackmail!"

"It's not blackmail, Jane. It's just me making sure you follow the rules."

"Let me get this straight. I play DH's game, go for this psych counsel and tell them whatever they need to hear . . . just like Chris did? And then I can come back and fig-ure out all those baffling murder mysteries?"

"Putting your pointed sarcasm aside and taking the ses-sions seriously, yes, that's what needs to happen for you to see the inside of this department in the near future."

"Uh-huh," Jane muttered, her eyes canvassing the ceil-ing. "Well, I'll go to that psych counsel when pigs fly out of my ass." Jane started for the door.

"You know, Jane. One day that stubborn, insolent streak is going to get the better of you."

"What makes you think it hasn't already?"

# Chapter 4

"Jane!" Chris said, barreling over to her from his desk. She was out the door and headed for the elevator. "Jane, wait!" He caught up to her as she was slapping the "down" button at the elevator. "What in the fuck's going on? Why haven't you answered my twenty plus phone messages? I came by twice and your old neighbor lady said you were inside but you weren't answering the door."

Jane stared ahead, ready to explode. "Leave me alone, Chris."

"We need to talk."

"Talk about what?" Jane said, turning and glaring at Chris.

"The fuckin' price of rice in China! What do you think?" Chris furtively looked around, making sure their conversation was still private. "We gotta talk about *us*," he said, softening his stance.

Jane looked at him in silence, shook her head and turned back to the elevator. "Jesus! You really do think you're God's gift but you're just a fuckin' boot licker!"

"*Excuse me?*" The softness quickly dissolved.

Jane slammed the heel of her palm against the elevator button. "You tell them exactly what they want to hear in your psych counsel and you kiss their asses—"

"Oh, I'm sorry I'm not a maverick like you! I just come in here day after day and do my job and put the occasional son-of-a-bitch behind bars whenever I can!"

"Save that shit for the media, Chris!" Jane gave up on the elevator and turned toward the stairwell. Chris followed, determined to get in the last word. Jane headed into the stairwell, digging into her satchel for cigarettes. Popping one out of the pack, she lit up as she made her way down the stairs. The sound of their footsteps and voices resounded throughout the cement structure.

"Are you crazy?" Chris yelled out.

"The jury's still out on that one!" Jane replied, keeping a good ten steps in front of Chris as she puffed on her cigarette. "Get off my back, Chris! I mean it!"

"Jesus Christ, don't you ever turn it off?" Jane neared the heavy security door that led into the Denver PD lobby. Chris bounded down the stairs and blocked Jane's ability to open the door. They stood face-to-face, inches from each other. Perspiration poured from Chris' forehead, causing a minor rash to become redder around his hairline. His fair skin and ruddy complexion always made it look as if he'd run a marathon after only minor exertion. Between his wired persona and his aggressive, take no prisoners demeanor, it was all Chris could do to keep his natural rash outbreaks to a minimum. "I said wait!" Chris demanded, out of breath, as he slapped the palm of his hand across the door.

Jane took a long drag off her cigarette. "Is it that you like to hear the sound of your own voice or is it that you just don't hear?"

"Jane, we fucked up the case. Okay?" Chris said, confidentially.

Jane was taken aback by Chris' statement. He was never usually one to admit wrongdoing. Jane studied his eyes. "You mean it?" she asked with a softer tone.

"Of course I mean it."

"Why didn't you say that to Weyler?"

"I told him I blamed myself!"

"You said you blamed *Stover!*"

"Jane, Weyler just made me point person in a double murder I can really put to bed. But you and I have to work together on it. This case, Jane, is gonna put me . . . *us* back on top."

Jane regarded Chris with an incredulous glare. "You go from 'We fucked it up, Jane' to 'Let's figure out how to put Chris back on top?' What is up with you?"

Chris moved closer, tilting his head in an awkward manner. "I need you—"

"Get away from me." Jane pulled her body away from him.

"Jane! I'm not kidding!" Chris yelled in a desperate tone. Jane spun around and continued down the stairs to the basement where the evidence room was located. Chris leaned over the railing. "Jane! *We can make it right!*"

Jane swung open the basement door and entered the huge evidence entry area. There was always that smell down there. Jane figured you could be blindfolded and when you got to the basement, you'd know it by the odor of over one million pieces of evidence—all crammed into metal shelves and waiting to be called up to solve a crime. Bloodied baseball bats used to bash in a husband's head lay next to carefully sealed plastic K-Paks bags of cocaine, marijuana and meth.

Ron Dickson, one of the evidence technicians, stood behind a metal security grating, signing out one of the detectives from burglary. The place was unusually still and silent. Ron wasn't the kind of fellow Jane would have talked to outside the office. Maybe it was because Ron was very obviously a Pentecostal Christian. Or perhaps it was because he always had a smile on his face and something positive to share with Jane. He'd brag about one of his three kids winning a league soccer tournament or that he collected more money than anyone else at Headquarters for D.A.R.E., a group he held in high esteem. Jane wondered at times how he made it through life so trusting and somewhat gullible. He worked amongst the blood and the drugs and the obscene photographs and he somehow remained cheerful. When Jane finally asked him one day how he did it, he shrugged his shoulders and said, "It's a God thing!"

Jane leaned against the door and took a long drag on her cigarette. She figured that Chris had headed back upstairs or out to the double homicide. The detective from burglary walked to the elevator and disappeared behind the large steel doors.

"Detective Perry?" said Ron, his cheerful voice bringing Jane out of her slight daze. "I sure don't mind if you smoke but if they find you down here with that cigarette, I'll be in a world of trouble." He pulled out a large coffee can with a handmade note taped across it that read "PUT YOUR BUTT IN HERE." Jane reluctantly sidled over to Ron and took one last long drag before plopping it into the can. Ron was wearing a perfectly pressed pair of chinos to go along with his perfectly pressed navy polo shirt. On the shirt was a discreet button that said, "D.A.R.E. to keep kids off DRUGS." Jane imagined Ron's ivory-skinned wife dutifully pressing his pants and shirts, affixing either his D.A.R.E. or "Proud Soccer Parent" button onto his shirt and sending him off to work with a gentle kiss. When Jane was around Ron, she always felt very loud, very crude and very lost. "I'm sure I'm not the first to say this, but welcome back!" Ron said with an honest smile.

Jane tried her best to twist her lips into what could pass for a smile. "Thanks, Ron." She dropped her leather satchel against the counter. When Ron spoke to you, he always looked you straight in the eye, no jittery shifting back and forth. It was a sign to Jane that he was honest and speaking from the heart.

"Are you feeling alright, Detective Perry?"

Jane could have said a million smart-ass answers, but between feeling the need to censor her vocabulary with him and still stinging from Weyler's suspension, she decided to settle on the truth. "No, Ron. I'm not feeling alright."

"Is it your hand? If it is, my wife makes an herbal salve that works wonders."

"The hand's fine. I just have a lot on my mind."

Ron hesitated. "I hope you don't think I'm too forward but when I heard about what happened to you and Detective Crawley and that poor family, I asked our faith circle to include you in their prayers. My wife and I also prayed for you."

Jane leaned on the steel counter and turned to Ron. "What did you ask for?"

"We prayed that you would be protected, and for God to give you direction."

Jane's eyes trailed off to the side. "You think God heard your prayers?"

"Yes, ma'am. And I know in my heart He will give you the answers you need very soon." Ron placed the palm of his hand over Jane's bandaged hand. "He works in mysterious ways, Detective Perry." Jane stood still, taken aback by Ron's bold gesture. His clear, blue eyes seemed to look right through her. It might have been the end result of her five-day drinking binge but she felt as though Ron knew things about her that she buried long ago. The elevator doors opened and two detectives from assault emerged, chatting loudly and carrying bags of evidence. "Excuse me," Ron said, gently withdrawing his hand and attending to the detectives.

Jane grabbed her leather satchel and moved aside. Her head spun with various forms of strategy that would convince Weyler to put her back on the board without having to endure hours of psych counseling. This kind of deep thinking required tobacco, however. She headed back into the stairwell and lit up a cigarette. Leaning on the railing, she lost herself in thought. Jane heard the big steel door open from the lobby entrance and the patronizing voice of Martha Durrett. It was hard for Jane to concentrate on her thoughts while Martha was chattering. The 47-year-old worked for the Department of Social Services and was a constant thorn in Jane's side. Part of it was Martha's voice, a strident and annoying one. It was hard enough to stomach her voice when one was feeling normal but it was especially brutal with a hangover. Martha had a habit of clipping her words with the precision of a sharp knife as she moved through the world as though she owned it.

"Come along, dear," Jane heard Martha say in that ever-condescending tone. "It's just two quick flights up. Come, come!" Jane shook her head in disgust at Martha's schoolteacher manner. She didn't know who she was talking to but she felt sorry for them. The stream of smoke from her cigarette drifted up from the basement. Like a human smoke alarm, it didn't take Martha long to blare. "*Is someone there?*" Martha leaned over the railing. Silence. "I say, is someone down there?" Martha sounded more agitated. Silence. "Wait right here," Martha said to her hushed companion. Jane heard the sound of Martha's sensible rubber soled shoes scuffing across the floor and tramping down the stairs until she lit on the landing above where Jane stood. "Ah-hah!" Martha dug her fists into her wide hips and drew herself up to her full five-foot frame. She looked down at Jane with a scowl and a chiding "Tch, tch, tch" with her tongue. "Detective Perry. You know smoking is forbidden inside all Denver County and City buildings! Put that awful thing out before you set off the sprinklers!"

Jane leaned back against the wall, took a long, exaggerated drag off her cigarette and let the smoke slowly curl from her lips in a continuous ribbon. "You know, Martha, standing there like you are in that light, I can't decide whether you look more like Napoleon or Hitler. Either way, fuck off!"

Martha quickly looked up the stairs and then bounded halfway down toward Jane. "Detective Perry!" Martha said in a hushed tone, "curb your language! I have a young child up there!"

"Does she realize what a complete asshole you are?"

"Detective Perry! I will not say it again! Please refrain from—" Martha's attention was drawn upward as the child peered over the railing, her brown hair hanging softly in midair. Jane looked up at the girl and moved away from the wall to get a better view. "Emily," Martha chided. "Step back. I'll be right there."

Emily Lawrence started to retreat when Jane spoke up. "Hey, Emily! Don't listen to her! Run like hell and don't look back!"

Emily stared at Jane in stunned fascination. Martha grabbed Jane by her elbow and brusquely took her aside, out of Emily's view. "Detective Perry, you are *very much* out of line!"

Jane replied in the same clipped manner. "Get your hand off me, Martha, or I'll knock you on your—" Jane peered around Martha. Emily stood on the landing above her. In her left hand, she clutched onto her navy blue vinyl case that held the Starlight Starbright projector. Jane felt an unnerving jolt of recognition. There was something vaguely familiar about the kid—*strangely* familiar.

"That's it!" Martha announced. "I'm reporting you to your sergeant." Martha spun on her sensible shoes and walked up several steps toward Emily. "You are foul-mouthed and inappropriate!" Martha exclaimed, speaking over her shoulder to Jane. But Jane didn't hear a word of it; she was still trying to shake the odd feeling churning her gut. It was as if a memory suddenly surfaced without any lucid connection. "Come along, Emily!" Martha barked at Emily. Martha was halfway up the second set of stairs, issuing orders to Emily but the kid didn't move. She stared undaunted at Jane.

Jane leaned against the wall. She wanted to say something to the child but . . . what? She figured a mild caveat might be appropriate. "Hey, kid," Jane said in a half-whisper. "Don't let her jerk you around."

"*Emily!*" Martha beckoned from one flight above. "*Come up here now!*"

Emily stood for one more long second staring at Jane

before she made her way back up the stairs and into Martha's waiting hand.

Jane waited as the echoing clip-clop of Martha and Emily's footsteps climbed the stairs. A dull sound of steel against steel penetrated the stairwell when Martha opened the door leading onto the third floor and let it slam shut. Standing in the sudden silence, she tried to contend with the elusive sense that something extraordinary was happening. She felt detached from her body but also filled with a palpable sensation that she knew more than she consciously realized. Given that she'd been blitzed on booze and blacked out many times over the last five days, she worried her current state might precede a complete breakdown. The thought of losing her mind forced the need of nicotine to suffocate the sharp edges. Jane took a long drag on her cigarette. The smoke caressed her throat and penetrated her lungs. She closed her eyes to drink in the sweet anesthesia. But suddenly, a disjointed series of stark images flashed in front of her. There was an outstretched Glock, a flash of blinding light and the genuine sensation that someone was desperately grabbing her right hand. Startled, Jane opened her eyes expecting to see someone holding on to her. But she stood alone.

"Shit," Jane muttered under her breath. The walls closed in on her. She had to get out of the stairwell. Jane wanted more than anything to run upstairs, sit at her desk and focus . . . focus on *anything* mundane that would force the booze-induced images out of her head. Her ego quickly took hold when she remembered her suspension. Jane wasn't about to go upstairs and negotiate with Weyler. A psych counsel now might prove her worst fears. She would do what she always did: bury the trauma and move forward. If she talked to Weyler, she had to be tactful. However, tact was not something Jane had mastered in her 35 years. Tact, as she was fond of saying, was for people who didn't have the balls to speak the truth. She grabbed her leather satchel, pinched what was left of her cigarette between her lips and plodded up the stairs with purpose. Jane had no idea what she was going to say to Weyler but she figured the right words would spill out at the precise moment. She was so deep in thought as she climbed the steps toward the third floor door that she didn't hear the loud voice of a woman yelling on the other side of the door. She flicked her cigarette butt to the floor, smashed it with the toe of her boot and swung open the door.

The grating pitch of the Mexican woman she'd seen earlier in the elevator with the scared little girl greeted her. The woman held on to her daughter with one hand and used the other to gesture excitedly toward several of the detectives from Assault. She spoke rapidly and hysterically in Spanish, adding a sentence here and there in English. "You don't know!" screamed the woman, during an interlude of English. "He hurt my baby! My baby girl!!!"

As determined as Jane was to get to Weyler's office, she couldn't help but take in the scene. Down the hall, twenty feet away, stood Martha, her hand tightly clasped around Emily's wrist. Several detectives and police personnel poked their heads out of their offices. Even Weyler looked outside his office door to catch the action.

Jane started to move around the woman when out of the corner of her eye, she saw two officers escorting a slightly built Mexican man in his mid-twenties down the hallway. He wore a stained T-shirt, baggy tan pants and sported endless tattoos that flowed from his wrist to his neck. Even though he was cuffed from behind, he walked with an arrogant, cocksure swagger and held his head high.

Jane was about two feet from the screaming woman and in direct line with the approaching suspect when it happened. The woman caught sight of the fellow and, in one desperate stroke, withdrew a Glock from a passing patrol officer's holster and pointed it at the Mexican suspect in cuffs. "No!" the woman screamed as she stood firm, both hands clasped around the gun and holding it outstretched toward the suspect.

Jane turned toward the woman and took a quick step back, within arm's reach of the weapon. Every officer on the floor reached for their firearm. Martha pulled Emily down onto the carpet and shielded the child's head with her body.

Weyler moved forward into the hallway and yelled toward the officers, "Stand down! Stand down!" Everyone took a step back except for Jane. Her eyes were locked onto the woman, who by now was shaking and choking back tears. As strong as the woman was trying to look, every fiber of her being was seized in terror. Jane carefully took her eyes off the woman and slid her glance toward the suspect who was frozen between the two officers not more than fifteen feet away. "Ma'am?" said Weyler quietly, his voice cutting through the tension. "Put down the gun."

"No!" she screamed in her thick accent. "You don't know what he did to my baby! No father should do those things to his little girl!"

The suspect smirked, sticking his chin defiantly in the air. "You lying *bitch!*"

The woman moved her finger onto the trigger. Everyone in the hallway stiffened. "I don't lie!" the woman screamed as her daughter buried her head in her mother's hip. "You broke her! She's just a baby!"

"Ma'am, please," Weyler insisted. "*Put down the gun.* Let's talk about this."

"No talk!" the woman yelled defiantly, her eyes burning holes toward the suspect. Jane drew her attention back to the woman and stepped toward her. The woman kept her eyes forward. "Don't you try nothing!" she screamed at Jane.

"I'm not gonna do anything," Jane said, an eerie calm to her voice. "I'm on your side."

"Don't you play no game with me!"

"I am not playing games. I'm serious. I want to help you."

"How you help me?"

"Well, for starters, you've never shot a gun before, have you?"

"No," the woman said, her throat choked with emotion.

"That's okay," Jane said offhandedly. "You've got the right idea. You just don't have the right control. I need to move closer so I can give you some pointers, okay?"

"Don't you try nothing!" the woman yelled.

"I'm not gonna stop you," Jane said, almost insulted. "You want to do this right, or do you want to make a mess? *Relax.*" Jane slid her body next to the woman so that she could see down the barrel of the extended pistol. "You gotta stop shaking. Take a good, deep breath." The woman drew in her lungs. "Now, let it out slowly," Jane counseled. The woman followed suit, letting out a long stream of air. "Good. You're not shaking as much. Okay, there's several ways you can do this." Jane directed her attention toward the suspect. "You can aim for his head," Jane gently placed her index finger under the woman's wrists and slightly moved the gun sight in line with the suspect's forehead. "That'd be a sweet shot. However, we're about fifteen feet away and even the best cop could miss. Your second option is to bring the gun down here." Jane gently directed the woman's aim to the suspect's groin. "That's a tempting shot. You hit the mark dead on and he never hurts anyone else like that again. But, tempting as it is, we're still fifteen feet away and there's a good chance you'll miss. So there's option three." Jane directed the pistol at the suspect's chest. "That's what we call a 'center punch' and it always works. You fire a magnum plug right there and you solve your problem in less than a second." Jane turned to the woman. "I'd go with option three if I were you."

The woman thought for a second, then nodded. "Okay," she said calmly.

"Now, before you plug him, I need to know if you have a safe place for your daughter to stay."

The woman furrowed her eyebrows as if irritated by the question. "What?"

"Is there a safe place for the kid to live? A family member you trust? Preferably not one on *his* side of the family. A sister? A brother?"

"She live with me!"

"Well, of course, I'll do everything I can in court to make that happen."

"What you saying?" The woman started shaking.

"Relax! It's going to be okay. It's just that after you kill the son-of-a-bitch, I'm going to have to arrest you and take your daughter away from you."

The woman started to cry. "What? You can't! *She need me.*"

"I know. But that's why I need to know about a trusted family member who can look after her—"

"How long?"

"I don't know. Conservatively, probably six months to ten years."

"*Ten years!*"

"I'm just throwing out numbers. I don't know for sure. Hey, I don't make these rules. If it were up to me, I'd say shoot the asshole and I'd buy you dinner. But I'm not in charge. So, again, have you got anyone you can trust with your kid?"

The woman started shaking violently and sobbing. "*No!* I can't let her be away from me. She need me now!"

Jane let out a long breath of air coupled with a sigh. "Well then . . . you better not shoot the bastard. It'll just get too complicated."

For the first time, the woman took her eyes off the suspect and looked at Jane, tears streaming down her face. They stared at each other for what seemed like eternity until Jane moved closer to the woman's ear and whispered, "I'm sorry."

The woman lowered the pistol. Jane carefully slipped it out of the woman's sweat-soaked hands and gave it back to the patrol officer. She turned to Weyler. He didn't say a word—he just stared at her with a look that bordered somewhere between apprehension and disbelief. Jane picked up her leather satchel and walked to the elevator, punching the "down" button with the side of her fist.

Everyone turned their attention to the woman. Everyone, that is, except for Emily, who watched Jane enter the elevator and disappear behind the steel doors.

# Chapter 5

It was just after 10:15 a.m. when Jane sped out of the DH parking garage. As she rounded her Mustang onto 14th Street and curved around the Civic Center, she noted that it had taken just over an hour for her life to fall apart.

Jane saw the look on Weyler's face after she disarmed the Mexican woman. She noted how he appeared genuinely guarded by her actions, as if it was something only a nutcase would do.

Nothing made sense to Jane anymore. When she woke up that morning, she had a plan. She always had a plan. It may have been a little blurry due to the alcohol burn off, but there still was a plan. Jane figured she had three or four legal-sized yellow pads filled with angles, motives, wild theories and other sundry notations regarding the death of Bill Stover, his wife and daughter. Every time Jane awoke from that blistering nightmare filled with fire and Amy's dying eyes, she'd jot something down on one of those pads. When she'd reread her scribble in the morning, sometimes she could only make out a word here and there.

One thing was for sure, if this was the work of the Texas mob, it went against their usual pattern. Then again, it was hard to pin a hard-and-fast MO on a group that was still an unknown to law enforcement. In the end,

Jane had only her gut intuition that had never failed her. After all, it was her gut intuition that told her that Mexican woman was up to something. That same gut intuition told her the Stovers' death was not entirely the work of the Texas mafia. There was something or someone else. She could feel it.

She could also feel that numinous nudge creeping up on her—that sensation that she was balancing on a slim blade between sanity and illumination. She thought back to the Mexican woman and the outstretched Glock. Twice before that morning, the image of an outstretched Glock flashed like flint in front of her eyes. But there was something attached to the jarring, disturbing image—a swath of navy blue and bright lights. And that sharp tug on her sleeve; the tug she physically felt in the stairwell.

Jane pulled in front of her house just past 10:25. It was six hours before RooBar, her nightly watering hole in the center of Cherry Creek, opened for business. She hadn't been there in a few days, preferring to get a load on at home. But most drunks like the comfort of a familiar bar and RooBar fit the bill for Jane. There was never a chance of running into fellow cops since they were more partial to the gritty downtown taverns. And it didn't hurt that RooBar was located about a mile from her house.

She sat in her car and stared into the void. A gentle breeze slipped through the car bringing with it the sweet smell of lilacs that were coming into full bloom. Jane started out of her car when she felt the concentrated beat of her pounding head. She cradled her forehead in her hands, attempting to press the pain back into her body. That eerie disconnect began to surface again but this time she fought hard to drown it. An old cop adage crossed her mind; a saying that was bandied around the Department when joking about borderline loonies: "They're not crazy enough to check into the nut house, but they can see the front door from where they're standing!" At that moment, Jane could clearly see that door.

Standing on the front porch, Jane stared at the collection of rolled up newspapers, along with clumps of wind-blown leaves, dandelion fuzz and the mass of cobwebs. If her dad could see the mess, he'd have something to say about it. "Clean up your fuckin' mess," is what he'd say. Jane quickly shut off his voice. It was bad enough that she was going to have to visit his house at 6:00 that night. She didn't need to have that voice inside of her head just yet.

Once inside the house, Jane quickly poured herself two shots of Jack Daniels, downing them one after the other. Within minutes, the ache in her head became bearable. Jane opened the living room windows to release the pent-up stench of beer, rotting leftovers and other debris. She moved with purpose around the living room and worked her way into the kitchen, collecting discarded beer and whiskey bottles, cardboard take-out boxes and chucked them into a large garbage bag. As always, the repetitious movement put her into a kind of Zen state. Once there, her focus was on whatever memory chose to rear its ugly head. To drag her out of this trance was pointless. She was thrust back in time to a place that was as real as when it happened. The smells and sounds were as acute as when the misery was fresh. It had gotten so bad lately that anything could trigger the memories. To be back in the moment again—this time as a witness to the vicious beating—was like reliving the trauma anew. Every time she emerged from the memory, she felt that she was missing a piece of herself. *Post-traumatic stress disorder*. That's what the psych counselors at DH called it. But Jane balked at the label. For her, it was just another tight fitting box that somebody wanted to force her into.

Suddenly, another memory snuck up on Jane. It wasn't the usual one that haunted her soul. She's twelve. She and her father, Dale, are in the living room watching *To Tell The Truth* on the TV with the tobacco-stained screen. They sit apart, Jane on the sofa and her father in his re-cliner, puffing on his cigarette and knocking back his fifth whiskey of the night. It's not just a television show; it's a study in human personality traits. It's two people lying and one telling the truth.

"Watch the fucker on the left," her father says pointing at the screen with the lit end of his cigarette. "See how he licked his lips when Kitty Carlisle asked him that question about how long he's been in business? That's nerves. It's a simple question. *And there!* Watch! Did you see that? The fucker looked to the left for a second. He's not telling the truth. Neither is the bastard in the middle. It's the one on the right. The one on the fuckin' right!" he yells toward the screen.

Young Jane leans forward, elbows embedded into her thighs, studying the television screen and waiting patiently for the subtle nuances that pinpoint those who lie from those who don't. She is learning at the foot of the master. Her father lights another cigarette off the one that's about to go out. It's time to find out who is telling the truth. Finally, the man on the right stands up and her father lunges forward. "I told you! The goddamn fucker on the right!"

He never missed an episode of *To Tell the Truth* and he always picked the right guy.

As quickly as that memory clicked into Jane's head, it was over. She was in her bedroom and all the scattered debris was in the trash bag. She stood silently for a moment and felt the numbness wash over her.

Jane left the house at 4:30 to beat the traffic out to her dad's place. Before leaving, she changed the bandage on her burned hand and coated it with the burn gel. It was a good hour's drive to her dad's house and she had to pick up the beer. She knew Mike would drag his heels after work. The only thing that guaranteed her brother's appearance at their father's house was a cold, six-pack of Corona. Call it bait to the trap.

At thirty years old, Mike was five years younger than Jane, but he acted more like twenty years her junior. He had a reticence to his step and a soft, unassuming voice that spoke volumes to anyone who was perceptive. Mike had shuffled from one construction job to another, always cutting out when the boss got too demanding. No matter how often Jane encouraged Mike and told him to stand up to whomever was bothering him, Mike never followed through. She was his older sister but she was really his mother and she treated him as such.

The traffic going east on I-70 toward Tower Road was surprisingly light for a Monday night. By the time Jane drove past the Denver International Airport exit, there were only a few other cars sharing the highway with her. By this point of the drive, the scenery became desolate and isolated. Flat, dry plains stretched into the distance until they met the cloudless sky. There was a starkness and emptiness to the area, even back twenty years ago when Jane called it home. Turning off on Tower Road, Jane gunned the Mustang down a lonely ribbon of road dotted by rural electric light poles, precariously balancing the never ending miles of electric lines that looped one after the other. The soulful voice of Gladys Knight singing "Midnight Train to Georgia" blared from the Mustang. Jane drove on Tower for several miles, almost to the line that separated Denver City and County from Adams County, and turned right onto a dirt road. She passed several old homes before turning left into the gravel drive, past the black mailbox that said "DALE PERRY" in stark white block letters.

Her father's bleached, single-story white house stood on the left side of the wide driveway, shaded by a ring of weeping willows. Directly ahead of the driveway was a narrow, wooden building with small windows that served as her father's workshop. When he wasn't knocking back booze or hunched over the kitchen table perusing photographs of mutilated bodies, you could find him inside the workshop. It was a place where he could clean his guns and listen to eight tracks of Tony Bennett, Nancy Sinatra and Dean Martin. Jane brought the Mustang to a halt ten feet from the workshop and turned off the engine. It was 5:30—a good forty-five minutes before Mike would wander down the road in his beat-up pickup truck. Forty-five minutes to be alone in a place she despised.

Jane got out of the car, grabbing the Corona from the front seat. She stared at the workshop. Her pulse quickened and that familiar rage welled up inside of her. She canvassed the squares of dusty windows and finally the tin roof, searching for "the mark." Through the filtering rays of the setting sun, she found it—a hole just big enough for a .38 bullet to exit.

Her dad bought the house and the weed-filled acre it sat on for $25,000 in the early sixties. That was back when Denver detectives weren't given city parameters in which they had to reside. There was a small circle of neighbors who lived nearby in this desolate corner of Denver County. As Jane liked to put it when she was growing up, you were close enough to the neighbors to ask for help, but far enough away so they couldn't hear you scream. Dale Perry didn't care if his wife had to drive over 30 miles one way to pick up a quart of milk or that his son and daughter had to wake up an hour and a half early each morning to make the long journey into school. In Dale's world, he was king and the human beings who were unlucky enough to exist in his shadow were told to do whatever he said and then shut up.

Jane entered the house, letting the screen door slam shut. Everything was in a kind of suspended animation—a visual portrait of the moments leading up to the heart attack. There was the half-washed pan in the sink. The dishcloth on the floor. The half drunk whiskey teetering on the arm of the recliner. The littered ashtray filled with cigarette butts. The three-week-old newspaper, opened to the "Crime Blotter." For Jane, it was like visiting a crime scene, except this victim unfortunately didn't die. There was an uneasy silence in the room that lay heavy in the air. Jane turned on the TV, flipped over to the Denver early evening news report and adjusted the volume so it was just loud enough to create background chatter.

Checking out the hall closet, Jane found stacks of cardboard boxes filled with the remnants of homicide notes, photos, and volumes of crime scene textbooks. It was the stuff of her childhood. She popped the lid off one box and uncovered a neatly arranged selection of old homicide manuals. Hoisting the box off the stack, she took it into the kitchen and set it on the tiled sideboard near the sink. The homicide manuals covered everything from crime scene surveillance to protecting the integrity of evidence. Interspersed between the dry text were pages of black-and-white crime scene photos, depicting gunshot wounds, stabbings, hangings and the occasional decapitation.

Jane lit a cigarette. As she lifted a large manual out of the box, several dozen color Polaroid photos slid out from the book and spread across the kitchen floor. The photos showed in great detail the dead, decomposing bodies of a husband and wife in bed. The husband had shot the wife and then turned the gun on himself. They'd been dead for three weeks in the middle of July before someone found them. When Dale Perry arrived on the scene, a bedroom taken over by thousands of cockroaches and maggots greeted him. They were everywhere—on the walls, the ceiling, the floor, the bed and inside of each black, blood-ied and bloated victim. The roaches had made a permanent trail inside the head of the husband, entering through his eyes and nose and exiting through his mouth and the hole where the bullet entered. It was all there in each grisly close-up, down to the trace markings of excrement left by a roach on the woman's wedding ring. The photos were twenty-one years old, but they were as disturbing as the first time Jane saw them. Instantly, it triggered the memory.

She's in the same kitchen with the same furniture, except she's fourteen years old. She's seated at the kitchen table under the piercing overhead lamp she half-jokingly referred to as "the third degree bulb." Her brother, nine years old, is seated next to her. Her father sits across from her. The Polaroid photos of the roach-covered bodies are strewn across the table. It's February and there's an icy chill in the air. Pellets of hail mixed with snow bounce off the kitchen window in a steady rat-a-tat-tat. Jane is serving her father and Mike dinner, doling out macaroni and cheese onto mustard yellow plates. Her father's cigarette dangles precariously from his lips, heavy ash hanging from the tip. He examines the crime photos as Mike grimaces at the gruesome images.

"I don't feel good," Mike says with a soft whine.

"What the hell's wrong with you?" Dale says, eyes still examining the Polaroids.

"My tummy hurts," Mike says, sitting back in his chair.

"There's nothing wrong with you!" Dale says brusquely. "Eat your food!"

"Come on, Mike," Jane quickly interject. "It's okay. Take a little bite."

"*Noooo*," Mike replies.

Dale smacks Mike's head. "Stop whining and eat your goddamn dinner!" Mike reacts with a muffled cry. "*Did you hear me?*" Dale screams as he leans over to Mike, inches from his face. "Shut up! You understand? *You understand me?*"

Mike sinks down into his chair and cries out, "Don't. Don't . . ."

Dale stands up and his chair skims across the floor. Jane bolts out of her seat.

"Goddamnit, you weak little fuck!" Dale yells. "You want something to cry about?" Dale grabs Mike by the back of his shirt and yanks him out of his chair.

"Janie!" Mike screams, trying to reach out to her. "*Janie!*"

Dale gives Mike a hard slap across the face, sending his son onto the floor. "I said shut up! *You understand?!*"

Mike screams as he rolls into a fetal position and covers his ears. "*Janie!*"

"Janie?" Mike's voice shook Jane out of her daze. "You okay?"

It took Jane a second to put herself back into the moment. "Sure," she said, quickly gathering up the fallen photos from the kitchen floor.

"Here, I'll help," Mike offered.

"No!" Jane barked. "I'll do it."

Mike stood in the doorway, wedging his body against the frame. "Sorry I'm late. Traffic, you know?"

"Right. Traffic," Jane said as she slid the last Polaroid off the floor and buried the bundle in the box.

Mike looked around the room with an uneasy stare. His thick shock of blond hair fell over his eyes. With a nervous jerk, he flicked his head backward, forcing his hair in place. Although Mike was thirty, he still had that doe-eyed, innocent look, with a tinge of adolescent awkwardness. Even his body, with its soft muscular tone, seemed underdeveloped. "It feels weird in here. I mean, like, him not being here, you know?"

Jane slammed the lid onto the cardboard box. "He might be horizontal in a hospital bed right now. But take my word for it, the bastard's still here."

"You bring the Corona?" Mike asked, keeping his priorities straight.

"Have I ever let you down?" Jane said, pointing to the six-pack.

Mike broke into a wide, toothy grin. "I can always count on you." He crossed in front of the television. "Hey, Janie, look! Chris is on TV."

Jane let out a long sigh. "Oh, God. Turn off the asshole."

Mike was drawn into Chris' commentary. He was standing outside a home, a mass of microphones in front of him, addressing the media. "Hey, Janie. You know anything about that double murder last night?"

"People get killed every day. Turn him off!"

Mike poked his head into the kitchen. "Think that little girl saw anything?"

Like an irate parent, Jane walked with purpose into the living room. "Jesus, Mike! Turn it off!" With that,

Jane angrily slammed off the TV.

Two hours later, the hall closet was empty of all the boxes. Jane pulled out a few classic crime scene text manuals for her home library and dumped the leftovers into garbage bags. The rest of the house would have to wait for another day. Besides, after she and Mike downed three Coronas each, there wasn't much desire to continue.

They sat outside on the cement steps that led from the kitchen to the workshop. The heat of the late May day had burned off, leaving a stippled layer of Denver pollution against the pink-stained sky. Jane lit two cigarettes, handing one to Mike. She took a swig of Corona and let out a low sigh.

"Does your hand still hurt?" Mike asked.

"I don't know. I stopped connecting to the pain a few days ago."

Mike grinned. "Thanks to a fifth, eh?"

"You got it," Jane said with a half-smile as she took another sip of beer.

There was a moment of silence between them before Mike spoke up. "Hey, I got news for you!" Mike said brightly. "I made a decision."

"Oh, god, you made a decision. And what would that be?"

"I'm gonna ask Lisa to move in."

"Who's Lisa?"

"You know . . . *Lisa*. We've been seeing each other for two months. Well, technically, six weeks. But I'm gonna do it. I'm gonna ask her."

"Mike, that's not a good idea. It's six weeks. You've spent half of those six weeks at my place. So, technically, it's three weeks and that's not long enough."

"Janie, I think she's the one—"

"You thought Kelly—"

"Karen," Mike interrupted.

"*Karen*. You thought Karen was 'the one.' You thought Lori was 'the one.'"

"Okay, yeah, at the time. But Lisa's different."

"They're all different. And then it falls apart, you get hurt and it's a mess."

"Fuck, Janie. Sometimes you act like my warden."

"That's my job, Mike." Jane cast her eyes toward the ground.

"Don't you want me to be happy?"

"Happy? Mike, the only happy people are the ignorant. Nobody with a functioning brain is happy. They know better." Jane looked over at Mike who was sinking into himself. "I don't want to see you get hurt. We've got each other. That's one more person than a lot of people have. I'll never hurt you and I'll never let you down. You can't say that for all the Lisas out there."

Mike thought for a second before he spoke. "You got Chris."

"Fuck Chris! I'm getting rid of Chris!"

"I thought you and he were—"

"We're nothing!" Jane felt herself slipping. She didn't know whether it was the beer or the end of an awful day but she had to drag herself back into the moment. She took a deep drag off her cigarette. "Sometimes I'm talking to Chris and it's like I'm talking to Dad." Jane looked off to the side, lost in a pocket of emotion.

Mike seriously considered what Jane said. "Shit . . . That's gotta suck." He downed another gulp of beer. "You still having those dreams about the explosion?"

"Yeah. Sure."

"I thought so. When I tried to wake you up this morning, you were *really* deep sleeping."

"You should have gotten me up. I was damn near late to work."

"You were talkin' weird again!" Mike chuckled.

Jane turned to Mike with a puzzled expression. "Huh?"

Mike grinned. "When you were sleepin' these last few days, you were quite the Chatty Cathy doll. It didn't make a shitload of sense."

Mike's jovial recollections of her blackout irritated Jane. "*What did I say?*"

"It was all disjointed. But . . ." Mike suddenly remembered, "I wrote some words down that you kept repeating." He pulled a wad of receipts from his jeans pocket and sorted through the disorganized bundle. "Here it is. You explain this to me: 'Navy blue . . . Glock something or another . . . Bright light . . . Hold on to me—'"

Jane snatched the corner of paper out of Mike's hand. Her heart raced as she read the words. Except for "Hold on to me," it was a printed repeat of the odd staccato visions. "When did I say this?"

"You said it lots of times over the last few days. You said other shit, too, but I couldn't understand it." Jane stared uneasily at the piece of paper. Mike's happy-go-lucky countenance melted into a look of concern. "You okay?"

Jane took a final swig of beer, finishing off the bottle. "Of course I'm okay," she replied, as if saying that statement would make it true. "Come on, let's get outta here." Jane collected the empty Corona bottles.

"This is a shitload of trash. I don't want to drag it to the curb," Mike said, a slight whine to his voice. Jane instructed him to snag the dolly from the workshop. He disappeared into the small, dirt-floored side building, leaving one of the large wooden doors wide open. "I can't find it!" he yelled out to Jane.

"Keep looking," Jane said with an edge.

"Man, it's a fuckin' mess in here. This is gonna be a bitch to clean out, Janie!"

Jane felt her body tense up and her jaw clench. She stared at the open door to the workshop and wished Mike would find the dolly and come back. "Forget cleaning!" Jane yelled. "We'll burn the fucker down!"

Mike emerged from the workshop with the dolly. "Cool!" He rolled the garbage bags to the curb while Jane locked up and turned off the lights save the outside porch lamp. She felt the urge to break the stonecold silence so she popped a CD into the car's player. Turning up the volume, the gritty voice of Bob Seger sang

"Katmandu." She picked up the six-pack of empty Corona bottles and walked around the car. Mike propped the dolly against the house and crossed over to Jane. She reached down and grabbed one of the Coronas by its long, thin neck and looked up at her dad's workshop, the red glow of the setting sun darting across the glass windows. Reeling back her arm, she eyed one of the workshop's windows and tossed the beer bottle toward the target. It crashed through the glass, leaving a crystal echo and a huge hole. Mike turned to her, his mouth agape. She pulled another Corona bottle from the pack and picked out another window. Hurling it through the air, it burst through the glass with a defined clatter. Jane handed Mike one of the bottles. He took it but hesitated. "Go on," Jane insisted.

"But it's his—"

"Fuck him, Mike," Jane said with a merciless tone. "*Fuck him.*"

Mike broke into a mischievous grin and hurled the bottle toward the workshop, leaving a hole in a side window. He grabbed one bottle and then another, cheering like a kid after each explosion of glass. Mike was so into the moment that he didn't see Jane pull out her pistol from her shoulder holster. When he finally turned to her, she was focused straight ahead, both hands extended, her finger brushing the trigger. He stood perfectly still, eager to find out what Jane would do. Mike watched as her eyes zoned in on a target and a peculiar look came over her face. She squeezed the trigger with precision and blew a hole the size of a baseball in the center window. Jane calmly lowered the gun, still staring straight ahead. After several seconds, she turned to Mike. "Ready to go?"

It was after nine o'clock when Jane turned onto Milwaukee Street. She'd stopped at the liquor store to pick up a fifth of Jack Daniels and consumed a good six swigs by the time she neared her house. As she drove closer to her home, she saw a figure seated on her front steps. At first, she thought it was Chris, but the build was wrong. It wasn't until she pulled in front of her house that she realized it was Sergeant Weyler.

# Chapter 6

Sergeant Weyler looked just as dapper in his suit and tie as he had over twelve hours earlier. Jane felt a rush of heat hit her head—partly from the three Coronas and whiskey she had just consumed and partly from the irritation at seeing her boss waiting for her on her own front steps. Weyler sauntered over to Jane's car as she carefully slid the brown bag that held the Jack Daniels under the front seat. He leaned over on the passenger side of the Mustang, addressing her through the open window.

"Good evening, Detective Perry."

"Hello," Jane said, staring Weyler in the eye, trying to mask the slight buzz.

"How are you?" Weyler said pointedly.

"How am I supposed to be?"

Weyler briefly surveyed the inside of the car, like a hound dog on the trail. "Have you been drinking, Detective Perry?"

Jane was a bit put off. "I've had a beer," she said with a touch of sarcasm.

"*A* beer?"

"Am I a suspect in a crime? Because I sure feel like one right now."

"Just a simple question—"

"Well, sir, I don't know why it matters. After all, I am on suspension."

Weyler regarded Jane very carefully. "Yes, you are."

There was an awkward pause between the two of them. Jane got out of her car. "Shouldn't you be home with your wife watching *Prime Suspect* on PBS?" Jane said, undaunted, as she lit a cigarette. "What are you doing here?"

Weyler stood straight as an arrow, pulling himself up to his full 6'4" height. "I am here, Detective Perry, to make an assessment."

"On what? My character? My integrity? My sanity?"

"Yes."

"If you don't know those answers by now, then I guess you don't really know me." Jane headed toward her front door.

"I know you better than you think I do."

Jane stopped, her back to Weyler. She half believed him as a shudder raced down her spine. Jane turned back to Weyler. "What do you want?"

"I had a visit from Martha Durrett today. She was complaining about certain obscenities."

"You'll get no arguments from me. Martha Durrett is as obscene as they come."

Weyler chose to ignore Jane's evasive reply. "You made quite an impression on someone today. *Quite* an impression."

Jane took a long drag on her cigarette. "Did you arrest her?"

"Who?"

"*Who?* The Mexican woman."

"Oh. No, I did not. As far as I'm concerned, it never happened."

Jane's eyes trailed off. "I saw her in the elevator. And I knew. She had that look. So did the kid." She looked at Weyler. "Make sure that son-of-a-bitch husband of hers suffers for what he did to his kid. Put him in a cell with five angry queers. Make him feel the same terror and pain his little girl felt." Jane sensed the warmth of the alcohol taking effect and wanted to be alone. "I have to go. I've got things to do."

"After you left, certain things transpired regarding a high-profile case."

Jane jumped to attention. "You got a lead on the Stover case! I *knew* it!"

"Think you can make it to the office by 10:00 tomorrow morning?"

"I'll be there at 8:00!"

"Ten is fine."

"Sure. Ten o'clock. I'll go over the file tonight and organize my notes."

Weyler stared at Jane with a careful eye. "Get some sleep."

"I don't need sleep—"

"*Get some sleep.*" Weyler turned and started toward his sedan. "Oh, Jane? I came here tonight against my better judgment. The case is highly sensitive. I need you to be functioning at peak performance tomorrow morning. Please don't make me regret this."

"You will not regret this, boss. You have my word."

Jane waited until Weyler's headlights turned off Milwaukee before she retrieved the bottle of Jack Daniels from her car.

After an improvised dinner of macaroni and cheese, Jane situated herself at the dining room table and spread out the pages of notes and files from the Stover case. Perhaps she'd discover something new—something she'd missed before. But after four hours, everything felt like a blur. Jane stood up, stretching her back and peered at the kitchen clock. *1 a.m.* She was tired but her mind was racing too fast to allow sleep—not an uncommon problem for Jane Perry. There were two ways to quell the insomnia: a healthy glass of whiskey and the drone of a late night radio show she'd come to depend on called "Night Talk." It was an eclectic mishmash of politics, philosophy, rhetoric on current events and anything else the female host could dredge up for the legions of insomniacs that depended on the program. After several sips of whiskey, Jane turned on the radio and returned to her seat at the dining room table.

"Good evening to all you junkies of the night . . ." Jane stared at the radio, perplexed. It wasn't the same host. "I'm Tony Mooney and this is 'Night Talk.'" His timbre was low, warm and intoxicating. Jane wasn't sure if it was the whiskey, but she found herself drawn into Mooney's enigmatic voice. "I'll be hosting the show for the next six weeks or so, while your regular host is on maternity leave." Jane took another sip of the whiskey and arched an eyebrow. Six weeks off, she thought. She couldn't fathom a six-week break from her job. "Many of you know me as a researcher and lover of the paranormal side of life—the elusive, mystical side of our consciousness that hovers behind that fragile veil we call reality . . ." Jane regarded the radio with suspicion. Perhaps the whiskey was responsible but a sense of paranoia tightened around her. "Do you ever feel like you're going crazy? Maybe you are. Or maybe . . . maybe you're a genius. There's a thin line, my friends, between genius and insanity." Jane rubbed her head and knocked back the glass of whiskey. A pervasive blanket of sweet numbness washed over her. She poured another glass of the amber nectar and blearily dug her hand in her pants' pocket. Feeling the edge of the small piece of paper, she withdrew it and held it under the piercing glare of the overhead light. She read the words to herself: "Navy blue . . . Glock . . . Bright light . . . Hold on to me." She stared at the paper, her eyes moving in and out of focus. Mooney's voice hovered in the background, a melodic, concomitant soundtrack for the drugged sensibility engulfing Jane. She felt herself falling into the words when the sharp sound of a child screaming quickly spun her around. With eyes wide open, she stared into the kitchen where the crisp scream still lingered.

Morning came far too early. Jane awoke under the

burning glare of the overhead dining table light. The fifth of whiskey was almost drained and the nearby ashtray filled with the burned out remnants of a cigarette pack. Outside, the sound of a car alarm suddenly went off, jolting Jane out of her slumber. She steadied herself between the eye-piercing overhead light and the streaming morning sun that filtered through her two large front windows. After a few seconds, she squinted toward the kitchen clock to check the time.

*9:00 a.m.*

"Shit!" Jane exclaimed as she gathered together the mass of paperwork and crammed it into the files. Between gulps of strong black coffee, she raced through the house getting ready. Her head pounded from the hangover as she heard Weyler's warning: "Don't make me regret this." She was damned if that was going to happen.

Her bandaged hand looked a bit soiled from ink stains and smelled of whiskey and cigarette smoke. She figured she'd do her best to hide the hand from Weyler. After all, he wasn't interested in her injury. Together, they were about to break open one of the most frustrating cases of Jane's career.

Jane squealed into the DH parking garage with five minutes to spare. She grabbed her leather satchel, papers and files bursting from its seams, and caught the elevator. Jane hit the third floor button with the heel of her boot. As she puffed nervously on her ash-heavy cigarette, she shook her head from side to side in an attempt to throw off the heavy, throbbing aftermath of booze. Jane squashed her cigarette on the elevator wall as the doors opened onto the third floor. As she headed toward Weyler's office she nearly ran right into evidence technician Ron Dickson.

"Detective Perry!" Ron exclaimed. "Excuse me!"

"It's okay, Ron," Jane said, trying to maneuver her way around him.

"I know you're in a hurry, but I wanted to remind you

about the fundraising campaign for D.A.R.E. Can I put you down for your usual donation?"

"Yeah, sure. But not now. I gotta be somewhere," Jane said as she made her way to Weyler's office. She hit his office with one minute to spare. Weyler looked up from his desk, assessing Jane's appearance.

"Good morning, Detective Perry."

"Morning," Jane said as she slid into a chair and unloaded paperwork.

"Close the door, would you?"

Jane pushed the door shut with her hand. The sound of the sudden slam caused her to grimace in pain.

"How are you this morning?" Weyler said haltingly.

"Fine, sir," Jane said, keeping her eyes on her files and avoiding Weyler's glare.

Weyler leaned over and turned on the radio to an easy listening station. Jane's attention was immediately drawn to the music. Weyler gradually cranked up the volume on a particularly high-pitched Bee Gees tune. To Jane, it was like fingernails on a chalkboard. She grabbed her head in pain. Weyler quickly turned off the radio.

"You're hungover!" Weyler said angrily.

"No! I fell asleep on the dining room table. My neck's stiff. I'll be fine."

Weyler rose from his chair and leaned across his desk toward Jane. "I told you this was important! I told you this was a highly sensitive meeting. And you *still* got drunk!" Weyler's voice had a nervous edge that Jane had never heard. "You're going to make me look like a damn fool, Detective Perry. I'm putting my ass on the line for you! I expected a little more cooperation!"

Jane was taken aback by Weyler's sudden anger. He seemed overly concerned, in her opinion. "Sir," she said carefully, "it's just you and me sitting here, throwing possible scenarios back and forth."

Weyler stared at Jane, his anger still evident. Jane nervously pulled out more files. "Put your files away, Detective Perry."

"I need notes, sir. I don't have it all memorized."

"Put your files away. *You will not need them."* Weyler said with emphasis.

"Sir?" Jane said confused and flustered. "What's going on?"

Weyler composed himself and sat down, adjusting his freshly pressed dark suit. "I came to your house last night to make an assessment as to your ability to function. It was vital that you appear in the office this morning sober, not smelling of whiskey and not looking like you've spent the night slumped over furniture. Your appearance and capacity to think clearly is of utmost importance in this sensitive issue."

"If I'm supposed to address the media today, you should have told me!"

"It's not the media! And it's got nothing to do with the Stover case."

Jane sat back, totally perplexed and feeling uneasy. "What the hell is it?"

"How much of the news have you caught the last couple days?"

"None. I've been occupied."

"You are completely unaware of the leading news story on every local network?"

"I've been busy—" Jane said, annoyed.

"Well, allow me to fill you in on what everyone in Denver is talking about. Two nights ago, on the evening of May 23, a little girl named Emily Lawrence, age nine and a half, barricaded herself in her bedroom closet while her parents were brutally stabbed to death downstairs in their living room. The living room was torn apart, as though the killer or killers were looking for something. The only incriminating evidence found at the house was a mound of cocaine weighing in at nearly five ounces. This occurred in the Washington Park neighborhood where instances such as murder and high stakes drug trafficking are about as common as a comet hitting a large city."

Jane quickly digested what she heard and shrugged her

shoulders. "Alright. Fine. Two people dead. Drug deal gone bad. I'm sure you have everyone and their brother out there doing their job."

"Oh, yes. Chris . . . you remember Chris?" Weyler said sarcastically. "He's lead detective on the case. He's also fielding the media's questions. I have about three quarters of our staff out there. Emily is in protective custody. Between her guardian adlitum and her appointed psychologist, she's not short on company. And your good buddy, Martha Durrett? The Department of Social Services has given Martha the job of tending to the child's welfare and safety."

"I'm sure they'll bond like oil and water," Jane said with a smirk.

"Actually, that's exactly how Emily Lawrence is bonding with *all* of her caregivers, Martha included. In short, the child is not talking. Except, of course, for the occasional question of 'Where's my mommy and daddy?'"

"You didn't tell the kid they're dead?"

"I leave that up to the experts. The child psychologist felt it wasn't appropriate for the girl to know right now. Martha agreed."

"Oh, sure." Jane crossed her arms defiantly and shook her head in disgust. "Being evasive is always good with kids. Lying is, too. Martha should tell Emily that her folks are camping. Then in, I don't know, three years, figure out a way to work it into the conversation that they're dead. That should ease the kid's pain."

Weyler pinched the skin between his nose. "Detective Perry, must you?"

"Kids aren't stupid, sir. I may not have any of my own, but I was one. And I can tell you that they know things. Lying to them just screws them up."

"Martha will inform Emily when she feels the child can handle it. Let's get back on point." Weyler leaned back in his chair, his hands folded against each other. "We are ninety-nine percent certain that Emily saw something."

"You said she was barricaded in her closet upstairs. What did she see?"

"Evidence points to a couple possibilities. First and foremost, Emily's palm and fingerprints were found in the streaks of blood along the wooden banister. The killer or killers wore gloves and dragged their bloody hands up the banister on their way, presumably, to Emily's bedroom at the top of the stairs. We know that one of them entered her room and stood approximately in eyesight of the closet door that was slightly ajar when patrol officers found her the following morning. Blood droplets were found on the bedroom carpeting that probably came from the tip of a knife. It is only by the grace of God that the individual who was in that room was somehow distracted from finding the child. Either way, there's a good chance she saw him from in there."

Jane's head began to beat from the hangover. Trying to intelligently debate with Weyler was proving difficult. "Okay, maybe I'm missing something here. How can she be hidden in her closet and also be touching a bloody banister?"

"She obviously didn't stay in the closet the entire time," Weyler said irritated. "Do a little crime scene math! Or is your head pounding too much?" Jane instinctively grabbed a cigarette from the pack in her shirt pocket. "You can't smoke in here!"

Jane jabbed the cigarette back into the pack. She could feel herself becoming edgier. "Okay, so, she's in the closet and she possibly sees the perp. He leaves the scene for whatever reason. She gets up, walks downstairs and sees mom and dad on the living room floor. Then she goes back up—"

"No, she does not go back up right away. She walks over to her parents, their blood pooled together, and stands there in her bare feet for an undetermined amount of time. We know that from the trail of her bloody footprints that lead back up the stairs. The front of her nightgown was also partially stained with their blood as were the palms of her hands."

Jane listened, unable to stop the gory visuals. As much as she tried to remain detached, she could feel herself falling into the child's body, standing in her parents' blood and looking down on their mutilated corpses. Jane collected herself. "It sounds like you know a lot already about this case. I'm sure the kid will tell you the rest."

"As I said earlier, she's not talking except to ask if her parents are dead. She stood in their blood and she doesn't remember any of it. Martha says it's deep post-traumatic stress. When you see or experience something so utterly destructive and shocking that you simply turn it off, you black out in a way and bury it somewhere deep down in your psyche."

Jane looked Weyler in the eye. "Sounds great. Some people aren't given the gift of blacking out memories."

"According to Martha, it's never completely blacked out."

"Wait a second," Jane interrupted. "Since when did Martha become an expert trauma psychologist? Isn't she just a glorified government babysitter?"

"She's read books on the subject—"

"*Oh, spare me!*"

"She works with children who have been traumatized! Children just like Emily Lawrence who bury ghastly images deep in their mind and can't remember. However, the research shows that slices of those memories fall between the cracks of the child's subconscious. With the right stimulus, they reappear, allowing for a full reconstruction of the events. For the time being, it might just be a memory of, say, a face. Maybe the face of the killer."

"That's asking for a lot, don't you think?"

"It's all dependent upon what the child is willing to share. Martha is of the opinion that Emily has something to say."

"So, now Martha's psychic?"

"In the few words that Emily has said to her, she has made it crystal clear that she has some kind of information to offer us."

"Why don't you just leave the poor kid alone?"

"Because two innocent people who had no criminal history were savagely stabbed to death in their comfortable Washington Park living room. Because I am drowning in a case that is quickly becoming as high-profile as the JonBenet murder. And because I don't give up or give in when I have a viable witness to the crime. In short, I am in the business of solving homicides. And so are you."

Jane started to shove her files back into her satchel. "Well, good luck."

"Remember last night when I told you that you made quite an impression on somebody? I was referring to Miss Emily Lawrence." Jane looked at Weyler in confusion. "For whatever reason, you appear to have captured the child's attention. First in the stairwell and more importantly, in the hallway when you talked the Mexican woman out of killing her husband. I'm not sure what Emily sees in you, but it makes no matter to me. You've been personally chosen by this child as the only individual she will talk to."

Jane could not believe what she was hearing. "You have *got* to be kidding! She's nine and a half. When did we start giving nine-and-a-half-year-olds the power to tell us who they will only speak to?"

Weyler leaned forward. "When that nine-and-a-half-year-old can solve a crime!"

Jane folded her arms tightly across her chest and met Weyler's piercing glare. "I won't do it."

"Then your suspension becomes a termination. Effective immediately." Weyler's tone was firm and etched with anger.

Jane bristled. Her whole body tightened. "You can't do that."

"*Watch me!*"

"You can't fire someone for refusing to interrogate a witness!"

"Someone with a hangover shouldn't question my administrative power. Now, what's it going to be?"

She looked away from Weyler as her heart began to race.

Jane stopped by the coffee maker on her way to the interrogation room and poured herself a cup. She wasn't sure whether her head was pounding from the hangover or from the anger she felt at being blackmailed into talking to Emily. The interrogation room was just down the hall from homicide. It was a tiny room, about eight by ten feet square, designed to make suspects feel pinned in and anxious. The walls were painted lime green, or as some called it, "D.O.C. green" for Department of Corrections. The floor was covered in tough, "industrial-strength" carpeting. The walls were empty save for a corkboard where evidence was placed, a writing board for the suspect, a nondescript clock, a calendar and a "No Smoking" sign in bright red lettering. Fluorescent lighting beamed down on the suspect, who sat across from the interrogator at a small table. Hidden in the corner of the small room was a camera and microphones that videotaped the entire scene. A computer monitor sat nearby, connected to a keyboard in the narrow observation room on the opposite side of a two-way mirror. During questioning, an observer who was monitoring the interrogation, could type a question into the computer for the interrogator to ask.

Sergeant Weyler stopped first at the observation room and poked his head in. "Here she is."

Chris popped his head outside the door. He looked weary with bloodshot eyes and tousled hair. It was obvious to Jane that the Lawrence case was occupying his nights and days, leaving little time for sleep. Chris acknowledged Jane with a tinge of attitude in his voice. "Glad you could make it to my case!"

"I'm not grandstanding, Chris," Jane said, irritated as

she leaned her leather satchel against the wall. "I'm only here because Weyler strongly suggested I help out."

Chris moved closer to Jane, catching a whiff of her boozy aroma. "You're fucking hungover!" Chris addressed Weyler. "*She's hungover!*"

"Hey, why don't you talk to the kid?" Jane yelled back. "You're such a people person, I'm sure you'll bond!"

"Alright, you two!" Weyler said. "That's enough! Jane is not going to screw up your case, Chris. The child simply asked to talk to her and not you."

"Fine," Chris said, sounding like a petulant child. "Just find out what she saw and whatever important thing she has to tell you so I can solve this crime and get the media off my ass."

"Oh, like you don't love having your face splashed across the local news shows!" Jane exclaimed.

"Did it ever occur to you that maybe I don't like being hounded by the media? Constantly being asked if we're as inept as we appear?"

"Have I got to pull the two of you apart?" Weyler interrupted.

"No, sir," Chris said, scowling at Jane. "Just get the information we need. And keep your eye on the monitor in case I come up with questions. Don't act like some one-woman renegade in there!"

Jane turned toward the interrogation room. "Your confidence overwhelms me."

Weyler gently knocked on the interrogation room door. Martha Durrett opened the door and slipped out, closing the door quietly behind her.

"Detective Perry! You don't look well," Martha said, her voice laced with apprehension. "What's wrong with you?"

"Oh, Christ," Jane said, turning to Weyler. "I don't need this shit!"

"There you go with that inappropriate language again! You can't say those words in front of that child!" Martha turned to address Weyler. "Sergeant Weyler, I don't feel this is a good idea. I'm almost positive that with a little role playing, engaging the child in some sort of artistic endeavor and maybe incorporating dolls that represent her family, I can convince Emily to disclose information to me."

Jane rolled her eyes. "I can't believe the state allows you anywhere near a kid!"

"Sergeant Weyler, the detective is out of order!"

Jane grabbed her throbbing head. "Hey, am I going in there or not?"

"I don't think this is a prudent idea!" Martha exclaimed.

Weyler took Martha by the shoulder and ushered her into the observation room. "Martha, go inside and wait for me." Martha reluctantly disappeared inside the narrow room. Weyler turned to Jane with a frazzled look. He grasped Jane's shoulder tightly and looked her in the eye. "All I ask is that you do your job." Jane nodded. Weyler turned, went into the observation room and closed the door behind him.

Jane walked into the interrogation room and shut the door. Emily was seated across the table from the two-way mirror. A stuffed animal shaped like a brown bear sat on the table in front of her, next to the computer.

Emily looked up at Jane, a look of slight surprise on her face. The girl seemed out of place in the room, sitting there in her denim jumper and cheerful yellow-and-red polka dot, short-sleeved shirt. "You're here!" Emily exclaimed.

"In the flesh, kid," Jane said as she slid into the chair opposite Emily.

Emily intently stared at Jane in utter fascination. After a second, all the kid could say was, "You're here´. . . in the flesh." Emily looked stunned. The seeming worship by the kid made Jane feel uncomfortable. Nervously, she rubbed her head with her bandaged hand and let out a sigh. "Are you okay?" Emily asked Jane, genuinely concerned.

"Of course I'm okay."

"You look kind of sick."

"I'm not sick."

"What's that smell?"

"Excuse me?"

"You smell like my daddy when he gets drunk."

"Oh, this is great," Jane said as she pulled out a cigarette from her shirt pocket and lit up.

"I don't think they let you smoke in here," Emily said, motioning to the "No Smoking" sign.

"Is that a fact?" Jane said, taking a deep drag on her cigarette.

From inside the observation room, Chris buried his head in his hand and muttered, "I knew she was going to fuck this up."

Emily's eyes were drawn to Jane's bandaged hand. "What happened to your hand?" she asked.

"It got burned."

"In the kitchen?"

"No. In the line of duty."

Emily looked at Jane, examining her face very closely. "What happened to your head?"

Jane was caught off guard. "What?"

"The scar on your forehead."

Jane readjusted herself in her seat nervously. She could feel the prying eyes of Weyler, Martha and Chris behind her. "It's just a scar."

"How'd you get it?"

"I got it . . . in the line of duty."

"That must have hurt really bad."

"You're a real detail-oriented person, aren't you?"

"Huh?"

"You see small things in a big picture."

"I guess so."

Jane felt uneasy and took another drag. "What's your bear's name?" she said pointing to the stuffed animal.

"I don't know. Martha gave it to me. I'm supposed to talk to it and tell it secrets."

"Really?" Jane wanted to roll her eyes but restrained herself. "You doing that?"

"No. Why would I tell a stuffed animal secrets? It's not real."

Jane could feel a slight smile forming on her face but did her best to hide it. She looked over to the monitor. A sentence scrolled across the screen in capital letters: ASK HER WHAT SHE SAW! Jane knew the message was from Chris. "So, you got something you want to talk about?"

Emily sat for a moment, composing her thoughts. "That lady yesterday with the gun. I saw what you did and I heard what you said to her."

Jane turned her head to the side and spoke, directing her response to Martha without Emily realizing it. "Yeah, well, you were not supposed to be up there."

Martha turned to Weyler. "Was that comment directed at me?"

Weyler, eyes focused on Emily, ignored Martha.

Emily leaned forward a bit. "Well, I was there. *Were you scared?*"

"No."

"How did you know what to say to her?"

"I just told her the truth." Jane took another nervous puff on her cigarette.

Emily leaned forward. "But you knew how to save her?"

"From doing something stupid? Yeah. Look, if you wanted to talk about that Mexican woman, you could have chatted up anybody around here!" Out of the corner of her eye, Jane saw the frantic typing of Chris transferring another message: ENGAGE HER, DAMMIT!!! Jane slammed her hand against the monitor and pushed it away so the screen faced the wall.

"What the hell is she doing?" Chris yelled.

"She knows what she's doing," Weyler said, keeping his eyes forward.

Emily sat back, sizing up Jane. "I can't talk to just anyone," Emily said softly. "Most people lie. My mommy lies and so does my daddy. My best friend moved away and they wouldn't tell me why. And when I ask them if they love each other, they say they do, but I know they're lying."

"Yeah, well, if everybody told the truth, there would be no secrets. And I can't imagine a world with no secrets, can you?"

Chris pressed his forehead against the two-way mirror. "Is she seriously trying to kill my case?"

Emily leaned forward. "You know stuff, don't you?" Emily questioned. "Important stuff?"

"Yeah, they call me an encyclopedia of knowledge here at Headquarters."

"If I ask you a question, will you tell me the truth?"

Jane took a hard drag on her cigarette. "If I know the answer, yeah, sure."

Emily leaned her body against the table, resting her elbows on the edge. She hesitated and then spoke. "Are my mommy and daddy dead?"

Jane looked Emily straight in the eye. "Yes," she said quietly.

Emily's eyebrows arched upward ever so slightly. Her body tightened as her eyes traced the top of the table.

Martha turned to Weyler in a rage. "My God! How could she do that? The child is not ready to hear that! Didn't you advise Detective Perry of this? *Pull her out of there!*"

"Let's see where it goes," Weyler instructed. Jane carefully watched Emily's every move. "I'm sorry, kid," she said in earnest.

Emily looked up at Jane, eyes wide. "Who's gonna make my lunch?" Jane was caught off guard. She searched for something to say. "Somebody will make your lunch and your breakfast and your dinner and you will be okay."

Emily looked off to the side. She seemed to go into a

daze. Jane sat back, waiting and hoping that whatever was buried within Emily would stay buried. As the child zoned out, her breathing became slightly heavier and her eyes stayed fixed on her reflection in the two-way mirror.

The trio of onlookers in the observation room stood transfixed.

"Jesus," Chris said quietly to Weyler. "The kid *does* know something."

Emily came out of her daze and stared at herself in the mirror. "I know a secret."

Jane felt her body stiffen. "Is that so?" was all she could manage.

Emily got up and slowly made her way toward Jane. She hesitated briefly before cupping her hand to Jane's ear and whispering.

Weyler and Chris strained to hear the microphone pick up any sound but it was useless. "What in the hell—" Chris said under his breath. As Emily whispered into Jane's ear, Jane remained stonefaced. When Emily finished, Jane kept a poker face but turned her head slightly toward the two-way mirror. Chris shook his head in frustration. "I don't fuckin' believe this."

Emily pulled away from Jane, never once taking her eyes off her. Jane gathered her thoughts. "Is that all you have to say?"

Emily stared, absolutely transfixed by Jane's face. "It's really . . . weird . . ."

Jane's gut unexplainably clamped down. Staring back at Emily, she felt slightly disoriented. "What's . . . weird?"

Emily looked off to side as if she were trying to remember something. "I can't explain it." She carefully crossed back to her chair and sat down.

Jane did her best to shake off the disjointed sensations competing for her attention. *Damn, the booze.* "Well, I'll leave you be." Jane plopped the cigarette butt into her coffee cup and got up. But before she could take a step, Emily reached out and tightly grabbed her hand.

An electrical jolt raced down her spine as she locked eyes with the child. The deeper Jane sank into those eyes, the closer she came to losing control. She had seen the exact same eyes filled with fear looking back at her more than twenty years ago. But there was something else—something closer that tugged at a fresh memory. She could feel herself falling into herself. It was all she could do to yank her hand out of Emily's grasp and head out the door.

Jane slammed the door shut and pressed her back up against it. She grabbed her head as a jumbled blur of blurry images raced in front of her. Weyler emerged from the observation room, followed closely by Martha and Chris.

"What have you done to that child?!" Martha barked at Jane as she pushed her aside and went into the interrogation room.

Jane kept staring straight ahead, still not able to focus.

"What the hell did she whisper, Jane?" Chris yelled. "Goddamnit, Jane! I'm lead detective on this case. Not you! What the fuck did she say?"

Weyler stood waiting, observing Jane and her reaction.

Jane turned to Chris, clearly unsettled. "Fuck you." With that, she turned, grabbed her satchel and headed toward the elevator. Weyler followed.

Weyler turned back to Chris. "Let me handle this!"

Jane slammed her hand against the "down" button on the elevator. The doors opened and she got on. Weyler slid into the elevator just before the doors closed. Jane pounded the button that was marked "parking."

"What happened in there, Jane?" Weyler asked in a probing manner.

"Leave me alone!" Jane was still shaking and trying to keep herself together.

"When she grabbed your hand, something happened."

Jane pounded the "parking" button harder and harder. "Nothing happened!!!"

"I was standing on the other side of the wall! Don't tell me nothing happened!" The doors opened onto the parking level and Jane burst off the elevator. Weyler stayed close on her tail. "If it was nothing, then why are you shaking? Why can't you look me in the eye? Why can't you tell me the truth you're so fond of telling?"

Jane stopped several feet from her car and turned to Weyler. "You want to know what she said? She said, 'I know they're watching us from the other side of that funny mirror.' Satisfied?!" She swung open her unlocked car door and got in.

Weyler leaned his hands on the open window. "Alright. But that doesn't explain your present behavior. What are you not telling me?"

"Boss, I swear to God, if you don't take your hands off this car . . ."

Weyler stood back. Jane shifted her car in reverse and screeched out of the parking lot, leaving a trail of blackened rubber on the cement and the lingering echo of screaming tires.

# Chapter 7

Jane slammed her Mustang into gear the second she cleared Headquarters. She looped around the Civic Center, changing lanes erratically. Angrily, she slapped her head several times trying to bury the emerging memory. A pitter-patter of fat spring raindrops dotted the windshield as Jane curved around Cheesman Park. The rain began to fall with vengeance, making it difficult to see more than a car's length in front. Jane pulled over to the side, under a "No Parking" sign as the rain beat like fists on the roof. Jane grabbed the steering wheel, stared into the oncoming storm and gave in.

"*Janie!*" Mike screams.

She is fourteen and back in the kitchen staring at Mike who is in a fetal position on the floor where he landed after Dale slapped him out of his chair. A steady pit-pit-pit of hail mixed with snow hits the kitchen window.

"Shut up, you weak fuck!" Dale screams as he leans over Mike.

Mike cups his hands over his ears and holds his breath. Dale punches Mike hard in the head as Mike lets out a bloodcurdling wail.

"What the fuck's wrong with you!" Dale screams, moving closer to Mike's face.

Mike holds his hand out to Jane, his eyes filled with terror. "Janie! Help me."

Jane grabs his hand and jerks him off the floor. Mike retreats behind Jane's body.

"I'm not fuckin' done with the little faggot!" Dale yells.

"Yes, you are!" Jane yells back, meeting his angry pitch.

Dale turns over the kitchen table sending the macaroni and cheese across the room. He storms toward Jane, backhanding her hard across the face, but she stands her ground. "Don't you fuckin' raise your voice to me!"

"He doesn't want to look at photos of dead people while he's eating," Jane says, her voice more controlled.

"Get outta the way!" Dale bellows. Mike stays pinned behind Jane, his head buried in the center of her back.

"Mom hated having those pictures at the table but she never told you!" Dale smacks Jane across her other cheek with the flat of his hand. "She just kept it inside but she hated it!" Dale lays another hard slap across Jane's face. "She hated those pictures, she hated this house and she hated you! That's why she died! To get away from you!"

The blood wells in Dale's face. "You fuckin' bitch!" he screams as he grabs Jane by the hair and punches her across the face. Blood spews from her nose and onto Mike as he takes refuge against the doorjamb. Jane starts to fall to her knees but catches herself. She looks at Mike. "Go to your room, Mike."

Dale pulls Jane upward then slams her flat against the wall. "Don't you ever say that kind of shit to me again! *You understand me?*"

Jane pushes her face just inches from her father's face. "It's fuckin' true!"

Dale lets go with a punishing series of slaps to Jane's face. Mike still stands paralyzed in the doorway.

Jane falls to her knees, blood trailing from her nose and into her mouth. She screams at Mike. "Go to your room!"

Mike tears across the living room and races up the stairs to his bedroom.

Dale leans down, barking in Jane's ear. "You think you're so fuckin' smart? You don't know shit!"

Jane pulls herself up, fists clenched. "I know more than you'll ever know!" Jane swings at her father's face but Dale grabs her arm before it makes contact.

"You wanna play hardball?" Dale uses one hand to jerk Jane's arm behind her back and the other to pull her head backward with a clump of her hair. "You wanna play hardball, bitch! You got it!"

Jane tries to break free as Dale shoves her forward to the kitchen door that leads outside. "Get your hands off me!" Jane screams.

Dale kicks the screen door open wide. "Shut up! You understand me?" He pushes his body against Jane's, forcing her outside in the fast-falling snow. The snow flies against her face, the icy cold stinging her flushed cheeks and cut lip. Jane digs her heels into a patch of snow as Dale tries to push her closer to the workshop door that stands ajar. He swings open the wooden workshop barn door with his foot.

"Move!" Dale yells.

"No!" Jane shouts before shooting a thick wad of spit mixed with blood at her father's face. Dale rears back, his rage at the boiling point. With all his strength, he pushes Jane forward into the workshop. She skids across the soft dirt floor on her shoulder. Dale closes the door behind him, whipping off his thick black belt. He lunges toward Jane and . . .

"Hey, you can't park here!"

Jane snapped out of her daze and turned. A Denver patrol officer pounded on her window trying to get her attention. The heavy rain continued to fall relentlessly.

"This is a tow-away zone, ma'am! You have to move your vehicle!"

Jane, still in a daze, reached over and grabbed her badge. She slammed it hard against the driver's window.

The patrol officer backed off. "Oh, sorry! I didn't know!"

As the officer got back into his patrol car, the rain let up. Jane popped the Mustang in gear, Dale's voice still screaming in the distance.

It was noon when Jane pulled in front of her house on Milwaukee. Out of the corner of her eye, she could see her neighbor Hazel watering her lawn. Jane braced herself for the inevitable questions as she made her way to the front door.

"Home again so soon?" Hazel said, looking surprised. "Are you sick?"

"Not now, Hazel," Jane said, unlocking her door and walking inside. Jane slammed the door behind her. She scooped the near empty fifth of Jack off the dining room table and took a swig as she made her way to the kitchen. Poking through the freezer, she pulled out a frozen macaroni and cheese dinner. It was covered in ice. Jane slammed it hard against the counter top, sending the chunks of ice flying across the kitchen. She shoved the frozen entree into the microwave, set the timer and headed down the hallway to her bedroom.

After shuffling through an eclectic tangle of CDs that ranged from country rock to classical selections including Pavarotti singing selections from *Turandot* and *La Bohéme*, Jane selected Grieg's *Peer Gynt* and placed it into her CD player. As the haunting melody lay heavy in the bedroom, she set the bottle of whiskey on her dresser and kicked off her boots. Jane sat on the edge of her bed, staring into the void. She was a prisoner of her own head and she was the jailer. Unlocking the demons that raged inside her would be akin to lighting the fuse to a powder keg. Jane was sure of it. But the unholy trap of holding on to the discordant memories and sounds was proving equally dangerous. And now there was this new twist to the on-going madness—this disorganized flash of images that hung just beneath her conscious mind. Jane flexed her right hand, recalling the tight, desperate grip of Emily Lawrence in the interrogation room. It was exactly the same wraithlike sensation she felt brush her hand as she stood in the stairwell at Headquarters. Jane, still blanketed in a slight daze, considered the most insane inference: the idea that she was sensing and seeing things that had yet to occur. She caught herself, almost embarrassed by her absurd reasoning. It was the booze. It had to be. No cop worth her salt would entertain such an insane notion unless said cop was going insane.

After a lunch of macaroni and cheese interspersed with hearty swigs of whiskey, Jane sorted through her notes on the Stover homicide. The hours passed quickly as she read and reread notations she'd all but committed to memory. However, after turning the last page on one of the yellow pads, a black pen fell from the center of the pad. A shock of emotion caught in Jane's throat. The words: WOLF FACE were written in large capital letters over a crude drawing of a wolf's face. At first, Jane feared that someone else had written the words and drawn the picture. But she quickly realized that it was indeed her own handwriting and novice attempt at artwork. Touching the drawing, Jane noted that the ink was still wet in spots where the pen had leaked. It was the same pen she had been using the night before when she passed out at the dining room table. But she had no memory of either drawing the picture or what prompted her to it.

Jane checked the time. 5:10 p.m. She needed to escape. RooBar was finally open. If she walked down there—just over a mile—she could be playing pool at her favorite table by 5:30. She strapped on her Glock, grabbed her beat-up leather jacket and headed down Milwaukee Street. When Jane arrived at RooBar, the place was empty, save for two guys at the bar and a young couple playing pool. Supertramp's "Dreamer" played loudly on the CD jukebox. RooBar reminded Jane of a cave, albeit a cave with dim lighting, red vinyl booths, purple pool tabletops, dark walls and flooring and television sets

perched in every corner. It was a cocoon of security—
something she needed right now. Once ensconced in a
game of pool at her favorite table on the landing away
from everyone else, Jane felt safe and able to zone out
the madness. For Jane, pool was like meditation—a Zen-
like endeavor, a game of chess with a stick and fifteen
balls. She set down a row of twelve quarters on the edge
of the table; a universal signal that she "owned" that table
for at least twelve games. She played eight ball and she
always played alone unless Mike was with her. The wait-
resses didn't know her name but they knew her pattern.
They'd bring her a basket of hot wings and a slice of
pizza along with two shots of whiskey. Jane lit a cigarette, racked them up and was just about ready to break
when a largeboned, flannel-shirted fellow lumbered up
the steps and set his beer down on the pool table. Jane
looked up at the guy, sizing him up.

"How 'bout a game?" he said with a cockeyed grin.

"No, thanks," Jane said, irritated.

"Would a hundred bucks change your mind?" he asked,
licking his lips.

Jane stood up and assessed the guy as if he were a suspect down at DH. "You got a hundred?" she asked.

"Right here," he said, patting his shirt pocket and then
covering his mouth with his hand. "It's all yours if you
win two out of three."

Jane knew the guy didn't have a hundred dollars in his
pocket. His body language gave him away. He covered
his mouth when he spoke and licked his lips, two signs of
deception. "Well, I say you don't have a hundred bucks in
that pocket or any other pocket."

"Hey, sweetheart," he said, tapping his shirt pocket,
"I'm tellin' the truth."

Jane pulled back her leather jacket to reveal her Glock
pistol in the shoulder holster. "And I'm telling you that
you're lying."

The blood quickly drained out of the guy's face. He put
up his hands as if surrendering. "Oh, shit. Sorry to bother

you," he said, walking quickly away from the table.

Jane turned her attention back to the table and smacked the cue ball hard, sending the five, ten and twelve balls scattering into the side and corner pockets. By 6:00, Jane had played two games and was starting her third when the waitress came by to drop off a new basket of wings and two more shots of whiskey. As she gathered up the empty shot glasses, she looked up at the muted corner television set directly above the pool table. It was the start of the local Denver newscast. The words "TOP STORY" were splashed across the screen, followed by "DEATH AND INNOCENCE."

"Hey, Billy!" the waitress called out to the bartender. "Turn up the sound! Maybe they found the killers!" Jane finished racking the balls and tried to ignore the waitress. "That poor little girl," the waitress said quietly as she watched the TV. "I guess they're not showing her face to protect her. What she must be going through."

Jane chalked up her stick as she felt her jaw tightening. Keeping her back to the TV, she knocked back a shot of whiskey and slammed the glass on the felt.

"It is still not known how much the nine-and-a-half year-old girl witnessed in the horrific Washington Park murder that occurred two nights ago," the newscaster reported with a dour look on her face. "The girl's parents were stabbed to death in a downstairs living room while the child slept upstairs."

Jane turned to the TV and said under her breath, "While she slept?"

"Oh, my God," the waitress said, shaking her head. "I can't even imagine going through something like that. She's ruined for life!" She turned to Jane. "Another shot?"

Jane looked at the TV. An exterior shot of the Lawrence house surrounded in yellow police tape flashed on the screen, followed by Chris addressing the media's questions. He looked even more bedraggled than earlier in the day. "We're doing everything possible to find the perpetrators of this crime," he said, stopping to clear his throat and then continued. "The child has been talking extensively to several detectives and has revealed certain information that could lead to arresting a suspect or suspects fairly soon. However, I can't go into any more detail at this time," Chris concluded, shifting his eyes from side to side and licking his lips.

"You lying son-of-a-bitch!" Jane said, her voice more audible.

The waitress turned to Jane with an uncertain look. "Just give me a holler when you need a refill," the waitress said before she turned and left.

The bartender muted the sound on the TV. Jane kept her eyes focused on the screen as images of the crime scene with its yellow tape blowing in the breeze flashed across the television. "Talking to several detectives, my ass," she said softly. "*You wish!*"

In the background, the voice of Nancy Sinatra singing "These Boots Are Made For Walkin'" played on the jukebox. Jane turned her attention away from the television and toward the sound of the music. "What the fuck—?" Jane glanced around the bar. She leaned her pool stick against the wall and walked down into the bar. Turning to the left, she saw the same boorish, flannel-shirted guy with the fake hundred in his pocket leaning against the machine, punching in different selections. "Hey, smart-ass!" Jane yelled out at the guy. The guy turned around and backed up a step when he saw Jane. "Did you punch this fucking song into that machine?"

The guy looked around helplessly. "Yeah. Is there a problem, officer?"

Jane moved closer to the guy in a threatening position. "Yeah, there's a problem! This song sucks! Anyone with half a fucking brain knows that!"

"Look, officer, I don't want any trouble, okay? I'm sorry."

"Fuck you!" Jane was almost two inches from the fellow's face when she looked over to the side. Mike was standing several feet away, obviously distraught. As quickly as Jane turned on the intimidation with the flannel-shirted guy, she turned it off and quickly walked toward her brother. "Mike! What's wrong?"

"I figured I'd find you here," Mike said, holding back tears. Jane threw thirty bucks on the tray of a passing waitress, grabbed Mike gently by the arm and left the bar. The second they walked outside, he turned to the wall and buried his head against the brick. "I fucked up bad, Janie!" Mike said, tears streaming down his face.

"For God's sake," Jane said, trying to turn Mike toward her, "what happened?!"

"I asked her, just like I told you I would . . ."

"Asked who? What are you talking about?"

"*Lisa!*" Mike said, turning to face Jane. "I asked her to move in with me!"

"Oh, shit. Mike, what did I tell you? I said you were going to get hurt!"

"No, it's not what you think!" Mike whined as he slid down the wall and sat on the pavement.

"Mike," Jane said, not sure what to make of her brother's behavior, "what happened?" Jane knelt down, resting her hands on Mike's shoulders.

"We went to dinner and I had a few beers to get a buzz on and get the nerve up. I told Lisa that I wanted her and I to move in together..."

"And she said 'no'," Jane said matter-of-factly.

"Actually, she said she was gonna ask me the same question."

"I'm lost, Mike."

"She has some reservations about . . . me . . . and certain things I do."

"Everybody's got reservations about everybody else. So what?"

"That's not the biggest part, Janie," Mike said, burying his face in his hands and crying. "Oh, God, I'm so fucked up!"

"Mike! What's the biggest part?"

"We talked about stuff. About our future, you know? Her and me together and what she wanted in life . . . She wants kids, Janie!" Mike blurted out.

"So?"

"*Kids.* I'd be a father. The more she talked about it, the more scared I got."

"I don't understand."

"If heart problems and strokes can be passed from one family member to another, maybe mental shit can too."

Jane tried to process it all. "I don't know—"

"What if it turns out I'm just like him?" Mike started to bang on his head with the flat of his hands. "I've got to get him out of my head!"

Jane pulled his hands away from his head. "You're not making sense!"

"She wants me to be the father of her kids. I can't do that! It's just another goddamn thing I'm never gonna be!" Tears rolled down Mike's cheeks. "Oh, Janie, you and me, we're fucking damaged goods. I'd love to be a dad, you know? I think part of me could be real good with kids. But I'm scared that I'd snap one day for no reason and become him."

"Mike, look at me. You will never be him. *You understand me? Never!*"

"Don't you ever wonder if it's like a curse in our blood?"

"Mike—"

"You're lucky you can't have kids. You don't have to worry about shit like this."

Jane stiffened. "Yeah, Mike," Jane said quietly. "I'm real lucky."

Mike's eyes trailed off as a pensive look came over his face. "Every time I make a wish, you know what I wish for?"

"What?"

"Freedom," Mike declared. "I want to be free, Janie."

Mike grabbed hold of Jane's jacket sleeve and dissolved into a flood of raw emotion.

Jane called a cab for Mike and promised to phone him when she got home. She walked around block for half an hour, puffing nervously on cigarettes. It seemed to Jane that keeping the pieces of her life together was proving more and more difficult. "Freedom," Jane thought, as Mike's pronouncement rung in her head. "Good fucking luck," she surmised. She was on her fifth cigarette by the time the sun sunk behind the tall buildings and she headed back up Milwaukee to her house. Jane was still lost in her own world when she neared her house. Suddenly, from behind her, a set of headlights from a parked car flicked on. Jane turned, blinded by the brightness. Instinctively, she opened her jacket and touched her pistol. A car door opened and closed.

"Jane."

"Chris? Turn off your lights!"

Chris sauntered over to Jane and stood next to her, spot-lighted in the glare. He looked weary, with dark circles under his eyes. "You're home early."

"What's that supposed to mean?"

"I've dropped by here over the last week after work and you're never here. Maybe if you'd ever have given me a fuckin' key—"

"What do you want, Chris?"

"Oh, fuck, Jane. We're not at DH. You can take off your balls." Chris crossed over to the steps by Jane's front lawn and sat down. He ran his fingers through his tangled blond hair. "Let's not play this game. I don't know what happened between us that made you so hateful to me. We're not perfect, but we still have something going for us. At least I think so." Jane lit a cigarette and said nothing. "Look," Chris continued, "I've been pulling doubles ever since this Lawrence case. Weyler said I'm almost maxed on overtime. So, I was thinking. We got Memorial Day this weekend. How about you and me take off on Saturday and go up to Lake Dillon and christen my new boat." Chris pulled a set of keys out of his shirt pocket and tossed them to Jane.

"Boat?" Jane said, unimpressed.

Chris leaned back on his elbows. "What can I say? Off-duty jobs pay good bank. Hey, I even treated myself to a pair of custom cowboy boots." His ruddy face flushed with self-importance. "*Custom boots*, Jane. Wait'll you see 'em, babe. They're wild. Hey, maybe if you jumped on the off-duty honey wagon, you could afford to put some money into this place. Make it look like somebody important lives here."

Jane tossed the keys back to Chris. "No, thanks. I couldn't juggle all those important responsibilities." There was a hard sting to her voice. "How are you keeping up with your many side jobs, Chris? Aren't you overwhelmed with all that information Emily Lawrence is giving you and the other detectives? I saw you on the news tonight. Anybody with half a brain could see that you were lying through your goddamn teeth."

"You and your fuckin' body language," Chris said in a dismissive tone.

"Your shifting eyes and lip licking gave you away when you launched into that bullshit about Emily confessing her secrets to detectives. *I'm* the only one she's willing to talk to!"

"You mean '*whisper.*' What the fuck was all that about anyway? I asked Weyler when he came back up and he just blew me off." Chris' demeanor quickly turned ugly. "I'm lead on this case and suddenly you're getting buddy-buddy with the kid."

"If you weren't such an asshole, I'd tell you what she said—"

"So, suddenly you and the kid are great buds, huh?"

"I want nothing to do with your case!" Jane started toward her front door. Chris stood up, preventing her from moving.

"Hey, Sherlock, maybe I stretched the truth with the media to create a certain amount of fear on the part of the killers. If they think that this kid is spilling her guts to us, they're gonna get nervous. And if they get nervous enough, they might start making mistakes and talk to some people. And those people might just come talk to us."

"What kind of screwed up reasoning is that? They might get *nervous*? How about if they get so nervous that they track this kid down and kill her so she permanently stops talking to us! Ever think about that?"

"'*Us?*' I thought you wanted nothing to do with it!"

"You know what I mean!" Jane tried to move around Chris but he grabbed her arm.

"And how would they find her? She's in protective custody! Even I don't know where she is half the time!"

"They didn't have any trouble finding Amy Stover. And they sure didn't think twice when they blew her up along with her parents!"

"Christ! Here we go again with the Stovers! You can't let that go, can you? *Don't compare the two cases!* Amy Stover and her parents were in protective custody until Mr. 'methamphetamine' Stover got the bright idea to go get ice cream! *He* got his family killed because he was 'tweaking' and didn't want to stay put. There's a load his mother should have swallowed! I don't have any sympathy for that asshole."

Jane looked at Chris, not quite sure what to think. "Jesus, Chris. You saw Amy Stover burning to death in that car just like I did. You saw her eyes. She was pounding her fist on the window and she knew she was going to die—"

"Jane, they all start to melt together after a while. All the bodies. All the weeping relatives. All the perps that get off. You gotta let it go."

"I can't let it go! It was so simple, Chris. All we had to do was sit outside in that goddamn car and watch out for them—"

Chris grabbed Jane by her shoulders. "Let it go, Jane!"

"S*top saying that!*" She angrily jerked away from him.

"You are going over the fucking edge!" Chris said. "I'm worried about you. Weyler is, too."

Jane felt exposed by the revelation. "Weyler said that to you?"

"He thinks you need help. So do I." Chris let out a deep sigh. "Look, you and I are still partners. What happens to you affects me. And I'm telling you right now, I am not going to watch everything I've worked for all these years go into the shitter because you can't move forward! Think of your career!"

"I don't have a career! I have a day-to-day existence that the Department can snuff out like that!" Jane snapped her fingers to punctuate her point.

"The Stover case is over!"

"No, Chris!" Jane yelled, waving her bandaged hand in his face. "It's right here every goddamn day! I look at this and I remember that I couldn't save Amy Stover. The only way I have a career left is if I solve the Stover murders!"

A wellspring of rage engulfed Chris. He angrily yanked Jane's wrist toward his body and spoke with vitriol. "You think your career is fucked? You don't know what fucked is! I took it in the ass with the Stover case just like you did. But open your eyes, Jane! We caught the fuckin' golden goose with this Lawrence murder! It's our opportunity to rise above all the shit and make *better* than good. But I can't do it alone. I need you and *only* you to help me on this case. We gotta work like a team . . . like the old days, right? We put aside our differences . . ." Chris loosened his grasp on Jane's wrist and pulled her closer to him. "We work the angles . . ." He brushed the palm of his hand against Jane's breasts. "We get back in sync . . " Chris seductively slipped his hand between Jane's legs, stroking her prominent mound. "And maybe it all works out for us . . ." Chris pressed his fleshy mouth against her lips. "Maybe even a promotion . . ."

Jane was just about to fall under Chris' spell. She wasn't sure whether the booze was wearing off or if the stench of his toxic body odor combined with his metallic breath had awakened her. Either way, she pulled back, regarding him with renewed disdain. "That's what this is about? A promotion!"

Chris looked at Jane, suddenly all business. "Sergeant Hank Weiting is retiring next month. I want his job." Chris hesitated a moment, "No . . . I *am* his job. I'm not some fucking errand boy detective. I'm going to call the shots. I'm going to have the power that I deserve. All I need is the kind of case that makes the Brass sit up and take notice. That's why I've got to nail this Lawrence murder."

"Somewhere in there, 'us' turned into 'I.' You'd cut in line in front of starving Ethiopian children to get a second plate of food."

"You do what you gotta do in this world. That's my *new* motto. Hey, babe, you know how to play the game. Don't you?" He winked at her in a knowing way.

Jane suddenly felt very dirty standing in Chris' shadow. "Assholes and cream," she said, heading toward her front door. "Eventually they all rise to the top."

"Don't you fuck up this case for me, Jane!" Chris bellowed as Jane kept walking. "We've all got our demons! You're no exception to that rule!" Jane stopped in her tracks as Chris' words cut to her core. Chris moved toward his car and swung open the driver's door. "Take a good look in the mirror, Jane. You and I are two of a kind!"

Jane turned and stared into the piercing glare of Chris' headlights. As he sped away from the curb, she wondered what it would feel like to kill him.

Inside her house, the answering machine light flashed two messages. The first voice was Mike.

"It's me. I got home okay. I gotta get some sleep. Talk to you tomorrow."

The machine beeped and the second message started.

"Hello, this message is for Jane Perry. My name is Zoe. I'm the head nurse here at the hospital where your father is staying. I'm in his room right now and he asked me to call you to find out if you could come by tomorrow afternoon. He'd like to discuss some things—"

The nurse's voice was interrupted in the background by Dale Perry's voice, slightly slurred from the stroke. "Give me the phone!" Jane stared at the answering machine as the phone was passed to her father. "Jane! Where the fuck are you? I want you over here tomorrow! Bring your brother!"

# Chapter 8

Sleepless nights were getting to be a habit for Jane. When she did sleep, it was fitful and splattered with the bloody, charred bodies of the Stover family. Tuesday night was no different. The combative message from her father on the answering machine didn't abate the insomnia. It was closing in on 2 a.m. when Jane grabbed a pack of cigarettes and walked into the living room. After wearing a tired path around the dining room table while sucking the nicotine out of a cigarette and downing two shots of whiskey, she flicked on the radio.

"Welcome back to all you travelers between twilight and dawn . . ." Tony Mooney's voice lay like black velvet across the shadows in the living room. Jane lit another cigarette and poured a third shot of whiskey. "Things are not always what they seem, my friends." Mooney's cadence felt comfortable to Jane; like an old friend she hadn't yet met. "I'm exploring this fascinating idea tonight . . . the interconnectedness of souls. It is a foundation of so many esoteric philosophies and an integral concept explored in the Hindu texts known as the *Upanishads*. For those of you new to the mystical path, the *Upanishads* are considered the doctrine that espouses the interconnectedness of separate phenomena. In effect, what appears to be separate, is in fact, intertwined within a giant, infinite web that we experience on many levels of consciousness." Jane downed the whiskey, waiting for the heat of the alcohol to mend her fractured psyche. Mooney leaned closer to the microphone, his persuasive voice urging naysayers to pay attention. "We truly are *all con-*nected to each other. We dip into that collective uncon-sciousness whether we want to believe in it or not. In doing so, we constantly attract specific souls within that web that call to us like cosmic magnets. And in a heart-beat, we know the stranger's thoughts and we feel the stranger's fears. They become us and we become them because, in the end, we are all one . . ." Jane quickly turned off the radio as a cold shiver ran down her spine.

Morning came too quickly. Jane called Mike at 5:30 Wednesday morning so she could catch him before he headed to his job site. "Take a half day. He wants to see us," she said to him, "and meet me at Duffy's no later than 1:00." Jane wasn't going to go into the tone of the message or exactly what their father said. Mike would have a hard enough time knowing that in less than nine hours, he'd be face-to-face with his father.

Duffy's was a bustling restaurant located in Cherry Creek North. It was where locals mixed with business-men who mixed with the occasional tourist. The red-topped bar greeted one upon entering the establishment. Nine booths lined up against the pea green walls. Tables with the occasional wobbly fourth leg sat crammed together in the center of the place as the jukebox played eclectic selections that ranged from Adam Ant to Randy Travis. Duffy's was nearly packed to the gills when she walked in at 12:55. She looked around for Mike, not expecting to see him. As usual, he would be late. If the get-together had anything to do with their father, Mike would always drag his heels. The hostess seated Jane at the far corner booth. She sat down, grabbed a menu and kept one eye on the door. Mike wandered in nearly 15 minutes later, looking about as lost as he did the night before at RooBar. He meandered over to Jane and sank into the booth with about as much energy as a slug.

"Glad you could make it," Jane said eyeing him carefully.

"Sorry," Mike said under his breath. "Traffic, you know."

"Yeah, right. I ordered a beer. You want one?"

"No. I'll just get a Coke."

"A Coke?"

"Yeah," Mike said slightly irritated. "*A Coke*."

Jane regarded her brother with a raised brow. The waitress delivered Jane's beer. "He'll have a Coke," Jane said in a slight mocking tone as she slid the menu to Mike and took a sip of her beer.

"So, how you doing?" she asked.

"The same, I guess." Mike scanned the menu quickly and tossed it aside. "I'm not hungry."

"I know your stomach is in knots, but you have to eat."

"I'm not hungry, Janie." Mike's voice raised a few decibels.

"Fine. Go ahead and starve."

There was an awkward silence until the waitress arrived. Jane ordered a French Dip. She took a sip of beer and studied her brother. Mike always had a difficult time whenever he had to see his dad but something seemed different about his melancholy mood. He sat staring at the tabletop, rolling the edge of the paper napkin back and forth with his thumb. Jane could sense a boiling tension below the surface. It took several more minutes of silence before he finally spoke up.

"You sleep much last night?"

"No," Jane replied.

"Me neither. I did a lot of thinking." Mike looked off to the side in a half daze. "Do you still believe in God?"

Jane was slightly taken aback by the question. "Yeah. Sure. Everything has its opposite and I know for sure there's a devil so I'm sure there's a God somewhere."

"You ever pray to Him?"

"What's all this about?"

"Do you pray to Him?" Mike repeated with emphasis.

Jane was getting weary of the odd exchange. "No, Mike. I don't. I used to when we were kids but then I got tired of Him never answering my prayers."

"Oh...Maybe He did answer and the answer was 'no.'"

Jane leaned forward, speaking quietly but directly. "What's all this God shit?"

"You shouldn't say 'God' and 'shit' in the same sentence, Janie."

"Mike, what the fuck is going on?" He let out a deep breath and kept his eyes pinned on the paper napkin. Jane was at a loss to understand his behavior. "Hey," Jane said trying to sound empathetic, "I know you're nervous about seeing the son-of-a-bitch. And I know it's short notice—"

"Janie—"

"Look, you don't have to go in. Just stay in the car. I'll tell him you're sick."

"Janie, that's not all of it."

"Of course it is, Mike!" Jane said, sounding more like a tired parent.

"Oh, Janie . . ." Mike's voice trailed off as he stared off to the side again. "Do you believe that everybody has a defining moment in their life? You know, something that alters the course of their existence? Something that turns them into a completely different person? And afterward, nothing is ever the same. Is that possible?"

Jane felt an uncomfortable tremor in her belly. "Yes! We all have defining moments."

"You think it's possible to have more than one defining moment in your life?" Mike seemed to struggle with the concept but pressed on. "Like, do you think that you could have a defining moment when you were young and then have another moment that defines you all over again? Does that make sense?"

"I don't know. Maybe. You're giving me a headache. What's all this about?"

Mike stared down at the napkin. "I'm not sure I can talk about it just yet."

Jane leaned forward. "What do you mean?"

"I need to think about it some more."

"Think about what? Come on, you always tell me everything." Jane reached across the table and touched Mike's hand. "Mike, talk to me. Whatever it is, I'll fix it."

Mike looked at his sister with a guarded eye. "I don't think you can, Janie."

The one-hour drive out to their father's rehabilitation nursing home in the Denver suburb of Wheatridge was completely silent. Jane finished off a half pack of cigarettes while Mike stared out the window, lost in his own world.

It had been over a week since Jane drove out to see Dale. When she'd arrived, her father was fast asleep so she quickly left, not even alerting the nurses to her aborted visit. Prior to that, the last time she had seen her father was weeks before his illness. He'd demanded that she come out to the house after a power outage and reprogram his VCR. That visit lasted less than twenty minutes before she lied about having to get back to work. She knew Dale was aware it was a lie. He could always read her and destroy that carefully constructed wall of protection. From what she had been told by the nurses, Dale's stroke was enough to permanently place him in a 24-hour care facility for physical reasons, but not so disabling to destroy his mental faculties. Jane wasn't sure if h                         e                         r father knew she was suspended from the Department but she figured the news would be plastered all over her psyche when she walked into his room.

Jane parked her Mustang across the street from the care facility. She turned to Mike who stared out the window. "You coming in?" she asked. Mike kept his eyes fixed outside and shook his head. "Okay. I won't be long." Jane took one long, penetrating drag after another on her cigarette as she neared the front door of the facility. Tossing the butt on the ground, she entered the building. The hallway reeked of ammonia, urine and overcooked broccoli.

"Miss Perry?" a voice called out. Jane turned just in time to encounter the head nurse, Zoe. "Thanks for coming. I know it's difficult when it's last minute."

Jane looked down the hall toward Dale's room. "What's going on with him?"

"He has good days and bad days. Today seems to be a good day."

"Really?" Jane said, not impressed. "What makes it a good day?"

"He's lucid. He was able to walk to the bathroom with very little help this morning. I don't want to give you the impression that he could ever return to his home. Even though things are improving, his health is still fragile. Another stroke or heart attack could put him in I.C.U." Jane nodded. "I want you to know we're doing everything possible to keep him happy and comfortable."

Jane lost herself for a moment. "Well, that's great," she said with no emotion as she stared down the sterile hallway.

"I'll let you visit with your dad."

"Uh-huh," Jane replied. Zoe walked back to her station but Jane didn't move. She started to turn back toward the front door but stopped when she saw several nurses looking at her. Reluctantly, she walked down the hall to her father's door and stood to the side, out of his view. Jane let out a deep breath and crossed the threshold.

Dale Perry was propped up in bed, eyes glued to the television screen that was tuned to Court TV. The sound was muted. Dozens of greeting cards were pinned to the wall on either side of his bed. Vases of long stemmed flowers graced both bedside tables. A banner stretched the length of the opposite wall. In red and black letters it read, "GET WELL, DALE!" which was followed by "Your pals at Denver PD!"

Her father was hooked to an IV and heart monitor. An oxygen tank sat nearby. Jane stood inside the doorway, waiting. Dale turned his head on his pillow and looked at her. He appeared to have aged ten years compared to the day Jane went out to his house to fix the VCR. The only thing that remained sharp and stoic was his grey, regimented buzz haircut. It reminded Jane of the quills on a porcupine—sharp, rigid and ready to attack.

"You got the message," Dale said, his speech slightly slurred. "I bet that nurse ten bucks you wouldn't show. Make sure you pay her the money on the way out." Jane didn't move a muscle. "You gonna plant your ass in a chair or are you gonna just stand there like some retard?" Jane carefully moved to a bedside chair and sat down. "You look like hell," Dale said, eyeing Jane like a perp. Jane looked off to the side, pursing her lips, as Dale glared at Jane. "Where's your brother?" he said, his voice slightly raised.

"He couldn't make it," Jane said, looking at the television screen.

Dale stared even more intently at Jane. "He's in the car, isn't he?"

"Yeah."

"The weak little fuck is hiding out. Shit."

Jane kept her eyes glued to the television. Her heart raced and her head pounded. She figured that if she avoided his eyes, he wouldn't be able to drill into her head. "Why do you have the sound off?"

"I don't need sound to hear a fuckin' lie. It's not what they say, it's what they do. Didn't you learn anything?"

"What's the case?" Jane said, still focused on the television.

"The defendant is charged with murdering his wife and kids. But they can't find the bodies. The fucker on the stand is a defense witness. He's a friend of the fucker who killed his wife and kids. Look at him. *There!* Look how he touched his mouth and glanced over to the defendant. I bet that asshole helped him dump the bodies. It's so obvious. He's like one big open sore and nobody can see the pus. They're blind!" Dale screamed at the television. "They miss what they don't want to see." Dale looked over at Jane and her bandaged hand. "Christ, you still have that goddamn hand bandaged? That was one of your less intelligent moments."

Jane took her eyes off the screen and turned toward her father. "Trying to get a kid out of a burning car?"

Dale let out a slight snicker. "The fucking car's engulfed in flames and you decide to suspend common sense and try to punch a fucking hole in the window with your fist. Jane, do the fucking math. That kid was gonna die either way. You should have saved your hand." Dale turned to Jane, meeting her eye to eye. "But you actually believed you were going to be the hero, didn't you? Didn't I teach you that lesson a long time ago?"

Dale's words cut to the bone. Once again, she'd let her guard down and he was worming his way back inside her head. She quickly turned back to the TV. A smile creased Dale's face. "You're so *easy*," he said, the venom dripping from his mouth. "You don't know who blew them up, do you?"

"No," Jane whispered.

"That's because you haven't followed the right road. You take what you know and find the right road and it always leads to the killer. *What you know* is that it was a hit. That's obvious. *What you know* is that Stover, 'Mr. Fuckin' Entrepreneur of the Year,' was a coke and meth addict. *What you know* is that Stover and the Texas mob were in bed together. Stover let them launder drug money through his businesses in exchange for all the free meth and coke he could sniff up his nose. Over time, he got to hear all their important secrets. You also know that the Texas mob offers under the table protection for all the 'Gooks' and 'Chinks' in Denver. Every single one of those is an undeniable fact. So, then Stover gets his ass caught by the cops and he has to make a big decision. Do I lose everything I've worked for, my reputation, my fam-

ily and get plastered across the front of every newspaper
or do I tell the cops everything I know about the mob and
their connections? Do I name the players and take away
their mystery? Maybe Stover wasn't the only one with a
lot to lose. Maybe there were other people just like him
with reputations to uphold that didn't want the spotlight.
Other people with businesses that are really just fronts.
People who live two lives." Dale leaned closer to Jane.
"Who did Stover know and who knew him? Ask yourself
that question! Follow the protection money and you'll
find your killer. Of course, that means you have to cut
through all the bullshit and have the guts to see what's
smack in front of you. I'm not sure you know how to do
that. You'll always miss what you don't want to see. Then
you'll be just like those assholes up on that TV."

Jane may have had her eyes on the TV the whole time,
but she didn't miss a word of her father's speech. "I gotta
get going," she said.

"Hold your fuckin' horses. I told you I wanted to discuss some things with you. I understand from the boys at
DH that you and Mike are going through the house and
cleaning it out. I got some things that I want to sell to
some of the guys. They've been hounding me for years
about my tool chest and guns. Your lover boy Chris wants
that old hand drill for his boat. Go over to the house
tonight and get the stuff and take it to DH. They'll settle
up among themselves and Chris can bring me the
money."

"Where is it?"

"It's in the workshop. Take care of it tonight." Dale
sunk his head into his pillow and watched the television.
Jane sat motionless in her chair. "I thought you had to
go," Dale said. Jane gradually got up. "Tell your brother
he's a fuckin' coward." Jane moved toward the door. "Oh,
and Jane?" Jane turned around. Dale moved his right
hand up to his face, stuck out his thumb and first finger
to look like a gun and pointed it at Jane's head. He peered
at her and then quickly flicked his thumb to mimic a

trigger. A grin crept across his face and he quietly said, "Bang!"

Their eyes locked and Dale shot into her head.

Jane dropped Mike off at Duffy's to pick up his car. She didn't say a word to him about getting the tool chest and guns from the workshop. Mike was so far gone into his own world, Jane wasn't about to broach the subject with him.

She stopped at the corner liquor store and picked up a six-pack of Corona. By the time she hit the turnoff on I-70 to her father's house, she had knocked back two bottles and was on her third. No matter how loud she cranked the volume on her radio, Dale's voice continued to play loudly in her head. "Follow the protection money" and "You actually believed you were going to be the hero, didn't you?" blended into "Didn't I teach you that lesson a long time ago." The last sentence stung. This was where the madness always began. And to compound matters, she was less than five minutes away from the present melting into the past.

Jane pulled into Dale's gravel driveway and turned off the engine. She drained what was left of the third Corona, popped open another and lit a cigarette. Jane stared ahead at the workshop, standing starkly against an aqua sky. The alcohol gave her a slight buzz—a welcome effect that she had hoped would dull the process and make it easier. But instead, it was as if her senses were heightened. She tried shaking it off as she popped open the car door and got out.

As she walked toward the workshop, a cacophony of screeching birds welled up from the surrounding willow trees. She reached the workshop and waited before clinking open the broken, rusty lock and letting the battered door slowly creak open.

Immediately, Jane was greeted by that familiar odor of wet wood, dirt floor and old paint curled at the edges. Sharp shafts of sunlight beat down from the slanted win-

dows on the roof. She crossed inside, minding each step
on the dirt floor that lay littered with the broken glass
from the impromptu bottle and bullet vandalism she and
Mike enjoyed a few days ago. Jane regarded her father's
worktable where parts of a .22 rifle were strewn. Dale's
reading glasses were perched next to a can of gun lubri-
cant oil that was missing its red plastic protective tip. Her
eyes scanned the table until they rested upon Dale's dusty
eight track stereo player with the bent handle.

Jane took a long swig of her beer and turned to face the
opposite wall. Several boxes sat on the dirt floor in front
of a rectangular object covered by an old blanket pad. She
nervously dragged on her cigarette for several minutes,
staring at the blanket pad. Finally, Jane scuffed toward it,
gingerly lifting the padding to reveal the end of a five foot
long, unframed mirror. Along the corner section was a
curved crack that ran from top to bottom. She pulled the
padding off the mirror and sunk to the floor. The fracture
across the mirror sliced her reflection in half, distorting
her image. It was no use fighting it any longer. So, she
decided to give in and live her nightmare to its conclusion
once again.

It's that same snowy night in her 14th year. Dale pushes
Jane forward into the workshop. She skids across the soft
dirt floor on her shoulder, her face bloodied. Dale closes
the door and snaps off his thick black belt. He lunges
toward Jane and lays a hard crack of the belt across her
back.

"Who the fuck do you think you are!" Dale screams
before moving closer to Jane and nailing her with another
lick of the belt. Jane covers her head with her arms and
tries to get up, but at each attempt, Dale's belt whips
down harder. "You don't fuck with me, bitch!" Down
comes another lash of the belt. "*You understand me?!*"

Dale hovers over Jane's crouching body and showers
her with a series of punishing blows from his belt. By
the ninth stroke, Jane begins to lose consciousness. She

fights the feeling and rolls up on one knee, ducking the continuing lashes. She reaches out toward the oncoming belt. Connecting with it, she grabs the belt with both hands and pulls herself up on her feet jerking the belt from her father's hand and throws it against the wall.

"Asshole!" she screams, slightly dazed.

The words no sooner stumble from her lips when Dale backhands Jane hard across her face. She spins to her right and careens headfirst into Dale's worktable. As she makes contact with the table, she feels a surge of excruciating pain in her right temple. At the same moment, her hand reaches out to break her fall and hits the "play" button on Dale's tape player. The voice of Nancy Sinatra fills the workshop, singing "These Boots Are Made For Walkin'."

*"You keep saying you got something for me*
*Something you call love but confess*
*You've been a'messin' where you shouldn't have*
*    been a'messin'*
*And now someone else is getting all your best."*

Jane's back is to Dale. Blood drips from her right temple and into her eye. The room spins wildly. In the distance, she can hear the faint sound of his voice screaming at her but can't make out the words. Nancy Sinatra's recording drones loudly in her ear as Jane tries to focus on the object directly in front of her on the table.

*"Well, these boots are made for walkin'*
*And that's just what they'll do*
*One of these days these boots are gonna*
*    walk all over you . . ."*

Jane tips her head to the right to force the blood out of her eye and makes out the object that sits within her reach. It's a Smith & Wesson, 357 Magnum revolver and the chamber is fully loaded. She carefully drags her hand a few inches and wraps it around the butt of the gun. Her head pounds and the searing pain in her temple permeates her entire being. She gathers her strength, lifts her head, scoops the gun off the table and spins around to face her father. She stands, both arms outstretched, hands wrapped tightly around the grip of the gun. Blood streams from her temple, down the side of her face and gradually works its way into the corner of her right eye. Through the glaze of blood, she aims the shiny black barrel at her father's head. Dale stops screaming and stands firm. The only sound between the two of them is the incessant blare of Nancy Sinatra's voice and Jane's labored breathing.

> *"You keep playing where you shouldn't be playing*
> *And you keep thinking that you'll never get*
>   *burnt (Hah!) . . ."*

"What the fuck are you waiting for, you little cunt!" Dale yells over the music. "Go on. Pull the fucking trigger! I dare you." Jane slides her finger onto the trigger. The workshop rotates around her. "*You don't have the guts,*" Dale screams.

Jane can hardly see out of her right eye which is now completely flooded with blood. She blinks hard in a wasted attempt to clear it. "You don't . . . know me . . . very well," she manages to get out.

"I know you better than anyone. You think you're tough, but *you're nothing!* You think you know how to win, but you'll *always* fail."

"I'm going to kill you now," Jane utters, with no emotion.

"Is that so? You'll go to prison."

"I'll go to 'juvie.'. . . I'll fake insanity . . . I know the ropes. . . I'll be out. . . when I'm 18 and you'll still be dead." Jane feels the sweat of her finger against the steel trigger and starts to put pressure on it.

"What about Mike!" Dale yells. "When you're stuck in juvie, who's gonna watch out for him and protect him?" Jane stands firm, still pointing the barrel at Dale's head but saying nothing. "You don't have an answer for that, do you?!" Dale screams. "Stupid bitch didn't think about that! You know where the little fuck's gonna end up? . . . A foster home! And the guy who runs it will butt fuck him every night because he knows Mike won't fight back! You want that on your head the rest of your life? If you do, you dumb bitch, then shoot me! Shoot me!"

Jane can hardly see through the blood. The more she tries to think rationally, the cloudier her perception gets. Dale's face waves in and out of focus as the gun becomes heavier. And through it all, the song plays against the moment.

> "These boots are made for walkin', and that's just
>    what they'll do
> One of these days these boots are gonna walk all
>    over you."

Jane strains to focus. She can see that Dale is slowly moving toward her. As the blood clears from her eye, she can clearly make out that he is smiling.

With a sudden jolt of movement, Dale slaps her arms off to the side. Jane pulls back on the trigger and blows a hole in the ceiling. Dale grabs the revolver from Jane's weak hands and throws it on the ground behind him. It falls against the rectangular mirror that leans against the wall, forging a deep crack in the glass. Jane stumbles backward. With his right hand, Dale grabs her by the throat and pulls her upright. She gasps for breath as she attempts to pull his hand away. "You are nothing! You understand me?" he screams. "*You understand me?*"

Jane manages to pull several of his fingers away from her throat. She looks Dale straight in the eye. "*Fuck you!*"

Then, another power suddenly enters Dale's body—a power so destructive that it will stop at nothing until it shatters its target. Dale balls his fist and nails Jane hard against her cheek, sending her to her knees. Before she knows what hit her, she feels Dale's boot kick her hard in the stomach. She falls to the side, trying to protect her body. But no matter how much she tries to take cover, Dale is relentless. He kicks her hard repeatedly in the groin.

The pain crescendos and then . . . nothing.

Jane opens her eyes and sees her reflection in the cracked mirror. She observes her father's boot contacting with her body but feels nothing. There is no sound. There is no pain. There is no grief. There is no emotion. There is a cocoon of emptiness and she sits in its void. She watches as a trail of blood travels from the cut on her head and into the corner of her mouth. That's the last thing she remembers before she loses consciousness.

Hours pass before Jane wakes up on the dirt floor. She is alone. The snow outside has turned to pellets of hail that beat a drowning rhythm on the workshop roof. At first, she wonders if she is dead and that Hell looks just like her former existence. She starts to move but feels a bolt of pain in her tailbone that works its way down both legs. Jane looks in the mirror and sees the dried cakes of blood smeared with dirt crisscrossing her face. She remains on the floor for another hour, considering her next move. About five feet away from her, she spies a gallon jug of whiskey hidden underneath a chair. She drags the bottle closer and pops the cork. Jane looks around for a clean cloth but finds nothing. She tips the jug and pours a handful of whiskey into her palm. Jane then holds her palm against the deep gash on her head. A low, guttural moan emits from her throat but she continues to bathe the wound in the whiskey.

Jane uses what is left in her palm to wash away part of the blood on her face. She pours another handful into her palm and rinses off the thick crusts of dried blood that settled in the crease of her lips. A few drops make their way into her mouth and she winces at the bitter taste. She continues to cover her face in whiskey. Each time, more of the liquid makes its way onto her tongue. She shakes off the flavor, but then begins to notice a comforting warmth enveloping her injured body. Jane takes a small sip from the jug and then another, until she swallows several ounces.

She starts to free-float. The pain in her tailbone fades. A penetrating heat surrounds her body. For the first time in her short life, she feels safe and protected.

Jane drinks another few ounces of whiskey before shoving the cork back into the bottle and sliding it under the chair. Using the chair as support, she pulls herself up to her knees. Jane looks down and catches a glimpse of dark, dried blood in the crotch of her jeans. She unzips her jeans and pulls them down to reveal her underwear soaked completely through with bright blood. She stares at her body but cannot connect with any emotion. There is blood and yet there is no feeling attached to it. She zips up her jeans and drags herself to her feet. Jane makes her way carefully outside the workshop, closing the door behind her and enters the house. The morning sun is cresting in the distance, allowing slivers of light to illuminate the landscape.

Jane makes her way through the kitchen and enters the living room. Her father is sound asleep in his barcalounger, a bottle of whiskey precariously propped up in his hand. Carefully, Jane walks around the chair and starts up the stairs toward her bedroom. The stairwell is dark and full of early morning shadows. The top step creaks and a door slowly opens. Jane looks over to see her brother peering from around his bedroom door.

"Janie?" Mike asks quietly.

"It's okay, Mike," Jane whispers. "Go back to bed."

Mike closes his door and Jane softly pushes open her door. She walks inside, but before closing it, she peers outside into the hallway one last time. The stillness of the house blends with the long shadows. It draws her into its grasp. Jane records the memory before closing the door and going to bed.

Jane sat on the dirt floor of the workshop, staring

straight ahead. She didn't jolt out of the memory this time. It was more like sliding out of it, while making sure to leave the door open so she could return to the nightmare.

She finished off her Corona and threw the bottle against the mirror. Jane stood up and grabbed a nearby cardboard box. She dumped every gun from her father's collection into the box, including the ones he had taken apart to rebuild. Wedging the box of guns under her arm, she snapped the lid down on the tool chest and walked out.

On her way home, Jane finished the sixth bottle of Corona. It was pitch dark by the time she pulled up in front of her house. She had driven slowly on the way home due to the buzz she felt from the beer. Jane grabbed the box of guns and the toolbox and got out of the car, stumbling up the curb toward the house.

The sound of a car door opening and closing, along with footsteps approaching her, caught Jane off guard. She dropped the toolbox and box of guns and spun around. "Goddamnit, Chris!" she yelled. "I'm not in the fuckin' mood!"

Sergeant Weyler emerged out of the shadows. Jane took a step back and tripped over a sprinkler head on her lawn. She tried to stay upright but gravity pulled her down to the grass.

"Well, Detective," Weyler said matter-of-factly. "Did I catch you at a bad time?"

# Chapter 9

Jane tried to get up from the lawn where she fell, but her head spun like a top.

Sergeant Weyler peered down at Jane's flaccid body. "Detective Perry, exactly how much have you had to drink tonight?"

Jane looked up at Weyler. She could feel her blood pressure rising and knew that her ability to censor her mouth would be difficult. "Gee, Dad, I'm not sure! Why don't you look inside the car and count the goddamn bottles for yourself!"

"My God, Jane! How in the hell can you drive in this condition?"

"Oh, fuck, boss. You should give me an award. Most people in my condition would have taken out at least five cars on the way here."

"Get up!"

"No, I think I'll just sleep here tonight." Jane rested her head on the moist grass.

"Give me your hand!" Weyler commanded, holding out his hand. "Get up!"

Jane reluctantly held out her hand to Weyler, who quickly pulled her to her feet. "What in the hell are you doing here?" Jane said, irritated.

"I'm worried about you." Weyler steadied Jane's

shoulder with his hand. Jane let out a loud cackle. "I'm standing here looking at somebody who is drowning and hasn't got the sense to cry out for help!"

"Oh, Christ—"

Weyler grabbed Jane's shoulders. "Is this the way you want it to end?" Weyler's voice was stern and abrupt.

"My career or my life?" Jane yelled in a slurred tongue.

"Both!"

"Well, let's see. My career is pretty much fucked. As for my life, well, I died a long time ago. It's just that nobody noticed." She felt herself slipping into herself. "At least I think I died . . ." Jane's voice trailed off. "I have to keep checking, you see?" Jane looked Weyler in the eye. "Sometimes, boss, we have to keep hurting ourselves just to make sure we're still alive."

"You're very much alive, Jane and you still have a lot to offer."

Jane pulled away from Weyler's grasp and stumbled backward. "Look at me! I'm a fucking drunk! *I'm nothing!* And I don't care! You know what would make me happy? To wake up truly dead! I want the pieces that are left of me to finally die!" Jane slumped down on her front step. "I'm gonna regret this conversation in the morning, but it's the God's truth. Everything I touch ends up destroyed. All the blood . . . and the bodies. We're supposed to act like we don't care. Like they're all just collateral damage. But we're kidding ourselves." Jane looked off to the side. "Then again, there's always going to be that one son-of-a-bitch who really doesn't feel anything. You know, boss, there's a thin line between the mind of a cop and the mind of a criminal. Do you have any idea how often they are one in the same? And how they can hide it so well?"

Weyler stared at Jane. "So? . . . How is your father?"

Jane turned to Weyler in shock. "What?"

Weyler moved closer to Jane. "I have no idea what happened to you. But I have met your father on brief occasions. Just because the rest of the crew puts him up on a pedestal doesn't mean that I do. I didn't get to the position I'm in because I kissed someone's ass. I got here because I know things about people. Just like you do. I can look into someone's eyes and paint a portrait of who they really are. When I looked into your father's eyes, it was a very dark portrait. I cannot imagine what you went through growing up. But then I look into your eyes and I don't see the shadow of your father anywhere. You're not your father, Jane. Deep down, I think you're afraid that you are." Weyler leaned down toward Jane. "You think you're weak, but you're one of the strongest people I know. The fact that you survived all that hell and can still function is a testament to who you are. I've told you that I think you're one of the most intelligent people I've ever known and *I mean it*. You've got a kind of sixth sense that defies explanation. When you combine that with your inner strength, you're a very powerful person. Unfortunately, the booze prevents you from seeing that." Weyler stood straight up. "I'll tell you one thing, Jane. As long as I'm in charge, I will not let you destroy yourself. You're far too valuable to me."

Jane sat stunned. There was a long stretch of silence between them. For a brief moment, she felt as if should could trust him. "Boss . . ." Jane struggled with revealing herself, "I've . . . ah . . . had some weird shit happening lately . . ."

"What is it?" Weyler asked compassionately.

Jane traced the grass with her eyes, realizing that to divulge the splintered images and odd notations with drawings of wolf faces would be career suicide. She shook her head. "Nothing . . ." There was a moment of silence.

"Can you pull yourself together by 9 a.m.?"

"Why?" Jane quietly asked.

"I want to take you to the Lawrence crime scene. I'd like to get your impressions."

"It's Chris' case and I thought I was suspended."

"Technically, yes."

Jane looked up at Weyler. "What does that mean?"

"It means that I'm in charge. And I say that I'm going to pick you up at 9 a.m." Jane nodded. "Oh, I almost forgot," Weyler said, turning to his car, "Emily Lawrence asked about you. She wanted to know if your injured hand felt better." Weyler got into his car and drove down Milwaukee.

Nine o'clock came quickly. Jane only woke twice during the night. Both times, it was the result of her recurring nightmare of the Stover murder.

The nightmare always followed the same pattern. She and Chris are sitting in the unmarked sedan across the street from the Stover's house. Stover and his family have just left the location in their SUV to get ice cream, flanked by two police cars. All is still and very dark around them. Jane, sitting in the passenger seat, is trying to get the lid off her thermos of coffee. She is wondering how she is going to tell Chris that she wants to end their relationship.

Chris is edgy and irritated as he calls one of the flank vehicles on his cell phone. "Yeah, it's me. I can't believe Stover was so stupid! He drives off with his family for ice cream so he can get thirty minutes in the outside world! Thirty fucking minutes! It looks all clear from here but hurry up!"

In the dream, Jane thinks to herself how arrogant and self-important Chris sounds on the phone. Like he's ordering people around that he has no authority over. Chris enthusiastically engages Jane in conversation about himself. He drones on about how he's getting a plasma TV along with mega-sized speakers. He offers to help her get the lid off the thermos and they concentrate on that for several minutes.

The dream accelerates in time and Jane sees three sets of headlights in her passenger mirror coming down the street from behind their parked location. Stover's SUV is sandwiched between the two police vehicles. Jane turns toward the oncoming cars. This is where it all slows down in her dream. The Stovers' SUV creeps up the street and stops briefly in front of Jane and Chris' sedan. Amy Stover is seated in the backseat, behind her father who is driving. Amy presses her face against the car window and makes eye contact with Jane. She waves toward Jane and smiles warmly as Stover pulls the SUV into the driveway.

There is complete silence until the explosion cracks into the night air and the car goes up in flames. Jane charges out of the sedan toward the SUV. Chris chases after her. Jane stands several feet from the burning car and comes face-to-face with Amy. Her palms are pressed against the window as she screams in terror. Chris tries to hold Jane back but she breaks free of his grip and tries to open the door. The handle is red-hot. She bangs on the window with her fist. The whole time, Amy Stover is wailing words that cannot be heard above the roar of the fire.

Jane punches the window with her fist, ignoring the fact that the skin on her knuckles and the side of her hand is peeling off due to the intense heat. Another series of explosions ricochet through the car, sending Chris and Jane backward onto the lawn. Jane looks up and sees Amy looking down at her. It takes a full minute for the life to completely drain from her eyes.

And that's when Jane always wakes up.

Weyler rang the doorbell at the stroke of nine. There he stood on Jane's front porch, dressed in another one of his dashing, conservative suits from Nordstrom. His trademark narrow tie was pinned discreetly with a gold-plated clip he got as a perk from Denver PBS after contributing ten dollars during one of their many pledge drives. "Good morning, Detective," Weyler said.

"Morning, Sergeant," Jane said, walking outside, leather satchel in hand and locking her front door.

"How are you feeling this morning?" Weyler carefully eyed Jane.

Jane, feeling his intrusive stare, focused on the door lock. "Right as rain, boss." She spied the box of guns and toolbox from her father's workshop on the front porch. "Could you put those in your trunk and take them to DH? Apparently the guys down there want to buy them from my father."

Weyler collected both boxes and put them in his immaculate trunk. His black Ford Taurus was spotless. The wax job was so slick, Jane could see her reflection in the door twenty-five feet away. Weyler slid into the driver's seat and turned to Jane. "You like Dinah Washington?"

"Sure," she responded.

Weyler slipped a CD of *Dinah Washington's Greatest Hits* into his car player. Her silk voice softly filled the car with "What A Difference A Day Makes."

"I got this CD as part of a package deal from PBS during their last pledge drive. Five classic jazz CDs for a two hundred and fifty dollar donation to the station."

"Gee, that's fifty bucks a CD, boss. You sure know how to shop."

Weyler smiled at Jane's retort as he drove down Milwaukee and wound around the one-way streets until heading straight on University. "The Lawrence house is about four miles from your place." Jane remained quiet, staring out the window. "Oh, I have something for you." Weyler removed a small envelope from his jacket pocket and handed it to Jane. "Ron Dickson from the evidence lab asked me to give that to you."

Jane examined the outside of the envelope. It looked like Ron's wife's curly-cue handwriting where it said "Detective Jane Perry."

Stamped across the sealed flap was the word "D.A.R.E." in bold red letters. Inside, Jane found a folded note. It was a short, cheery note from Ron's wife, Sarah, reminding Jane of her regular contribution to the D.A.R.E. program. A self-addressed envelope was tucked around the note. Jane marveled to herself at the fact that Ron's wife was so diligent in helping her husband take care of his charity obligations. What a sweet, sheltered life they had, she thought. Jane dug through her leather satchel for her checkbook.

"I didn't tell Chris about bringing you to the house today," Weyler offered.

"Why not?"

"As lead on the case, he's a bit possessive of it. I'll let him know about our visit after the fact. I think he'd like to solve it by next week but that's not going to happen."

"What about the Stover murder?" Jane brought a cigarette out from her satchel. "You're not turning that over to cold case, are you?"

"I'd appreciate if you wouldn't smoke in the car."

Jane stuffed the cigarette back into the pack. "Don't toss it to cold case, boss."

"Let's focus on the Lawrence murder right now."

Jane jotted out a check for fifty dollars to D.A.R.E., put the check in the envelope and handed it to Weyler. "Did anybody follow up on the protection money trail?"

"How's that?"

"With Bill Stover. Did anyone flush out all of the other businesses that give protection money to the Texas mob?"

"I'd have to check on that. Why?"

Jane wanted to make the idea sound like her own but was having a difficult time formulating it. "I just wonder if there's a lead buried somewhere in that. It's a needle in a haystack, but it's worth considering."

"I'll check into it." Jane looked outside as Weyler turned down Exposition. "You know, Emily Lawrence hasn't stopped talking about you. You made a tight connection with that child."

"I just talked to her. No big deal."

Weyler observed Jane's obvious withdrawal. "I'm sure it'll pain you to know that Emily's interest in you is driving Martha Durrett crazy." Weyler stole a glance at Jane.

"Humph!" Jane enjoyed the image in her mind. "So, how's the kid doing?"

"Alright, I guess, considering. Apparently, she's still

extremely disconnected from the event, mentally and emotionally. No tears, Martha reports, even after you informed her of her parents' death."

"That doesn't surprise me. When you can't feel...you can't feel."

"I don't think I told you that the DA asked us to put Emily under hypnosis to see if her subconscious mind could tell us anything about that night."

"Great," Jane said sarcastically. "She hasn't been traumatized enough—"

"She wouldn't cooperate. No matter how hard they tried, they couldn't get her to go under."

"Smart girl."

"From what I hear, Emily has disassociated from the murders and what she witnessed. She's acting distant and disinterested in the whole thing. Martha says it's normal behavior, even though it makes the child come off as rather cold and detached."

Jane listened to Weyler but wondered why he was reporting the details of Emily's emotional response to the murder to her. It wasn't Jane's case. She didn't want to come off sounding interested in Emily so she put on a casual tone. "What's going to happen to the kid?"

"In what way?"

"Family. Does she have family nearby to take her in?"

"She has an aunt and uncle up in Cheyenne."

"Cheyenne?" Jane said under her voice as Weyler turned onto Franklin. "The kid's going from Washington Park to Cheyenne, Wyoming? That's gotta suck."

"You almost sound worried about the child."

"Worried? Please. Just making conversation, boss. Look at this neighborhood." Jane motioned outside of the car. "It's great. It's comfortable. Cheyenne, Wyoming is like going to Mars. It's not that I care! It's just an observation."

Weyler pulled up in front of the Lawrence crime scene and parked the car. "Me thinks thou doth protest too much, Detective." Weyler motioned around the house. "I want to take you around the perimeter first."

The Lawrence house stood in the middle of the tree-lined block, facing Smith Lake. It was the kind of neighborhood that reeked of solid, middle-class comfort. The Washington Park area of Denver was an enigma to Jane. If you snapped a photograph of the streets in summertime and asked someone to guess the location, she figured that Colorado would be low on their list. It was a secret pocket in the Mile High City that felt more like a West coast retreat. Of course, now with the bright yellow police tape surrounding the Lawrence house, the neighborhood vibe had taken a downward turn. Vicious double murders just didn't happen in Washington Park.

Jane looked across the street to an unmarked police car. "What's up?"

"We put a 24-hour watch on the house," Weyler said, picking up a large envelope marked "Crime Scene Photos" from the backseat of his car.

"Chris' idea?"

"No, just an insurance policy."

"You think the killers are coming back to grab a souvenir?"

"It's more to appease the neighbors. These people are like one big family. They have block parties and babysit for each other's kids. This tragedy has turned the whole place upside down. Come around this way. I'll show you the backyard first."

The two-story Lawrence house stood fifty feet from the sidewalk. The entry walk was lined with neatly trimmed juniper bushes and colorful flowers. The house was built mostly of brick except for the upstairs addition that was trimmed in dark wood. It was deceiving in size. From the road, it looked like a little saltbox, no more than 1,500 square feet. But as Weyler and Jane walked up the spotless driveway on the right side of the house, it was evident that the house stretched farther back than it appeared.

Weyler unlatched the side wooden gate and waved Jane

into the backyard. A deep green carpet of manicured grass filled the space, along with a large Sycamore that grew against the back of the house and tickled the rain gutter with its strong branches.

"There's a back door here," Weyler said, pointing to an entrance to the right rear of the house. "But we don't believe the suspect or suspects entered that way because it was locked from the inside. All the action took place in the living room, as far as we can determine. Over there," Weyler said, directing Jane's attention to the rear, "is the back gate that leads into the alley. The alley was clean. No fresh tire tracks or prints. We feel the perps entered through the front door."

Jane looked up at the second floor. "That's a small second story."

"It's just got one room and a separate bathroom that belong to Emily."

Jane stood back and noticed what looked like scuff marks and footprints on the sloping roof that jetted away from the window. "Are those footprints up there?"

"Yes. They belong to Emily."

"She ran out on the roof that night?"

"No, neighbors say she liked crawling outside her window and watching the stars at night. The child has quite a fixation on planets and such."

"Her parents let her walk out on that roof? She's nine years old! That's dangerous. There's nothing to catch her fall except that damn Sycamore."

"Apparently, it wasn't an issue for them."

"Well, that's just stupid." Jane mumbled to herself as she focused on the top story. Whenever she visited a crime scene where a homicide took place, she could always feel the vibration of the death. The Lawrence house was no exception. It was as though a thick cloud descended upon the dwelling that only Jane could sense. She had an uncanny ability to dissect a crime scene. Jane used hard-and-fast procedures like everyone else, but then she took it a step further, letting her psyche connect with the murderous energy still swirling at the scene. Somehow, she was able to tune into a hidden energy field that permeated the walls, ceiling, floors and every last piece of minutia of that space. Years ago, when she first experienced the sensation, she chalked it up to just another bad booze reaction. But the feeling continued and what was both amazing and disturbing was that her heightened perception always proved to lead her to the answer. Weyler—the only soul Jane shared this odd phenomenon with—called it a gift. But to Jane, it was just another curse.

Jane and Weyler walked up the three steps that lead to the rear door and entered the small kitchen. The narrow room was lined with floor to ceiling cabinets. A wooden farm table sat in the center of the room with four heavy chairs encircling it. There was the stainless steel refrigerator with the obligatory notepad attached to it with a magnet. The words "Pick up Brie" were scrawled across the pad. An assortment of family photographs filled the right side of the unit. As Jane stood back and observed the room, she felt she was looking at a page from the Pottery Barn catalog.

"They were out of Brie," Jane said, pointing to the note.

"Is that a clue, Detective?"

"No. They were people who ate Brie, not Velveeta. Just an observation." Jane glanced over to the photos on the refrigerator. Most of them were of Emily. There was Emily in her ballerina Halloween costume, Emily with Santa, Emily in the park and Emily holding a doll. There was only one photo of Emily with her parents. It looked like it was snapped at the park across the street from the house. Jane took the photo off the refrigerator and turned it over. The imprinted development date was May 2, three and a half weeks old. Emily was sandwiched between her parents wearing a half-smile. Jane couldn't help noticing that Patricia had a strained look on her face and David looked preoccupied. Jane mused it was an odd family photo choice to display on a refrigerator. But then again, she figured, most people were not as observant as she was.

"This door leads into the living room," Weyler said, pointing to an adjacent door. "But if you go down that corridor and turn right, you'll come upon the entry hall and stairway. There was no trace of an intruder in this area." Weyler lead Jane down the short corridor and stopped at the staircase. Jane looked over and noticed an old desk standing several inches away from the side of the stairs, in a direct line with the front door. She stopped momentarily and scanned the desk with her eyes as Weyler started up the stairs. "Stay there for a second," he said.

Weyler ascended the staircase that was conspicuously missing patches of carpeting. He stopped on the darkened landing in front of Emily's bedroom door and awkwardly lowered his 6'4" frame. "If I hunch myself down so I'm about Emily's height, it's conceivable that she could have stood here in this shadowy area and witnessed the murder. The bodies were found approximately twelve feet behind you where that carpet section has been cut out." Jane turned around to face the cozy living room, filled with several overstuffed chairs, a comfortable dark green sofa, cherry wood coffee table, central fireplace and a handsome liquor cabinet. The plush carpeting where the bodies fell had been cut away and taken to evidence, exposing a twenty-five foot square section of dark wooden flooring. "Back up ten feet," Weyler instructed. Jane complied. "Now, look up here. Can you see me?"

"No, boss."

"That's what I thought. That's a possibility right there." Jane raised her eyebrows slightly as she entertained the idea of Emily standing in the dark recesses and watching her parents being butchered to death. "Come on up." Jane reluctantly joined Weyler upstairs. "The child's bedroom door was open when police arrived." Jane followed Weyler into the bedroom. He flicked on the light switch. They were greeted by plush ever-so-pink carpeting that complemented both the pale pink walls and rose print comforter edged with ivory lace. A curved section of carpeting was removed that trailed from the outside landing and into the closet. A trio of windows graced the wall in front of them. Jane couldn't help but notice that the center window had shoe scuff marks and a few scratches on the bottom section, telltale signs of Emily's nocturnal visits onto the roof. Sundry toys and dolls dotted the floor. A cream colored nightstand sat next to the bed. Upon it sat a small lamp with a lampshade that had cutouts of stars encircling it. Jane walked over to the lamp and turned it on while at the same time, turning off the light switch on the wall. Thanks to the innovative lampshade, a band of star shapes projected their illuminated bodies across the wall and ceiling.

"I guess this brings the stars inside," Jane said.

"That's nothing. The kid's got this projector called Starlight Starbright. They found her with it in the closet. It was turned off but when you put it on, these ethereal sounds come out of the speakers and it projects a revolving display of stars across the walls and ceiling. It's quite impressive." Weyler smiled. "Emily's very covetous of it. She carries it around in a little navy blue case."

Suddenly, a swath of dark blue flashed in front of Jane's eyes. It was the exact fragment of navy blue she'd seen before in the staccato blast of images. But *this* time she could clearly make out the outline of a carrying case. Jane closed her eyes, pressing the heel of her hand against her forehead.

Weyler observed Jane. "What's wrong?"

Jane kept her eyes closed, realizing that a fragmented connection had been made; a connection between a split-second of color and the accompanying image it belonged to. Jane felt her heart beat faster. At that moment, she was certain she was slipping out of her body and into a precarious dark hole where one questions their sanity. She opened her eyes, still feeling as if she were balancing between two realities. "It's nothing," Jane uttered, flicking on the bedroom light and turning to a side door. "That's the closet?"

"Yes." Weyler opened the closet door to reveal a single row of tightly packed clothing on one side, a neat line of shoes underneath and a bevy of oversized bed pillows scattered on the floor. "The door was slightly cracked. Emily was found completely buried in the center of the pillows. The patrol officer who came on scene didn't see her at first. He had his gun drawn as he searched the house. When he opened the closet, he had to look twice before he saw Emily staring straight at him with, what he called, a poker face. No emotion at all on her part. A box of coloring pencils were strewn across the floor right here." Weyler pointed to the front of the bedside table. We believe the perps caused that to happen when they bumped against it. If you go into that closet and hunker down and crack the door just exactly like it was when they found her, it's possible to assume she had clear line of sight on their faces." Weyler directed Jane's attention to a three-inch square of pink carpeting in front of the table that had been removed. "Right here is where we found drops of blood that fell off one of the knives. We theorize the perp was standing still when the blood dropped from the knife tip. In other words, there could have been a good ten, fifteen, maybe twenty seconds of him standing in one spot in direct line with where Emily was hiding. Enough time for her to clearly see the perp."

"That's just wishful conjecture," Jane replied in a dismissive tone.

"It's a possibility, Jane."

Jane felt herself thankfully slide back into her body. She could now be all business again. "From what you said, the individual or individuals did not leave a trace of their presence, right?"

"Correct."

"So that means they probably covered their shoes to hide footprints, wore gloves and most likely covered their face with something to prevent us from finding sweat and hair and getting a DNA sample."

"That's what we're thinking up to this point."

"Okay, then you have to assume that certain things follow. First, they are professionals. They know the drill. They know what cops are gonna look for at a scene. Second, the killer or killers knew Emily existed or why would they bother to come upstairs? Oh, and by the way, Chris really fucked up when he told the media that Emily was in this house during the murder! That's the kind of information the perps don't need to know! That's also the kind of info that'll keep that kid in protective custody for a lot longer!"

"Point noted, Detective," Weyler said wearily.

"So the killer or killers come up to this room. But Emily's not in her bed like she should be and it doesn't follow to them that she'd be anywhere else in this room. They figure the kid's not here. She's at a friend's house. End of story. They're hyped up. They just killed two people downstairs. They're flying a million miles an hour. Neither one of them is going to stand still after all that and contemplate what he just did, even if he thinks he's alone. *They want out of here!* But let's just say for the sake of argument that the killer or killers did stop for five or ten seconds. And, as luck would have it, they just *happened* to stand still right in line with Emily's point of view. So what? They're wearing masks! They could have stood in front of this door for hours and it still wouldn't make a damn bit of difference because she couldn't see their faces anyway. In my opinion, I think the whole thing is far too speculative."

"It's only speculative if you're not willing to think outside the box. Remember, Detective, Emily's prints are on the staircase. And her bloody footprints trailed blood from the head of her mother's dead body, up those stairs and into this closet." Weyler waited for a response but was greeted with stony silence. He leaned closer to Jane. "She stood in their blood, Jane!"

"She saw her parents! That doesn't mean she saw the killers! Those two pieces of information don't fit together!"

"You just don't want them to fit."

Jane held firm. "They don't fit because they don't fit. Are we done in here?"

Weyler straightened his body and stared at Jane. "Let's go downstairs."

Jane followed Weyler down the stairs and into the living room. She spotted two rolled sleeping bags in the corner of the entry hall—one adult size and one child size. "Who was Emily going camping with?"

"Chris noted that. The neighbors said that Emily and her mother had just returned on May 22 from a nine day camping trip to Moab, Utah."

"They decide to go on a nine day camping trip in the middle of May while school is still in session?"

"Perhaps they wanted to avoid the summer rush of tourists."

"Why didn't David join them?"

"Maybe it was one of those mother/daughter bonding experiences."

Jane stared at the sleeping bags, feeling a nagging sense of something being off creep into her psyche. Weyler stood near the front door. "The front door was wide open when the next-door neighbor found the scene the following morning. Based upon the lividity of both victims, estimation of death is put between nine and eleven the previous evening. Both victims were dressed in street clothes and from all appearances, opened the door quite willingly to the suspects. So did the Lawrences know the perps? It's after nine in the evening. You're typically not going to open your door at that hour to somebody you don't know or you don't trust. Thus, we throw out the idea that this is a random crime."

"Okay."

"Take a look at the scene," Weyler pulled out several color photos from the large envelope and handed them to

Jane. "The living room was in shambles. Lamps broken and overturned, there was an overstuffed chair that sat over there that was cut open with one of the knives. That white fluff in the one photo is the polyester filling from inside the chair. Most of the glass vases and knickknacks were either chipped or smashed. The scene was totally disorganized and trashed. Then of course, there's this."

Weyler handed a photo to Jane. It was a close up of the coffee table. A mound of five ounces of cocaine was piled on the table. Jane examined the photo closely then handed it back to Weyler. "That's convenient," Jane said with a smug look.

"How's that?"

"Look closely. It doesn't fit into the scene. It isn't affected by any of the surrounding debris. If this is a drug deal gone bad, the coke is already going to be on the table before the carnage starts. If it's already sitting there and all hell breaks loose, the coke is not going to stay in a neat little mound! I'm telling you, after all the shit went down, the coke got put there to throw us off."

"I'll have to think about that one."

"Hey, boss, I'm thinking outside the box!" Jane rejoined.

Weyler looked tiredly at Jane, aware she was sarcastically referring to his earlier remark. "We questioned the neighbors about the Lawrence's overt behavior. They all reported the same thing. Nice couple. He liked to drink a lot at block parties but none of the conspicuous late night drug pickups were ever witnessed. And believe me, these people watch each other."

"There's a Hazel in every neighborhood . . ." Jane said.

"But take a good look at this." Weyler held up a large color photo of David Lawrence sprawled facedown across the living room floor. His throat is deeply slashed, exposing muscles and bone. "You tell me a hyped-up drug addict didn't carve up that man?" Weyler dropped the crime scene photo of David's bloody body onto the floor. "David fell here. Patricia was here," he dropped her photo less than three feet from the other one. "David was stabbed over ten times with a double edged knife. The first cut was to the throat, obviously to disengage him from saving his wife. The final kill was to his heart. Patricia Lawrence was stabbed with a single edged knife approximately seventy-five times. Her first cut was also to the throat. Not enough to kill her, but enough to knock the fight out of her. Half of her seventy-five stab wounds were to her face. This photo here shows how the knife entered her left eye and popped part of it out." Weyler layered the close-up photo of Patricia's face on top of her full body photo. Jane regarded the photos with cool detachment. "You want to hear Chris' theory?"

"Sure."

"One of the killers was a woman. The final kill to the heart on David Lawrence and the mutilation of his wife's face led him to that possibility."

"Both of those MOs can reflect a female killer but each was killed with a different knife. So, is Chris saying that two women did this?"

"He speculated it could be a jealous woman and a man."

"Oh, sure. David's having an affair with the woman and he won't divorce Patricia. So his lover hauls ass over here in tow with her boyfriend or husband who conveniently just found out about the tryst and together they decide to take care of business in between snorts of cocaine. Yeah, that makes perfect sense. Or how about this? Maybe it's like a roaming Bonnie and Clyde duo? If so, 'Bonnie' must have the upper arm and wrist strength of a Romanian weight lifter to plunge that knife in Patricia's eye and pull it partly out of her head. Not to mention that Bonnie continues this onslaught seventy-five times on Patricia or over ten times on David. Now, there's a broad you want to have on your office softball team!"

"You can drop the sarcasm. What's your point?"

"A woman played no part in this murder. This is a professional kill. How many male/female teams are out there? I'm not saying that can't happen. I'm just saying it didn't happen here. The other reason I don't think a woman was involved is that pile of cocaine. If this was a drug deal gone bad—and I'm telling you it wasn't—no *woman* is going to forget what she came here for!

"So, it's two men."

"I don't know. Is it two men who know enough about the MO of a female killer that they *consciously* create the outward appearance of female involvement? And if so, *why?* That's on par with premeditated manipulation. Manipulation of us who are standing here and trying to figure out what the fuck happened! Boss, I know you don't want to hear this, but nothing fits in my opinion. The whole thing feels *purposely* disjointed. It's like three or four different murders that DH has investigated, but suddenly they're all wrapped up into one house. Is it a man making it look like a woman? Is it one person making it look like two? Is it two making it look like one? I don't know. All I know is that whatever it turns out to be, it's not at all what it seems." Jane's eyes rested upon the desk in the front hallway.

"What is it?" asked Weyler.

"My mother had a similar desk." Jane crossed toward the desk, gently skimming her finger against its rolled edges. "You don't see a lot of these."

"Are they worth a lot?"

"I don't know. They were more a novelty item. I used to call it the 'riddle desk.'"

"Why's that?"

"That's where the novelty part comes in. Every time you think you've found a drawer or cubbyhole, you get tricked. I'll show you. They must have hired world-class artists to do the three dimensional designs because they're so lifelike. See these drawers?" Jane pointed to a series of four slender drawers aligned on the top left of the desk. "Try pulling one of them out."

Weyler reached over and tried to grab on to the knob but then realized it was only painted on. "Humph!"

"Lifelike, eh? Try opening what looks like a cubbyhole, and it's not."

"What the hell good is a desk you can't use?"

"But you can use it. You just have to know what buttons to push."

"Buttons?"

"They're hidden. I'm not exactly sure where they are on this one. My mom's had a couple on the side and some underneath." Jane moved her face closer to the surface of the desk, slowly running her index finger along the middle of the desk. "You just gotta look real closely and if you're lucky . . ." With that, her finger wedged into an indentation in the desk and the front door popped out like a cashier's drawer. "Abracadabra!"

"Anything interesting in there?"

Jane rummaged through the near empty drawer and came up with a handful of paper clips, pencils and erasers. She slid the flat of her hand beneath the underside of the desk. "Sometimes if you feel underneath the front of the desk, you might find a little depression . . . like there." She pushed her finger into the depression and a quick *click-click* sound triggered the two smaller front side drawers to unlatch. Jane pulled them both out to find them completely empty. "Have you ever seen a cleaner desk than this one?"

"I don't get it. It's got all these secret compartments and hidden buttons, how do you find anything? How do you know where they all are?"

"Only the owner of the desk knows what button goes with what drawer. The rest of us just go about blindly."

Weyler eyed the five wooden compartments that lined the top of the desk. "Are those real?"

"Yeah. My mom's desk had seven of them. One for every day of the week. I used to leave her a little piece of paper in one of those slots every day with a message on it. You know, 'Hi, Mom,' 'Have a good day,' 'Please get well,'" Jane's voice trailed off.

Weyler broke the silence. "You oughta take your

mom's desk down to that *Antiques Roadshow* on PBS when it comes to Denver. Maybe it's worth something."

Jane stiffened. "It's long gone. Dad sold it two days after she died. He got a whole forty bucks for it," Jane declared sarcastically. She turned away from the desk and sauntered into the living room. After surveying the area, she let out a deep sigh. "What do you know about David Lawrence?"

Weyler pulled a small notepad from his jacket pocket and flipped it open, scanning the scribbles. "He was Assistant VP of Technical Development for *Crimson Technology* in Denver."

"What's *Crimson Technology?*"

"It's an Internet networking firm. They're troubleshooters. David was apparently the quintessential computer geek. But in the words of one employee our detectives talked to, he was a 'geek who made it good.' This same guy said David reminded him of someone who was awkward and an outsider, but a guy who carefully rose to the top of his company. Someone who could afford to send his daughter to a private school."

Jane brushed up against the Lawrences' glassed liquor cabinet. "You said, 'carefully rose to the top.' Why '*carefully?*'"

"I'm going by the words used to describe David." Weyler read from the pad. "'Careful,' 'Methodical,' 'Deliberate,' 'Safe.' One woman at the company threw in the word 'boring.' He arrived at the office at 8:30 a.m. and left promptly at 6:00. Kept a tidy desk, emptied his 'in' box every day, left nary a scrap of refuse on his office carpet."

Jane stared at the liquor cabinet in a daze. She was taking in every word but, at the same time, developing an internal sense for David Lawrence.

"Bank accounts?"

"We checked. No unusually large deposits or withdrawals. He paid his credit cards in full and always at least ten days before they were due. No debt, except for his mortgage. His new Audi was paid off as was his wife's brand-new Toyota 4-Runner."

"Other women in his life?"

Weyler smiled. "We asked about that and we were laughed at."

"Why can't a rich computer geek have an affair?"

"They can. But David Lawrence did not."

"What about the hard drive on his home computer? His personal e-mails?"

"Chris said there was nothing incriminating."

"So, after all the prelim, nobody found *anything* odd?"

"The only somewhat odd comment one of his coworkers made was that for a couple months this spring, David was acting . . . how did he say it . . ." Weyler referred to his notes. "Like a guy who finally got picked for the school team."

"What does that mean?"

"He walked around with a cocky strut. The fellow wondered if David had landed another promotion and was keeping it quiet. We asked about a promotion and there was none. Apparently, the cocksure attitude didn't last more than six weeks. He suddenly became edgy and anxious with his coworkers. Talked on his phone in hushed tones. Seemed preoccupied at staff meetings. Showed up at work smelling obviously of whiskey."

Jane took Weyler's comment as a backhanded, personal affront. "He showed up at 8:30 and left at 6:00 and paid his bills ten days before they were due. Who gives a shit what he does on his off time? Alcohol isn't illegal."

"But cocaine is."

Jane chuckled. "A by-the-book computer nerd turns into a cokehead overnight?"

"It's not impossible."

"No, it's not. But the way everything is laying out around this strange scenario, it's too convenient—too 'Movie of the Week.' Calculating outsider who hasn't a blemish on his record, in the space of a month or two, decides to turn to cocaine to . . . what? To add excitement to his regimented life? And then, he screws up a huge score with his dealer inside his own house and he and his wife pay with their lives. Pure fiction! Boss, the missing chunks in this case are so big that trains could drive through them! No one point leads effortlessly to the other." Jane approached Weyler, joining him on the landing near the front door. "Why *does* a careful, boring, financially secure computer geek who's an outsider get slaughtered alongside his lovely wife? What is David's dirty little secret?"

"What do you mean?"

"Everyone's got at least one dirty little secret. And those who say they don't, have some of the best secrets. The Lawrences might have looked clean to their neighbors at block parties, but most people judge you by your outward appearance. And even then, people don't really pay attention. The neighbors know that Patricia and Emily are away on an off-season, nine-day camping trip during school but no one asks 'Why?' It's not about *seeing* the little things as much as it's about *feeling* the little things. It's listening to the spaces in between the words. It's understanding what a lie sounds like. It's taking a step back and watching. Let's face it, boss, everyone is far too busy to sit back and watch! The Lawrences may look clean on paper, but it's what they whisper to each other in bed. It's what they scream at each other when their kid is at a friend's house. It's what they don't write on the Christmas card letter. It's the dark, rotten family secret that everybody has but no one talks about. Because, if anybody really knew your little secret, you'd be an outcast. And nobody wants to risk that. I don't know what their secret was, but I know it *wasn't* cocaine." Jane casually turned her gaze to the rest of the room. "Well, you asked for my assessment and my assessment is . . ." Jane found her gut tightening. She tried to cover it up but the visceral response was overwhelming. She walked away from Weyler, trying to get centered. The more she looked around the room, the deeper her gut moved into it. Holding back was pointless because it only seemed to deepen her attachment. It was as though she could almost hear the walls talking, vibrating, whispering, longing to blare out what they saw. Suddenly, a splash of blood flashed in front of Jane's vision. In less than a second, Emily's face appeared through the disappearing crimson haze. Then, unexpectedly, Emily's face warped into Amy Stover. Her pleading eyes beckoned Jane as her deafening scream pierced the room. Jane grasped her forehead to shut out the disturbing hallucination. Icy sweat beaded across her face and neck. She needed a drink and looked at her watch. It was 11:00 a.m. If she left the house now, she could be downing a bottle of Jack Daniels in less than twenty minutes. "My assessment is that we don't have all the pieces," Jane said urgently. "And the kid probably doesn't either." Weyler remained silent, staring intently at Jane. She avoided eye contact as she moved to the front door. Pursing her lips, Jane turned to him with an indignant air. "What?"

"Are you done bullshiting me?"

Jane anger peaked. "Look, what the fuck do you want me to tell you? You got no prints except for the occupants . . . no incriminating evidence . . . no witnesses."

"We do have a witness."

"We *don't!*" Jane felt cornered. She started to open the front door when Weyler moved quickly and slammed it shut with the flat of his hand.

"What are you so damned afraid of?" Weyler yelled. "The truth!"

"The truth is all I care about! But sometimes it's better to let certain things stay buried in people."

She tried to open the door but Weyler kept his hand firmly against it. "You can't tell me that you believe that in your heart."

Jane looked Weyler in the eyes. "Yes, I do."

He scrutinized Jane for a second. "That's too bad. But that doesn't change the fact that Emily trusts you and *only* you. You're the only one she'll talk to. Whether you want to accept it or not, the two of you made an odd little connection. What draws the two of you together is what she knows deep down and what you can get out of her. And that's exactly what you're going to do."

Jane's eyes widened, an anger edged with fear. "No!" Jane bolted toward the center of the living room.

"Whatever she knows or saw is asleep inside of her. Only *you* can wake it up."

"*Absolutely not!*"

"I want you and the child alone in this house for twenty-four hours. Maybe longer. It goes against all policy but I'll take care of the details."

"Have you lost your mind?"

"I'm not expecting you to probe her with questions. Just be with her and pay attention to what she says or what she can remember."

"You will never convince Social Services, not to mention her guardian adlitum and the court psychologist to agree to that deal! They'll take it in front of a judge!"

"I know my way around the system. I have a lot of friends who owe me big favors. I'll take care of it. I have a strong feeling that when Emily returns here, she might get a glimpse of what she saw that night."

"This is Chris' case! Have him talk to her!"

"She won't talk to anyone but you."

"I won't do it."

"You're on shaky ground with the Department, Jane—"

"Wait, the Department says that I'm too fucked up to solve other crimes but I'm *not* too fucked up to hang out with a nine-year-old kid and somehow manipulate her to tell me what she possibly did or didn't see? Is that what I'm hearing? Because if that's what you're telling me, I want you to think how that's gonna play back at DH!"

"Like I said, I can be very convincing with the higher-ups when I have to be. Besides, they don't know how often you attend 'choir practice.' I've done everything I can over the years to keep your self-medicating as quiet as possible."

Jane looked at Weyler, stupefied. "You don't get it, boss. You want me to lead that kid straight down to hell. Down in the sludge and the blood and the outright fear of it all. And you buy into all that psychobabble shit that if she helps us solve this mess, she's gonna magically wipe away all those demons in her head and get healed. Well, that's not the way it works! You can't draw that hell out of somebody and expect them to ever be normal again. Because they will *never* know what normal feels like. I will *not* be responsible for fucking up the rest of that kid's life."

"I think you want to know."

Jane exploded. "I know what she sees!" Her voice caught suddenly. "What she . . . saw."

"Good! That's why you're the only one I can trust."

"Boss, listen to me. What she saw should be forgotten!" Jane turned away from Weyler, her chin trembling. Inside her head, it felt like a million electrical lines had crossed and ignited simultaneously. She wanted out of that house and to feel the burn of a whiskey shot on her tongue.

Weyler leaned on the front door, crossing his arms. "Okay, let's look at this your way and follow it through. We drop the case, not wanting to cause any more pain to Emily. We pat her on the head, wish her luck and send her to the aunt and uncle in Cheyenne. Life goes on for her. She makes new friends, starts a new school, sleeps in a new bed, plays with new toys. But somewhere inside, something is never quite right with her. She can feel it. It's like she has the answer to a million dollar question on the tip of her tongue but she just can't quite remember what it is. So the years pass, but still that nagging feeling never leaves her. Then one day, she's driving her car down the street and she sees something—something insignificant by itself, but for whatever reason, it triggers her memory. And in a split second, what she sees in front of her is no longer the street she is driving on but the memory, played out as though she was thrown back into time. She pulls the car over and she is scared out of her wits and all alone. She wonders if she's going crazy. But once her mind is unlocked, it's a free-for-all and those memories just keep coming. This happens at the market, in the shower, while she's waiting for the toast to brown, when she's in line at the bank. And the more they come, the crazier and more alone she feels . . . until that insanity becomes the only world she knows. She wants the memories to stop more than anything. So one day, she does the only thing she knows to make it go away. She blows her brains out. You want that on your head?"

Jane turned to face Weyler. The words, "You want that on your head?" brought back the memory of the dialogue that lead to her blood-soaked confrontation with her father. A gnawing indignity engulfed Jane. "Someone used those same words to manipulate me a long time ago. I should have ignored them back then and saved myself a lot of grief. It's *not* on my goddamn head what happens to that kid! *I don't know her!*"

"Yes, you do. The two of you are already linked by some unknown force." Jane looked at Weyler with an incredulous glance. *Linked by some unknown force.* Jane wondered if he realized how prophetic his words truly were. "You look at her and you see yourself. She's that moment in time between all that was good and all that went terribly wrong. If you can help her, maybe you can help yourself." Weyler smoothed his jacket and straightened his tall frame. "You want her to pretend like it never happened. But it did. And so we go from that point. One way or the other, she's going to remember. And when she does, I want you to be with her."

Jane always hated it when Weyler won.

# Chapter **10**

Less than thirty-six hours after leaving the Lawrence crime scene, Jane was on her way back to it. Weyler picked her up at her house at seven o'clock sharp and drove the four mile route in near silence. It was thirty-six hours of heavy thought for Jane. Thirty-six hours of feeling stark and exposed. Thirty-six hours of debating how to get out of the assignment. Thirty-six hours of Jane wondering how far she could have driven away from Denver in that space of time. More than anything, it was thirty-six hours without a drop of alcohol and that was thirty-six hours too long.

It wasn't that Weyler threatened her if she took a drink. For Jane, it came more from an odd sense of duty—a time to set aside one's personal desire to become numb for the good of another. There was a kind of righteousness in it. However, it couldn't assuage her desire to feel the sting of a whiskey shot against the back of her throat. By the time Weyler and Jane pulled onto Franklin and neared the Lawrence house, the mere thought of booze was as addictive as the thing itself.

Jane spotted two unmarked cars parked across the street from the house. Weyler pulled up alongside one of the cars and rolled down his window. The other driver, a

Denver patrol officer, leaned out the window. "Give us ten minutes." Weyler said to the officer, who nodded in response.

Jane noted that the backseat window was rolled down several inches. Like a jack-in-the-box, Emily popped up out of her seat and framed her eyes and nose in the window opening. Jane could hear the distinct voice of Martha Durrett admonishing the child to sit down. "What's Martha doing here?" Jane asked with an irritated edge.

"Part of the deal with the Court," Weyler said as he pulled his sedan across the street and parked in front of the Lawrence house.

"What about all those 'favors' you said they owed you?"

"There are certain things favors don't cover."

"If that bitch is required to be in the house with us, I'm out of here—"

"Calm down, Detective! Martha stays in the car with the officer, strictly as an observer and as backup if you need it. Same goes for the other car which holds one detective at all times."

"What's all this 'backup' shit? I don't need to be observed!"

"Hey, the police presence is a request from the neighborhood. As far as Martha's role, it's what I had to do to get the 'okay.' You'll also notice a black-and-white patrolling the alley behind the house every twenty minutes or so."

"Isn't this overkill?"

"It's precautionary." Weyler pulled a small cell phone out of his coat pocket and handed it to Jane. "Take this. Phone service was cut inside the house."

Jane took the phone. "What aren't you telling me?"

Weyler let out a sigh that was more irritated at others than at Jane. "The Court felt there was a certain degree of concern regarding the child's welfare."

"Psychological or physical?"

"Maybe a little bit of both."

"Well, I got the psychological figured. What's the physical?"

"Like I said, it's precautionary."

"Whoa! If you think for one second that someone is stalking this kid and might come after her, what the hell are you bringing her back here for? What is she? *Bait?*"

Weyler turned to Jane. "My God, of course not! You know this is a rare and delicate situation. We have a nine-year-old child who may have important information to share with us. Look, I don't like this any more than you do. Of course, you tell anybody that, and I'll deny it. But my hands are tied. The Department is coming off a case where a family of three who we were hired to protect is blown to bits in their own driveway. And when one of those victims is a child, well . . . I don't have to tell you how that makes us look. We need a tally mark in the 'win' column. We need to show this city that we don't have our heads up our collective asses. So, desperate times call for very desperate measures. And one of those measures is bringing a traumatized child quietly back to a crime scene and seeing if we can shake some of that memory loose. Bottom line, Detective, you have to *make* this work."

Jane looked straight ahead. "So, is she or is she not being stalked?"

"I honestly don't know. But I sure as hell am not going to take any more 'ice cream' chances," Weyler stated, alluding to the Stovers' side trip to the ice cream parlor that eventually cost them their lives. "Are you?"

"We wouldn't need to ask that question if Chris kept his mouth shut about how Emily was in the house when all the shit came down. I want that on the record."

"Duly noted."

Weyler dipped underneath the yellow police tape and entered the front door of the house followed by Jane who set her leather satchel near the staircase. At the sound of the door closing, Chris called out from inside the kitchen.

"It's us!" Weyler yelled back.

"What's he doing here?" Jane said, muffling her voice.

"He's the current shift detective positioned in the other vehicle."

"Why's he in here?"

"I asked him to go get you and Emily some food."

"Wonderful." Jane said, knowing how Chris must have reacted when he was sent to the store. Jane stood on the landing that overlooked the living room and surveyed the area. There was a smattering of knickknacks. The balance, along with the missing pieces of carpet, had been taken into evidence. The room looked cold and disturbed. "You should have had Chris pick up some stuff to fill in the place. And couldn't you have had someone cover up the carpet cutouts? That's going to freak out Emily."

"It's all I could do on short notice." Weyler's cell phone rang and he answered it.

Jane wandered across the room and into the kitchen where Chris was putting the final item into the refrigerator. "I thought you were going to Lake Dillon."

Chris kept his back turned to Jane. "I did, too. But Weyler figured out a way to squeeze more blood out of the overtime fund." He slammed the refrigerator door and turned to Jane. "But I shouldn't complain. I get to shop for you and the kid and then I get to sit out in that car until my shift's up at 10:30. I'm one lucky son-of-a-bitch."

"You want to go one-on-one with the kid, Chris? Be my guest!"

"No! She picked *you!* You're the star of the fucking show. Just do me one favor. Cut to the chase and figure out this fucker! I don't give a shit what you have to do to jar her memory. Whatever it takes, *do it. Understand me?* But you keep me informed. *I'm* the one who has to solve this case, one way or the other."

"Whatever it takes?" Jane retorted. "Want me to pry off her fingernails?"

"Do your fucking job so I can end this." Chris started out the back door and turned around. "I'm still going to Lake Dillon after the shift tonight. Tomorrow, when I'm

on the water with my new boat and starin' at my new custom boots, I'll pop open a beer and think of you. I bet a
cold one sounds pretty good to you about now, eh?" A
sadistic smirk crossed his face.

Weyler called in from the living room. "Let's do this!"

"Showtime!" Chris whispered as he turned and walked
out the back door.

Jane secured the lock on the back door, still stinging
from Chris' comments. She then joined Weyler who was
standing at the front door.

"You ready?" Weyler asked. Jane nodded. Weyler
opened the front door. Framed against the filtered light
of the setting sun, stood Martha Durrett holding tightly
onto Emily's hand.

"Good evening, Sergeant," Martha said, haltingly.
"Detective."

"Hello, Emily," Weyler said, lowering his angled frame
and holding out his hand. Emily withdrew her hand from
Martha's tight grasp and shook his hand. "Come in,"
Weyler beckoned as the child crossed the threshold and
stood next to Jane. Emily was dressed in a denim jumper,
red short-sleeved blouse and dark blue cardigan. She held
tightly onto her Starlight Starbright projector, safely
ensconced in its navy blue carrying case.

Martha knelt down in front of the child. "Remember
what I told you," she said with her trademark patronizing
tone. "If you get those scary feelings in your tummy, you
are allowed to leave. Okay?" Emily nodded. Martha
pulled out a pocket-sized flashlight with a key chain
attached—the plastic covered kind that, when squeezed,
produces a bright LED blue sapphire light. "This is a
*very special* flashlight, Emily. Four squeezes will be our
special signal." Jane couldn't believe what she was
hearing. Martha angled the flashlight up in the air and
squeezed it four successive times as she said with
each squeeze, "H-E-L-P." Without realizing it, the pointed
sapphire light was pointing directly into Jane's eyes.

Jane turned away and walked into the living room,

mumbling under her breath, "Oh, S-H-I-T."

"We need to move along, Martha," Weyler said gently.

Martha attached the small flashlight onto the right strap of Emily's denim jumper. "I'm putting this here so that you can use it at a moment's notice. Just go to one of the front windows and flash our special signal out to the car and I will be at your side within seconds." Martha awkwardly patted Emily on her head and reluctantly returned outside to her observation vehicle.

Weyler bent down toward Emily so he was on her eye-level. "Everything's going to be fine, honey." Weyler nodded toward Jane and left.

Emily stood on the hard wooden floor, facing the living room. Her expression reminded Jane of the term "poker face."

"You can call me Jane."

"Okay," Emily said quietly.

Jane felt a swell of irritation build in her stomach. Another minute of deafening silence passed between them. "Look, kid, I just want you to know that I think bringing you back here is a stupid idea and a waste of our time. As far as I'm concerned, you can sit on the couch and watch TV."

Emily glanced around the living room. "I can't. The TV's gone."

Jane turned around and realized Emily was right. "Oh, shit."

"Where's all the stuff? Why's the carpet missing?"

It took the child less than one minute to observe the one thing that had concerned Jane from the outset. Jane clenched her jaw and let out a deep sigh. "A lot of things, unfortunately, had to be removed so the police could look at them."

"Are they going to put them back where they got them?" said Emily, with a slight indignant sound to her voice.

It would have been easy to lie to the kid and placate her with some dressed up answer, but that just wasn't Jane's style. "Probably not."

Emily took several steps into the living room, noting every crevice and cranny. "I don't feel anything."

"I told you. You don't have to feel a damn thing."

"No. I mean I don't feel anything at all. I know my mommy and daddy are dead. I know 'cause you told me. But I can't feel sad. I can't cry."

Jane was taken aback by Emily's directness. She had hoped that by letting the kid off the hook and telling her not to worry that this whole thing would be painless and over in a matter of hours. Obviously, it was heading in a very different direction. "Hey, crying is overrated."

"Martha says I'm in . . ." She tried to remember the word. "Shock? She says I'm sleeping real deep and part of me doesn't want to wake up."

"I don't think that's a bad thing."

"But Martha says I—"

"You know," Jane interrupted, feeling a surge of anger. "Forget Martha! Martha is not the end-all, be-all! She's not even all there! She's like the tin man in *The Wizard of Oz*, you know? If she only had a brain!"

"The scarecrow," Emily said succinctly.

"Huh?"

"The scarecrow didn't have a brain. The tin man needed a heart."

"Whatever. The point is, I don't want you to buy into her psychological crap."

"How come you don't like Martha?"

"She's a pain in my ass. What? Are you two pals?"

"No. I don't like her, but I don't hate her."

"Okay. Fine." Jane felt her nerves tweak.

"You okay?"

"I'm fine!"

"How come your hands are shaking? Are you nervous?"

"Of course not!"

"Are you scared?"

"No!"

"Are you cold?"

"*No!*"

"Well, then why are you shaking?"

"Stop it," Jane said directly and to the point. "I said I was fine and I'm fine."

"Okay," Emily replied, not completely buying Jane's answer.

Jane nervously looked around the room. Her eyes rested briefly on the liquor cabinet against the far wall. Emily watched Jane intently. Jane turned back and saw the look on Emily's face. "*What?*" Jane said, defensively.

"Nothing." Emily looked down at Jane's leather satchel that lay against the wall. "Is that yours?"

"Yes." Jane moved into the living room and pulled out a cigarette pack from her shirt pocket. "Look, why don't you come in here and sit down or something."

Emily set down her Starlight Starbright projector and sauntered into the living room. "Does your hand still hurt?"

Jane searched throughout every pocket, trying to find matches. She looked at her left hand. She suddenly realized she hadn't changed the bandage in two days. "Nah." Digging into her trouser pocket, she came up with a box of matches from RooBar. She lit up and took in a meaningful puff on the cigarette.

There was thick silence as Jane positioned herself on the couch and Emily slid onto the facing chair. Emily looked at Jane with the same fascination she had in the interrogation room. It made Jane extremely uneasy. "What are you doing, Emily?"

The child struggled to reconcile what she saw with what she was thinking. But there was no way to explain it. "When did you start smoking?" Emily asked.

"When I was 14."

"Why did you start?"

"Because whiskey tastes better with a cigarette."

"Huh?"

"It was just something to take off the edge."

"What edge?"

"An edge is like a feeling, you know? Feeling edgy. Irritable. Frustrated. *Edgy.*"

"Like you're feeling now?"

"Yeah. *Exactly* like I'm feeling now." Jane sucked in another dose of nicotine.

"So, I guess it doesn't work."

"What?"

"You said you smoke to take off your edge. But you're still feeling your edge. So I think the smoke stopped working. Maybe if you stopped smoking—"

"Look," Jane said, leaning forward, "rule number one: don't hassle me about smoking. Understood?"

"Understood."

Jane peered around the room once again, zoning in on the liquor cabinet.

"You keep looking over at Daddy's liquor cabinet."

"I am observing the room. *Period.* Don't keep staring at me." Jane took another drag on her cigarette. "Don't you have some toys you can play with?"

"I've got my Starlight Starbright but it's not dark enough yet to use it."

"Is that all you have to play with?"

"It's all I *want* to play with."

"I see," Jane said, leaning back into the couch. Emily mirrored Jane as she, too, fell back into her chair and crossed her arms.

"Well, I guess this conversation is over," Jane surmised, observing Emily.

"What do you mean?"

"Your arms told me."

Emily looked down at her arms folded across her chest. "What'd they say?"

"You're cutting me off. You're feeling defensive."

Emily thought about it. "What's defensive?"

"It's like you're building a big wall around yourself so no one can find you."

Emily slowly uncurled her arms. "What does this mean?"

Jane looked across at Emily who was almost sharing her identical pose. "That's what you call 'mirroring.' It's that I look like you and you look like me."

Emily carefully observed Jane. "Oh, yeah . . . Is that good?"

"Well, you changed your position to mirror mine, so that means you're trying to make me feel more comfortable."

Emily considered the idea. "Is it working?"

Jane looked at Emily and felt a slight smile come up on her lips. "Maybe."

"What does this mean?" Emily slid her index finger down to her tummy and gently poked it again and again.

"You're telling the pitcher to throw a fast ball," Jane said with a deadpan expression.

Emily smiled at the joke. "It means I'm hungry. Would you please fix me some scrambled eggs?"

"Eggs?"

"Yeah, eggs."

"Okay," Jane said, getting up and heading toward the kitchen. Emily quickly followed behind her. Jane opened the refrigerator and found a carton of eggs that Chris bought. Setting the carton on a nearby counter, she contemplated what to do.

"Mommy and I made eggs every morning on our camping trip! I'll get you a bowl," Emily said, opening a cabinet and removing a white bowl.

"Okay." Jane awkwardly grabbed an egg and broke it over the bowl, landing most of the yolk on the table. "Shit," she said under her breath.

Emily opened a drawer, pulled out a towel and diligently sopped up the mess. "Try it again," Emily said quietly, her eyes pinned onto the bowl.

Jane cracked another egg against the bowl and the same thing happened, this time knocking some of the yolk onto her hand. "Oh, for Christ's sake!" Jane grumbled. Emily quickly swept up the residue. "I'll try it this way," Jane said, slamming the egg against the inside of the bowl, scattering tiny flecks of the smashed eggshell into the broken yolk.

"You got to pick those things out," Emily said, looking into the bowl.

"Yeah, yeah, yeah!" Jane said, digging for pieces of the eggshell.

"This isn't the way Mommy does it."

"Look, it's been a long time since I made scrambled eggs and I've pretty much forgotten how it's done."

"Don't you cook at your home?"

"Not really."

"How do you eat?" Emily asked, astonished.

"I know how to put food in a microwave and I've got Domino's on speed dial."

"Are you joking?" Emily said seriously with a semi-shocked look on her face.

"No. How does a pizza sound?"

"How about a sandwich?"

"*Pizza.*"

Emily held her fist in the air. "Rock, paper, scissors. If you win, pizza. If I win, sandwich." Jane rolled her eyes and held out her fist. "Okay, on three," Emily instructed. Jane and Emily brought their fists up and down in unison as Emily counted it out. Emily made the form of a pair of scissors and Jane kept her fist clenched. "Rock crushes scissors," Emily said, defeated. "Pizza."

Jane rifled through the nearby phone book until she found the number for a pizza parlor. Pulling the cell phone from her jacket pocket, she dialed and rattled off her order like a seasoned pro. Emily slid onto one of the kitchen chairs and watched Jane intently. She noted that Jane's navy blue pants were wrinkled, her denim shirt had a spot on the pocket and that her tan leather jacket looked as old as her leather satchel. Jane removed her jacket, tossing it on a chair. Emily immediately eyed Jane's shoulder holster and black pistol. "No anchovies, right?" Jane asked Emily, lowering the phone.

"Huh?" Emily said, still in awe of Jane's pistol.

"Never mind." Jane lifted the phone, continuing the order. Emily crept out of her chair and worked her way around the kitchen table toward Jane. She stood next to Jane, her eyes on the same level as Jane's Glock. Jane snapped the phone shut and looked down at Emily, just in time to see Emily's hand reach up toward her gun. "Hey!" Jane said brusquely. "Don't you ever touch that!"

Emily was taken aback by Jane's voice. "I just wanted—"

"I don't care! You *never* touch my gun! That's rule number two! Understand?" Emily nodded. "Let's just sit down and wait for the pizza."

Emily took a seat. Jane lit another cigarette off the ember that was dying and crushed out the old one in the sink. She took a deep drag and sat across from Emily. "I need to ask you a question," Emily said quietly.

"What?" Jane said, sucking in another good drag.

"Did you ever kill anybody?"

"What kind of question is that?"

"Well, did you?"

"*No,*" Jane stressed.

"*Could* you kill somebody?" Jane sat back in her chair, surprised by the question. "I have to know when they come back to get me—"

"No one is coming to get you!"

"But they are—"

Jane was incensed. "Who told you that? Martha?"

"Nobody told me. I . . . I just know."

Jane leaned forward. "No one is going to get you," she stated with conviction. Emily remained silent, not buying Jane's reassuring statement. "Look, you've got two cars out front and a black-and-white out in the back circling the alley every half hour—"

"You didn't answer my question? *Could you kill some-body?*"

"That's not a question a nine-year-old should ask!"

"Nine and a half."

"Oh, shit—"

"You're not gonna answer my question, are you?"

"No, I am not."

After about a minute of silence, Emily spoke up. "How old are you?"

Jane took a drag on her cigarette. The smoke curled out of her nostrils as she leaned across the table toward Emily. "I'm 35 . . . and one-quarter."

"You're older than my mommy," Emily replied reflectively.

Jane felt as though the wind had been knocked out of her. She sat back in her chair, nervously filling her lungs with more smoke. "Look, kid," Jane said in a subdued voice. "You're safe. Okay? No one is coming to get you. I would never let anything happen to you . . . Ever."

Emily sized up Jane and liked what she saw. "Okay." A thought crossed her mind. "Do you know what Venus looks like in the sky?"

Jane wasn't prepared for the sudden shift in conversation. "Do I . . . huh?"

"It's real pretty," Emily said, standing up and taking Jane's hand. "Come outside. I'll show you!"

"We're not going outside."

"Why not?"

"Because I said so. You stay in the house with me unless I say differently."

"But I can't show you Venus from in here—"

"I said you're not going out and I mean it!"

"My mommy lets me go out on my bedroom roof and look at the sky—"

"Well, that's not right. I saw that roof back there. You could slip and fall!"

"I never slipped."

"Listen to me, Emily. *You do not go outside of this house unless you are with me.* That's rule number two."

"No, it's not. Rule number two is don't touch your gun. Rule number *three* is don't go outside."

"Don't be a smart-ass. You're not going outside. Understand?"

Emily appeared genuinely defeated. "You say 'understand' a lot."

"I said don't be a smart-ass!" Jane felt her nerves fraying.

Emily leaned closer to Jane, speaking in a whisper. "Are you scared?"

"You already asked me that question. I told you I'm not scared. What's to be scared of?"

"Things," Emily said quietly, almost in a confidential way. "Like when people yell at each other but you can't see them. And they yell louder and louder . . . and you can't make them stop." Emily turned away from Jane and looked off to the side as if her words triggered a mental picture in the distance. The front doorbell rang and Emily jumped, grabbing instinctively on to Jane's arm. She quickly came out of her daze. "The pizza's here."

# Chapter 11

"Stay here," Jane instructed Emily. "I'll get the pizza."

Emily slipped into the chair and watched Jane leave the kitchen.

Jane pulled her wallet out of her leather satchel and opened the front door. There was Chris, holding the pizza. "What the hell are *you* doing?" Jane said, irritated.

"What are you doing ordering a pizza, for Christ's sake? It's a fucking crime scene! You can't have a pizza guy delivering to a place with fuckin' yellow tape surrounding it!"

Jane stepped outside and shut the front door part way. "Keep it down?"

"What's going on in there?"

"Nothing. Give me the goddamn pizza!"

"Don't tell me 'nothing!'" Chris said, pulling the pizza carton away from Jane. "Dammit, Jane! Don't be a cunt!"

A bolt of hot rage shot through Jane as she lunged toward Chris, grabbed the pizza and slammed the door in his face. Jane stormed into the kitchen, still steaming from Chris' remarks.

"Who was that?" Emily asked.

"Nobody!" Jane said, flipping open the pizza carton and grabbing a piece of pizza. "Here you go."

"Aren't we gonna use plates?"

Jane let out a sigh. "Where are they?"

"Behind you, second cupboard from the right."

Jane brought down two plates and slapped pizza slices on both of them. She sat down to eat when she caught Emily looking at her. "What is it now?"

"We need napkins. I don't want to get sauce on my jumper."

"You're a little hothouse orchid, aren't you?"

"Huh?"

Jane got up and grabbed the roll of paper towels near the sink. She tore off several pieces, stuffed them into the collar of Emily's shirt and placed the roll on the table. "That should take care of any major spillage." Emily looked down at her impromptu bib, not knowing what to make of it. "Eat your pizza, Emily."

Emily took a bite of pizza and looked at Jane's bandaged hand. "Are you gonna tell me what happened to your hand?"

"It's not important."

"You told me in that little room that you got hurt in the line of duty. What does that mean?"

"It means it happened while I was working. Like right now. This is called being on duty."

"It is?" Emily sounded surprised.

"Yeah. What'd you think this was?"

"I thought we were having dinner."

Jane realized she'd backed herself into a corner. "We are . . . and I'm also working at the same time."

"Did you hurt your hand in a kitchen trying to fix food?"

Jane looked at Emily, thinking she was being a smart aleck and then realized she was serious. "No, I did not."

"Did you hurt it—"

"Look, kid," Jane said, putting down her pizza slice and sitting back in the chair. "There are certain things you don't need to know and this is one of them." Emily looked deep into Jane's eyes, not saying a word. "Did you hear me?" Jane asked, agitated.

"You were scared when that happened, weren't you?" Emily said softly.

Jane was jarred by Emily's words but tried not to show it. "Can we talk about something else?" she said with less of an edge.

"Okay," Emily said, taking a bite of pizza. "Guess what my middle name is."

"I have no idea."

"Just guess."

"Bertha."

"*Bertha?* No! Guess again!"

"Why are we doing this?"

"Are you gonna try to guess my middle name?"

"I'm going to have a headache soon if this continues."

"Grace."

"What?"

"Grace. That's my middle name. E.G.L. Those are my initials. Grace is my grandmother's name. Mommy says she gave me the name so that I take a part of my grandmother with me everywhere I go."

Jane took a bite of pizza. "Anne."

"What?"

"Anne. That's my middle name."

"That's pretty. I like it."

"It's my mother's name."

"Where does your mommy live?"

"She's dead."

Emily's eyes lost some of their luster. "When did she die?"

"A long time ago. I was ten. Just a little older than you are right now."

"How did she die?"

Jane felt her stomach tighten. "Cancer. But I told people she killed herself."

"Why?"

"Because," Jane said quietly, "That's exactly what she did. She hated her life. She made herself sick so she could get out."

Emily thought for a second. "We have a lot of things that are the same. Your mommy died when you were little, just like me."

"That's one thing, Emily. That doesn't mean we have lots of things."

"I think we do."

"You have no idea what you're saying." Jane looked Emily straight in the eye. "You don't want to have anything else in common with me." Emily observed Jane carefully. "You finished with your pizza?"

"Yeah." Jane ripped off several feet of paper towels and wrapped the uneaten pizza in it. "Do you have kids?" Emily asked.

"No," Jane said, opening the refrigerator door.

"Do you want to have kids?"

Jane jammed the pizza into a vegetable bin. "It doesn't matter whether I want them. I don't have them today and I won't have them tomorrow." Jane slammed the refrigerator door shut. "Isn't it time for you to take a nap or something?" Jane lit a cigarette.

"You don't babysit, do you?"

"Never."

"So you don't know any games?"

"No."

"You like to play cards?"

"Yeah, but I don't think you're ready for five card stud."

"How about board games?"

Jane grimaced.

"Pleeeese . . . " Emily begged.

Jane let out a weary sigh. "What's the board game?"

"I'll get it!" Emily jumped off her chair and ran into the living room. Jane reluctantly followed her and sat down on the couch. Emily opened up a wooden trunk that was wedged across the far wall near the fireplace. After rummaging through the trunk, she brought out a large white box with blue stars across lid. She slammed the trunk shut and ran across to the chair opposite from Jane.

Emily opened the board game on the coffee table that sat between them and arranged the playing pieces. "The game's called 'Think!'"

"'*Think?*' What the hell is that?"

"I don't know. It belongs to Mommy and Daddy. I just liked the box cover." Emily proudly held the cover up to show Jane. "It's got stars all over it!"

"What about Monopoly? Or checkers?"

"Mommy and Daddy don't have those." Emily was quickly separating the colored pieces and sliding Jane's share across the coffee table.

"So, what's the point of this game?"

"I've only seen Mommy and Daddy play it when A.J.'s Mommy and Daddy were over here."

"Who's A.J.?"

"She was a friend from school. She doesn't live here anymore."

"I see." Jane might have engaged Emily more but she found herself fixating on the taste of whiskey. Normally, after dinner, she'd down a beer or two, followed by a shot or more of whiskey. Her eyes trailed over to the Lawrences' liquor cabinet.

Emily was deeply engrossed in setting up the game board. "You roll the dice and that tells you how many squares you can move on the board. But first, you have to answer one of the questions from this deck of cards." Emily gathered together the deck and placed it in the center of the board.

Jane quickly turned her attention back to Emily. "What kind of questions?"

"I don't know." Emily picked up the instruction booklet.

Jane examined the board, trying to understand the direction of the game. "This looks ridiculous. It goes in a circle. There's no 'Lose a turn' or 'Go to jail' squares—"

Emily read from the instruction booklet. "'The game of Think has no winners or losers.'"

"Oh, shit. When did the Communists start designing board games?"

Emily continued to read. "'It is a way to in . . . inter . . .'"

Jane took the booklet from her and continued reading aloud. "'It is a way to interface with other players and gain insight into their lives.' Oh, Christ! It's not the Communists! It's the American Psychiatric Association!"

"Here's the dice. You be green."

"Are you sure there's not a little tiny therapist that comes with the game?"

"No, everything's out on the table," Emily said seriously. "You go first. Roll the dice!" Jane took a deep drag on her cigarette and rolled the dice. Emily picked up a card. "Okay, the first question is . . ." Emily looked up, just in time to see a ribbon of cigarette smoke pour from Jane's nose. "How do you make the smoke come out of your nose like that?"

"That's an easy question! Practice, practice, practice!" Jane took her green playing piece and started moving it across the board.

Emily placed her hand on top of Jane's hand, preventing her from moving to the next square. "That wasn't the question on the card. Put that back on the first square." Jane begrudgingly slid her playing piece to square number one. "Okay," Emily said, reading the card. "'What is your biggest regret and why?'"

"My biggest regret was five minutes ago when I agreed to play this stupid game!" Jane once again started to move her playing piece.

"Are you gonna play this game right?"

"Wait! Wait! I'm not ready for question number two!" Jane said sarcastically.

"You're not playing fair!"

"Okay!" Jane once again shoved her playing piece to the first square. "Give me another damn question!"

Emily discarded the first question and pulled another

card. "'When were you the happiest recently?' *And be serious.*"

Jane sat back, pondering the question. "Well, let's see." Her thoughts drifted off into the distance for a second. "Happy . . ." Jane tried her best to connect *happy* with anything in her life. "I don't know," she replied, temporarily lost in the moment.

"Can't you think of something?"

"Apparently not," Jane said, surprisingly annoyed at the sudden revelation. "Give me the deck."

Emily discarded the last card and handed the deck to Jane. Her eyes traced the top of the table. "You wanna know when I was the happiest most recently?"

"When?" Jane said, shuffling the deck.

"When I saw you walk in that little room at the police station where you work. The room with the funny mirror and green walls." Jane stopped shuffling the cards and paid attention to Emily, who turned and met Jane eye-to-eye. "I asked to talk to you 'cause I knew . . ." Emily hesitated.

"You knew what?"

Emily stared at Jane. "I knew . . ." Again, she hesitated, not sure she wanted to reveal her true feelings. "I knew you were . . . special. But I didn't know if you'd say 'yes.' So, when you walked in that little room, I was so happy." Emily smiled at the memory.

They sat in silence for several minutes.

"What do you say we put this game back in the trunk and get you out of here?" Jane's tone was subdued.

"Can't I stay here with you?" Jane was at a loss for words. "I don't want to go back to the foster house. They don't talk to me and they watch stupid TV shows," Emily said in earnest. "I want to stay with you. *Please?*"

"You don't have pajamas or a toothbrush—"

"Yes, I do. They're upstairs." Emily walked around the coffee table and placed her hand on Jane's shoulder. "Please let me stay with you. I promise I'll be good." Emily smiled softly.

Jane sized up Emily and let out a deep breath. "Alright," she said, giving in.

Emily threw her arms around Jane's neck, hugging her tightly. "Thank you!"

The gesture caught Jane off guard. She haltingly patted Emily on the back. "Okay, alright, that's good. Why don't you go change into your pajamas."

Emily walked across to the staircase. Jane pulled out another cigarette and lit up, her eyes resting once again on the liquor cabinet. "Jane?" Jane abruptly turned to Emily. The child was staring at the floor where the carpeting was cut away—the same spot where her parents met their death.

"What is it?" Jane asked.

"There used to be a big piece of carpet there."

"Uh-huh," was all Jane could manage.

Emily stared at the floor, her face expressionless. "Is that where they died?"

Jane realized she was holding her breath and let it out slowly. "Yes."

"You know what?"

"What?" Jane asked, expecting the worst.

"My mommy never liked that carpet." Emily turned to Jane, her face still devoid of emotion. "Would you please go upstairs with me?"

Jane stuck the cigarette in the corner of her mouth and stood up. "Sure." As she approached Emily, the child held out her hand. Jane grasped it and proceeded up the stairs. They stopped at the top of the stairs on the landing in front of Emily's bedroom. The door was shut.

"Let's get some light here," Jane said, flicking on the switch and illuminating the landing.

Emily stared at her bedroom door, not moving an inch. "I need to go to the bathroom," Emily said, her eyes pinned on the door. Jane led her several feet to the left and opened the bathroom door that sat adjacent to Emily's bedroom. She flipped on the light and released the child's hand.

Emily quickly grabbed Jane's hand. "Could you come in with me, please?"

"I'll wait out here. Nothing's going to happen."

Emily surveyed the bathroom from where she stood. "Please?"

The thought of '*This is not in my job description*' flashed across Jane's mind for a millisecond. "Okay."

They walked into the cramped, black-and-white tiled room, Emily still holding tightly onto Jane's hand. "Keep the door open!" Emily said in a nervous tenor.

"You need to let go of my hand so you can do your business."

Emily reluctantly let go and pulled up her denim jumper. Jane turned to face the sink. Scanning the small space, she was reminded of a case she had worked years ago where a father hid his drug stash in the medicine cabinet of his child's bathroom. The SOB figured that the cops would never look in his kid's bathroom. He was right. The cops didn't look in there. But Jane looked and found the father's secret cache of cocaine, which blew the case wide open. If Emily's father really did die because of a drug deal gone bad—a theory Jane wasn't willing to accept—there had to be pockets in the house where he stored his coke. It was a pattern of drug users. But the longer she stayed in the Lawrence house, the more Jane felt that Emily's father wouldn't go to any great lengths to hide drugs—if, indeed, there were any drugs to be found. Sweet Jesus, Jane thought, the man played a game called "Think." Was that the MO of an intrepid drug addict?

Nonchalantly, Jane uncovered the hamper lid and looked inside. Nothing. Not even a lonely sock. She popped open the medicine cabinet and found Emily's toothbrush, toothpaste and a bottle of children's aspirin. Emily flushed the toilet and crossed to the sink to wash her hands. "Brush your teeth," Jane instructed, handing Emily the toothpaste and toothbrush. Emily brushed her teeth as Jane turned to look out the small diamond shaped window that overlooked the backyard and alleyway. She watched as the appointed patrol car crept slowly down the alley, its lights radiating fifty feet forward. "See you in another half an hour," Jane said under her breath toward the patrol car. Emily turned to Jane, dribbling toothpaste down the front of her jumper.

Jane grabbed a hand towel. "Hey, watch what you're doing. Rinse your mouth." Emily complied. Jane knelt down so she was eye-to-eye with Emily and wiped the toothpaste off her jumper. Emily's attention was instantly drawn to Jane's scar on her right temple. She pulled Jane's hair away from her forehead. "What are you doing?"

Emily examined the scar, brushing her finger across the surface. "That really hurt, didn't it?" Emily said quietly.

Their eyes locked for only a second, but to Jane, it felt longer. It seemed that the stronger she built her comfortable wall, the more Emily was able to break it down. "Get your pajamas on."

Emily took hold of Jane's hand and walked back on to the narrow landing with her. Jane opened Emily's bedroom door and started to turn on the light switch when she turned to the child. "There's some carpet in there that's missing. I just wanted you to know that before you walked in there." Emily nodded apprehensively. Jane turned on the light. The ever-so-pink colors of the room felt startling to Jane. It also felt tainted. A cold-blooded killer stood in this room with a knife, dripping the blood of Emily's parents all over the plush, pink carpeting.

Emily carefully moved into the room, still holding onto Jane's hand. Her eyes followed the missing trail of pink carpeting that ran from the door to the closet. She stared at the closed white closet door and noted the residue left behind from where detectives dusted for prints. "Why's it all dirty?" Emily asked.

"That's not dirt. That's just something the cops did."

"People were in my room?" Emily said, her voice raising an octave. "*Why?*"

Jane promised herself she wouldn't take Emily down that rocky emotional road. She had no intention of making the kid remember anything about the crime, no matter how much Chris or Weyler persuaded her. Screw 'em. Screw the media. For that matter, screw the city. She walked into this assignment completely against her will and she was not going to cooperate and drag Emily through hell. So when the kid asked why the cops were in her room, Jane did what she hardly ever did. She lied. "Just procedure," Jane said, avoiding eye contact with her.

"How come you're lying to me?"

Jane turned to Emily. "What do you mean?"

"You're lying. I can tell. When I ask my mommy a question and she doesn't want to tell me the truth, she looks up in the air or she turns away."

"I—"

"I thought you didn't lie! That's why I picked you."

Jane's head started to pound. Her forced sobriety was beginning to hurt. The general numbness she had come to embrace over the years was quickly wearing off, leaving raw, exposed nerves. She wanted out of that little pink room, out of that house, out of that neighborhood and to fall back into a comfortable state of intoxication. The answer was going to call for tact and tact wasn't her forte. But she also knew her typical response of "fuck off" wasn't the way to go with the kid. "Okay," Jane said, "You really want the truth?"

"Yes," Emily said with an uneasy edge to her voice.

"Do you remember where you were when the policeman found you last Monday morning?"

"In my closet," Emily said, pointing to the door.

"Right." Jane struggled with putting her words together. "And that's the last thing you remember?"

"Yes."

"Well, you see, the police believe—and I'm not saying this is true—but they believe that possibly some person came up here. So that's why they had to come in and check out the room."

"Who was in here?" Emily's eyes widened.

"We're not sure. Just someone who didn't belong here."

"Well . . ." Emily looked at the carpet, trying to process everything. "Who was it?" Jane turned away and let out a deep breath. "Jane?" Emily said, her eyes still wide with concern. "*Who was in my room?*"

Jane turned back to Emily. "The person . . . or persons who . . . killed your parents."

Emily moved closer to Jane, still gripping her hand. "They were *here?*"

"I don't—"

"Is that why my carpet pieces are cut out?"

"Yes."

"Why just that part of the carpet?" Emily asked, pointing to the floor.

"Because they had to test that part of the carpet."

"Test it?"

"Footprints," Jane said without flinching. There was no way she was mentioning blood. "They have to match footprints."

"Footprints? Match them from where?"

"The stairs that lead up here. They took some carpet from there, too. They want to see if the footprints they found there are the same as what was in here."

Emily considered the idea and figured it seemed logical. She glanced toward the closet door. "So, they were standing here when I was in there?"

"That's what the cops think."

Emily buried her head in Jane's stomach. "I don't remember anything."

"I told you before, you don't have to remember a thing. How about if we get out of here? What do you say we go downstairs and you flick that little flashlight you've got out the window and see how fast Martha can get her ass in this house?"

Emily threw her arms tightly around Jane's body. "I want to stay with you."

Jane steadied herself as Emily leaned into her body. "Okay. Fine. We'll stay here. Where are your pajamas?"

Emily stayed glued to Jane's body. "In the top drawer over there."

Jane gently peeled Emily off her and motioned to the bed. "Sit there."

Emily sat on the bed as Jane shuffled through the bureau drawer. Upon finding the pajamas, she returned to Emily's side and helped her undress. There was stone silence between the two of them as Jane pulled off Emily's jumper and shirt and dressed her in a matching set of white pajamas, decorated with hundreds of blue and pink stars. When Jane finished, Emily looked up at her. "What if I can't remember ever?"

"You don't have to remember, Emily. Some things in life are better left forgotten. Believe me, kid. That's the God's truth."

"But I'm already forgetting what Mommy and Daddy look like."

"That's easy to fix. You've got photos of them. There's that photo downstairs on the refrigerator of the three of you. Remember?"

"Oh, yeah." Emily leaned over to the side table next to her bed and pulled out the overstuffed drawer. "Where's my pack of photos?" Emily said, clearly upset.

"Is that where you left them?"

"*Yeah,*" Emily said, growing more annoyed.

"Well," Jane said, wedging her hand way back in the drawer. "Sometimes when a drawer is overfilled, items on the top can get caught in the back." After a few moments of pulling and readjusting the drawer, Jane withdrew the crumpled photo pack. "Is that what you're looking for?"

"Yes!" Emily exclaimed, holding the packet to her chest. She slid the photos out of the envelope and looked at the top picture. "There they are."

Jane glanced down at the photo. It looked like the same one on the refrigerator. "Keep those pictures with you and you'll never forget them."

Emily stared at the photo, becoming lost in it. "That was a fun day."

"How about if you put that top one right here by your bedside so you can see it when you wake up." Jane started to take the photo off the stack when Emily quickly placed her hand over Jane's hand.

"I can't sleep up here!" Emily said, her voice filled with fear.

"Nothing is going to happen to you. I'll be downstairs."

"Then *I* want to be downstairs. I want to be with you." Emily grabbed on to Jane's sleeve as if she were drowning and Jane was her life preserver.

"Well, I'm not—"

"Please let me be with you."

Jane realized that Emily was genuinely scared and that the child was not taking "no" for an answer.

Downstairs, Jane fashioned the couch into a bed using sheets and blankets from the hallway closet.

"Hey," Emily said, safely securing the pack of photographs inside the vinyl case that held her Starlight Starbright projector. "It's dark enough to show you my Starlight Starbright. Turn off the lights!" Emily grabbed the case and skipped over to the couch.

Jane went around the room turning off the various table lamps. When she reached the final lamp that sat next to the couch, her eye glimpsed something against the metal side of the lamp's center post. At first Jane thought it was a large black fly. She squinted through the blinding light. It was a bug, alright, but not the insect kind. Jane carefully removed it and recognized it as the kind of apparatus that the police use for surveillance. She handled it very discreetly as she walked across to the front window. Jane could make out Chris sitting in his unmarked car with the interior light on. He was drinking coffee with one hand and holding his earpiece with the other. Jane purposely ran her finger over the bug and watched Chris readjust his earpiece.

A flash of hot anger surged through Jane's system. She turned to Emily and spoke in as calm a voice as she could muster. "I'll be right back."

Emily watched as Jane crept to the front door, opened it quietly and walked outside leaving the door slightly ajar. Emily slunk off the couch the second Jane was out of sight and crossed to the front door, peering outside into the darkness. Jane walked across the lawn, safely hidden in the dark shadows. She brought the tiny microphone bug to her mouth and spoke into it as though she were having a covert conversation. "Okay, Emily, I'm back. Now, I want you to listen to me very carefully. What you just told me upstairs about how you know who killed your mommy and daddy . . ." Jane stopped walking and watched as Chris immediately held his earpiece closer to his head. "I want you to know that's going to be our little secret. No one ever has to know a thing. Especially not my fucking partner who's sitting across the street and getting a hard-on listening to what we're saying!"

Chris jerked forward and turned toward the house just in time to see Jane bolt across the street and head right to his car.

"Roll down your fucking window!" Jane screamed. Martha turned around in the other car to see who was yelling. Chris rolled down his car window. "You got a lot of fucking nerve, cowboy!" Jane screamed at Chris who looked as though he'd been caught with his hand in the proverbial cookie jar.

"Yeah, well, call that a little insurance!" Chris yelled back.

"*Insurance?*"

Chris got out of the sedan and stood his ground. "Insurance that I know everything so I can solve this case!"

"Jesus, Chris! You're turning into a paranoid little fuck!"

"You think I'm paranoid? Well, just because people call you paranoid does not mean other people aren't out to get you!"

"What in the hell are you talking about?"

"Oh, fuck, Jane! Do the math! I catch a huge, career-making case that I can solve and then suddenly I'm pushed aside because some kid dictates who she will and will not talk to! Maybe that kind of shit doesn't set well with me!"

"She's a kid!" Jane screamed, slapping the roof of the sedan for emphasis. "She's not a fucking case notch on your belt!"

"And you're gonna make damn sure of that! *Fuck!* Why Weyler ever gave you this case is beyond me! You have zero ability when it comes to dealing with children!"

"Oh, I don't know about that. I thought I'd learned a lot dealing with *you!*"

"You don't have to be such a fucking cunt!"

Jane's eyes filled with rage as she went for Chris. "Stop calling me that!"

Chris grabbed Jane's arms before she could touch him and physically held her back. "I know you and I know what you're up to! You are willing to sabotage this case because you can't handle it! Fuck, Jane, I heard you say it to the kid in there, so don't deny it! You want this case to disappear because you can't wrap your head around it. Well, that doesn't cut it with me! My ass is on the line, not yours! I will not sit back and let you fuck it up! That kid knows something! She may be in some psy-chological trance, but with the right prodding, she will wake up. And when that happens, she will tell you what she saw! So I put in a bug in there! So fucking what! I did that because I want to hear all the shit. Not just the shit you deem me worthy of hearing! *Get it?*"

Jane shook off Chris' tight grip and stuck her face inches from his face. "You want to hear all the shit?" she said confidentially. "Stick this bug up your ass and you'll hear more than enough!" With that, Jane threw the bug into Chris' car, turned on her heels and headed back to the house.

Martha popped out of her car and called out to Jane. "Is everything all right?"

Jane never turned around as she yelled, "Fuck off!" She reached the front door and found Emily standing on the outside front porch. "Hey! What did I tell you about going outside?" Jane's voice was edged with fury.

"I just—"

"Just nothing! Get your butt back in there!"

Emily quickly turned around and went inside. Jane stood on the front landing and looked back at Chris. He was still glaring at her, pissed off that she got in the last word. Jane walked into the house, slamming the door behind her. She stood in the entry hall, arms folded across her chest, trying her best to cool down.

Emily was propped up on the couch, her Starlight Starbright at the ready. "Why was that man yelling at you?"

"Did I not specifically tell you to stay in this house?"

"Yes," Emily said softly.

"Then what the hell were you doing on the front porch?"

"He was yelling at you and I was worried—"

"That is not an excuse! I told you to stay inside and I mean it!" Jane stood still, saying nothing, her arms still tight across her chest. All she could really think about was the in-your-face, brazen nerve it took for Chris to plant that bug in the house.

"I'm sorry I went outside," Emily said without hesitating. Jane, still seething, turned away. "Don't cut me off."

"Cut you off?" Jane said, not understanding the child.

"You got your arms crossed. You're building a wall."

Jane looked at Emily, partly in amazement and partly in exasperation. She relaxed her arms, sauntered into the living room and pulled the drapes across the front window. "What's rule number one?"

"Don't hassle you about smoking," Emily said, without missing a beat.

Jane pulled out her Glock, crossed to the coffee table and set the gun down before removing her shoulder holster. "What's rule number two?"

"Don't *ever* touch your gun," Emily said on cue.

"And what's rule number three?" Jane said with emphasis, tossing her shoulder holster on the coffee table next to her gun.

"Don't ever, ever, *ever* go outside unless you say so."

"Good." Jane slumped onto the couch, arranged the pillows and then pulled off her cowboy boots. "You got that thing ready to roll?" Emily nodded. Jane pulled up the makeshift bedding on the couch and turned off the table lamp. Emily turned on the Starlight Starbright. In an instant, the floors, walls and ceiling were covered with pinpoint stars that slowly turned clockwise around the room. Emily moved another knob and the soft sounds of crashing waves and distant seagulls calling their partners gently issued forth. Underneath, the moody melody of "Nessun Dorma" filled the room. Emily spooned her body in front of Jane's and pulled the covers up around her neck.

"Isn't it pretty?" Emily quietly said.

"Yeah. It is."

There was a calm silence between the two of them. Both were drawn into the rhythmic sounds and twinkling stars that floated across the ceiling.

"What does it feel like to die?" Emily asked in a whisper.

Jane thought for a second. "It gets very quiet. So quiet

that you can't hear yourself trying to breathe. There's no pain. No sadness. You just float far, far away. Until the you that was, no longer exists."

Emily felt herself drifting off to sleep. "Okay," she said quietly as her eyelids got heavy. It was so very peaceful—so serene. She was just about to drift off to sleep when she was jolted awake by the sound of a bloodcurdling scream.

"What is it?" Jane said, herself jumping to her senses.

"You hear that?" Emily arched her back, peering around the darkened room.

"Hear what?"

Emily scanned the room and waited. She sunk back into the couch, closely nestling her body to Jane. "Nothing," she whispered.

# Chapter **12**

It had been a long time since Jane dreamed of her mother. Twenty-five years had passed since her death and along with it, the distinct memory of her appearance and the sound of her voice. So on the rare occasion when Jane would catch a glimpse of her mother in a dream, there was a faraway, unfamiliar resonance to the experience.

The dreams were always the same—pinpointed moments in time that flashed like a video. Anne standing at the sink in the kitchen looking out the window. Anne hanging sheets on the clothesline. Anne sitting in a chair reading a book. Anne staring into the air with that trapped look on her face. They were crisp images that lasted mere seconds but conveyed years of emotions and an underlying deep sadness. The dream invariably culminated in the final moments of Anne's life.

Anne Perry was propped up in a hospital bed that had been wheeled into the living room. Her gaunt, pasty white face blended into the dingy sheets that covered her body. Her sunken eyes fixated on a spot above her as ten-year-old Jane encouraged her mother to take one more spoonful of soup. Outside, Dale Perry shoveled snow in the late February shadows while five-year-old Mike played alone in the drifts of snow. Pavarotti sang "Nessun Dorma" on the radio that was sitting next to Anne's bedside. There was a plaintive sense in the air that winter day. To Jane, it felt as if the tentacles of heaven were impatiently reaching down to collect another soul.

Even at Jane's young age, she knew her mother was giving up and that it was only a matter of time before she would die. Jane hated her for that and yet, could not bring herself to let go of her mother.

Anne pushed the soup bowl away from her. "That's enough," she whispered.

"You gotta eat more," Jane admonished her mother.

Anne turned her attention to Pavarotti's tenor voice on the radio. "I love 'Nessun Dorma.' I looked up the translation of the words once. It's a beautiful story. Listen to the way he feels the words, Jane." Jane let the haunting melody engulf her. She could sense the passion and depth of emotion that 'Nessun Dorma' evoked. "Promise me you'll look up the words in English one day, okay?"

"Okay," Jane said, feeling as though 'Nessun Dorma' was becoming a backdrop for a tragic event. "Come on, Mama. Eat more soup," Jane urged Anne.

"I'm tired, Jane. *Bone tired.*" Her mother's voice filled with an undercurrent of rage. "I want you to really listen to me."

Jane backed away. She knew what was coming. "Take a nap, okay?"

"Jane Anne Perry, come back here now!" Anne demanded in the strongest voice she could muster. Jane reluctantly moved back to the bed. "I want you to promise me that you will always be strong." Anne's bony hand took hold of Jane's hand and held it tightly. "You've got an inner strength that you don't even know you've got. Promise me you'll dig deep and use it."

Jane held on to her mother's hand. "I promise."

Anne tried to crane her neck to look outside but didn't have the energy. "Where's your father?"

"Outside with Mike."

"Good. I want you to promise me something else. Watch over your brother."

"Watch over?"

"You're going to be the only one left who can protect him. He's not as strong as you are. He'll *never* be as strong as you. You've got to make sure he's always safe. Do you understand what I'm saying to you?" Jane stole a glance outside the window at her father as he angrily shoveled a pile of snow and yelled over at Mike. She lowered her head. "Jane? Do you understand what I'm asking you to do? You do whatever it takes to protect him. *Whatever it takes, Jane.* Will you promise me that?"

"Okay. But Mama, you can't leave us. I still need you."

"I can't do it anymore, Jane."

"You want me to be strong but you won't do the same for me! It's not fair!"

"No, it's not fair. But there it is." Anne winced in pain as she grabbed Jane's hand even tighter than before. "You promised me, right?"

"Yes, Mama, I promise."

Jane watched helplessly as an enormous wave of pain entered her mother's body. Pavarotti swelled into the climactic finale of "Nessun Dorma," "*Vincero! Vincero! Vincero!*" he sung with an unsettling fervor. "Vincero!" Anne whispered, wincing in pain. "You must seek that in your life, Jane. *Vincero!*"

"Do you want me to get Dad?" Jane asked, terrified.

"No!" Anne yelled. "Pull me up!"

Jane grabbed on to Anne's wrists and pulled her forward. Once her mother was in a sitting position, Jane quickly slid pillows behind her back to support her. "What is it?" Jane said, her voice shaking. Anne's body went into a mild seizure as her eyes fixated on the wall. "Mama, please, don't do this! Mama? *Don't do this!*"

The more Jane pleaded, the more her mother's seizure grabbed hold of her body until the spasms became unrelenting. Anne jerked her head forward, opened her mouth and projectile vomited the soup across the sheets. She started to choke and gasp for air when a surge of energy enveloped her chest. A gush of blood spewed from her throat, covered her white cotton nightgown and dribbled down her chin. Jane stood paralyzed. The smell was acrid and toxic. Anne held her arms out in front of her with her palms upward and whispered in a rattled voice, "Take me . . ." With that, her head tilted backward against the pillows. There was a futile gasp for air and then nothing.

The silence lay heavy in the room. All Jane could hear was the swift beat of her heart and the shallow breaths she was taking. Her mother lay frozen in the moment, arms against the sheets with her palms facing the ceiling. Her head bent back, mouth open and pooled full of blood; her eyes wide open and dead. Jane looked outside to where her father was shoveling snow, completely unaware of what just happened. It was at that point when Jane looked down at her shirt and found bright red splatters of her mother's blood across the fabric. She reached over and gingerly tried to close Anne's eyes. But no matter how hard she pressed her fingers against her mother's rubbery eyelids, she could not get them to stay shut.

A few hours later, from her perch on the staircase, Jane watched the mortician and his assistants slip her mother's emaciated body into a heavy dark plastic bag and zip it shut with a quick jerk. Dale stayed outside smoking cigarettes. After they left, the house seemed cold and full of strange echoes.

The graveside service was quick and over before it started. There were no speeches or tributes—just an abbreviated prayer from the minister and then they lowered the casket. Only a few of her dad's fellow detectives were there—not because he invited them but because they had found out on their own and made the long drive out to the cemetery. There was no gathering afterward. No sandwiches. No soft whispers. No chance to catch your breath. Within days, everything that belonged to Anne Perry was gone from the house. Dale washed down everything with bleach—the walls, the floors, the shelves. "Gotta get rid of the goddamn stench," he angrily announced. The house was sterile. Not even her scent was allowed to linger. "She's gone," Dale told Jane and that was that. Dale only took one day off work and allowed the same for Jane and Mike. There were homicide cases to solve and he was needed back at Denver Headquarters. Three days after Anne died, there was no trace that she had lived.

It was the end of Anne Perry and it was always the end of Jane's occasional dream. When Jane awoke, a sense of coldness overcame her.

The early morning light filtered through the living room curtains, casting a creamy lemon glow across the couch where Emily lay fast asleep in the crook of Jane's arm. Jane snuck a look at a nearby clock. 7:45. Too damn early. Her head pounded relentlessly—a physical consequence of cold turkey sobriety. She carefully pulled her arm out from underneath Emily's head. The child stirred before going back to sleep. Jane sat up and rubbed her forehead, trying in vain to push back the pulsating pain. It was then that she realized her hand was shaking. She stared at her trembling hand as if it belonged to someone else. Finally, the tremor stopped. The day wasn't starting off well. At least, Jane surmised, the disturbing, staccato visions had thankfully stopped.

She stood up, taking care not to make any sudden movements that would wake Emily. The soft morning light slowly expanded, illuminating the entire room with a gentle warmth. Jane canvassed the room, taking in every silent detail. She tried to imagine Patricia and David Lawrence sitting on the couch bent over a line of cocaine. The more Jane attempted to force the scene into her head, the more ridiculous it felt. She had never met Emily's parents and yet, she felt she knew them intimately. They were still in the walls, the floor and the fabric of the house. Their energy occupied every seam. Most of all, their imprint was cast upon their daughter. It was a difficult feeling for Jane to distinguish, let alone explain to others. Suffice it to say that their essence lingered and that essence was not resonating a coked up persona.

Jane felt the need to poke around the room. She walked up onto the landing, brushing her hand against the desk that sat against the staircase. Something called out to her gut that she could not comprehend. There was a strange pull that tugged on her senses, like the eight ball dropping into the corner pocket with a resounding plop. It was the solution to the riddle. It was so close and yet so hidden. The more Jane tried to catch hold of what she was feeling, the farther it slipped from her mental grasp.

Her eyes came to rest again on the liquor cabinet across the room. She moved toward it, quietly creeping across the rug. The cherrywood unit held five shelves of every imaginable alcoholic beverage—everything from Dewar's Scotch to Bailey's Irish Cream. She scanned the bottles and noticed something odd on the E&J Brandy bottle. About an inch above the alcohol level there was a black pen mark that looked to be from a thick tipped permanent marker. A careful examination of a nearby Smirnoff vodka bottle showed the same type of black mark on the bottle. Jane scanned every other bottle in the cabinet and found the same markings.

Who marks liquor bottles? Not the drinker. The one who marks the bottles is the one who feels a need to track their partner's habits. Jane always regarded the act as a somewhat passive/aggressive type of conduct. So what if you mark the bottles and you note a change, she thought. It just proves what you knew already. Then what do you do? Show your partner the bottle with the black marks and raise hell? What's that supposed to accomplish? Jane scowled with derision at the cabinet. From the little Emily had said about her parents, it seemed that the child made mention of her father's "smell of liquor." That could only mean that the pen-wielding culprit was Patricia. Jane found it even more difficult to pin the label of "coke fiend" onto Patricia. A woman who takes the time to mark liquor bottles is probably not allowing cocaine in the house.

Jane started to turn away when she spied what looked

like a plastic baggie protruding from a dark corner of the top shelf. She strained to make it out but between the lighting and various bottles, it was impossible. The front door was locked but Jane knew the key couldn't be far away. As a teenager, she learned to first skim her hand across the top edge of any liquor cabinet. That was the first place where parents stashed keys. No luck with this cabinet, however. The second most popular place to hide the key was underneath the unit, secured with a piece of tape. Jane knelt down. Without her realizing it, Emily quietly awoke just as Jane was probing underneath the cabinet. Emily didn't move a muscle. As Jane got up empty-handed, Emily quickly shut her eyes, pretending to be asleep.

"Shit," Jane whispered to herself. "Where are you?" Jane wedged her hand across the rear left side of the cabinet and ran her fingers up and down the cabinet. Emily opened her eyes and took in the scene. Jane switched to the right side of the unit and continued to search. Suddenly, her hand hit a taped protrusion. Jane peeled the tape off of the object and pulled a key from behind the cabinet. She gently unlocked the door and slid her hand across the top shelf of the cabinet toward the suspicious protrusion. She grasped it awkwardly and began pulling on it. From Emily's perspective, Jane's actions took on a dubious appearance. Jane continued to tug on the plastic baggie until it gave way and she was able to remove it. What looked from the outside as a hidden baggie of contraband turned out to be a three by five inch size card inside the plastic baggie that outlined *Five Handy Tips to Preserve the Fine Wood Finish on Your New Wood Cabinet*. "Oh, for God's sake," Jane whispered to herself.

Emily continued to observe the scene, still unsure what to think. Jane replaced the plastic baggie, locked the cabinet and secured the key back into its taped spot. Emily decided it was time to "wake up" and let out a fake yawn. Jane turned around just as Emily opened her eyes.

"Hi," Emily said.

"Hi," Jane replied. The two stared at each other amidst an awkward silence. "What are you doing?" Emily asked with care.

"Just looking around."

"Oh." Emily was not convinced.

"You awake?"

"Yes."

"I need to ask you a question." Jane sat on the couch as Emily worked her way up. "I know you're a very observant kid. This is going to sound odd, but did you ever catch your dad or your mother sniffing something up their nose?"

"Sniffing . . . Like smelling, you mean?" Emily said, not quite grasping the idea.

"No . . . like snorting. Maybe off a plate or the top of their hand?"

"You mean cocaine?"

Jane stopped for a second. "Yeah . . . You know what that is?"

"Sure. I've seen it."

"Where?"

"On TV."

"TV? What kind of shows did your folks let you watch?" Jane said, a slight indignant tone creeping into her voice.

"I've seen *Cops* a bunch of times. People are always getting in trouble for having cocaine on that show. But they're always from Florida and California."

"Is that right? No one from Denver, Colorado?"

"No. They only showed the cops in Denver a couple times and that was just all about people getting drunk and driving their cars into trees and one park bench."

"I see. So, the only place you've ever seen cocaine is on *Cops?*"

"Yeah. But only when they're in Florida and California."

"Right. Denver just has the drunks. Okay." Jane stood up, rifling through her jacket in search of a cigarette.

"Are you gonna ask me if my dad was a drunk?"

Jane lit her cigarette. "No."

"Oh." Emily glanced at the liquor cabinet, then back to Jane. "'Cause if you were going to ask me that, I'd say yes."

"That's not important to me." Jane moved toward the kitchen. "What do you usually eat for breakfast?"

"I think that's why Mommy took me on that camping trip. She wanted to get away. He got really drunk a lot this year."

"It's not important, Emily," Jane said succinctly.

"But it *was* important. Every time they fought, Mommy would always say something about how daddy was drinking too much and making bad . . ." Emily searched for the word. "Decisions . . ." She turned her head to the side and furrowed her brow. "Hey . . . you know what?" It was as if a lightbulb started to go from dim to bright. "Mommy and Daddy were fighting that night. I was in my room and I heard their voices get louder." Emily looked at Jane. "Is that when I went in the closet?"

"I don't know. Maybe."

As quickly as Emily's memory wrapped around that moment in time, it abruptly ended.

Jane managed to whip up a mediocre breakfast of scrambled eggs and half-burnt toast. Instead of her usual no frills coffee, she had to settle for the Sumatra Blend from Starbucks. Emily poked at her breakfast with her fork, arranging the eggs in little piles across her plate.

"Stop playing with your food," Jane admonished. "If you don't want to eat it, there's always cold pizza."

"For *breakfast?* No, thanks. I'll eat this. It's just not how Mommy makes it—"

"Well, that's because I'm not Mommy!" Jane brusquely got up from the table and washed off her plate. Her teeth clenched. What she wouldn't give for a taste of whiskey. Her sudden sobriety was playing havoc with her senses. Lights were brighter, sounds were more intrusive and time seemed to drag.

"I didn't mean to hurt your feelings," Emily said softly.

"You didn't hurt my feelings," Jane said abruptly.

"Then how come you're mad?"

Jane turned to Emily. "Look, kid, it's too damn early in the morning for this. You done with your food?"

"Yeah."

"Okay, go upstairs and get dressed."

Emily slid off the kitchen chair and headed toward the stairs via the kitchen hallway route. Jane stood at the sink in a half-daze. Suddenly, the sound of her cell phone pierced the silence. She tossed her cigarette into the sink and followed the annoying chirp-chirp ring to her jacket pocket that lay over the living room couch.

"Yeah?" Jane answered the phone.

"Jane, it's me," said Sergeant Weyler. "Can you talk freely?"

"Yeah, sure."

"What's happening?"

"Nothing. Absolutely nothing."

"No memories?"

"Not unless you count 'Mommy and Daddy were fighting.'"

"Fighting about what?"

"Who the fuck knows?"

"It could be important. Ask her more about it."

"People fight. So what?" Jane wandered over toward the staircase where the desk stood. She wove looping patterns into the surface with her finger.

"We have to start making connections, Jane. Maybe they were fighting about drugs. I know you think that cocaine was a dead lead—"

"This has nothing to do with coke!" Jane said, guarding her voice so Emily couldn't hear. "I asked the kid point blank. The only coke she's ever seen is on *Cops*."

"What cops?"

"The television show? Well, it's not on PBS, so of course, you've never seen it."

"What makes you think Emily would be aware of her parents doing coke?"

"Kids know things. They may not tell their friends about it but they know things. They *see* things. Any guy who traffics in the amount of coke that was left behind that night would be sloppy as shit. This kid doesn't miss one damn thing. She watches you and I mean, *she watches you fucking constantly!* There's no way her parents could hide a coke habit that stretched into late night deals that turned sour." Jane ran her hand over the top of the desk that held the cubby holes. "Look, none of it makes any sense. It's like I told you. The whole crime scene was misleading. Whoever did this was smart and cunning. They made sure that it looked like something it wasn't." Just then, her finger hit one of the hidden buttons on the desk and a side drawer popped open. "Shit!"

"What is it?"

"It's this desk." Jane opened the drawer and looked inside. It was empty, save for an eraser. "Boss, there's nothing this kid can give us. Call her aunt and uncle and—"

"We made an arrest last night in LoDo," Weyler quickly interjected.

"What arrest?"

"There might be a connection to the Lawrence murders. The perp was arrested for public drunkenness and pissing on the sidewalk. When PD searched him during booking, they found an item on his person that sent up a red flag."

"What item?"

"A silver cigarette case with the inscription 'Wedding Blessings. David & Patricia Lawrence.' I paged Chris and told him to come back from Dillon. He's been talking to the guy for the past half hour. I want you to come down and check out this guy. Chris thinks this could go somewhere. I'll call Martha and tell her to watch Emily while you're gone. Have one of the cars bring you over."

Weyler hung up. The whole thing felt wrong to Jane. But she couldn't back up her gut feeling with practical analysis and so she was stuck. Jane felt two eyes staring at her and looked up the staircase. There Emily sat on the top step in her denim jumper with the straps undone. "How long have you been sitting there?"

"What's going on?"

"It's nothing." Jane started up the stairs toward Emily. "I have to go see my boss for a little bit. But your good buddy Martha is going to hang with you."

"When are you coming back?" Emily sounded anxious.

"Couple hours probably. Your straps are all twisted around."

"I know. I can't button them."

"Stand up." Emily complied as Jane tried to untwist the child's straps. The tiny flashlight that Martha had fastened on the jumper was the root of the problem. "You want to keep this thing on here?" Jane said, poking at the flashlight.

"I probably should. She'll wonder what happened to it if I don't."

Jane continued to unwrap the cotton strap from the flashlight. "Stupid flashlight," Jane mumbled under her breath. "I'm surprised Martha didn't ask you to talk in code to her so I couldn't understand your conversations!"

"Code?"

"Yeah. Cops do it all the time between each other when they don't want perps knowing what they're saying." Emily placed her hand on the railing and gently rubbed her hand up and down the wood. Slowly, she became transfixed with the movement until she zoned out. Jane caught a glimpse of Emily. "Hey!" Emily did not respond. "*Emily!*"

Emily looked up, still in a half-daze. "Mommy and Daddy were fighting. Then somebody else showed up . . ."

"Somebody else?"

"I listened through the door." Emily was silent for a

second. "There was an accident!" she recalled, with a tinge of fear.

"Accident?"

"That's what the man said. He walked over there," Emily pointed toward the kitchen, "and into the kitchen."

"How do you know?"

"I heard the kitchen door close up in my room," Emily replied in a slight trance. The child fell deeper into the memory. "It was quiet. But when he came out of the kitchen, the yelling started. And then . . . I don't know . . . everything's dark." There was a loud thump-thump on the front door. Emily jumped and grabbed hold of Jane.

"*Emily?*"

The voice outside belonged to Martha Durrett. She had obviously received the call from Weyler and was wasting no time coming to the child's aid.

"Can I go with you?" Emily said, still hanging on to Jane's shirtsleeve. "I promise I won't say a word!"

"Emily, you can't come with me. Why don't you pull out that 'Think' game. That psycho-babble shit is right up Martha's alley!"

Thump-thump-thump! This time the knocking on the front door was louder. "*Emily!*" Martha's voice was deeply concerned. "Please come to the door!"

Jane turned to Emily. "I'll be back in a couple hours."

"Okay," Emily said, discouraged.

Jane started down the stairs then turned back to Emily. "Hey! What's rule number three?"

"Don't go outside unless you say so," Emily replied softly.

"Don't you ever forget that."

# Chapter 13

Saturday traffic around DH was usually insignificant. However, since this was Memorial Day Weekend, the parks were full of families and various roads were closed off to accommodate the street festivals. The patrol officer and Jane pulled into the DH underground parking structure almost a half hour after Weyler had given her the news about a possible suspect in the Lawrence murder. In her mind, that had given Chris a full hour to screw around with the subject in the interrogation room.

The third floor of DH was like a ghost town when Jane got off the elevator. She made her way down the hallway to the first interrogation room and knocked on the opposite observation room door. Weyler opened the door and stepped into the hallway.

"So, what's going down?" Jane said apprehensively.

"The guy's pretty incoherent," Weyler said to the point.

"Are you talking about Chris or the perp ?" Jane said, taking a jab at Chris.

"You know, I'm aware that things are not working for the two of you on a personal level, but he's still your partner."

"We need to discuss that. When the dust settles on this case, I'm putting in for a new partner. It's a trust issue, boss. He's gone paranoid on me."

"That's a strong word, Jane."

"You don't know what he did last night—"

Chris' voice exploded in anger toward the suspect in the interrogation room.

"Fill me in afterward," Weyler said.

Weyler and Jane walked into the narrow, claustrophobic observation room with the two-way mirror. Chris stood with his back to the mirror, leaning over the table and jabbing his thick finger toward the suspect. As for the suspect, he looked as if he hadn't seen a bath since the '80s. His long, salt-and-pepper hair was pasted together with grease, dried chewing gum, leaves, strips of newspaper and anything else that he happened to roll into while sleeping in the alleys. He was Caucasian—at least, he appeared to be a Caucasian. Between the dense grime and his suntan, he could have passed for Mexican. His shredded clothes hung over his bony body. He wore only one shoe that was two sizes too big and secured on his foot with layers of duct tape. The chest pocket on his shirt was torn off. The only other pockets were in his pants and they, too, were full of holes. Jane noted every single detail in less than thirty seconds. "Is this a joke?" Jane said, facing the two-way mirror.

"Chris seems to think he's worth pursuing. The guy's had plenty of time to dry out but he's still not making much sense," Weyler said.

Chris moved away from the table and Jane caught a glimpse of the silver cigarette holder on the table—the supposed link to the Lawrence murder.

"Was the cigarette case stuck up his ass?" Jane asked Weyler.

"How's that?"

"I'm just curious since there isn't a pocket on this guy that would hold a Kleenex, let along a heavy, silver cigarette container."

Weyler opened a small manila file folder and searched the pages. "The PD report shows that the container was found 'near his person.'"

"So he found it in a dumpster or on the side of the road. It doesn't tie him to anything. The person or persons who did this murder are smart, clever and cunning. Tell me how this guy fits that description?"

"You're holding back from me!" Chris yelled, angling his body over the suspect.

"Hey, dude, I don't know what you want me to say," the suspect replied, his bloodshot eyes widening in fear.

"How about the fucking truth!" Chris screamed back. Jane noticed that Chris' shirt wasn't tucked in on one side and his tie was askew. He looked unkempt—a result she surmised from being abruptly pulled away from his vacation at Lake Dillon and having to throw on the same attire he was wearing the night before.

The suspect looked at Chris as if he was trying to make an association. "Hey, dude, you look familiar. You were in my high school, right?"

"Stop fucking around!" Chris yelled, slamming his fist on the table. He grabbed the cigarette holder and held it up. "Where did you get this cigarette case?"

"I'm not sure—"

"Don't lie to me! A little girl saw you. She was hiding in the shadows watching you take a knife and rip her parents to death!"

The suspect's face fell in sorrow. "A little girl saw that? God, that's awful."

"You were so out of it. It's obvious. You forgot the coke, but like an idiot, you took this little trinket instead. But their fucking names are written on it!"

"I didn't take that thing. Somebody gave it to me—"

"You expect me to believe that someone gave you a silver cigarette case!"

"Yeah, dude. This guy just gave it to me last night. Hey, man, I gotta get outta here. I gotta go to Atlanta. I'm catchin' the dream weaver train."

Jane turned to Weyler. "How much more of this do we need to watch?" She walked out of the narrow room and stood nervously in the hallway. Weyler followed and pounded his fist three times on the interrogation room door to alert Chris. Chris emerged, flushed in the face and reeking of body odor.

"What is it?" Chris asked Weyler, almost out of breath.

"Let him go."

"Boss, the guy's got a piece of property on him from the scene! We can't kick him!" Chris stole a glance toward Jane. "Goddamnit, Jane! Don't fuck this up for me!"

"I'm not fucking it up for you! You're doing a fine job all by yourself!"

"He's got crime scene property on him, Jane!" Chris yelled.

"And I'm wearing Eddie Bauer pants! That doesn't make me his cousin!" Jane replied.

"Alright, you two!" Weyler said loudly. "Chris, let him walk."

"Yeah," Jane interjected. "He's gotta get up early and go to work at NASA!"

"My God!" Weyler said in an angry tone, "you're like two belligerent children! Chris, I know you want to solve this case. I know you want to make the department look good. But you're shadowboxing with ghosts in there."

"Then explain how he got the cigarette case! Maybe this asshole hangs with the guys who did it. There could be a viable link here, boss!"

"He couldn't find the fucking hole in a donut!" Jane said, under her breath.

"Kick him out of here, Chris," Weyler said, turning toward his office.

"Boss!" Chris urged. "You're worried about the possibility of that kid being stalked! Well, who's to say he's not the guy that tips off the stalker?"

Jane's ears perked up. This was the first time she had it confirmed that Emily was in physical danger. She turned to Weyler, "So she *is* being stalked?"

"There's a possibility but we can't confirm it," Weyler said wearily. "Chris got a call several days ago that alluded to a possible situation."

"When were you planning on sharing this information with me?" Jane pointedly said to Chris.

"Maybe when you shared what the kid likes to whisper to you!" Chris replied with a mean twist to his voice.

Jane looked at Weyler. "If Emily is in real danger, I need to know about it."

"It was one call," Weyler said. "Chris tried to trace it but it was from a phone booth somewhere in . . . where was it?"

"Littleton," Chris quickly replied.

"More than likely it was some freak," Weyler assured Jane.

"Boss," Chris said, "I know this guy's fuckin' crazy, but we have to turn over every rock just in case it leads to something significant. If we kick him, put a car on him. Find out where he's going . . . who he's talking to . . . We've gotta figure this out, dammit!"

Weyler rested his hands on his hips and stared ahead deep in thought. "I appreciate your steadfast determination, Chris. But I just don't feel it's worthy of pursuit." Weyler turned and headed into his office.

Chris looked at Jane, burning holes of red hot anger into her. "If something happens to that kid, Jane, and it comes back to this guy, it's on *my* head, not yours!"

"He wants a one-way ticket to Atlanta! Or was it Atlantis?"

"So he's fucked up! That doesn't mean there isn't some weird connection!"

"Exactly what connection would that be? Have you thought about what you were going to tell the DA's office when you presented this character to them? Let's see, he knows a bum who knows another bum who knows a guy who works at Starbucks who found the cigarette case in a dumpster behind Safeway. The one bum stole it from the guy at Starbucks, then that bum traded it to the other bum who then gave it to the guy sitting in there who's catching the dream weaver train to Atlanta!"

"We *have* to solve this crime." Chris' voice was tired and hoarse. "You just don't get it. I'm going to lose every goddamn thing if I can't put this case to bed. I'm working my ass off while you're sitting back and chatting up the kid!"

Jane moved closer to Chris and spoke in a confidential manner. "I never wanted anything to do with this case. I'm just doing what I'm told to do. And you, more than anyone, should understand that!"

Chris regarded Jane with a quizzical eye. "What do you mean?"

"Figure it out." Jane turned away.

Tension gripped Chris. "If you know something and you're not telling me—"

Jane wearily faced Chris. "I know a lot of things."

"That kid *did* tell you something—"

"Maybe she did. But if I told you, I don't know that you'd have the necessary discernment to evaluate it. God, Chris, look at you! You smell like piss and you look like shit. And you have the nerve to say that *I'm* fucked up?"

There was an uneasy silence between the two of them. Chris sized up Jane. "You think you're smarter than me?" Chris asked.

"Right now? Yes."

"You don't know everything, Jane."

"I know a shitpot more than you and that's all that counts." She turned on her heels.

Chris stared at Jane with penetrating anger. "Where are you going?"

"I need to talk to Weyler *alone.*"

"Why alone?"

"Chris, you really gotta take something for that paranoia."

"Like a drink?" Chris replied. Jane froze. Chris knew he hit a soft spot. "What's it been? Two? Three days? That's a fucking lifetime for you. Has your skin started to crawl yet? Has your head started to pound? Are your hands shaking? 'Cause I know how addicts get when they're jonesin' for a fix. And I'm looking at a walking example of it right now."

Jane turned around to face Chris. Everything he said was true but there was no way she would own up to it. "Fuck you."

Chris grabbed Jane by the arm. "No, Jane. *Fuck you.*" His cutting stare lingered before he headed down the hall and disappeared around the corner.

Jane spun around and made her way into Weyler's office. She closed the door and stood against his desk in an aggressive stance. "As far as I'm concerned, this case is over. Call Emily's aunt and uncle in Cheyenne and get her out of this city!"

"I'm not ready to cut and run. It was one phone call, Jane. *One.* And it was probably just some nutcase."

"You really believe that?"

"Pretty much."

"Yeah, well, I've 'pretty much' had it with the direction of this investigation. I've been lied to. I've been spied on. And I've been stuck in a house with a kid who's got a puzzle piece memory and tells me stories of how her daddy liked to drink and how her parents liked to yell a lot."

"What else is she saying?" Jane hesitated for a second, but it was long enough to garner suspicion from Weyler. "What did she tell you, Jane?"

There was no way Jane was going to bring up the whole "third voice" that Emily said she heard on that fateful night. Jane wanted the whole thing to be over and she was determined to do anything to make that happen. "It's like I've said before. There is no justice or righteousness in making this kid remember what happened that night."

"That's where you and I disagree. I say there's no justice or righteousness without it! And *I* have the final word on this matter. So I suggest you turn around, go back to that house and continue to draw out what you can from that child's memory. Do I make myself clear?"

Jane stared at Weyler, gradually realizing that any attempts to argue were futile. She was stuck. Trapped. Lured into a situation that repelled and sickened her. All she wanted to do at that moment was to get in her car and drive and keep driving until she was a million miles away from that place. She wanted to numb the monster that was waking up inside her. Walking back into that house and facing Emily was like volunteering for torture. And yet, there were no words that would convince Weyler to change his mind.

Jane instructed the patrol officer to stop by a sandwich shop en route to the Lawrence house. The way she was feeling, there was no way she was going to cook lunch. She arrived back at the house just before one o' clock. Neighborhood kids gleefully rode their bikes alongside the pathway that edged around the glimmering lake. It was as though the world outside the Lawrences' house was blissfully unaware of the nightmares that lay within the walls of that dwelling.

Jane stopped at the front porch, gathering her reserves and turned the doorknob. The door was unlocked. She walked into the house, slamming the door behind her. Emily and Martha were seated at the coffee table. They turned around quickly in surprise. "The door is unlocked!" Jane yelled.

"Oh," Martha uttered, half-startled from Jane's sudden entrance. "I went outside to pick some flowers to brighten up the room and I must have left it unlocked."

"Is that your story?" Jane said, moving into the living room toward Martha. "Because if that's your story, I could get your ass fired for doing that!"

"Detective! Your language!"

"Fuck my language!" Jane countered. Her head spun in a disorienting haze.

"*Detective!*"

"Look, Jane," Emily said, trying to break the tension. "I drew some pictures." She held up a piece of art paper.

"Martha told me to draw a picture of my feelings."

"A picture of your feelings? What the hell is that supposed to mean?" Jane dropped the sandwich bag onto the coffee table. "I picked up sandwiches." She turned to Martha. "Two sandwiches. One for her and one for me."

"Lunch!" Emily exclaimed.

Jane walked into the kitchen and came to a sudden halt. The back door was wide open. She walked into the living room, hell-bent for action. "Who left this door open?"

Martha stepped forward. "I did! We needed some cross ventilation!"

Jane looked down at Emily who was busily opening up one of the sandwiches. "Did you go outside?"

"No," Emily said offhandedly.

"Why are you causing such a scene, Detective?"

Jane stormed into the kitchen, slammed the back door and locked it. Martha followed, irritated that she was being ignored. "Detective! I asked you a question!"

Jane could feel herself slipping. She was seconds away from cold-cocking Martha across the floor. "Listen to me very carefully," she said pointedly. "You know nothing about law enforcement and you know nothing about this case. I'm not sure what your job is, but as far as I'm concerned, you are a glorified babysitter and you're not even good at that. Now, I'm back. That means you go!"

"Detective, I do not know what has made you so upset or why you are demonstrating aggressive postures—"

"Don't analyze me!"

"All I am saying is you need to get ahold of yourself and not project your anger onto that innocent child."

Jane leaned in close to Martha and spoke quietly but directly. "Martha, if you don't get your fat ass out of here in the next five seconds—"

"I will not be moved by threats!"

Jane jerked forward and Martha quickly jumped back. "Get out!" Jane ordered.

Martha turned around, slightly shaken, and walked into

the living room. She gathered her belongings and crossed to Emily who was eating her sandwich. Martha leaned down and touched the flashlight that was still attached to Emily's jumper strap. "Remember, Emily. Four quick flashes of light are our little signal."

Emily, her mouth full of bread and meat, could only nod her head and offer a slight smile to acknowledge Martha's statement. Martha patted Emily on the head and left the house. Jane crossed toward the front door and locked it. She stood still, feeling trapped like a rat in a maze.

Emily spoke up cheerfully. "You picked a good sandwich!" Jane didn't move. Emily put down her sandwich. "Is everything okay?"

Jane turned to Emily and stared at her. "This is not a game, Emily," she said quietly. "We're not here to have fun. We're not here to get to know each other. They put you back in this house for one reason only. They want you to remember what happened the night your parents were killed so they can catch whoever did it. They know that you know some things based on certain evidence that was found in this house. I was put here to find out what you know. I'm not here to bond with you or tell you stories or play board games. Now, if any of that upsets you, that's too damn bad. I'm here to do a job. So, I suggest you start thinking real hard so I can tell my boss something that will impress him so much that he'll give the all clear and get us the hell out of here. There it is. *Deal with it.*" With that, Jane walked down the hall and into the kitchen, leaving Emily alone in gritty silence.

The hours dragged on that Saturday afternoon. Shifts changed outside and the Memorial Day holiday weekend patrol went on duty. Two cars stayed out front and the police cruiser made its rounds down the back alley every thirty minutes. The whole thing was monotonous for Jane. With every hour that went by, she could feel herself sinking deeper into a dark pit. By sunset, a slow rain fell outside. It quickly turned into a steady downpour that pelted the windows and added an extra dose of misery to the scene.

There had been few words exchanged between Emily and Jane after Jane's abrupt statement to the child. Emily busied herself drawing pictures and later, taking a nap on the living room couch. It was when Emily lay fast asleep that Jane found herself staring with greater interest at the living room liquor cabinet. The longer she went without a drink, the more she couldn't shut out her father's berating voice. "You are nothing! You understand me?" There was no escape for Jane and it was driving her into a primal place of existence.

By 7 p.m., the house felt cold and lifeless. A strong wind whipped the treetops outside the back door. Emily sat quietly on the living room couch, playing with the mini-flashlight Martha gave her. At one point, she was able to get the flashlight halfway into her mouth. She delighted in squeezing it with her teeth and making her cheeks glow red.

"Stop it," Jane said tiredly.

Emily popped the flashlight out of her mouth. She turned on her side and looked at Jane's bandaged hand. "Do you ever change that bandage?"

"Of course I do."

"It looks real dirty—"

"I change it, Emily." Jane lit yet another cigarette. After taking a long drag, she nervously rubbed her fingers across the scar on her right temple.

"Does your scar hurt?" Emily asked.

"What?" Jane said, unaware of her actions.

"The scar on the side of your head. You're rubbing it." Jane jerked her hand away from her head and let out an exasperated breath. "You think if you rub it hard enough it'll disappear?"

"Emily, stop it!" Jane was at her wit's end. Emily watched Jane with renewed intensity. Jane stared straight ahead, all too aware of the child's prying eyes. *"And stop watching me."*

"You're the only other person in the room. Who am I—"

"Don't be a smart-ass, Emily!" Jane's voice raised an octave. "I said to stop watching me and I mean it!"

Emily sat up, confused by Jane's confrontational behavior. She directed her glance across the room and spoke, "Why are you so nervous?"

Jane turned to Emily. "What are you looking at?"

"You said not to watch you," Emily said, her eyes pinned across the room.

"Hey!" Jane slapped her hand across the couch. Emily slightly jumped and turned to face Jane. "I also said don't be a smart-ass."

Emily felt cornered. "I'm sorry. I'm not trying to be a—"

*"Don't argue with me!"* Jane felt the walls closing in on her.

"Okay," Emily said almost inaudibly. "How come you're scared?" she whispered.

"I am not scared! Stop asking me that!"

"But your hands are shaking . . ."

Jane looked down and saw that, indeed, her hands were trembling. She stood up and walked across the room, taking hard drags on her cigarette and stealing a peek at the liquor cabinet. "I'm fine!"

"Maybe you should change that bandage. Maybe your hand got infected—"

"My hand is not infected!"

"Tell me how you got hurt."

"You want to know?!" Jane screamed. "I fucked up! Okay?! I tried to save her and I fucked up!" Jane felt light-headed.

"Who were you trying to save?" Emily said in a hushed tone.

"It doesn't matter. I didn't save her."

A wave of fear hit the child. "But you *can* save some-body, right? I mean, if you had to—"

"She *died,* Emily! She burned to death in a fucking car! *And it's all my fault!*" Emily froze. "And *this,*" Jane held up her bandaged hand, "is what I've got to show for it!"

Emily stared at the living room floor. She wanted desperately to explain what she felt inside but she knew Jane was too angry to hear it.

Her mind drifted to her best friend, A.J. She wished A.J. was still in town so they could talk. No matter what the problem was, Emily felt she could always share her troubles with her. *It wasn't fair.* Emily thought. A.J. and her family quickly moved away and didn't even say good-bye. For a moment, Emily felt anger toward her chum but that soon dissipated into sadness and a longing to know why she left so suddenly. Emily fell back against the couch, fighting the loneliness that tugged at her heart. "I wish my mommy was here right now."

"You and me both, kid!" Jane nervously adjusted her shoulder holster.

"Everybody is going away. Are you going to go away and not come back?"

"Well, yes. This is not a permanent situation!"

"Right," Emily said dejected. "You want me to remember something big so we can get out of here—"

"Exactly!"

"So I can go live with my aunt and uncle in Cheyenne—"

"When did you hear that?"

"When you were on the phone this morning with your boss."

"So, you were eavesdropping?"

"I go live with my aunt and uncle and then you can have a drink."

Jane stopped dead in her tracks. She turned to Emily, rage boiling underneath her skin. "What in the hell is that supposed to mean?"

"You keep looking at Daddy's liquor cabinet—"

"So what!"

"I saw you open it up this morning—"

"Now you're spying on me, too!"

"I smelled it on you the first day I saw you. You're just like my Daddy."

"Who in the hell do you think you are? Where do you get off judging me?"

"Mommy said she could smell Daddy across the room when he drank—"

"You think you're so smart? Well, you're not! You think you know people? Well, you don't! You are way out of line! *You hear me?*"

"I just know—"

"You don't know anything!" Jane screamed, her voice vibrating against the living room walls. "Get away from me!"

"Why?"

"Go upstairs!"

Emily got off the couch. "I'm sorry," she pleaded.

"I don't give a shit!" With that, Jane kicked over the coffee table, sending all of Emily's art pictures scattering. "Go upstairs!"

Fear gripped Emily. "Please, don't. You're the only one who can—"

Jane cut her off. "Upstairs! You hear me?"

Emily skirted the periphery of the living room and scooted up the stairs to her bedroom, slamming the door behind her.

Jane's pulse raced. She ran her fingers through her hair and let out a loud grunt of anger mixed with frustration. She plopped down onto the couch, sucking the last bit of life out of her cigarette. Jane briefly turned toward the liquor cabinet. Her head pounded in punishing syncopation. If she could sleep, maybe the pain would subside. *Sleep.* What a wonderful concept. To sleep with no dreams, no nightmares . . . if that were only possible. Jane felt herself slipping away as the couch embraced her body. Within less a minute, she was fast asleep.

Upstairs, Emily stood in her perfectly pink bedroom, not sure what to do. If she could only talk to Jane. *Really* talk to her. If there was a way to make her understand . . . She wished she had her Starlight Starbright projector to keep her company. She half-considered walking back downstairs to retrieve it but decided against the idea. To make do, she flicked off the ceiling light and turned on the tiny lamp next to her bed that sported the star cut outs across its shade. The splash of projected stars momentarily warmed her heart before she lost interest. Emily turned to her bedroom window. The occasional pitter-pat of rain could be heard against the glass. It sounded like the last sputtering of action before the storm moved toward the east. If the clouds were parting just right, there was a great possibility that the quarter moon could be seen shimmering against the night sky.

Emily crossed to the window and gingerly opened it. She strained her neck outside the window. Unfortunately, the large sycamore tree obscured her view. The air was sweet and slightly cool. She turned back to her closed bedroom door and considered her options. She had made that promise to Jane about never going outside. But all she wanted was to sit out on the roof outside her bedroom window. Technically, that wasn't "going outside," she convinced herself, since the roof was attached to the house. And those stars and that quarter moon were calling her.

The decision was made. Emily rotated the window open and quietly undid the screen, setting it onto the carpet and out of sight. She crawled out onto the damp roof and pulled the window shut. As she scooted her butt across the wooden shingles, she looked up at the night sky. Emily watched the moon duck behind a bank of clouds. The sound of a car caught her attention. Looking down into the alley, Emily watched the high beams of the patrol car come into view. Even though the sycamore tree obscured her, she flattened her body against the roof until the car rolled past her house.

She sat up as a strong wind blasted across the back-yard. Within seconds, the clouds completely obscured the moon's radiance. Several minutes later, Emily felt the plop-plop of fat raindrops falling on her head. Discouraged, she made her way back up the roof and pulled on the bedroom window. But the window wouldn't budge. This had happened several times before due to a defect in the window's rotation bar. The answer? She would crawl down the roof and grab hold of the large sycamore branch that rested against the house. Then, she could creep across the branch and make her way down the tree. Once on terra firma, she would cross to the kitchen door, lift the planter pot that sat by the door and pull out the hidden key. She'd unlock the door, replace the key, walk in, lock the door and sneak back upstairs to her bedroom via the slender kitchen hallway instead of through the living room. It was all so simple and a great plan in Emily's young mind. If she did everything right, she figured Jane would never know she snuck out of the house.

*Crack!*

Jane woke up with a start. The sound of an angry wind combined with the fast surge of rain greeted her. She was pissed with herself for falling asleep and checked the nearby clock. Her best guesstimate was that she'd been asleep for less than ten minutes. The house was stone-cold quiet—the antithesis of the fury that whirled outside the window. But something didn't feel right to Jane. Jane got off the couch and walked to the bottom of the stairs. She stared up at Emily's bedroom and the closed door before ascending the stairs.

Outside, Emily carefully inched down the roof and crawled onto the sycamore branch. Like a skilled climber, she maneuvered her body down the branch, slid onto the lower branches and finally jumped the few feet to the wet lawn. As she hit the earth, the sky opened up and released an enormous torrent of rain. Her denim jumper quickly became soaked as she crossed to the back door. The kitchen light was turned off. Emily craned her neck to see if she could detect Jane's location. Unfortunately, her diminutive height prevented her from fully canvassing the entire area. She uncovered the hidden key from underneath the planter and quietly unlocked the door.

Jane arrived at Emily's bedroom door. "Emily?" she said softly. "Are you asleep?" No answer. Jane opened the door. She was immediately greeted by the eerie shadow play of cutout stars across the walls and ceiling that emanated from the bedside lamp. "Emily?" she said with an edge of concern. Jane flicked on the overhead light. "Emily!" Jane lunged for the closet and threw open the door. "*Emily!*" She dropped to the floor and looked under the bed. Her heart pounded and her breathing became labored. A million thoughts raced through her head, none of them pleasant. Her head spun so frantically that Jane failed to see the window screen leaning against the wall underneath the unruly window.

*Crack!*

Jane turned quickly toward the sound. She leaned her head outside the bedroom door. "Emily?" No response.

Emily made it through the kitchen in the darkness when she realized she forgot to replace the hidden key. Cautiously, she walked back to the door and turned the knob slightly. It was at that exact moment that she heard Jane calling her from upstairs. Emily jerked backward, unlatching the door halfway. She panicked and crossed back into the shadows of the kitchen.

"Emily!" Jane stood on the landing outside Emily's bedroom. The wind howled outside, bending tree branches and slapping rain against the front windows.

*Crash!*

Jane spun around. She leaned over the staircase and yelled. "Emily!"

*Crack!*

Jane felt beads of cold sweat inch across her neck. "Shit!" she exclaimed. She leapt down the staircase, hitting the bottom with a hard skid.

*Slam!*

Jane turned toward the sound. It came from the kitchen.

*Tat, tat, tat, tat, tat!*

Jane stiffened. She looked down the hallway that led into the kitchen and saw only darkness.

"Emily!" she yelled, her voice filled with terror. The wind came up again.

*Bam!*

Jane unsnapped her shoulder holster and carefully pulled out her pistol. She positioned herself against the living room wall, sliding her body toward the kitchen entrance. Upon reaching the light switch, she flicked it off, leaving only the dim lamp by the couch to illuminate the house. When she was about three feet from the open doorway that led into the kitchen, she stopped and listened. The wind and rain sounded closer.

*Slam! Tat-tat-tat!*

Jane quickly realized the source of the sound. The back door had swung open and was banging against the kitchen wall. But how could that happen? Jane thought. She locked it. Jane steadied herself, then curved her body around the doorjamb, stretching her Glock in front of her. The room was pitch-black. The kitchen door slammed hard against the wall as another powerful gust of wind blew through the house, sending in a flurry of leaves and debris from the backyard.

Jane waited, Glock outstretched. She tried to adjust her eyes to the darkness but it was useless. Nothing made sense. Her head pounded and her stomach churned with the ominous possibilities. The sound of cracking and crashing reached deafening levels. She could stand there with her pistol forward or she could make a bold move. Jane opted for the latter and reached over to the light switch.

*Flick!*

The kitchen shone with light. Suddenly, there was movement to her right and Jane lowered her gun to the target, pressing her finger against the trigger.

"No!" Emily screamed.

Jane caught herself a millisecond before pressing the trigger. Still in a state of shock and confusion, Jane kept the pistol outstretched toward Emily, who stood paralyzed with fear, dripping small puddles of rainwater from her soaked clothes onto the kitchen floor.

It took Jane a good second or two to sort out the scene. Her heart was beating so rapidly that she was sure Emily could hear it. Jane lowered her Glock, never taking her eyes off of Emily. The silence was thick against a backdrop of chaos from the wind and rain. Jane secured the pistol in her holster as a growing rage swelled inside her. "*I could have killed you!*" Jane seethed. Emily stood still, staring at Jane. "What in the hell are you doing?!" Jane screamed. Emily tensed up. "I asked you a fucking question!" Jane yelled as she reached out and grabbed a clump of Emily's hair, pulled her head back and got into her face. "What is wrong with you?" Jane exploded. She pulled harder on Emily's hair. "I told you *never* to go outside and what do you do!"

"I . . . I . . . ." Emily stumbled on her words.

"I, I, I what? What part of 'don't go outside' do you *not* understand?"

"I'm sorry—"

Jane let go of Emily's hair and held her hard by the shoulders. "Sorry, my ass! I called out to you and you said nothing! I could have killed you! Do you understand? *Do you understand?*"

And that's when it happened. Those three words ignited an inferno within Jane that separated her from her body. She slammed Emily against the kitchen wall. "*Do you understand?*" Jane pulled Emily away from the wall and pushed her backward toward the open kitchen door. Emily regained her balance and walked backward as Jane moved toward her. *"Do you understand?"* Jane lunged toward Emily, pushing the child near the open kitchen door. Emily fell against the wall as Jane came straight at her. In an instant, Emily fled to her right into the living room.

The child quickly walked backward through the living room, bumping into chairs and tables. Jane stood in the doorway that led into the living room. "Don't you walk away from me!" Jane hollered above the roar of the punishing storm. She raced through the living room after Emily. The child stumbled, allowing Jane to get closer. She snagged Emily by the straps of her soaked denim jumper and shook her. "I'm not fucking done with you! You understand me?"

Emily jerked free of Jane's grip and jumped onto the couch. Jane tried to grab her but Emily was able to swing her body over the back of the couch, avoiding Jane's grasp. "You want to play hardball?" Jane yelled. "Is that what you want?" Emily shot around the couch to her right. Jane was way ahead of her. As Emily rounded the corner of the couch, Jane caught her by the back of her jumper. "You think you can run from me?" Jane screamed as she jerked Emily back toward her. Emily's back fell against Jane's chest. Jane held tightly onto the back straps of Emily's jumper, wedging her white-knuckled fist into the girl's spine. "What the fuck is wrong with you?" Jane kept her fingers wrapped around the straps as she forcefully pushed Emily forward, first several steps and then again, shoving her abruptly two and three feet at a time. "You think you're so smart!" Jane pushed Emily forward, edging her closer to the staircase. "Huh? You think you're so fucking smart?" Another sharp jab in Emily's spine forced the child another several feet. "Well, you're not smart! Do you hear me?" The two were now at the foot of the stairs. "I asked you a question!"

With that, Jane let go of Emily's straps and angrily turned her around to face her. "I asked you a question!" she screamed. Emily said nothing. With that, Jane shoved

Emily backward. The child fell on the inclining stairs. Jane leaned down, grabbed Emily by her shoulder strap, inadvertently also clutching the small squeezable flashlight that was attached to the strap. Jane raised her right fist into the air and was just about to slam it into Emily's face when her left hand squeezed the flashlight. The pinpoint light shone directly in her eye.

Everything stopped.

Jane's fist froze in the air as the piercing light yanked Jane back into her body. She still felt anger but it was quickly tempered by a sudden awareness of what she was about to do. Jane lowered her fist and pulled away from Emily. As the moment crystallized and the realization of what just transpired sunk in, Jane began to shake. Emily reached out her hand to Jane. "Don't!" Jane said, her voice trembling. "Leave me alone!" Jane stood upright. "Go upstairs, Emily," she said, almost in a whisper. Emily sat up, deeply concerned for Jane. "Go upstairs," Jane whispered. "And stay there."

Reluctantly, Emily stood up and climbed the stairs, looking backward every so often before retreating into her bedroom and closing the door.

Jane closed her eyes, in shock by what occurred. After five minutes, she walked into the living room and pulled her cell phone from her jacket pocket. Slumping onto the couch, she dialed Weyler's home phone number. After two rings, he answered.

"Hello," Weyler said.

"You need to come over here," Jane said almost inaudibly.

"Jane? What's wrong? Are you alright?"

"I'm no good," Her voice was choked with emotion. "I'm no damn good."

And then she hung up.

# Chapter 14

Jane knew it was all over.

The career she had worked so hard for was about to end. Once Weyler found out from Emily that Jane had violently shoved her around and came within seconds of punching her in the face, it was only a matter of his signature on an official page of Department letterhead that would seal her termination. What else could he do? Jane was already on shaky ground. For Weyler to try and figure out another Department loophole or ask for another favor from Brass would only make him look ineffective.

Jane sat in the stone-cold silence, staring into the void. There was an eerie, pervasive calm within her. It was as though the rush of rage that welled up and exploded had perversely nourished her soul. Her hands were no longer shaking. Her breathing was back to normal. She felt strangely composed.

Was this what it felt like to go mad? Was this what it felt like to be evil? What was the next step? How completely would the darkness embrace her and drive her deeper into the black hole? When would the voices start telling her to do things to herself and to others and at what point would she comply? Those questions ran through Jane's mind as she sat on the couch waiting for Weyler. All she knew for sure at that moment was that the apple did not fall far from the tree. For better or worse, she was her father's daughter.

The kitchen door that led to the backyard was still wide open. The wind and rain had subsided, replaced by a sinister stillness. Jane checked the living room clock and figured it would take Weyler about ten minutes to arrive. She looked down at the overturned coffee table and the scattering of Emily's drawings and colored pencils strewn across the floor. A choice had to be made. She could turn the table upright, replace the drawings and pencils, close the kitchen door and make the place look presentable or she could leave everything as it was. What was the use? She was doomed anyway. She stood up and lit a cigarette and then for some reason, righted the coffee table. A few minutes later, she gathered the drawings and pencils. Another quick look at the clock. Weyler would be arriving in five minutes. It was like waiting for the judge to show up and declare your sentence.

Outside, Jane heard the patrol car roll down the back alley. She crossed into the kitchen and watched as the headlights bounced off the back fence before disappearing. Jane closed the kitchen door, locked it and started back into the living room when she turned back again. With an attitude of indifference, she secured the bolt on the door, took a look around the kitchen and flipped off the light.

Minutes later, Weyler knocked on the front door. Jane took a hard drag on her cigarette as she walked across the room and opened the door. Even though Jane was sure she had roused Weyler from a comfortable night in front of PBS, he looked as dapper as ever in his suit and silk tie. She regarded him briefly, saying nothing and walked back into the living room. Weyler entered, looked around the entry hall, closed the door and followed Jane.

"What happened?" Weyler said, concerned.

Jane couldn't look him in the eye. Instead, she puffed on her cigarette and kept her head bent toward the floor. "It's bad, boss," she said, humiliated, in a half-whisper.

Weyler tensed. "What is it?"

"I . . . I fucked up."

He closely observed Jane. "Did she reveal something to you?"

Jane let out a snort of contempt. "Oh, God. Are we back to that bullshit?"

"Jane," Weyler replied, irritated. "What happened?"

"Why don't you go upstairs and ask Emily that question." She turned away from Weyler, taking nervous drags on her cigarette.

"I'd rather hear it from you."

"No. You need to hear the whole mess from her."

Weyler weighed the situation before turning and walking up the stairs. Jane heard him knock on her bedroom door, announce himself, then open her door.

It was just about over for Jane. Thirteen years of hard work. Thirteen years of clawing her way into homicide and it was all going to be over in a matter of minutes. She heard the upstairs door open and close and the sound of Weyler's feet descending the staircase. He stood on the landing, staring at Jane. She flicked her cigarette into the fireplace and turned to Weyler. "So, how does this play out?" she asked.

"How do you mean?" Weyler said stonefaced.

"What's the protocol?"

Weyler casually crossed into the living room. "Protocol?"

Jane observed Weyler. He was far too calm. "What's the Department protocol to determine my removal?"

"Removal?" Weyler said confused. "If I removed detectives for yelling at their witnesses, I wouldn't have anyone left!"

"Yelling?" Jane was stunned and not sure what to think.

"Look, I'm not saying I approve of your shouting at the child for walking outside in the rain and tracking debris in the house—"

"Shouting at her? Wha—"

"Emily explained everything. She asked you if she

could go outside and look at the stars. You said 'no' and she bolted off anyway. You ran outside, brought her back in, yelled at her and sent her to her room. Frankly, I don't know why you called me."

Jane was shocked. Weyler continued to talk but his words melted into white noise. She wandered across the living room and stood by the front door. Jane felt two eyes watching her and turned to the upstairs landing. There was Emily, standing in the shadows. She had ditched her soaked jumper, dried off her hair and changed into her pajamas with the star design. As Weyler's voice droned in the distance, Jane looked up at Emily. The child stared at Jane with a look of utter forgiveness and unconditional love. Jane couldn't make sense of any of it. How could anyone feel like that toward her after what she did? Emily ducked back into the darkness and retreated to her bedroom, closing the door behind her.

"I understand this job is taking its toll on you." Weyler's voice bled back into Jane's consciousness. "And I'm aware that you're not used to working with children. But you must be doing something right. The child obviously has kind feelings for you. She said over and over how it was her fault that she went outside and that she doesn't blame you one bit for yelling at her. So, if that's all you need from me, I'll be on my way." Weyler started toward the front door.

"I can't stay here," Jane said quietly. "I can't do this anymore."

"Jane, the child isn't holding any grudge! Let's move on!"

"Boss," Jane reached out and grabbed Weyler by the arm. Weyler stopped, realizing she was serious. "I'm not asking to leave. I'm telling you that I'm leaving. Call her aunt and uncle in Cheyenne and take her up there."

"Tonight?"

"Yes! Tonight! It's a ninety minute drive. She'll be up there before midnight."

"Have you lost your mind?"

"Yes. Actually, I have."

"No one is driving that child anywhere tonight. You talk about protocol? I can't suddenly call up her aunt and say 'Make up the bed in the guest room. I'm bringing up your niece.' She is still in our protective custody and that's exactly where she's going to stay until we solve this damn case or I feel there's a justifiable reason to release the girl."

"Then take her to the foster home—"

"Jane. I have broken every goddamn rule with this case. I have stretched my leveraging as far as it will go. I am not going to be sashaying this child around Denver tonight and plopping her in some foster house."

"Fine. Go out there and get Martha and tell her she's spending the night on the couch. I'm going home." Jane opened the front door and walked into the darkness, leaving Weyler alone and stunned.

Jane did not say a word to Weyler during the ten minute drive back to her house. The Saturday evening traffic was a bit heavier than usual due to the Memorial Day Weekend events. As she stared out the window, Jane wondered if Emily had crept downstairs yet and found Martha sitting on the couch. Martha arrived at the door with a bag of oranges and apples, saying something about "It's my dinner" to Jane as they passed on the front porch. Perhaps Martha had made a beeline up to the child's bedroom to soothe Emily and ask her in a roundabout way the real reason Jane left. But she knew down deep that no matter how much Martha pried, that kid would never say a word about the physical altercation earlier that evening.

Jane was staggered and frustrated all in the same moment. Emily purposely covered up the violent event to protect Jane. *Amazing.* But why? It wasn't like they were friends, Jane thought to herself. There wasn't any kind of connection. *Connection?* It was too much for Jane to allow.

Weyler rolled up to Jane's front door but kept the motor running. He stared straight ahead, silent and etched with disappointment. "Okay," was all she could manage as she got out of his car. He drove down Milwaukee and disappeared into the darkness. After fishing her keys out of her leather satchel, she maneuvered her way up the short walk to her front door. Once inside, she dropped her satchel to the wooden floor and stood in the pitchblack. Within the threads of darkness, she felt herself coming apart bit by bit. There was nothing left to her life. After all the work and the years of struggle, she considered herself a total failure. Singlehandedly, she'd destroyed herself and her life with such precision that to bring back any semblance of order was impossible.

Feeling her way across the living room, Jane stumbled into the kitchen and tapped on the light over the stove. She swung open a cupboard door, brought out a fifth of Jack Daniels, twisted off the cap and took a long swig. At first, the liquid burn was comforting; a warm reminder of what it felt like to be numb and pain-free. She knocked back another swallow. Jane closed her eyes and waited to detach. But suddenly, she felt herself choking. Seconds later, she started to cough. She got her head over the sink just in time to spew the whiskey down the drain. Her body arced in violent waves as she threw up every drop of Jack Daniels. Once nothing was left inside of her, Jane sunk down to the floor, bottle in hand. She stuck her finger in the neck of the bottle, saturated it with whiskey and sucked on it. But moments later, the same gag reflex took effect. Jane threw the bottle across the floor and stared into the semi-darkness. Was this the way it was going to be from now on? If so, there was no good reason to stick around.

Jane unsnapped her holster and drew out her Glock pistol. It would be so easy. Just wrap her mouth around the tip of the barrel, tilt it at a forty-five degree angle and pull the trigger. One, two, three. No big deal. No one to mourn her. Well, maybe Mike. But he'd get over it with his new girlfriend by his side.

Jane brushed her finger against the barrel of the pistol

as an eerie sensation descended over her. She didn't hear voices—it was more like she felt them. They were coaxing her, encouraging her, goading her into doing the deed. No more pain. No more torment. No more guilt. No more regret. Just lift the pistol and do it.

Do it. Go on . . . *do it*, they urged.

Jane felt herself slipping into the warm, distant comfort of the intensifying voices. It's easy. *Do it!* She lifted up the Glock as the chorus of encouragement grew. Her finger touched the trigger. The barrel was less than an inch from her mouth when one, solitary voice yelled out among the din.

"*Jane!*"

She froze. "Emily?" she whispered. She turned her head to the sound of the voice, trapped in the sliver between worlds. It was too real, too bizarre. Jane rested the pistol against her thigh, her hand still clutching it. She sat up, squinting into the darkness around her. "Emily?" she yelled. Silence. She was still halfway outside herself but she was convinced she'd turned the corner on certifiably crazy. A groundswell of emotion overwhelmed Jane and her eyes welled with heavy tears. She grabbed her head. "No, God! *No!*" She broke down, gradually slumping across the kitchen floor sobbing and mumbling incoherently. The harder she cried, the more she felt her body being lifted into the air by the back of her neck. She floated high above herself, seized by the darkness and sure of her fast descent into madness.

Jane opened her eyes and inexplicably found herself sitting in the passenger seat of a patrol car. It was so real—so frighteningly palpable. Everything around her lay hazy as if a thick fog gripped the area. She turned to the driver's seat and saw Chris. He was staring straight ahead, completely paralyzed. Jane tried to roust him to no avail. She realized her body was moving in slow motion. Jane reached down to the door handle and unlatched the lock. She got out of the patrol car, still feeling as though she were floating. Standing outside the car, the thick fog embraced her body. Gradually, Jane caught a glimpse of two headlights coming toward her in the distance. As the lights came closer, the fog parted, exposing an SUV. Her rationale mind told her this was a dream—albeit, an odd, altered version of the usual Stover family nightmare. Jane strained to make out Bill Stover, the driver, but the fog would not allow it. Finally, when the vehicle was about thirty-five feet from her, the fog lifted just enough for Jane to look into the front seat of the car. There was no driver. No driver and yet the wheel kept moving and the car continued to eerily creep forward.

Jane started toward the car, her legs moving like jelly. She heard the muted sound of fists pounding on glass. Suddenly, she heard the isolated voice of a screaming child. The SUV continued inching toward her as the pounding fists and screaming grew louder. With one quick turn, the SUV changed course, turning right.

That's when she saw it. There, alone in the backseat of the SUV was Emily. She slammed her fists against the glass and screamed out Jane's name.

"*Jane!*" Emily shrieked. "*Help me!*"

Jane's connected with Emily's eyes just as a tremendous explosion rocketed through the fog and silence, blasting the SUV into a thousand tiny pieces.

Jane stood amidst the raining fire and screamed, "No! Emily!"

*Slam!*

Jane woke up on the kitchen floor with a core-rattling shock. "*Emily!*" Jane yelled into the darkness. Something was wrong—dead wrong. Her gut shouted a sick, twisted, dark warning. The more Jane leaned into the feeling, the more sinister it became.

Jane secured her pistol into its holster and rose quickly to her feet. Groping through the dim light, she snagged her leather satchel, pulled out her keys, bolted out the front door and raced toward her parked Mustang.

*Tat-tat-tat-tat-tat!*

Emily looked up toward her closed bedroom door.

"Emily?" Martha said, standing outside the door. "It's me, dear. Martha. May I come in?"

"Yes," Emily said, subdued.

Martha walked into the bedroom, carrying several oranges and apples. "Well, it looks like someone's all ready for bed!"

"Where's Jane?" Emily quickly asked.

Martha looked off to the side. "Detective Jane had a very important meeting."

Emily analyzed Martha's face. "You're lying."

Martha was caught off guard. "Why would you say a thing like that?"

"Your face told me," Emily said, not taking her eyes off of Martha. "She's not at a meeting. She left. And she's not coming back,"

Martha sat next to Emily on the bed, wrapping her arm around the child's shoulders. "Now, dear. Don't you worry one little snippet about Detective Jane. She can take care of herself—"

"No," Emily interrupted. "She can't!"

"Sweetheart," Martha tousled Emily's brown hair. "Did Detective Jane tell you that she couldn't take care of herself?"

Emily studied Martha's inquiring eyes and felt uneasy. "No. She's *strong*. She could fight anybody and win. If someone was trying to hurt me, she'd beat them up and save me."

Martha let out a little derisive chortle. "My! She certainly has told you a big barrel of bragging."

"She didn't say any of that," Emily pulled away. "I just have to know it."

"Well, okay," Martha said, not taking Emily too seriously. "I brought you some oranges and apples—"

"No, thank you." Emily stared out the window. Martha let out a low sigh. "Alright, then. I'll say good night." She got up. "I'll be downstairs, sleeping on the couch if you need me."

*Tat-tat-tat!*

Emily jumped to attention. "What's that?" she said, startled.

Martha opened Emily's door and peeked downstairs into the living room. "It's just the wind, dear. It's blown the curtain rod against the table."

"You've got the window open?" Emily said, concerned.

"Well, my goodness, yes. I have several windows open. It was so stuffy down there. You shouldn't sleep in a stuffy house. It's not good for you!"

"Please close all those windows!" Emily implored.

"Sweetie, fresh air—"

"You can't have the doors open and you can't have the windows open!"

"Emily, dear, calm down." Martha sat back on the bed, observing the child. "Look at you. You're shaking. What's wrong?"

"This isn't the way it's supposed to be," she said confused and scared.

"Whatever are you talking about?"

"Where's Jane?"

"There's no need to be frightened—"

"Where is she?" A mixture of fear and anger consumed the girl.

Martha let out a long sigh. "Jane had to go home. She's sick."

Emily stared into the void. "Something's wrong—"

"Wrong?"

Emily turned to Martha. "I have to call her!"

"Sweetie, you can't call her! Now, get into bed and—"

"I need to call her *now!*"

"Detective Jane has obviously upset you. Would you like to talk about it?"

"Are you gonna let me call Jane?"

Martha sized up Emily. "No. I am not. Come on, I'll tuck you in—"

"No! I just want to sit here."

"Well, okay. But the sandman will be here soon."

Emily regarded Martha with suspicion. "The sandman? Who's he?"

"Don't you know the sandman?"

An ominous dark cloud overwhelmed Emily as she looked at Martha. "No," she said softly, feeling a distinct terror bite into her stomach. "I don't think I want to."

"Good night, Emily." Martha turned to go. "You're safe, sweetheart. Perfectly safe." With that, Martha walked into the hallway, closing the door behind her.

Emily waited until she heard Martha's footsteps descend the stairs. She quietly crept to her window and pushed open the stubborn pane that had caused so many problems that night. Emily stuck her head out the window and peered into the night sky. The clouds were quickly clearing as a palate of twinkling stars blanketed the blue-black sky. In an instant, a shooting star dove across the horizon. Emily closed her eyes. "Jane," Emily whispered. "You're supposed to be here."

*Thud!*

Emily turned quickly toward her bedroom door. The sound came from downstairs. She stood perfectly still. Maybe Martha dropped something. Emily considered cracking her bedroom door to investigate but something held her back. She turned around to the window, feeling an uncommon draw to climb out on the roof. She pulled herself up onto the window ledge, knocking over the screen she'd removed earlier that evening. Once on the roof, she made a point of not pushing the window shut. She scooted her butt just a few feet away from the window and out of the sycamore tree's shadow. It was all so silent. So serene. So peaceful. And then . . .

*Bang!*

Emily jumped and quickly turned toward her bedroom window. The penetrating sound came from downstairs and echoed in the night air for several heart-racing seconds. Panic quickly set in. Without watching her step, Emily hurriedly got up. In a split second, her foot slipped on the wet roof. She reached out to grab the window ledge but it was too late. Emily slid down toward the edge of the roof on her stomach, desperately grasping for anything to stop her fall. The only thing she caught hold of was a vent pipe that protruded from the roof. Emily circled her arms around it and held on for dear life as her legs dangled helplessly forty feet off the ground. She looked down. If she let go, she had a fifty-fifty chance of landing either on grass or cement. Since she would be falling backward, gravity would determine which of the two she'd hit.

*Slam!*

Emily seized up when she heard the sound of her bedroom door being kicked in. Moments later, she heard the splintering crash of her bedside lamp as it was thrown against the wall. Her breathing became labored as she struggled to hold on to the air pipe. The individual in her bedroom moved toward the open window. Emily heard the person breathing and then slightly grunting as they hoisted themselves up onto the window ledge and out onto the roof. Emily closed her eyes, trying to hold her breath.

Footsteps moved cautiously across the roof. One, two, three steps then stopping. A careful turn and one, two, three, four steps and stopping. The intruder's breath came closer to where Emily's body hung. Keeping her head tucked inward toward the roof, she listened to every breath of the individual. The steps moved closer to Emily. One step, and then another.

A cruel gust of wind blew across the backyard. Emily heard the familiar *tap, tap, tap* of the sycamore branch beating against her bedroom window, followed by the slow roll of tires creeping along the back alleyway. The intruder made a determined step forward and Emily realized that the person was within a foot of her body. She pressed her forehead into the roof and waited for the worst.

Jane crisscrossed through traffic, ignoring the series of one-way streets and driving in the opposite direction. She jumped her Mustang over the center median on Eighth Street, stormed down the side streets and barreled through red lights. Once on University, she shifted gears, zig-zagged around vehicles and reached speeds of seventy-five mph in forty-five mph zones. An evil, foreboding feeling permeated her bones. Her gut twisted and a cold sweat broke out across the back of her neck. Jane peeled onto Exposition and continued clocking speeds of sixty to seventy miles per hour until she reached Franklin. She nearly lost control of the Mustang as she turned sharply to the right and came to a squealing stop in front of the Lawrence house.

Tearing out of her car, she pulled out her Glock. Both watch officers were already out of their respective vehicles and standing near the middle of the street. When they saw Jane's car swerve around the corner and come to a sudden halt, they automatically pulled out their pistols. "It's me! Perry!" Jane screamed.

"We think we heard a shot fired!" one of the officers yelled.

"Shit!" Jane yelled. She turned to the other officer "Call for backup! You—" she said, addressing the other cop, "follow me and cover!" Jane raced down the drive-way, her pistol clasped tightly between her hands. As she sprinted toward the gate, she noted that two windows were swung wide open in front of the house. Other than that, nothing seemed to be disturbed. The cop shadowed Jane as she kicked open the front gate and held out her Glock. The well-lit living room cast enough light into the area for Jane to see that there was no one there. Jane motioned to the cop to follow her alongside the wall, just under the windows that framed the fireplace. When she crept to a point where she felt safe, Jane lifted her body and peered into the living room through the gauzy drapes. The room outwardly showed no signs of struggle. Jane knelt down and moved toward the corner of the house, near the back door. She waited one second, then swung around, pistol extended. Nothing.

"Police!" Jane screamed out. She waited but heard nothing. Someone was out there. She felt it. Jane turned to the cop and whispered, "Where the fuck is backup?" Crashing into the house with the possibility of someone lurking in the shadows was not part of her program. But Jane felt an urgency to get inside the house. Keeping her pistol extended, she walked around the flowerpots by the back door. The patrol cop followed. She turned to the back kitchen door. It was wide open. A cold chill ran down Jane's spine as she peered into the darkened kitchen. She nodded toward the cop to follow her. Jane entered the kitchen, pistol still out in front. "*Police!*" she screamed.

Silence.

With the cop close behind her, she crept to the door that led into the living room. "*Police!*" she yelled out, maneuvering her body into the room. That's when she smelled it. The stench of blood and fear and death. Jane could feel her throat closing up—a visceral reaction she only experienced when she was virtually standing on top of carnage. She looked down and caught sight of a blanket draped across the end of the couch. With measured steps, she moved forward. The coffee table came into view. A freshly peeled orange sat alone amongst Emily's scattered drawings and colored pencils. One more step and Jane saw the entire bloody scene.

Someone lay covered under the blanket, curled up as though they were sleeping. The top of the blanket was soaked in blood from a single gunshot to the head. A knife—the same one used to peel the orange—had been shoved into the person's left cheek and through one of Emily's drawings. As Jane moved closer, she made out the words "PAYBACK!" written in red colored pencil across the drawing. Jane could feel herself about to lose it. "Please, God, no," she whispered under her breath. She gently pulled up the blanket. It was Martha.

Jane's body tensed as she turned to the staircase that led to Emily's bedroom. "God, don't you do this again," she whispered to herself with fear and anger. Without acknowledging the cop, Jane headed toward the stairs. When she reached the bottom step and looked up, she saw the door kicked in and the lights out. "Police!" Her voice cracked as she screamed the word. Skimming her back against the wall, she walked up the steps. With each step, her stomach churned. When she reached the top step, she reached around the wall and felt for the light switch. Jane flipped it up and snapped to attention, gun extended. She immediately noted the bedside lamp smashed against the wall. She looked to the closet and edged her way toward it. With a quick twist of the knob, she jerked the door open and shoved the pistol forward. Nothing.

Jane peered over to the bed. She wedged her boot against the bed frame and shoved it forward across the pink carpeting. No one hiding. The large sycamore branch tapped nervously against the far window, as if to alert Jane. Still moving with extreme caution, Jane stepped to the window and looked out into the darkness. But the shadows played tricks with her eyes. She looked down on the carpet and saw Emily's discarded jumper, wet from her outdoor adventure earlier that evening. The flashlight Martha had given her was still attached to the strap. Jane leaned over and ripped the flashlight off the strap, clamping it between her teeth. The bright sapphire colored light was surprisingly effective in illuminating the rooftop outside the window. Jane checked the area and listened intently for a sound but there was only silence.

She pushed her body up onto the window ledge and did her best to get through the open window and onto the roof without causing too much noise. Once outside, she hunkered down, pistol still at the ready. Pointing the flashlight across the roof, she looked for signs of a struggle but the darkness prevented her from picking up the subtle clues. Another skim of the flashlight to the right and then to the left and she stopped.

The vent pipe was obviously bent and precariously leaning across the edge of the roof. Jane flattened her body against the wet roof and carefully slid down to the pipe. As she came up on it, she examined it with the flashlight and realized it was a recent break. She looked out into the dense charcoal black darkness that filled the backyard. That same feeling came over her—the awareness that someone was out there. She craned her neck and removed the flashlight from between her teeth. Guardedly, Jane shone the pinpoint beam of light across the yard. Back and forth and back again.

Then, she saw her. There was Emily, directly beneath the edge of the roof, sprawled across the grass. She lay unconscious on her back, her head to the side, with blood pouring from a gash along her left temple. "Christ!" Jane said with a shudder as she threw the small flashlight to the side, secured her pistol and stood up. Without giving it a thought, she leapt onto the large sycamore branch and dropped down to the trunk of the tree. She nearly lost her balance, but she quickly recovered and continued down the tree. When Jane was about six feet from the ground, she jumped feet first to the grass and lunged toward Emily.

She immediately checked Emily's heartbeat. It was beating but it was very faint. Jane opened the child's mouth to see if anything was obstructing her breathing. "Don't do this to me!" she screamed in frustration. Without hesitating, Jane carefully scooped up Emily's frail body and cradled the child in her arms. She half-ran toward the back gate and tore down the driveway to her Mustang. Patrol cars zoomed onto the scene. Undeterred by their presence, Jane opened the passenger door on the Mustang and gently placed Emily into the seat, securing her with the seat belt.

A cop raced over to Jane. "Perry! Is that the kid?" Jane ignored him as she ran around to the driver's side. "Perry, you can't do this! It's against regulations!"

Jane slid into her car, slamming the door. "Fuck regulations! I'm going to Denver Health! Tell them I'm coming!" she yelled, peeling away from the scene. Jane tore down Franklin, ignoring every stop sign and hitting speeds well over fifty mph. She reached over and brushed the dripping blood out of Emily's eyes. "Don't you die on me, kid!"

Jane zoomed through red lights and crisscrossed around traffic, screeching her tires around the curves. She was within a mile of Denver Health Medical Center and continued driving like a maniac and screaming at Emily. "Come on, Emily! I know you can hear me! Come back!" Jane spun the Mustang into Denver Health, heading for the Emergency entrance. Skidding to a halt, she yanked out the keys and ran around to Emily's side. She undid the seat belt and hoisted the kid into her arms. "*Police!*" she screamed, racing to the doors. Several nurses ran up to her.

"Are you Perry?" one nurse quickly asked.

"Yes!" Jane yelled back.

A stretcher appeared and the nurses carefully placed Emily on it. "What happened?" the nurse asked as they dashed through the automatic doors and down the hallway to a curtained treatment area.

"I don't know," Jane said, her voice shaking as she ran alongside the stretcher. "I think she was on the roof and there may have been a struggle—"

"How far did she fall?" the nurse asked.

"Maybe thirty feet!"

"You shouldn't have moved her!" the nurse admonished.

"What the hell was I supposed to do? Watch her die?"

The nurse shot Jane an angry look as they swung the stretcher into the treatment area. A doctor made his way into the space and started checking Emily's vital signs. The nurse relayed the information given to her from Jane. Their conversation blurred into the background noise as Jane stared transfixed by Emily's tiny body on the stretcher. Her favorite pajamas with the star print were blotted with grass stains, dirt from the roof, leaves and splatters of blood.

The doctor fixed a bright overhead light above Emily's head. He checked for any fixation in her eyes. Turning to Jane, he asked, "What's her name?"

"Emily," Jane responded.

"Emily?" the doctor said, his mouth inches away from the child's bloody face. "Emily? My name is Dr. Brunler. You're in the hospital. If you can hear me, honey, wake up." He pried open Emily's mouth, felt around her throat with his gloved finger and turned to one of the nurses. "I think there might be an obstruction in her airway. We may need to intubate."

Jane reacted. She leaned down and whispered into Emily's ear. "Emily! Wake up *now* or they're going to stick a damn tube down your throat! Open your eyes!"

The doctor heard Jane and grabbed her by her shoulder. "Officer, I can't have you talking to her like that. I need you to leave."

A nurse tried to pull Jane away from Emily. "She listens to me!" Jane yelled.

"Nurse," Dr. Brunler said, irritated, "please show her into the waiting room!"

"Get your hands off me!" Jane shouted at the nurse. But the nurse kept moving her backward, away from Emily. Jane turned to Emily and yelled. "Goddamnit, Emily! Wake up! Don't let the bastard who did this to you win!"

"Officer, *please!*" the nurse implored Jane as she pulled her backward.

"Hey, hey!" the doctor said abruptly. "She's coming around!"

The nurse immediately let go of Jane and returned to the table. "Stay back!" the nurse cautioned Jane.

Jane stood away from the action, but positioned herself in a spot nearby where she could see Emily's face. Emily struggled to open her eyes.

The doctor pushed the light out of Emily's eyes. "Emily? Talk to me!" Emily darted her eyes from side to side. "*Emily,* can you move your head?"

Emily stared at the surrounding hospital staff. "Jane?" she whimpered. "Where are you?" Emily caught sight of Jane through the hospital crew. Immediately, she reached out her arm and lifted her body off the table, trying to get to her. "Jane!" Jane moved forward, grabbing Emily's hand. The doctor gently restrained Emily, encouraging her to lie back on the table. "Jane, I'm scared!"

"It's okay," Jane assured Emily. "Lie down. They're gonna fix you up."

Emily lay back down and reached up to her left temple, touching the gash and feeling the blood. She broke down. "I tried to hold on," Emily said through her sobs. "I was so scared. Somebody came on the roof. I slipped, just like you said I would. I tried to hide. I held my breath so he wouldn't hear me. He was so close. Then that car drove down the alley and he left. But I couldn't hold on anymore." She briefly looked up at Jane, tears intermingling with blood against her pale face. "I'm so sorry!"

The doctor retrieved a syringe from one of the nurses and looked at Jane as if to ask her to distract the child.

"Look at me, Emily," Jane said quietly. Emily turned to Jane. "I'm not mad at you. Okay?" The doctor injected Emily with a sedative. Emily screamed out in pain. Jane squeezed Emily's hand and gently touched her cheek. "It's all over! It's gonna be okay!" Emily stared into Jane's eyes as the sedative took effect. Jane leaned closer to Emily and whispered. "I'm not mad at you."

Emily's eyelids became heavy. She slid her hand from Jane's grasp and reached up toward Jane's forehead. The child ran her fingers across Jane's childhood scar on her right temple. In a soft voice, Emily whispered, "We're the same now."

# Chapter **15**

Jane held Emily's hand and stayed by her side while Dr. Brunler stitched the child's gash. Thanks to the mild sedative, Emily floated in and out of consciousness. As the bandage was placed over the wound, Emily finally drifted off to sleep. Jane released Emily's tiny hand from hers and the child was rolled into a secured area for recovery.

The nurse swept the white privacy curtain to the side, leaving Jane alone. But she sat motionless, shellshocked and still pulsating from everything that had happened that night. She leaned forward on the stool and buried her head in her hands. Behind her, a string of exhausted patrol cops began to arrive. Several of the cops positioned themselves outside the area where Emily rested. Within seconds, Chris appeared on the scene, racing down the corridor and out of breath. Just like the others, he looked like hell. As usual with Chris, whenever he sweated, the perspiration tended to exacerbate his springtime rash, which was currently making another appearance.

Chris looked around the hospital area and then spotted Jane with her back to him. He stared at her for several minutes, seemingly stunned before walking over to her. "Jane?" he said more as a question.

Jane lifted her head from her hands and turned to face Chris. "Jesus! Don't creep up on me like that!"

"Oh, my God," was all Chris could say as he began to tremble.

"What's wrong with you? You look like you've seen a ghost."

"I thought you were . . ." Chris' voice began to choke up. "I thought you were in the house—"

"I don't want to talk about it."

"When they paged me . . . they said there was an adult DOA on scene—"

"None of this would have happened if I had been there. Is it that Martha doesn't listen or was she not told to keep that place closed up?"

Chris ran his fingers through his dirty, rainsoaked hair, trying to get hold of himself. "I don't know." He steadied himself and looked at Jane. "You okay?"

"Am I okay?" Jane asked. "Well, let's see. Considering that I am responsible for this entire mess—"

"You?" Chris interrupted. "How are you responsible?"

Jane shook her head in slight disgust. "It's just a job to you, isn't it?" Jane let out a tired sigh. "Once again, someone died tonight because of my inability to follow through and see the signs. If it wasn't for some strange, freaky stroke of luck, someone else would have died." Jane looked off to the side, fighting back tears. "This is not my job, Chris. *This is my life.* And I'm not very good at it."

Chris got down on his haunches. "Don't beat yourself up. It's not your fault. Shit happens, you know? At least the son-of-a-bitch couldn't find the kid and had to take off. Don't blame yourself for this huge mistake." Chris placed his hand on Jane's leg.

Jane felt cold and vacant as she looked into Chris' eyes. It was so clear to her at that very moment why they could never again be partners on or off the force. "A mistake?" Jane said softly. "That's how you describe all of this?"

"Well, it was."

"Take your fucking cold hand off my leg and get out of my sight."

Chris pulled back. "Jane, I just—"

"Are you fucking deaf?" Jane yelled as she looked to her right and saw evidence technician Ron Dickson standing in the sterile hallway. She immediately felt embarrassed by her expletive, realizing that Ron heard her. "Ron," she said haltingly.

"Good evening, Detective Perry. Detective Crawley," Ron said.

Chris stood up and acknowledged Ron.

"What are you doing here?" Jane asked Ron. "I didn't know that evidence techs got paged for stuff like this."

Ron moved closer to Jane. She noticed that he seemed troubled. "Oh, it's actually an unfortunate coincidence."

Chris observed Ron. "You're shaking there, pal. You okay?"

"Oh, yeah. I've just had a rocky last few hours."

"What do you mean?" Chris said, closely watching Ron's every move.

"I was helping my wife cut up beeswax for her famous herbal salve and the knife slipped. I darn near cut off the tip of my left finger." Ron held up his bandaged hand.

"You okay?" Jane asked.

"Oh, it'll be just fine," Ron said, dismissing the question. "When I heard about your little girl in there—"

"My little girl?" Jane said quickly.

"Well, I mean to say you were looking after her and all." Ron quickly sniffed a ball of snot up his nose. "I'm sorry. I'm a little discombobulated. I just got word from one of the patrol cops about Martha. I'm in shock," Ron said, shaking his head.

"Yeah," Jane replied.

"I'll let you and Detective Crawley go about your business," Ron said as he stole a look in Emily's direction. "God bless you both."

Ron started off when Chris quickly spoke up. "Hey, Ron! You need a ride home? I could take you. It's no problem."

"No, thank you. My wife will take me home."

"Really?" Chris said, his voice becoming slightly intense. "Where is your wife?" Chris suddenly became an inquisitor.

Ron rubbed his hand in obvious pain. "Oh, she's gone out to get the car. She had to park pretty far away after she dropped me off. I'm sorry, I need to go. I'm not feeling very well. My wife and I will keep you in our prayers. Both of you." Ron turned and walked down the hallway.

Chris moved several steps into the hallway, watching Ron's every last move. "Yeah, bud, I'll bet you'll be praying real hard," Chris said under his breath.

"Chris, what's wrong with you?" Jane asked.

"Jane! Have you lost your touch? I thought you were a student of observation. Body language and the whole nine yards."

"What about it?"

"He's shaking like a fucking perp. And he's sniffing like a fucking coke fiend."

Jane stood up, disgusted. "You have got to be kidding!"

"There are no coincidences, Jane."

"You're not seriously trying to say that Ron could—"

"Jane, think about it! He cut his finger *chopping beeswax* for an herbal salve? What kind bullshit is that?"

"His wife makes the stuff! He offered me the salve for my burn. Ron is—"

"*Shhh!* Let's just keep this to ourselves until I can investigate further," Chris said in a hushed, confidential tone.

"My God!" Jane said, completely bewildered. "I've said it before, Chris, and I'll say it again. You have *got* to do something about that paranoia."

"No, Jane. I've got to do something about solving this case. You may not be able to see what's standing right in front of you. But I'm not going to make that mistake again." Chris turned to walk down the hallway, then stopped and looked back at Jane. "I've got some questions I want you to ask that kid. It can wait for a few days until she's back on her feet. Until then, I'm gonna do a little private investigation of Mr. Dickson."

"Chris, you're crazy."

"Crazy like a fox, kid. Wake up, Jane!" Chris said with a smirk. "I'm gonna solve this crime and I'm gonna put DH back in good favor. And I *will* get that Sergeant's promotion. Hey, when that happens, you'll be working for me. Won't that be sweet? Watch over that little girl in there. She's solid gold." With that, Chris walked down the hallway and disappeared around the corner.

Jane shook her head and pulled out a cigarette. She started to light up when a nurse spotted her. "Officer!" the nurse said, "you can't smoke in here!"

Jane walked down the hallway and out the automatic doors. A hospital traffic cop eyed her blue Mustang that was parked where she'd left it. "That's a police vehicle!" Jane yelled over to him. "Tow it and you'll be sorry!" Jane ducked around a corner and found a secluded area. She no sooner lit up when she heard her name quietly spoken. She turned. "Boss!" Jane said, semi-startled.

"I just came from the scene," Weyler said, subdued. "It's a goddamn mess."

Jane took a drag on her cigarette and looked off into the distance. "You know, I wanted Martha out of the picture. But I never wanted anything like this to happen to her. None of this would have happened if I hadn't left."

"How can you be so sure?"

"I'd have the good sense not to have the windows and back door wide open. Did you not express to her the possibility of a stalker?"

"Yes. I told her there was some concern in that area."

"That's it? Concern? Martha probably didn't equate the same meaning to that word. Did you tell her to keep the windows and doors closed?"

"I did. She said the house was stuffy and that she wanted to briefly open the windows to move the air around."

"How many people die for how many stupid reasons? So, who else knows about this mess?"

"We're holding off the media as long as possible. I'll have Chris handle that when I feel it's appropriate. I ordered a twenty-four hour police guard around Emily. Other than that, I haven't debriefed anyone. I was hoping you had information from the number one source."

Jane leaned against the wall and stared up into the starry night sky. "She was on that damn roof. I don't know whether she went out there to look at the stars or to get away from something. Either way, she was out there and slipped and caught hold of the vent pipe. She hung there while this fucking asshole crawled out on the roof."

"We know it's a guy?"

"She says she heard *him* breathing. That's how close he was. And then he left."

"Left?"

"Maybe the back alley patrol vehicle freaked him out. I haven't had a chance to figure out the timing but he must have shot Martha and then made a beeline up to Emily's bedroom and crawled out on the roof when he saw her open window. He had to know that we'd be in there when we heard the shot. He knew he had to work fast and get out. It was a helluva chance but it goes to show how desperate he was."

"Where did he go? He's on the goddamn roof."

"He didn't go back into the house through her bedroom because there were no signs of wet footprints on the bedroom carpeting." Jane thought for a second. "Come to think of it, I don't recall seeing any outside footprints on the carpeting except for Emily's from when she went outside earlier in the evening."

"So, he covered his tracks?"

"He covered his feet. Just like the first time when he took out her parents."

"This puts us back to the theory that one person killed two people—"

"One person *can* kill two people. You stun one and kill

the other, then turn around and finish off the first. This guy is smart. He's a pro."

"Are you forgetting that Emily's parents were killed with two different knives and two different kill patterns?"

"He planned it that way, knowing it would throw us off. This guy's sick but he's far from stupid."

"So, what's 'PAYBACK?' Weyler wondered out loud, referring to the ominous note left on the knife that cut through Martha's cheek.

"I don't know."

"I'm aware that you feel this case has nothing to do with drug dealing, but I think we should seriously reconsider that possibility."

"Boss, I told you, it doesn't add up—"

"I know. The kid told you that she never saw her folks doing coke. I don't think that's a good enough reason to dismiss the idea. 'Payback' is revenge."

"It's also used by the mob."

"Are you saying this is the Texas mob?"

"I'm saying it could be any mob and I'm not saying that a mob is involved."

"Why not?"

"What link would the mob have with this little family?"

"Maybe it's worth looking into. I can put Chris on it—"

"Don't bother Chris right now." Jane took another drag on her cigarette. "He's got his own suspect theory going."

"What's that?"

"Right about now, I imagine he's doing background checks on Dr. James Dobson and Pat Robertson. You know? The infamous 'Christian Cocaine Cartel.'" Weyler looked askance. "Don't worry, boss. Let him make a fool of himself. He wants to solve this thing and fuck the consequences."

"What do you want to do?"

"I want to make sure nothing bad ever happens to that kid again."

"Really? I was under the impression that you and she

had no connection whatsoever. Isn't that what you told me?" Weyler was testing Jane, goading her to see when she'd bite. "You know, I would never accuse you of caring for someone like Emily. But I have to assume that you've developed some extraordinary bond with that child for you to suddenly get off your ass, leave your house for no known reason and save that girl's life. How do you explain that?"

Jane searched the ground for answers. Her head spun as she recalled the disjointed, disembodied dream of Emily screaming for help. "I can't explain it, boss."

Weyler nodded. "Okay."

There was a moment of tense silence. "Boss?" Jane hesitated. "I haven't been completely up front with you." Weyler waited, a little uneasy. "Today, before I went down to DH to talk to that nutcase that Chris questioned, Emily told me something."

"Such as?"

"A third voice. She recalls her parents fighting and then hearing the sound from downstairs of a third voice."

"What was the voice saying?"

"Something about an accident. That was the way he got the Lawrences to let him into the house. You know, 'My cell phone's dead. Can I use your phone to report the accident?' Emily said she heard the footsteps of the stranger walking into the kitchen for a brief period of time. That's where the Lawrences' phone is located so it might fit."

"The crime scene evidence proves that the perp's feet were covered, he wore gloves and a mask. Certainly, he didn't show up at the door in that garb?"

Jane quickly started to formulate possible scenarios. "He didn't. He had it hidden somewhere on his person. When he was in the kitchen, he could change into it quickly and then reemerge. Emily remembered hearing a lot of yelling after the stranger walked back into the living room."

Weyler considered Jane's theory. "If that's what

occurred, then this guy is premeditated to a fault."

"This was not some dime store kill. Powerful people needed the Lawrences dead . . . But the Lawrences don't seem to know anybody." Jane tossed her cigarette on the ground, crushing it with her boot heel. "Anyway, I didn't tell you what Emily told me and so there it is. That's all she's been able to remember, but . . ." Jane began to struggle with the concept. "But I think she's going to remember more. When you send her to Cheyenne, make sure she gets some help, okay? She's gonna need it."

"Her aunt and uncle are not willing to take her back right now."

Jane was stunned. "Why not?"

"They're scared. Actually, they are terrified. They feel that whoever is after the kid is going to keep after her until one of them is dead. And after tonight, it only proves that whoever else might be with the child would also be in danger. They're not willing to take that chance right now."

Jane moved closer to Weyler, angered. "So what happens to Emily?"

"Do the math, kiddo."

"Protective custody?" Jane could hardly get the words out.

"Yes."

"For how long?"

"I'm not sure. Until we figure out this whole thing."

"You may never solve it! What's the kid supposed to do? Hide out in some town with a bunch of FBI agents until she's old enough to vote?"

"You've got the 'hide out' part right. But I'm keeping the FBI out of this." Weyler looked Jane in the eye. "There's only one person who I trust and who that child trusts."

Jane was dumbstruck. "What about my job? I still have a job. Right?"

"Right now, this is your job."

Jane tried to let the information soak in. "Okay, so, let

me get this straight. You're gonna . . . what? Find some
house in some town and I'm gonna take her there and
we're gonna lay low? Is that what I'm hearing?"

"I'll need to work out more specifics with the DA, but
that's it in a nutshell."

"For how long?"

"Not sure. I want you to keep this strictly confidential.
Just you and me and the DA will know where you're staying. Don't tell your brother or your father or Chris."

"I can deal with Mike and my dad, but what in the hell
am I supposed to tell Chris? He's going to go ballistic if
he thinks I'm showboating his case."

"I will tell him the same thing that I tell everyone else
who's involved in the case. As of this moment, you and
the kid are underground. For the child's protection, they'll
have to understand—Chris included."

"How in the hell are you gonna make this happen,
boss?"

"I'll pull some strings and we'll make it a special
request direct from the DA's office. It might take a couple days to clear it through the channels upstairs, but it
*will* get done. My advice to you right now is to go home.
Emily has twenty-four hour, armed protection. Get some
rest. See your brother. See your dad, too. You may be
gone for awhile."

For a change, Jane took Weyler's advice. She went
home and slept for twelve hours. It was past 1:30 p.m.
when Jane woke up on Sunday. She'd left several messages on Mike's answering machine, each one becoming
more and more insistent that he return her calls. He'd
been spending most Saturday nights at her place and Sunday was typically relegated to nursing their dual hang-
overs and watching whatever sport dominated the TV.
Jane had to assume that Mike had tied one on and was
passed out somewhere in the vicinity of the toilet.

Jane's sense of duty reared its predicable head. By five
o' clock, she was headed over to Mike's brick bungalow
located five miles across town. There was no sign of her

brother's pickup truck on the street. She figured it was parked at whatever bar he visited the night before and she would spend the remaining part of her Sunday tracking it down. Jane was just about to leave when Mike drove up, wedging his truck in a space behind her Mustang. She got out of her car just as Mike and a pretty, blond, long-haired woman got out of his truck.

"Hey, Janie!" Mike said with a happy sound to his voice.

"Hi," Jane responded, restrained and distrustful.

"Janie, this is Lisa." Mike turned to Lisa. "I've been telling Lisa all about you and how you solve murders and everything."

"Is that right?" Jane said, eyeing Lisa up and down.

Lisa moved closer to Jane. She was an attractive girl, neatly dressed in a modest white cotton top and pink skirt that skimmed her knees. Her straight blond hair was pulled back on the side with two barrettes. Jane noticed her shoes—a pair of espadrilles that matched her pink skirt. Lisa had a clear sparkle in her blue eyes and a sweet smile. Okay, Jane thought. What's the catch? Mike's choice in women had always proved tenuous at best. Usually, Jane could spot the weak link within less than a minute of meeting them. But this one was tricky. Jane wondered if her recent emotional upheaval was overriding her "bullshit radar" with Lisa.

"It's so nice to meet you, Jane," Lisa said, extending her hand. Jane hesitated before shaking Lisa's hand with the enthusiasm one would bestow on one's executioner. "Mike speaks highly of you."

"Uh-huh," was all Jane could manage.

"You know," Lisa continued, "it's ironic about you being a detective. My older brother, Jeff, is a private investigator. It's nothing too exciting, just fraud cases and husbands cheating on wives—"

"Her brother used to be a bounty hunter!" Mike interjected. "Isn't that cool?"

"He blew out his knee taking down too many outlaws

so he had to settle for a more sedate form of law enforcement. I bet you and he would have lots to talk about!"

Jane observed Lisa, reacting with a stone face. While she couldn't find anything wrong with the girl, Jane was damned if she was going to act civil. Jane turned to Mike, "I've been trying to get you on the phone for over four hours. I was starting to worry."

"There's nothin' to worry about, Janie," Mike said offhandedly.

"Well, I figured Sunday morning after Saturday night. You know the rest."

Mike looked over at Lisa, a little embarrassed by Jane's comment. "Oh, no . . ."

"What?" Jane said as she crossed her arms in front of her chest. She was starting to feeling like the odd man out and not enjoying it.

"We were at the art show," Mike quickly stated. "They got that Memorial Day Weekend thing in the park. Lisa makes this really cool jewelry out of copper and brass. You've got to see it sometime, Janie. It's just beautiful."

Lisa put her arm around Mike lovingly. "Mike's my biggest fan."

"Yeah," Jane said, treating Lisa more like a suspect. "I see that."

"Hey, I'm not the only fan!" Mike said, nudging Lisa. "Lisa's got these friends from her group who have a booth at the art show in the park. They're showcasing some of her stuff this weekend and she's already sold two neck-laces and three bracelets. I'm tellin' you, Janie, she's gonna be famous one day. You gotta get yourself one of her pieces while you can still afford it."

"Mike!" Lisa seemed genuinely chagrined.

Jane felt herself boiling inside as she watched the back and forth, flirtatious body language between Lisa and Mike. "Mike!" Jane said quickly. "I need to talk to you—"

"I'll go in the house and you guys can have some pri-vacy," Lisa replied, turning to Jane. "If I don't get a chance to say good-bye, it was a pleasure meeting you," she said with a sincere smile before heading to Mike's front door.

Mike watched her walk away, a sappy smile pasted across his face. He was totally in his own world as he turned back to Jane. "Isn't she great, Janie?"

"Let's go for a walk," Jane said.

Mike sidled up alongside Jane. "What's up?" he asked.

"I gotta go away for a while. It has to do with work."

"Where are you going?"

"I don't know yet. And even when I do, I can't tell you."

"Wow. Sounds important." Mike's attitude clearly demonstrated that he wasn't that impressed by the news.

"Mike? Did you hear me? I'm going away and I might be gone for a while."

"Yeah, okay, Janie. I'll go to your house and pick up your newspapers and water your lawn. Hey, you know what? Lisa has got a green thumb. How about if I bring her over to your house and we plant some pretty flowers around that pathway. I think it would really brighten it up—"

"What in the fuck has gotten into you!" Jane said, stopping in her tracks. "Jesus Christ! You're like some love struck puppy!"

"Okay, we won't plant any flowers! We'll just come over and water and—"

"You keep her the fuck away from my place!"

"Why?"

"Because, I don't know anything about her!"

"She's a good woman!"

"How the hell do you know, Mike? You've known her how long? She's like all your other girlfriends—"

"No, she's not!" Mike said defiantly. "I told you the other day, she's different!"

"Fuck that!"

"*She is!* Why can't you accept that?"

"Because that has *never* been the way it is!"

"Janie," Mike struggled a bit before he spoke. "Don't do this, okay?"

"Don't do what?"

"I don't need you to get in my face so much."

"If I didn't get in your face, God only knows what would happen to you."

"What's gonna happen to me?"

"Anything and everything! You have no idea, Mike!"

"Janie, you gotta pull back."

"I can't pull back!"

"What are you talking about?"

Jane looked upward, as if the right words were painted on the sky. "Things happen, Mike. Awful, sick things happen. It is my job to make sure you don't get hurt. It has always been my job. You'll never know how seriously I take that job."

Mike thought for a second and then spoke. "What if you just quit the job."

Jane let out an exaggerated groan. "Mike, when are you gonna grow up?"

"When are you gonna let me?"

"Excuse me?" she replied, sounding more like a parent than a sister.

Mike was reticent but forced himself to press on. "I have opinions about things that you might not agree with."

"Name one!"

"Well . . . I think . . . No. I *know* I have a drinking problem."

"A drinking problem? What the fuck are you talking about?"

"I think you do, too."

Mike's words hit Jane hard. "Really?" There was a sarcastic turn to her voice.

"You've got to admit that you . . . *we* have downed a lot of alcohol."

"We're white, single and over 21!"

"I think we're alcoholics."

Jane surveyed her brother carefully. "This is not you talking, Mike. This is someone else. Somebody has gotten to you. What? Have you found God?"

"There's nothing wrong with God, Janie."

"I knew it!"

"Janie," Mike said curtly, "there comes a time when you gotta say that you are no longer in control and that you trust in a higher power. That's the first step."

Jane could hardly believe what she was hearing. "Oh, shit. You went to a goddamn AA meeting."

"Yes. And it made sense—"

"Who in the hell dragged you to a fucking AA meeting?" Mike stared at Jane for a long second and then looked toward his house. "That bitch!"

"Don't call her that!"

"So that's the 'group' you mentioned. Has she got a bunch of useless AA members selling her jewelry at the art show? Oh, this is rich! Mike, she doesn't know you! She will never know you! But I do know you and I'll always be there."

"Lisa used to be an alcoholic and a drug addict. I told her about dad and how he drank and beat on us growing up—"

"What are you doing telling that bitch stories about our private life?"

"Stop calling her a bitch!"

"Those are personal stories, Mike! You had no right to tell a perfect stranger about what happened to us!"

"She's not a stranger!" Mike yelled. "You and me, we both have stories to tell! We lived in hell, Janie! Every second of every day was spent in fear of getting the shit kicked out of us. And when you moved out, you made sure you always had a bottle at the ready so you could drown yourself and not feel anything!"

"Stop it!"

"No!" Mike grabbed on to Jane's arm. "You gotta hear this! Part of you died growing up. Part of both of us died!

But we just kept digging holes inside of ourselves and burying it. But there comes a time when you can't stuff it inside any longer and pretend that it didn't count—that it didn't change you forever. That what happened didn't kill you." Mike's tears began to flow as he let go of Jane's arm. "As much as it hurts, I can't keep drowning in a bottle. I don't want to lie to myself anymore. I don't want to wake up and hate myself every fucking day. I'm thirty years old, Janie. I think it's time I stopped denying everything! I gotta take charge of my life. I need to find something wonderful in my life. And that's what I'm doing."

Jane turned to her brother, a pitiful look crossing her face. "Mike, this is an ugly, dark, awful world. It's full of people who want to destroy you. Can't you see that?"

Mike wiped away his tears. "There's beauty, Janie. There has to be."

A tear streamed down Jane's face. "No, Mike. There isn't."

Mike reached out to Jane, a profound sadness overwhelming him. "Oh, Janie. I'm so sorry you can only see the darkness. But I can't live like that anymore. I'm gonna find peace. I'd really like you to be part of it. But if you can't, then I'm doing it without you."

Jane stood still, completely unnerved. She'd lost control over the one person she had always been able to mold and dominate. "I have to go," she said, the strength sucked from her voice.

"Janie," Mike said, gently taking hold of Jane's arm. "Remember the other night when I told you about every time I make a wish, how I wish for freedom?"

"Yeah."

"I finally got my wish, Janie," Mike said, tears falling down his face. "And it's more than I ever dreamed about."

"I'm happy for you," she replied, not really knowing what to say.

"From now on, I'm wishing it for you."

Jane looked off into the distance, her heart empty. "Freedom? I have no idea what that means." She started toward her car.

"You're going away with that little girl, aren't you?" Mike said quickly. Jane kept her back turned and said nothing. "She's lucky to have you," Mike said earnestly. "I know that you won't let anything bad happen to her."

Jane closed her eyes tightly, steeling herself from that memory so long ago. She opened her car door when Mike called out to her.

"I love you, Janie!"

Without uttering a word, Jane got into her car and never looked back.

Jane spent Memorial Day packing her bags. Not knowing where she was going or for how long, she didn't know exactly what to bring. She filled one bag with clothes and a couple pair of shoes and a smaller bag with her collection of CD's. A third bag was crammed with piles of notes, yellow legal-size notepads and the sundry newspapers with feature articles on the Stover murder case. One of the newspapers sported both Jane and Chris' photos on the front page. When she caught sight of Chris' mug, she turned the paper over and stuffed it deep into the bag.

By noon, she finished packing and collapsed on the living room couch. The call from Weyler could come at any time. However, being a holiday weekend, Jane knew there was a good chance she and Emily would not be departing to their location until at least Tuesday. She couldn't tolerate just sitting still but she didn't want to go for a walk. She didn't want to watch television. She thought about downing a couple beers, but somehow the idea lost its appeal between the couch and the refrigerator. And so, she did the only thing she knew to do on a holiday weekend. She went to the firing range.

It was a way to focus, concentrate and blow off the compressed steam that was quickly building inside of her.

Jane always went to the same indoor range. It was located in the city of Englewood, southeast of where she lived. She was the only cop who frequented the place—a fact the owners of the firing range bragged about, but that her colleagues at DH always blasted. She wasn't going to frequent the cop bars so she sure as hell wasn't going to patronize the cop firing ranges.

Jane scanned the paper targets that were pinned behind the front desk. One drawing showed a lone male gunman pointing a weapon, another depicted two younger males pointing guns. A third target drawing caught her eye. "That's new," Jane said to Oscar, the owner of the range.

Oscar looked up at the drawing. "Yeah, we nicknamed that one 'The hostage.'"

Jane stared at it. The target showed a grizzled older man with one arm tightly around the neck of a frightened female hostage and the other hand pointing a large caliber gun at her head. The goal, of course, was to blow as many holes in the grizzled perp without touching the girl. "Give me a bunch of those." Jane said.

Once she was positioned in lane eleven—her favorite lane since it was farthest away from the other customers—Jane adjusted the protective ear cups and pinned her target on the screen in front of her. She drew out her pistol, laid it on the shelf and pushed the release button that drove the target six feet away, then twelve feet and finally twenty feet. Jane settled on twelve feet and focused. She stared at the target as she wrapped her fingers around the Glock. With split-second reflexes, Jane lifted the pistol and hammered a clip at the perp's head. She put down the gun and pushed the button, bringing the target closer. As it drew into view, she saw her handiwork: eight dead-on shots to the perp's forehead and two dead-on hits to the female hostage. "Shit," she said under her breath.

For the next hour, Jane replaced clean versions of the same hostage target and practiced at distances of six to twenty feet. As good a shot as she was, Jane kept nicking or nailing the hostage every time. She was just about to

put up another target when she felt two prying eyes behind her. Turning, she saw Sergeant Weyler on the other
side of the glass, motioning for her to come out and talk
to him.

"I figured there were three places to find you," Weyler
said as he met Jane outside the secured area. "Your house,
your brother's house or here."

"I could use about three more days of practice."

"Well, you're not going to get it. Let's go outside."

They walked outside and sat down on a bench. Jane lit
a cigarette as Weyler pulled a small pager from his jacket
pocket.

"This will be your only connection to me," Weyler said,
handing the pager to Jane. "It's one of those voice pagers.
I am the only one who has the number. If I page you, call
me back on a secure land line—preferably a pay phone."

Jane nodded, slipping the pager into her shirt pocket.
"So, where I am going?"

"Peachville, Colorado."

"You're joking!" was all Jane could muster.

"Do I look like I'm joking? It's a small town. The pop-
ulation is under three thousand—"

"Only if you count the dogs, cats and horses!" Jane
turned away trying to digest the news. "*Peachville?* The
town that celebrates fruit?"

"Better figure out a way to like it because it's going to
be your home for a bit."

"Exactly how long is 'a bit?'"

"Don't know. We're still going to be working the case
on this end. On your end, you'll have the child who will
hopefully continue to recall what happened that night.
Between the two of us, maybe we can wrap up this whole
thing in a month or two."

"A month or two?"

"Or three. I'm not putting a definite time on your stay."

Jane thought for a second. "What did you tell Chris
about my absence?"

"I haven't seen him. He's so maxed on overtime that

he's got to take several days off. By the time I tell him and the rest of DH of the situation, you'll be long gone."

"Well, good luck with Chris. He won't go down easy. Did you give a heads-up to Peachville's police about my presence?"

"The sheriff has jurisdiction there and, no, I didn't inform them. I don't want any leaks within their department that could end up compromising Emily's safety."

"What level of danger is Emily in?"

"I don't know. All I know is she's not safe in this city anymore."

Jane took a drag on her cigarette. "You don't think that there's any connection between that nutcase that Chris dragged in? The one with the Lawrence's silver cigarette case?"

"No. Like you said, whoever did this is smart and possibly a pro."

Jane took another puff on her cigarette. "Where are we living?"

"The DA's office has secured a rental house under the name 'Anne Calver.'"

Jane turned to Weyler, startled. "Anne Calver? That's my mother's name."

"I know. I ran across it in some of the old files from when your dad worked at DH. I can't have you using your real name. Protective custody means you alter everything, including names and relationships. I figured that Anne was a name you were more likely to respond to since you had some connection to it."

"Anne Calver," Jane mused.

Weyler handed Jane several stapled pages. "Here's the address of the house, how to get to the real estate office so you can get your house key and a map of the area. The individual from the DA's office who made the arrangements with the real estate company on your behalf—who, by the way, said she was a friend of yours—explained that you would be occupying the residence with your nine-and-a-half-year-old daughter."

Jane looked up from the papers and stared at Weyler. *"Daughter?"*

"Names *and* relationships must change—"

"Wait a minute. You said I was hiding out with the kid. Nothing was said about me pretending to be her mother! I should have a say in this! I mean, do I look like someone's mother?"

"You have to blend into the town, Jane. You want to avoid rumor and gossip. Easiest way to accomplish that is to make you mother and daughter. By the way, I didn't give Emily another first name because I wanted her to choose it. It's got to be a name that she responds to, so the two of you figure that out."

Everything was happening too fast for Jane. "Boss, we have to talk about this—"

"There's nothing to talk about. Anne Calver and her daughter are going to live in Peachville."

"And where in the hell is Mr. Calver?"

"I'll leave the details of your fabricated past up to you. He could be dead, you could be divorced or he could have been a one night stand. However, I would strongly consider against the one night stand option. This is Peachville, not Peyton Place."

"Have you informed Emily about this ruse?"

"Not yet. That's my next stop. I wanted to give her as much time to recuperate as possible before laying out the whole thing."

"You're expecting a helluva lot out of this kid! She loses her parents eight days ago and now she's being shuttled to some two-bit town and asked to call me 'Mom.' I'm sure your psychotherapist pals down at DH would have a field day with this one!"

"That kid is smart and you know it," Weyler countered. "I know that once I sit down with her and explain why we're doing this, she'll have no trouble playing the role. She already looks up to you as a protective figure. Calling you 'Mom' occasionally shouldn't be too difficult. You're just going to have to learn how to respond to it!" Weyler stood up. "We're shaking this thing down tomorrow morning at 8 a.m. sharp. I'll pick you up at the house and drive you to the drop point."

"I'm not driving my car?"

"No. I've secured a vehicle that we confiscated from a meth bust last year. It's the perfect cover for your new role."

"I'm more comfortable in my own car!"

"I can't have you zooming around Peachville in a '66 ice blue Mustang. You'd stick out like a sore thumb. Remember? *Blend* into the scenery. And circulate with the townsfolk. Let Emily play with the neighborhood children. But stay ever vigilant, with one eye on that child and the other eye out for any sign of trouble. Oh, leave your credit cards at home. I'll supply you with enough cash to get you through at least two months. And have your brother collect your mail and bring it down to DH once a week. We'll make sure all your bills are paid while you're gone."

"Any other orders, boss?" Jane asked, with a touch of sarcasm.

Weyler thought for a second. "Have you visited your father to say good-bye?" Jane shook her head. "Then you better get going. Visiting hours are up at eight." Weyler started to move toward his parked car but then turned back to Jane. He could see that the weight of the world was on her shoulders. "It's going to work out, Jane."

Jane looked off to the side. "You know what I find amazing, boss? You try to stay low your whole life and not stand out. But somehow the forces of the universe find you in the crowd and decide you're 'it.' And then for some unknown reason, they conspire against you until you either give up or give in."

Weyler was silent as he studied Jane's somewhat dejected body. "You want to know what *I* find amazing, Jane?"

"What?"

"How our fulcrum, the thing we hold onto and that gets

us through the day and night . . . how that thing often becomes our identity and is the one thing that can destroy us in the end."

The unannounced trip to visit her father went against her character. Whether she was going to his house or to the hospital, Jane always planned the visit days in advance. She needed time to get properly numbed in order to endure her father's wrath. But there she was sitting in her car outside the nursing home front door, sucking the nicotine out of every cigarette she had left in her pack. That familiar knot began to pull tighter in her stomach as she neared his open door. Cautiously, she moved forward and stood in the doorway. Her father was fast asleep in his bed with the television, tuned to Court TV, on mute. She stayed still and observed him. His head was awkwardly bent to the side and his mouth slightly parted. A prickly growth of beard covered his usually clean-shaven face. The razor-sharp buzz haircut was a little unkempt. His complexion was sallow and his cheeks slightly sunken. For the first time in her life, Jane felt a sliver of superiority in his presence. As quickly as she felt it, however, she wondered if the whole thing was some sort of trick and that he would suddenly awaken, bolt from the bed and attack her. It was that last thought that kept her positioned in the doorway.

"He's been sleeping on and off all day." Jane quickly turned to find Zoe, the head nurse, walking up to her. "It's not one of his better days," Zoe whispered to Jane, stealing a peek at Dale Perry's slumbering body.

"Okay," Jane whispered, "give him a message for me. I have to go away on business and I might be gone for a while. Tell him that—"

The clanging sound of a metal tray hitting the ground echoed through the hallway, startling Jane and rousing Dale.

"I guess you can tell him yourself," Zoe said turning to Dale. "Hello, Mr. Perry. Look who's here to see you!"

Zoe walked away, leaving Jane in the doorway. Dale squinted toward Jane.

"You gonna stay in the doorway?" Dale slurred in an acid tongue. Jane moved forward, stopping several feet from his bedside. "What in the hell are you doing here? If you want money, you're shit out of luck." Jane remained silent, standing stoically. Dale turned and watched the muted program on Court TV. "You pick up that stuff from the workshop like I asked you and give it to the boys at DH?"

"Yes."

Dale turned to Jane. "You didn't fuck with anything in that workshop, did you?"

Jane noticed his evil eye staring back at her, but somehow it didn't affect her. She felt a swell of indignity well up inside of her. "Why would I fuck with anything in there?" As the words came out, she realized how strong and unafraid they sounded.

Dale analyzed Jane. He tried to penetrate her being but his failing health made it difficult. "Don't use that asshole attitude on me. You know what it'll get you."

Jane moved closer to Dale's bed. "Why don't you tell me what it will get me?"

"You think you can fuck with me now. Is that what you came here to do?"

"No."

Dale checked out Jane's body language and realized she was not her usual fearful self. A slow smile, laced with a sneer, melted onto his lips. "I'll be in your head 'til the day you die." Dale waited for the words to sink in and watch his daughter's reaction. Jane stayed solid for a few seconds and then he could feel her beginning to doubt herself. "God, *you're so easy,*" he said with a delirious glint in his eye.

Jane felt herself slipping. "I'm going away," she blurted.

"Oh, yeah? Where?"

"It's confidential."

"Confidential?" Dale said with a heavy dose of mockery. "Well, let's see. It has something to do with that Lawrence double murder."

"Why would you say that?"

"The guys at DH keep me up to date with what's goin' on. You gotta hit the road after what went down two nights ago." Jane stiffened. She had no idea that Dale knew about Martha's murder. "You know, in all my years on the force, I never fucked up as bad as you did two nights ago." Jane couldn't argue with Dale's comment. She had been telling herself the same thing ever since it happened. "So, the Department is sending you away for a while." Dale surmised. "Or, maybe not just you. Maybe they're shoving the kid onto you. Yeah, that's how it works. That's how it *always* works."

Jane wasn't sure where she had lost control of the conversation but she knew that if she didn't get out soon, Dale would read her like an open book. "I have to go—"

"They're sending you away to some shithole small town," Dale declared with that same devious look in his eye. "They got you a house and they're giving you cash and they told you to 'blend in' for as long as it takes. What they didn't tell you is that you're walking into a fuckin' land mine."

Jane studied Dale's face. "What are you talking about?"

"It's gotten too messy. The whole Department will not be taken down because of your fuckup. Decisions had to be made." Dale's tone was succinct and brutal. "You take the two lambs and you sacrifice them for the good of the others."

Jane felt a shiver radiate down her spine. "That's not it at all."

"Don't be a fuckin' idiot, Jane. You mark my words. Something *will* go wrong. And you'll be all alone in some backwater town with no backup. Just you and that kid and the one who will finish the job."

Jane let Dale's words filter through her system. "What if I don't let that happen?"

"You think you got what it takes? You think you have the guts to point a loaded gun at someone and pull the trigger? Or would you rather just lay down and get the shit kicked out of you until you die?" Dale's eyes dissolved into a hateful glare. "Am I the only one who knows the answer to that question?"

# Chapter 16

Sleep was hard to come by the night before Jane's departure. No matter how much she tried to bar Dale's voice from her head, his words continually reverberated until she thought she'd go mad. "That's how it always works," he told her, referring to DH's relocation decision. What did he mean "always works?" Jane wondered. Was she really walking into a trap? Did DH have some hidden, sinister protocol for dealing with unruly cops? If so, who was behind it? Was it Sergeant Weyler? As much as Jane didn't want to pin Weyler with a secret agenda, she couldn't help but consider the possibility that he had some nefarious motive that Jane wasn't yet aware of. Behind that dapper, PBS-loving exterior could lurk a darker side. Jane recounted all the "connections" Weyler talked about—"connections with higher-ups" in the Department, "connections" with the DA's office. Just exactly who were these high-powered connections?

The more Jane pondered Weyler's behavior, the more questions she had. How was he able to pull off an overnight visit for a juvenile victim at the crime scene? That was strictly off the books. How did Weyler know exactly where to find Jane when he located her at the firing range? Was she that predictable in her comings and goings or was he having her followed? And then there

## Return Policy

With a sales r... any Barnes & Noble ...
will be iss... books (except ...
and ... audio made within (i) ...
my ...oble retail store (exc...
...th 7 days prior to the ...
...ery date for Barnes ...
will be issued for (i) ...
...rchases made via Pay...
prior to the date ...
within 60 days ...
within 14 d...
through ...
som...

...and unread books (except textbooks) and unopened
music/DVDs/audio made within (i) 14 days of purchase from a
Barnes & Noble retail store (except for purchases made by check
less than 7 days prior to the date of return) or (ii) 14 days of
delivery date for Barnes & Noble.com purchases (except for
purchases made via PayPal). A store credit for the purchase price
will be issued for (i) purchases made by check less than 7 days
prior to the date of return, (ii) when a gift receipt is presented
within 60 days of purchase, (iii) textbooks returned with a receipt
within 14 days of purchase, or (iv) original purchase was made
through Barnes & Noble.com via PayPal. Opened music/DVDs/
audio may not be returned, but can be exchanged only for the
same title if defective.

After 14 days or without a sales receipt, returns or exchanges will
not be permitted.

Magazines, newspapers, and used books are not returnable.
Product not carried by Barnes & Noble or Barnes & Noble.com will
not be accepted for return.

Policy on receipt may appear in tv. sections.

STR:2052 REG:008 TRN:1338 CSHR:Maggie S

BARNES & NOBLE MEMBER    EXP: 03/31/2011

Protector
9780981608747          N
(1 @ 7.99) Member Card 10% (0.80)        7.19
     7.19

                       N
                  10% (0.70)              6.29

was that pager he gave Jane outside of the firing range. He specifically told Jane that she was only allowed to contact him once she was in Peachville. Was that so only Weyler could feed her the information he chose to give her? And of course, his order not to tell anyone about where she was going. How convenient, she thought. She and the kid could end up dead and no one would know for weeks or possibly months. It could all be a string of innocent occurrences or it could be important clues that led to a fatal conclusion.

These were the troubling thoughts that haunted her throughout the night. And the more Jane fell into a pit of fear, the more her father's voice dominated.

*"You think you have the guts to point a loaded gun at someone and pull the trigger?"*

That was the one that stung. Jane's protective nature was ingrained into her being. It was not just something she did—it was who she was. She would protect someone at all costs, even if that meant dying in the process. But still, she hesitated long ago when she could have pulled the trigger. She let herself be tricked and paid a heavy price. Jane wanted to believe she had what it took to finish the job. She needed a guarantee that she could stand across from another human being and end their life in one millisecond. And if the person across from her ended up being Sergeant Weyler, Jane worried that she would repeat the identical outcome from years ago. If she allowed that to happen, it would end with her death. And after her demise, Emily would follow.

That sobering realization left her wide awake into the early morning hours. She stared at the radio next to her bed and turned it on, scanning the dial until she heard Tony Mooney's enigmatic voice. He was becoming a bad habit for Jane but something kept drawing her back to him.

"Welcome back to the second hour of the show. To all my soldiers of the star-soaked skies, doesn't it feel like déjà vu all over again?" Jane turned her head on the pillow and stared at the radio. "We're talking tonight about that giant web of unexplained interconnectedness that powers this solar system—that intricate and yet soul-specific generator that unites each of us with another. It's real, my friends. *Oh, yes.* It's *very* real. Your rational mind tells you it doesn't exist but your *heart*—which is your *true* mind—convinces you of its truth . . . It's the engine that drives our lives and dictates our evolution with another soul." Jane rolled over on her side, facing the radio. Mooney leaned closer to the microphone. "It's the unexplained bond between twins or a mother and her child. Like two hearts beating as one; two minds linked. Thoughts and realities, tightly interwoven like threads across the universe. We all experience it one time or another in our lives. It may only be for a brief moment or it can span a lifetime, but we all have the opportunity to dive into the pool of shared consciousness . . ."

Jane awakened at dawn. Filters of pink-tinged light radiated like fingers across her bedroom window. She turned to the right, expecting to see her clock but immediately felt disoriented. Jane lay on top of the covers and was catty-corner on the bed, her head resting in the bottom left corner of the mattress. Somehow in the night, she deduced, she must have gotten up and fallen back on top of the bed. The radio played low in the background, still on the same station that featured Tony Mooney's nightly program. Jane lifted her head. She felt drugged. It was worse than a hangover; she felt as if she'd run a marathon all night long.

Jane sat up and stared at the carpeting. Strewn across the floor were the stacks of legal-sized notepads, files of the Stover case and the newspapers that she'd stuffed into her bag for the trip. Her first nerve-wracking thought was that somebody had broken into the house during the night. Grabbing her Glock, Jane carefully made her way down the hallway and checked the front door. It was locked securely from the inside. Looking around the living room, nothing was askew. An icy quiver crept up her spine as she returned to her bedroom and stared at the chaotic splay of coveted case information. Setting the Glock on the bureau, she knelt down and collected the newspapers, files and notepads, replacing them in her duffel bag. Looking over to the side, just under the bed, she saw the corner of a yellow legal notepad. She pulled it toward her and felt an odd sense of recollection. A blur of images suddenly raced before her eyes. There was a flash of blinding light followed by the blistering outline of a Glock followed by the millisecond likeness of a wolf's face. Jane shook her head backward and the visions ceased. She thought the insanity was over—a lingering side effect of booze-fueled binges. But she was stone cold sober and the same bizarre, unrelated visual imprints had returned. Jane paged through the yellow notepad until she came upon the unexplained rudimentary drawing of the wolf's face and the two words, WOLF FACE, all in capitals. She still didn't remember drawing it—a fact that continued to disturb her. It was the last entry in the notepad. At least, it was to her knowledge. Jane turned the page. There, filling the next lined page was another crude drawing. This one depicted the palm of someone's left hand. Imprinted across the palm were numbers.

Jane stood up and held the notepad up to the mirror, revealing **10-24-99**. It seemed to obviously be a date but it held no significance to Jane. She stared at the drawing, realizing again that she was the elementary artist. Staring back at the floor, Jane surmised that she unexplainably awoke, rummaged through her bag and for some unknown reason, drew a picture of a hand with a backward date before collapsing on top of her bed. Cautiously, she checked out the remaining pages of the notepad and found them blank. "Oh, God," Jane whispered. "Please make it stop."

Jane waited until Mike was well on his way to work before leaving a message on his tape. Attempting to sound as ordinary and offhand as possible, she asked him to pick up her mail and take it to Weyler, per his instructions. She paused, trying to formulate some suitable good-bye, not knowing when or if she would ever return from her covert trip to that small-town, netherworld of Colorado known as Peachville. But before she spoke, Mike's machine abruptly cut her off.

The vehicle pulled up in front of Jane's house. Peering outside, she saw Weyler getting out of a car. Securing her shoulder holster and Glock, Jane grabbed her bags and turned around to face her living room. She gazed around the room and drank it in. If it was really good-bye, she wanted to etch the memory in her mind. Jane opened her front door just as Weyler walked up to the porch.

"Give you a hand?" Weyler asked, reaching for Jane's luggage.

"Sure." Jane felt her body tighten. Whether warranted or not, she regarded her boss with a modicum of suspicion.

Weyler trotted down the pathway and unlocked the hatchback of a station wagon. Jane walked toward the car with angst written across her face. "What's this?"

"This is your new car."

"Oh, dear God. Tell me you're kidding."

"It's almost a brand-new Subaru Outback wagon." Weyler slammed the hatchback shut. Jane moved closer, her mouth slightly agape. "It's not as bad as you're making it out, Jane. It's got cruise control, a sunroof and a CD player."

"Really?" Jane said, still not believing she was expected to drive what she considered to be a boring, cookie-cutter, assembly-line car. "Wow, I just got a chill."

"Save your sarcasm, would you?"

"What? I'm thrilled you decided you give me a vehicle that goes from zero to forty in no time flat! Where's the dog?" Jane asked.

"The dog?"

"Don't golden retriever/lab mixes usually come with the purchase of any Subaru wagon? I need a dog to complete the picture of the perfect single mom with her kid."

"Are you done?"

Jane walked around the rear of the wagon and noted a series of stickers on the bumper. One was a cheerful blue-and-white sticker that proclaimed "I Brake For Butterflies!" Another read "Love Mother Earth" while still another urged people to recycle and save trees. "Where did you say you got this car?"

"It was part of a drug confiscation. The woman was a 52-year-old meth dealer."

"A *meth* dealer owned this car? Well, glad to know there's one meth dealer out there who brakes for butterflies."

"We do need to get going." Weyler slid his angular body into the car as Jane followed. "We're meeting Emily at a drop point out by the old Stapleton Airport. I've asked one of the patrol officers to drive her there."

"How is she?" Jane asked, carefully choosing her words.

"Physically, she seems to be quite well. Emotionally, she's still shaken up. But I'm sure once she sees you, she'll calm down." Jane pulled out a cigarette. "I'd appreciate it if you wouldn't smoke while I'm in the car," Weyler stated.

Jane put the cigarette back in the pack and looked out the window as Weyler drove down Milwaukee Street. She debated how to handle their time together. She would have to tread a tenuous line between treating him like her boss and addressing him as if he were a suspect. More than anything, if Weyler was involved in a covert police deal, Jane wanted to make sure that she didn't let on. "So," Jane said, "does this happen a lot?"

"How do you mean?"

Jane kept looking out the window. She knew if her eyes met Weyler's, she could possibly give herself away. "You know, have there been instances in the past when detectives have had to lay low with a witness?"

"There's been a few," Weyler said, adjusting the rear-view mirror.

"I see. Do you pick the same town each time?"

"That's confidential information."

"Uh-huh," Jane responded, feeling very uneasy. While it wasn't in her to petition someone or beg them for forgiveness, somehow she felt that perhaps a last minute appeal might help. "You know, boss, I know I haven't been the model cop for a while. And I can understand if you . . ." Jane searched for the right words, "if you were so pissed off that you decided to teach me some sort of lesson—"

"This is not about teaching you any lesson, Jane—"

"I'm just saying if it were, so be it. But Emily doesn't deserve to be dragged into some sort of mess because of me." Jane knew if she went any further, Weyler would become too suspicious.

"As long as you do as I asked, you'll be fine." Weyler's response sounded oddly tart to Jane. "Keep the pager on and only call me when you absolutely have to. I'll do the same. Remember, do everything you can to blend in."

Jane's ears perked up at the same words her father repeated the night before. "Blend in. Right." Jane tried to shake off a sense of foreboding. "You talk to Chris?"

"No. He left a message on my voice mail that he was heading back to Lake Dillon. He mentioned something about having some guy up there install a more powerful motor on his new boat."

"A new motor? What kind of money are you paying this guy?"

"Between his overtime and off-duty jobs, he's putting in pretty good bank."

"Too bad he can't afford a personality," she muttered under her breath.

"He's going to be gone for another day or so unless his allergies kick up again. It seems good, clean mountain air always stirs up that rash of his."

"I've always said, he operates better in filth." Jane bit her lip. If Weyler was part of a corrupt police faction,

Jane's cutting words could come back on her. She quickly decided to change the subject.

"You ever pursue that idea of following the protection money in the Stover case?"

"Not yet. I've been a bit occupied."

"You know, it's a valid possibility that should be looked into. If we follow that trail, maybe we can find some common denominators."

"I can tell you right now that the most common denominator you're going to find is the Texas mob and then it always comes to a screeching halt."

"But maybe by questioning other businesses we could discover a link to a specific individual who—"

"Jane, I understand your desire to solve the Stover case. But right now, I need you to focus on the case in front of you. You see my briefcase?" Weyler asked.

Jane looked around to the backseat. "Yeah."

"There's a manila envelope in there with copies of the Lawrence crime scene photos. I made a set for you. Put it in your bag. Next to it, you'll find another envelope. There's five thousand dollars in it. Your rent on the house has been prepaid so that money should be enough to cover living expenses for you and the child."

Jane collected the two envelopes from Weyler's briefcase. As she slipped them into her leather satchel, two questions crossed her mind. How far in advance had the rent been paid on her house and how long was five thousand dollars supposed to last? "So, this is gonna cover everything I need?" Jane probed, trying to discern more information. "I don't want to suddenly come up short—"

"Don't worry," Weyler said, looking straight ahead. "You won't."

Jane didn't know what to make of Weyler's last comment. But even if she could have figured out a clever response, it wouldn't have mattered. Weyler turned a corner near the old Stapleton Airport and pulled up behind a parked, tan sedan. He turned off the motor and handed the keys to Jane. She started out of the car when

Weyler put his hand on her arm. "Whatever happens over there, whatever may come to pass, I want you to realize that it's not about blame anymore. It's about the job. You understand?"

Jane couldn't look at him. Her heart raced as a wave of rage welled inside. If she and Emily were being led to the slaughter, she had no intention of being knocked off without a good fight. "Yeah, boss, I understand." Jane said, with a defiant tone.

Jane and Weyler exited the Subaru. Almost simultaneously, Emily and the patrol officer got out of their vehicle. Emily stood by the side of the unmarked sedan, her Starlight Starbright navy blue, vinyl case clutched in one hand. She was dressed in a short-sleeved cotton dress with pictures of tiny daffodils plastered all over it. A gauze bandage covered the left side of her injured temple. To Jane, the kid looked as though she had been through a war and was the last soldier standing. Emily's face lit up when she saw Jane. In turn, Jane felt a sense of comfort when she locked eyes with the child.

Weyler conferred with the patrol officer as Jane walked over to Emily. "Hi."

"Hi," Emily replied with a soft smile.

"How are you feeling?"

"I'm okay. It only hurts a little. I can get the stitches out in ten days."

"Good." Jane glanced over at Weyler, who was still talking to the officer. She bent closer to Emily. "They explain everything to you?" Emily nodded. "You cool with this?"

"I guess."

"Alright." Jane patted Emily on the shoulder

"So, when are we leaving, Jane? I mean . . ." Emily struggled a bit. "*Mom?*"

Jane was caught off guard. "Look, you don't have to do that when it's just you and me. That's just for when we're in public. Where are your bags?"

"In the backseat." Emily seriously considered Jane's

words. "The thing is, if I only call you 'Mom' in public and 'Jane' when we're alone, I might forget and say 'Jane' when I should say 'Mom.' So, maybe I should call you 'Mom' all the time."

Weyler walked to the car as Jane pulled Emily's bags out of the car. "Ready?"

"Ready." Jane turned to Emily. "We'll talk about this later." Emily walked around the Subaru, leaving Weyler and Jane alone. "This whole 'mom' thing is ridiculous," Jane said confidentially to Weyler.

"It's important you play the part so we don't raise any suspicion. Treat it no differently than any of the under-cover roles you've played. You played that hooker way back when you were on patrol and some cops still talk about how realistic you were."

"A hooker and a mom. The only similarity is that it takes a big trick to pull them off successfully." Jane lugged Emily's luggage to the wagon and tossed it in the backseat. Emily sat in the front seat, her seat belt already fastened across her. She held open her Starlight Starbright vinyl case and looked longingly at several family photos.

Weyler held his hand out to Jane. "Good luck." Jane eyed him briefly before shaking his hand. She had reached a point where she wasn't sure of her own ability to judge another human being. Standing there with Weyler on that isolated dirt road, she wondered if she was shaking hands with her friend or her executioner. She looked over at Emily, still engrossed in her photographs. She surmised that from this moment on, it was the two of them against the world. Their ultimate survival would depend entirely on Jane's ability to stay focused, resolute and constantly on guard. "What route are you taking?" Weyler asked.

Jane opened the driver's side door. If Weyler was trying to garner more information so he could have some-body follow, Jane was damned if she was going to freely supply it. "Not sure. I was thinking I might go by way of Utah. Or maybe I'll go to Kansas first. I want to keep that mystery alive." Jane hoped that he would catch her drift that she was onto him. But all he did was turn away and smile.

"Just make sure you get there before five o' clock," Weyler said, walking to the sedan. "The real estate woman has to give you the house key. Her name is Kathy. Apparently, she's real perky and friendly over the phone. I know the two of you will hit it off like sorority sisters." Weyler's last sentence dripped with sarcasm. He got into the sedan and pulled away in a cloud of dust and gravel.

Jane got into the Subaru and secured her seat belt. She looked around the dash and then up at the closed sunroof. "Pathetic," she mumbled to herself.

"I'm glad you told me to keep these photos nearby."

"Why's that?"

Emily looked at the photos, brushing her finger across her dad's face. "That was a good day." Emily brightened a bit.

Jane reached into the backseat and pulled out her bag filled with CDs. "We've got a five hour drive ahead and we need the right tunes to get us there." Jane quickly lit a cigarette as she searched through the CDs.

"You know," Emily said carefully, referring to Jane's cigarette. "That's not good for my health."

"Yes. But forcing me *not* to smoke would be even *more* detrimental to your health." Jane rolled down the windows to let the smoke escape.

Emily pulled out a couple of the CDs. "Who's Joe Cocker?"

"You're kidding, right?"

"Is he any good?"

"Kid, if you don't feel this in your toenails, there's something wrong with you." Jane popped in Cocker's *Mad Dogs and Englishmen* CD. "Let's rattle this wagon." Jane turned on the ignition, turned up the volume on "Cry Me a River" and peeled down the road.

She headed westbound on Interstate 70. Her need for

extreme speed was only tempered by how fast the Subaru could climb the passes and take the curves. They stopped at the 11,000 foot Summit rest area so Jane could use the bathroom. While Jane ducked in to use the facilities, Emily stood outside and took in the high altitude view. It was one of those clear, late May days in the Colorado high country where patches of spring snow still stuck stubbornly to the north-facing grassy hills. Emily was drawn to a mound of snow nearby the restroom. She poked at the icy remains until she touched something hard. Carefully, she pulled the object out of the snow and found a metal bracket with a bright red edge of color encircling it. The object had fallen off someone's ski binding and wedged in the layers of ice. Emily examined the metal trinket, watching the sun bounce off of it. She was mesmerized by this seemingly innocuous find, and, within seconds, she fell into a trancelike state as the sun-lit glare reflected onto her face. Her heart beat faster and her breathing became labored. A well-defined sense of fear grabbed hold of her and yet she couldn't pull her eyes away from the penetrating glare. The feeling of doom strengthened. Then out of nowhere . . . "Emily?"

Emily spun around, her eyes wide as saucers, as the metal bracket flew out of her hand. Jane stood behind her, equally startled by the child's exaggerated response. For a split second, Emily was blinded by the sunlight and unable to make out Jane's face. In that second of time, Emily could swear that a large, indistinguishable man was standing over her.

"Emily?" Jane said concerned. "What is it?" At the sound of Jane's voice, Emily was slammed back into reality. She rushed forward and wrapped her arms around Jane's hips. "Emily, what happened?" Jane asked, canvassing the immediate area. The child grabbed Jane with an even tighter grip and mumbled indistinguishable words. "*Emily!*" Jane peeled the kid off of her. She knelt down on one knee so she could be on eye level.

"Did somebody bother you?"

"No," the child responded in a confused tone, still somewhat out of her body.

"Why are you shaking?"

"I don't know," Emily said, bewildered. "I saw that piece of metal in the snow and something happened. It was like I was somewhere else but I couldn't see anything. I just felt scared." Jane looked down and let out a deep sigh. "I'm not making it up!" Emily said, misinterpreting Jane's reaction.

Jane looked Emily in the eye. "I know you're not. Trust me. I know."

The two drove off, continuing their journey west on I-70. There was almost thirty minutes of silence until Emily spoke up. "Why are there bad people in this world?"

"I don't know," Jane said, lighting another cigarette and cracking the window.

"Have you met a lot of bad people?"

"Yeah."

"How many?"

"More than I can count." Jane took a hard drag.

Emily looked out the window as they descended down the mountain and into the Eagle River Valley. "Did you ever kill someone?"

"You already asked me that question. I'm not answering it. I don't want you thinking about stuff like that. All you have to do is get up in the morning, eat three meals, play with your toys and go to bed at night."

"I need to know you can if you have to . . ." Emily insisted.

Jane pulled onto the wide shoulder of the highway, bringing the Subaru to a stop. "A long time ago, I pointed a gun at someone. It was someone who deserved to die. You talk about bad, this guy was the definition of the word. A lot of people suffered because of what he did. I knew his death would make the suffering stop. I wasn't worried what would happen to me, because once he was out of the picture, I figured the world would be a better place. I had my finger on the trigger and I was going to do it . . ." Jane stopped, briefly reliving that moment.

"But you didn't?" Emily said quietly.

Part of Jane was still back in the workshop. "But I didn't."

Emily felt queasy. "What stopped you?"

Jane turned to Emily. "I was young and stupid. If I'd known then what I know now about how the world works, I wouldn't have hesitated a second. But I promise you, if it ever comes to that point again, I will not hesitate. You have my word."

They continued down I-70 for another hour before stopping for lunch in Glenwood Springs. On the way back to the car, Emily gazed longingly in the window of *Glenwood Shoe Service* at a pair of red cowboy boots. They got gas and headed down Highway 82, then took the turnoff at the town of Carbondale to Highway 133. For the next sixty-five miles, Jane drove through territory splashed with breathtaking, blue sky vistas, lush meadows and the occasional pasture of grazing cows. Jane always smiled to herself when she got into the far corners of Small Town, USA, because there was sure to be the obligatory trampoline stationed either in the front or backyard of the houses. It didn't matter where she traveled in America, that enormous trampoline could always be spotted from the highway. And it wasn't just one house; you could count dozens of them in the space of several hours. It was one of those mysteries of life that tugged at Jane. What started the trend? Why a trampoline? Was there some unconscious desire by these country dwellers to jump higher and higher until they touched the clouds and never came back down to their small-town existence?

Jane left the land of trampoline houses and drove toward the summit of McClure Pass. The white, chalk-barked aspen trees stood at attention, displaying their early summer explosion of quivering green leaves amidst slopes of cow parsnip and fuzzy mullein stalks. Jane slid open the sunroof as Emily held her hands against the stiff wind current. Thirty miles down the two-lane mountain road, construction crews were busy filling potholes. Jane's speedy journey came to an abrupt halt behind a truck hauling a horse trailer.

"You told me you were thirty-five and one quarter, right?"

"Uh-huh."

"When are you turning thirty-six?"

"January 11."

Emily did the calculations in the air with her finger. "That means you gave birth to me when you were twenty-five almost tweny-six." Jane regarded Emily with a questionable look. "If somebody asks, we have to get our stories straight."

"No one is going to ask you how old I was when I gave birth to you."

"Sergeant Weyler said you were taking me to a small town. People are nosy in small towns. That's what my mommy always said."

"Don't worry about it, Emily—"

"Where's your husband?"

"I have no idea."

"Shouldn't we make up a story so when people come to our house—"

"People come to the house? Hey, I'm not hosting social events!"

"Sergeant Weyler said we had to act normal—"

"Well, normal for me is not having a bunch of busy-bodies in my house."

"What if I want to invite somebody over?"

"That's tricky. My gut instinct tells me to keep people away from the house."

"What does your gut say about your husband?"

"Christ," Jane lit a cigarette. "Let's just take him out of the picture."

"He's dead?"

"Yeah, he's dead."

"Okay." Emily sat back and really thought about it. "How'd he die?"

"I don't know, he . . ." Jane looked at the trailer hauling the horses in front of her. "He got stomped on by a horse and died."

"That doesn't happen a lot."

"It can if you work the rodeo circuit," Jane said offhandedly.

"Was he a rodeo clown?"

"Oh, *please!* I would never marry a rodeo clown! I married the rodeo cowboy!"

"So you married a rodeo cowboy who fell off his horse, got stomped and died."

"There you go. End of story."

Emily considered the event. "Were you there when it happened?"

"Oh, shit. No! I wasn't there and neither were you. He was traveling on the rodeo circuit when it happened. In *Canada.*"

"Canada?"

"Yeah. It happened during the Calgary Stampede."

"So he died in the stampede?"

"Right. He got stomped in the stampede."

"In Canada?"

"*In Canada.*"

"So . . . was the funeral in Canada?"

"Emily, enough!"

The highway flagger waved the string of vehicles onward. Emily sat back and considered the entire phony story. "I sure hope they buy it."

Within the hour, Jane crested onto the mesa that overlooked the little town of Peachville. She pulled to the side and looked across the verdant valley. "Well, kid, say hello to your temporary new home."

"Hello."

"By the way, my boss decided to change my name to Anne Calver while we're here. That was my mom's maiden name."

"It's a pretty name."

"Yeah," Jane replied, a bit taken aback. "Anyway, your last name will be Calver while we're here, but you've gotta come up with a new first name for yourself."

"Gosh . . ." Emily pursed her lips, taking the assignment very seriously.

"It's got to be a name that you'll respond to. Maybe a name of a relative—"

"Patty," Emily said softly. "That's what my dad called my mom. You used your mommy's name and I'll use mine."

Jane nodded. "Okay, Patty Calver. Let's go get our house key."

# Chapter 17

Jane drove down the mesa that overlooked Peachville. Just outside of town on the rural highway loop, she slowed the Subaru to a stop. Emily gazed into the southeast and pointed out a blackened side of the far mountain range. Jane squinted into the distance. "You've got good eyes. That's the backside of the coal mine. Peachville has two industries: fruit and coal mining. There's a coal train that comes through here at night." Jane punched the Subaru into gear and drove down the hill that turned into Peachville's Main Street. A row of tiny, pastel houses lined one side of the road. A quick glance showed that the ubiquitous backyard trampoline could be spotted behind a few of the cookie-cutter homes. Jane slowed to a crawl as she came up behind a worn-out, Ford pickup truck that strolled at the approved twenty mph speed limit. "God help me," Jane mumbled. She could feel the noose tightening around her neck as she crept down Main Street. They passed Peach Street, Apple Court, Cherry Lane and Apricot Terrace.

This town that celebrated fruit also made a point to habitually name almost every shop and business with a fruity moniker. There was The Apple Cart, a hardware/gas station/convenience/video store, The Mountain Melon Market, a small supermarket that had eight aisles and felt a need to advertise the installation of "a brand-new frozen food section," *The Peachville Gazette*, a weekly newspaper that boasted an amazing 3,000 subscribers, The Orange Squeeze, a tourist trap that sold old postcards and camera supplies, and The Pit, a tiny movie theater. Across the street stood The Lemon Grill, a "high end" restaurant for Peachville as opposed to The Harvest Café—the down-home, vinyl tablecloth, greasy spoon where townsfolk congregated. Squashed in the middle of all this was the small, brick building that housed the County Sheriff. Jane made a special note of its location, quickly surveyed the structure and privately wondered if it resembled the fictional Mayberry Sheriff's headquarters, complete with two empty cells and an inept deputy. Finally, at the end of Main Street, stood Peachville Properties, the real estate office that served as the sole source for ranches, farms and rental units. Jane parked in front of Peachville Properties and turned to Emily. "Okay, let's keep this simple. I want to get in and out of here without a lot of talking."

A happy little bell attached to the front door signaled Jane and Emily's entrance. The white walled business was neat and smelled of rose potpourri and a fresh print run of the latest Peachville Properties Home & Farm Guide.

A young, bright-eyed girl approached Jane. "Can I help you two?"

"I'm looking for Kathy. She's holding a rental house for us. I need the key."

Jane's attention was drawn to the back corner of the office where a woman in her early thirties was talking on the phone and excitedly waving at Jane.

"She's just finishing up with a client," the girl said. "You can have a seat—"

"We'll stand, thank you," Jane said abruptly.

Kathy hung up the phone and sashayed around her desk. She was dressed in a pink skirt and matching blazer. Underneath the blazer was a simple white blouse that displayed a delicate gold necklace around her thin, ivory neck. Jane noted that Kathy's fingernail polish perfectly matched her pink blazer. Her hair was chin length, light brown and shellacked with so much hair spray that Jane figured it would take a Category 4 Hurricane to blow one hair out of place. While her facial features were ordinary, one could not help but be drawn to Kathy's wide, toothy grin that overwhelmed her narrow face. Kathy rapidly walked across the room, her arm outstretched toward Jane for a full twenty feet before reaching her. "Well, hello you two travelers! *Welcome to Peachville!* You must be Anne!" Kathy enthusiastically shook Jane's hand and then turned to Emily. "And you are?"

"Patty . . ." Emily said, haltingly, "Calver . . ."

"Well, good to meet you, Patty! How was your trip?"

"It was fine," Jane replied.

"You know, I don't even know where you two were coming from! When your girlfriend called to arrange the rental unit, I forgot to ask."

Jane realized the intrusion was already beginning. It made no difference where they came from, but somehow, it was vital information. "The Denver area."

"Oh, my goodness!" Kathy said with an exaggerated expression on her face. "Well, you two travelers must be tired!"

Jane pulled her hair away from her face with her band-aged hand. "Yeah, we're pretty *whipped*. You have the house key?"

"Oh, dear!" Kathy said, her eyes pinned on Jane's bandage. "What happened to your hand?"

"It's nothing. Burned it in the kitchen."

"An unfortunate cooking accident?" Kathy inquired. Emily stifled a laugh at the word "cooking." "Did I say a funny?"

"Just the cooking part," Jane said. "I'm not exactly Martha Stewart."

"Well, honey, we can do somethin' about that!" Kathy exclaimed. "A group of us girls get together every

Wednesday evening at a different gal's house and we trade recipes, dish the dirt and it's so much fun! We'd *love* for you to join us!"

"Oh, you know, I—"

"If you're worried about child care, bring Patty with you. I've got a daughter who is ten. I bet you girls would get on just like two peas in a pod!"

"Well, I—"

"Say you'll think about it," Kathy instructed, not giving Jane much choice.

Jane wanted out of that place. "We'll think about it," she said rigidly.

Kathy bent down to get closer to Emily's eye level. "Well, now sweetheart, tell me, what are you all bandaged up for?"

Emily started to respond when Jane quickly interjected, "She fell." There was an awkward moment of silence between the three of them. As soon as she said it, Jane realized that her spitfire response sounded forced.

Kathy looked up at Jane and then back to Emily. "Well, my, my, my. That's a big bandage for a little girl. Must have been quite a fall—"

Emily started to respond when Jane once again broke in. "She fell off her bike." Emily looked at Jane, not knowing what to say or do. "It was a tall bike," Jane added.

There was another awkward slice of silence between them as Kathy studied Emily's face. "Well, I know what will make you a happy girl." Kathy turned to Jane. "Mom, what's her favorite candy?"

Jane stood perplexed. Not only was this perky woman referring to her as "mom," but she was also asking a question that Jane couldn't answer. She turned to Emily. "What's your favorite candy?"

Kathy was slightly dumbstruck. "Oh, you're teasing me. Every mom knows what kind of candy their kids like!"

"Mounds," Emily quickly interjected in an attempt to rescue Jane's faux pas.

Kathy bent down toward Emily, "Well, this is your lucky day. If you go over to the front window, you'll find a big bowl of candy. And I bet if you dig around in there, you will find your favorite!" Emily crossed to the window and began rooting the Mounds out of the bowl. "Did she have to get stitches?" Kathy whispered.

"Yes," Jane whispered. "Why are we whispering?"

"I didn't want the child to think we're talking about her," Kathy said, her voice still in a half-whisper.

"She's not embarrassed about the stitches." Jane's voice leveled back to normal. "Now, if you don't mind, we're really tired."

"Of course," Kathy said, her toothy grin exploding across her face. "I'll get your key!" She scurried back to her desk and returned with two keys. "Here's one for you and one for under the mat! Of course, I have to tell you that no one in this town locks their doors. Or their cars. Or their tractors. Or anything!"

"Really?" Jane said, doing her best to squash her innate cop reflex. "Well, you oughta have your Chamber of Commerce publicize that fact so that all the burglars on the Western Slope can hit your town one night."

Kathy didn't understand Jane's response but she still erupted into a big, phony laugh. "That's a *funny!* Oh, say, I put together a little information packet for you." Kathy handed Jane a small envelope. "This'll give you the skinny on everything you need to know about our fruit festivals and community events as well as addresses and phone numbers for doctors and dentists and all that good stuff! There's also some 'Howdy!' coupons in the front from the merchants in town. When you're ready to hook up your telephone, just call this number—"

"We're not going to have a phone," Jane interrupted.

Kathy was caught off guard. "No phone? Well, that's . . . different."

Jane thought fast. "I have a cell phone with a great calling plan." It was a complete lie; Jane had a pager strapped to her waist and nothing else.

"Wow," Kathy searched for the proper response. "That's . . . so 21st century! Anyway, this little booklet has oodles of information. In the back, there's a section on our school system and the deadlines for enrollment." Jane's gut tightened. School was a good two or three months away. She was tempted to ask Kathy how long the lease on the rental house was prepaid. But she knew if she asked that, it would look strange. "It's super easy to find your house," Kathy said with giddy enthusiasm as she directed them to their rental across from the town park. "I don't mean to gab and rush off, but I've got to get over to Apple Cart Hardware. They're fixing a gash in our trampoline."

Jane and Emily drove back up Main Street in search of their new house. "That didn't go well," Emily said.

"What do you mean?"

"We should have figured out a story about my bandage before we went in. I don't think she believed you when you said I fell off my bike."

"Who gives a shit?" Jane lit a cigarette and rolled down the window.

"And the candy! Moms *know* what kind of candy their kids like!"

"Forget about it!"

"I think we should both make a list. On one side it says what we like and on the other side it says what we don't like. Then we trade lists and we memorize them."

"That's too much work."

"You can leave out the stuff I already know. Like 'I don't know how to cook.'"

"I could cook if I wanted to! I just don't have any interest in it. God invented frozen food for a reason. And restaurants? And pizza delivery?"

"God also invented kitchens, stoves, frying pans and food to put in them!"

"Emily, this is a battle you are not going to win. You're not gonna starve! We'll eat out and you can bring home the leftovers. Then the next day, we can warm up the leftovers and you'll feel like you're eating a home cooked meal."

"You mean a home *warmed* meal?"

"Don't push it, kid. And don't fret about what Kathy thinks. She's a nosy broad."

"I think she's pretty. She has a lot of teeth. Am I going to school here?"

Jane couldn't believe how fast the subject changed. "No."

"What happens if school starts and we're still—"

"Emily, this is just a temporary deal before you go to Wyoming."

"Okay," Emily said, slightly uneasy.

Jane spotted the town park on the right side and turned left into the driveway of the rental house. It was a small one-story wooden structure, painted white with violet trim. Two cottonwood trees provided full shade on either side of the central path that led to the front door. A white picket fence surrounded the freshly mowed front lawn.

"It looks nice," Emily said earnestly.

Jane looked around the area, noting the park across the street. "I wish they hadn't stuck us on Main Street and across from the park. This is 'laying low?'"

"What's laying low?"

"Staying under the radar. Blending in." Jane looked into her rearview mirror. A white Ford-150 truck was parked across the street. The single male occupant was slightly obscured as he sat back in the front seat eating a sandwich and listening to the country radio station. Jane turned around to read the signage on the driver's door.

"What is it?" Emily asked.

"I'm trying to read what that says," Jane said, squinting.

Emily turned around. "It says, 'Just Call Dan— 24-Hour Home . . . Main. . . . Main . . .'"

"Maintenance," Jane said. "So why in the hell is he sitting there?"

"He's eating lunch."

"It's way past lunch."

"Is something wrong?"

Jane turned back around. She recalled Chris' comment, "Just because people call you paranoid does not erase the fact that certain other people aren't out to get you!" Jane accused Chris of being paranoid and now she was proving to have the same behavior. Furthermore, she worried her paranoia was causing her to turn everything into a conspiracy and everyone into a conspirator. But still, it was her job to keep her eyes open to anything and anyone. "Let's wait here and see what he does."

"I have to go to the bathroom."

"Can't you hold it?"

"I don't think so."

Jane looked into the rear vision mirror and assessed the situation before they got out of the Subaru and headed toward the front door. The sound of a ringing cell phone could be heard coming from the parked truck. Jane spun around. The man inside the truck answered the phone and said, "I can be there in five minutes." With that, he turned on his ignition. A loud, whistling sound emitted from his engine as he put the truck in gear.

Emily turned to face the truck. The whistling sound drew her in as a trancelike expression descended. In her head, the whistling sound melted into a bloodcurdling, high-pitched scream. Her eyes filled with fear.

"Emily?" Jane said, unlocking the front door.

Emily slipped out of her daze. "Did you hear someone screaming?"

"Screaming?" Jane regarded Emily with care. "No, that's his truck whistling."

"Right. The truck." Emily tried to rectify what she heard as the truck sped up Main Street toward the mesa.

Jane entered the house followed closely by Emily. The place was outfitted with sturdy furniture, some of which looked as though it had seen better days. The walls were covered with framed prints of birds, paintings of fruit and needlepoint landscapes safely pressed between glass. A narrow hallway greeted them and led directly to a small bedroom. If you walked down the hall to the right, you'd find the only bathroom in the house. The living room was to the left of the front door. Just past the living room was a short hallway that led into the kitchen, which was decorated in bright shades of yellow. To the right of the front door was a hall closet and smaller bedroom with a window that overlooked the front yard.

The place felt like a tight box to Jane. But still, the house was clean and appeared to be well taken care of by the owners. While Emily went to the bathroom, Jane checked out the aged radio console next to the television. Scanning the dials, she discovered only a handful of static-free stations, only one of which featured a talk radio format. No chance of tuning in the velvet-voiced Tony Mooney late at night when she couldn't sleep, Jane thought to herself. Turning on the old television, Jane was greeted with one snowy picture after another.

"What's wrong with the TV?" Emily said, bouncing back into the room.

"It seems we have an amazing three channels to choose from. But before you get too excited, Channel 5 is the crop report, Channel 2 is the weather report and Channel 7 seems to be one of the networks. But that's only an assumption since there's no picture on Channel 7, just sound. So, basically, this thing is one big radio."

Jane and Emily dragged their bags into the house and did "Rock, Paper, Scissors" to determine who got the back bedroom down the hallway. Jane, as always, won the game. Checking the refrigerator, Jane found a lonely box of baking soda. The shelves were also bare, save for canisters of salt and pepper, a frying pan, two saucepans and assorted mismatched silverware. Jane jotted down a list of items to purchase at the local market.

"Hey, Jane!" Emily excitedly yelled from the backyard area. Opening the sliding glass door that led into the tiny backyard, Jane found Emily pointing eagerly across a thicket of tall grass. "I hear a creek running!" Emily said with adventurous eyes. "Let's go find out where it is!"

"Emily—"

"*Pleeeeese.*"

Jane surveyed the area and reluctantly trailed off into the tall grass with Emily. After about ten feet of wading through waist-high field grass and the occasional prickly bull thistle, the two emerged into a verdant, wildflower filled, soggy meadow that spanned a good seven acres. Emily ran ahead of Jane, skipping across the ground and picking a handful of wildflowers.

"I found the creek!" Emily yelled out. "And it leads into a huge lake!" Jane caught up with Emily and followed the creek around a bend of cattails that flowed into a stunning mountain lake that reflected the clear blue sky. "Hey!" Emily said excitedly. "There's fish in here!" Jane walked to the water's edge and noted a few large trout cavorting under the water. "I've never caught a fish!" Emily announced. "Have you?"

"Yeah, sure."

"Can you teach me?"

"Not without a fishing rod."

Emily's attention was quickly drawn to a glint of sunshine refracted off metal. She spotted the backside of an enormous, round metallic structure. "What's that thing up there on the hill?" Emily asked, chewing nervously on her bottom lip.

Jane strained her eyes against the piercing sun. "It's a water tower." The two then curved around the lake, ascended the gradual hill and came up on the immense tower. Standing beneath it, they felt dwarfed by its formidable exterior. Two ladders were built into the tower fifty feet tall and had a radius of at least thirty-five feet. Jane turned to Emily. "Come on, let's climb up. You go in front of me."

Emily stood paralyzed, her eyes scanning the sides of the tower. "No . . ." she said, turning away.

"Can you imagine the view? I bet you could see every fruit farm in this valley! Come on, climb up in front of me—"

"No!" Emily said defiantly, pulling away. She felt her heart racing and beads of cold sweat forming across her neck.

"What's wrong?"

The feeling was obvious to the child. She knew. At that moment, Emily understood everything. "I don't want to go up there, Jane." Emily took a step backward. "I'll . . . ah . . ." She searched for a suitable reason. "I'll fall."

Jane stood back for a second. "You weren't afraid to climb up on your roof."

"Maybe I should have been," Emily said quietly.

"Oh, God, Emily," Jane said very seriously. "Don't do this to yourself."

"Do what?"

"Don't allow fear to rule the rest of your life. Take my word for it, kid. It takes a lot of energy to be scared all the time. It wears you out. One day it's a water tower, the next day you don't want to leave your house."

"You were scared back at my house. You didn't want me to go outside."

"Hey, there's a big difference between being aware of bona fide trouble that's right in front of you and being afraid of what you can't see."

Emily stared at Jane. "I think you're afraid of what you can't see."

"Really? I think it's the other way around. I think I'm not lucky enough to be blind." Jane looked up at the tower. "You're just nine and a half. You could nip this fear in the bud before it gets out of hand. Think about it." Jane started up the ladder while Emily cautiously watched. "You see?" Jane said, turning her head back to Emily. "Just one step at a time." When Jane reached the top, she stood up and took in the view. "Oh, Emily, I'm telling you. You're missing a helluva view!"

"I can hear your voice echoing," Emily yelled up to Jane, feeling slightly queasy.

Jane hooked her two fingers in her mouth and let out an ear-piercing whistle. The sound reverberated from across the mesa. The wind carried the sweet scent of the early summer. There was a moment of peacefulness until Jane happened to look down on the metal surface of the tower. Sunlight bounced hard off the exterior, blinding Jane with its piercing reflection. Suddenly, staccato images flashed in front of Jane. First, there was an explosion of blinding light quickly followed by an outstretched Glock. The wolf's face flashed next before the odd appearance of the palm print with the backwards date, 10-24-99. Jane shook off the disturbing and seemingly unprovoked vision, holding her forehead in her hand.

"Jane?" Emily said with an uneasy tone. "Are you okay?"

Jane centered herself. "I'm fine." She lit a cigarette and descended the tower.

Emily stared at the ground in deep thought as Jane planted her feet on terra firma. "I'm starting to remember more," Emily said, out of the blue.

Jane took a drag on the cigarette. "Like what?"

"I can't explain it. It's like I see or hear things that are no big deal and then I feel things and then my head wants to make a picture out of it, but my eyes don't want to see it. Stuff like that happens almost every day."

Jane did her best to act nonchalant, the whole time trying to reconcile her own startling visions. "That's normal. I imagine you'll continue to get little memory jolts like that until the pieces come together."

Emily thought for a moment. "What am I going to see?" she said apprehensively.

Jane turned away. She knew the answer to that question all too well. To see the thing you fear the most . . . to go there the first time drives a knife through your heart that infects your soul. And if Emily ever remembered the brutal, bloody scene of her butchered parents . . . well, Jane couldn't let herself go there. Standing in the lush meadow with the warm summer wind blowing through the grass, Jane decided to lie. "I don't know what you'll see."

Emily looked deep into Jane's eyes. "Yes, you do." The

child scuffed her shoe against the wet dirt. "It's okay if you don't want to tell me." The two retraced their steps around the lake and across the soggy meadow. "Maybe you can tell me this," Emily carefully said.

"Is the person who hurt Mommy and Daddy the same person who was on my roof that night when I fell?"

"I would assume there's a pretty good chance of that."

"And we're hiding out here so he doesn't come and get me?"

"No, that's not it—"

Emily stopped in her tracks. "It *is* the truth!"

Jane turned back to her. "I genuinely do not know if that asshole has the energy and desire to find you."

"Yes, Jane. He does!" Emily's voice raised several octaves in fear. "And you *know* it!"

Jane gently took hold of Emily's shoulders. "Emily, I honestly don't know!" She paused, considering how to best approach the subject. "Look, we're masquerading as mother and daughter to hide your identity. That tells me that the Department senses a need for caution. So, I keep my eyes open, just like you should."

"But I don't know what he looks like! It could be anybody!"

Jane couldn't disagree with the kid. "That's why you stick close to me."

They headed home, locked up the house and drove the five short blocks down Main Street to the Mountain Melon Market. As they got out of the car, a voice sounding like coarse gravel rattled across the street.

"I like your bumper stickers!"

Jane quickly turned. It was the town sheriff, a large, meaty fellow with thinning hair and a sallow complexion. "Excuse me?" Jane said, catching herself.

"You brake for butterflies, eh? I've never seen that particular one!" the sheriff said in a throaty tone, observing Jane's car.

Jane remembered the annoying "I Brake for Butterflies" bumper sticker. "Well, I brake unless they smash into my windshield when I'm driving. Then it's just tough luck, you know?" Jane turned to Emily, "Come on!"

The ting-ting of the front door bell rang out a cheerful greeting when Jane opened the door. She quickly surveyed the store. It was your typical small, mountain town grocery store: eight aisles surrounded by purring frozen food units. Jane grabbed a cart and started down the far left aisle near one of the banks of frozen food that was next to an old refrigerator with the sign "BAIT" taped across the front. The sheriff entered the store and stole a glance at Emily, who looked back at him and smiled.

"Patty," Jane said abruptly, "come on."

The sheriff observed Jane's interaction with Emily before turning to the guy behind the counter. "How's it goin'?" said the sheriff with a jolly ring in his voice.

"Hey, Sheriff George!" replied the guy, putting down his newspaper.

"Startin' to feel like summer, isn't it?" the sheriff said, making conversation.

"Yup. I think the cherries are gonna be early this year."

The store was small enough that Jane could hear every word. The banal back-and-forth began to grind on her nerves as she plucked one frozen entree after another out of the case and tossed it into her cart.

Emily stared at the growing pile of frozen food. "We need vegetables."

"Okay," Jane replied. "Go pick what you want."

Emily trotted down the aisle and out of Jane's sight. Within seconds, Jane heard a saccharin voice coming from the produce department.

"Well, looky here! Patty Calver! We meet again!" Jane closed the freezer door and muffled a frustrated "shit" under her voice. "Are you down here all by your lonesome or is your mom with you?"

"She's over getting frozen food for us," Emily said.

"*Frozen?*" Kathy said, sounding a bit guarded.

Jane swung her cart around the produce aisle. "Patty!" Jane said abruptly. "Did you get what you need?"

Kathy stiffened slightly in response to Jane's crusty words. "Well, there's your mom!" Kathy said, false friendliness dripping from her cement smile. "How's it goin'?"

"Just great," Jane replied, grabbing a bag of chips and a large container of salsa from the shelf.

"My goodness!" Kathy said, looking into Jane's cart. "That's *a lot* of frozen food."

"Well, that house you got us has a *big* freezer!" Jane said, intoning her own version of false friendliness as she deposited two six-packs of cola in the cart along with a dozen eggs.

"Mom!" a child's voice rang out from another aisle.

"What is it, Heather?" Kathy asked.

"Come here!" Heather commanded. "I want you to see this nail polish!"

"Why don't you come over here and show it to me, darling?" Kathy replied.

An overexaggerated sound of exasperation came from the child as she pounded her little feet down the aisle and around the corner. Heather was one of those kids that adults refer to as "precocious" when they don't want to use the word "bratty." She was dressed in a trendy outfit with a country western flair. Her long blond hair was tied into a braid and secured with a red barrette that matched her shirt. She stuck her left hand out into the air, fingertips pointed down. Each fingernail was painted with a different color of fresh polish. "Which one of these is the prettiest?" Heather asked her mother in a bitchy tone.

"Heather," Kathy said, glossing over her daughter's behavior.

"I'd like you to meet Mrs. Calver and her daughter, Patty. They're living in the old Cooper house."

"Hello," Heather said with no enthusiasm. Turning to her mother, she jabbed her hand back into her face. "Mom! Which color do you like?"

"I think they are all very pretty colors."

"Don't be stupid! Which one will look best with my new line dancing outfit?"

Kathy turned to Jane. "Heather took up country line dancing three years ago. It's such a fun activity for kids! Do you line dance, Patty?"

"No," Emily said quietly, placing several bags of vegetables into Jane's cart.

"You *really* should give it a try. I'm sure Heather and her friends would love to teach you—"

"*Mom!*" Heather exclaimed, obviously not happy with her mother's invitation.

Jane could not stand another second. "It's okay, Heather!" Jane said, with a hefty dose of attitude. "We don't want to put you out!"

Heather glared at Jane, then turned to Emily. "What happened to your head?"

"*Heather,*" Kathy said, her smile grinding into her facial muscles.

Emily looked the girl straight in the eye. "I fell off my bike. My *tall* bike."

"It's gonna leave a scar!" Heather said with a tenor of righteous contempt.

"Now, sweetheart," Kathy said, gently touching her daughter on her shoulder.

"It's true! She's gonna have a big ol' scar on the side of her head!"

Emily pulled closer to Jane, who quickly moved her cart forward. "We've gotta get going!" Jane stated with agitation.

"Oh, wait!" Kathy said, pulling a business card from the side pocket of her purse. "Here's the number of our family doctor. Dr. Armstrong. He's a prince. When it comes time for Emily to have her stitches out, you call him."

Jane looked at the card. "Right. We better get this frozen food back to the house." Jane and Emily started down the aisle when Sheriff George rounded the corner. Jane quickly pulled her leather jacket around her chest to make sure her holster and Glock were covered.

"Well, we meet again!" Sheriff George exclaimed.

"Anne, this is our sheriff!" Kathy said, getting between the two of them. "Sheriff, this is Anne Calver and her daughter, Patty. They just took residence today in the old Cooper house."

Sheriff George shook Jane's hand with gusto. "Glad to have you two in town!" He bent down to shake Emily's hand. "And hello to you, Patty. My goodness, are you as smart as you are pretty?"

Emily looked at Jane for assistance, then turned back to the sheriff. "Yes?" she said, not sure of her answer.

The sheriff let out a hearty belly laugh. "I never had anyone answer that question before! Where are you two from?"

"The Denver area," Jane answered, playing it cool.

"Denver! Well, I guess you're in for a bit of a change livin' here in Peachville! Is there a *Mr.* Calver?" asked the sheriff.

Kathy looked eagerly at Jane. It was painfully obvious she wanted to ask the same question. Jane was just about to speak when Emily spoke up.

"He died in the Calgary Stampede in Canada and he's buried in Denver," Emily said, sounding overly rehearsed. No one said a word. The silence was so thick, you could cut it with a chainsaw. Emily decided to add information. "He wasn't a rodeo clown. He was a rodeo *cowboy*. Mom didn't want to marry the rodeo clown even though he made her laugh."

For once in her life, Jane was speechless.

"Well, Mrs. Calver," Sheriff George said, slightly stunned by Emily's information, "we're glad you chose Peachville to start your new life."

Jane nodded and pressed on. Emily tried to slide around the sheriff but his girth forced her to bump against a shelf holding pencil boxes. Her elbow dislodged several of the boxes, bringing them crashing down and spreading colored pencils across the linoleum. Emily turned to the falling pencils and fixated on them. Her pupils enlarged in fear as she stood paralyzed.

The child's awkward reaction didn't escape either Kathy or the sheriff. Jane noted their reaction and gently placed her hand on Emily's shoulder. She jumped and pulled away from Jane in a fearful posture.

"You alright there, sweetheart?" asked the sheriff.

It took Emily several seconds to get her bearings. She realized she'd zoned out and didn't know what to do. "Yes. I'm fine. Sorry about the pencils."

"Well, darlin', there's nothing to pickin' 'em up," the sheriff said reassuringly as he knelt down and collected the pencils.

Kathy stared at Jane, her smile slightly fading. Her look was one of concern mixed with apprehension. Jane caught Kathy's penetrating eye and felt her gut tighten. Jane somberly purchased the grocery items and quickly left the store with Emily.

"I'm sorry," Emily said quietly, upset with herself as she got in the car.

"It's okay," Jane replied in a gentle voice, putting the last of the food in the car.

Jane got in the Subaru, shoved the key in the ignition and quickly backed out of the parking space.

"I can't believe that happened in front of them," Emily said, deeply concerned.

"It's okay, Emily. You can't help it."

"They must think I'm weird."

"Oh, believe me kid, I have a strong feeling that at least one of them is more concerned about *me* right now."

# Chapter 18

By the time Jane and Emily piled all the frozen food from the Mountain Melon Market into their freezer and unpacked their suitcases, it was almost eight o'clock. For a house that sat right on the main drag, Jane had to admit that it was very quiet. Between the park across the street and their backyard that led into the open space, it could almost be considered pastoral.

When Emily announced that she was hungry, Jane let her choose which frozen entree she wanted. While it cooked, they sat across from each other at the kitchen counter and devoured a bag of tortilla chips with salsa. The entire time, Emily hardly said a word. Jane couldn't stand it any longer. "Emily, I told you back in the car, it's okay. I'm not mad at you for what happened at the market."

"I know you're not mad," Emily said, spinning her tortilla chip slowly through the salsa. "I'm mad at myself. What's happening to me?"

Jane looked at Emily and felt as though she were looking in the mirror. "Your mind is holding on to the memory of whatever you witnessed that night. But it's like a curtain comes down to protect you when you start to see certain things."

Emily thought for a second. "Did you see my mommy and daddy?"

Jane popped open a can of cola. "I didn't go to the house that night when it happened."

"So, you don't know what they looked like?"

"I saw photographs," Jane reluctantly offered, taking a sip of cola.

"*They took pictures!*" Emily was outraged.

"They have to take pictures. It's, unfortunately, part of the procedure."

"Where are the pictures?"

Jane hadn't yet looked inside the Lawrence case envelope that Weyler gave her but she hoped the crime scene photos were not included. "The pictures are in a file cabinet at Denver Police Headquarters."

"People just look at them?" Emily was incensed by the thought.

"They look at them so they can try and solve the case," Jane said in a gentle tone.

"You saw them?" Jane nodded. "Did Mommy look frightened?" Emily's throat caught.

Jane's memory flashed on the brutality of Patricia Lawrence's murder, with part of her eye cut out of her head. "Your mom looked peaceful. Like she was sleeping."

Emily relaxed. She bought the lie and felt a bit more at ease. Jane removed her jacket to reveal her shoulder holster and Glock handgun.

"Do you have to wear that all the time?" Emily asked.

"Yeah," Jane replied, laying the gun on the counter.

"You should hide it in another place. It's summer. People are gonna wonder why you're always wearing jackets."

Jane knew the kid was right. These smalltown folks were sure to question her penchant for bulky jackets on a hot day. "Maybe I could tuck it in my jeans."

"Or put it in your purse," Emily added.

"I don't own a purse."

"How about a fanny pack?"

"Don't have one of those either."

"I bet they sell them in town."

Jane agreed and passed a small notepad to Emily. "Make a note of it." Jane looked down at her bandaged hand. "I probably should lose this. Between your bandage and mine, we look like the walking wounded." Jane unwrapped her bandage.

"Shouldn't you go to the doctor for that?" Emily asked.

"I can't go to the doctor. And neither can you."

Emily looked astonished. "But Kathy gave you that card—"

"I know," Jane said. "But we can't do it. It's too risky. There'd be questions and I'm sure he'd ask for your medical records."

"Who's gonna take out my stitches?"

"You're looking at her."

Emily's eyes widened. "Do you know how to do it?"

"Sure."

Emily eyed Jane, full of skepticism. "Have you done it before?"

"No."

"So, how do you know you can do it?"

"It can't be that difficult. It's gotta be like sewing, just in reverse."

"*Do you sew?*"

"No. But I've seen people sew."

"You've seen people *cook*, too."

Jane rolled her eyes. "You have ten more days before they have to come out. It'll be fine. Trust me." With that, Jane unwound the last layer of her bandage and revealed her hand. It was slightly *pale,* but aside from a few small blisters, it was in fairly good shape. "I can take care of my hand and I can take care of your head."

"Yeah," Emily said, full of doubt. "You didn't have any stitches in your hand."

Jane and Emily divided the large chicken pot pie that the kid chose for dinner. By 9:30, Emily was tired and ready for sleep. After tucking her into her bed, Jane checked the lock on the front and back door, and walked down the hall to her bedroom. She slipped into a cotton nightshirt and propped some pillows on the bed. Dragging her leather satchel onto the bedspread, she lit a cigarette, pulled an ashtray onto the side table and lifted out the Lawrence case envelope from the satchel. Amidst the glut of paperwork, there were two line drawings depicting the multitude of wounds on both victims. On a separate sheet, Jane found a collection of photocopied crime scene photos. Jane made sure to place that page behind all the others and secured the envelope between other files in her satchel. Her hand brushed against the thick file on the Stover triple murder. She drew the huge folder from the briefcase and scattered the pages across the bedspread. The front page of the *Denver Post* that featured her and Chris' photos was set to the side along with the other news stories on the case. Photos of the burned out Range Rover and the charred bodies of the victims were placed into another pile. Intermingled between the two piles were sundry stacks of crime scene notes and obituaries from the *Rocky Mountain News*. She unfolded the newspaper and skimmed the obituary: "William 'Bill' Stover, 42 . . . Yvonne Kelley Stover, 41 . . . Amy Joan Stover, 10 were killed . . . tragedy . . . great potential . . . police looking into motives." Jane tossed the newspaper to the side and took a deep drag on her cigarette.

She pulled out two stapled pages of typed information on the elusive Texas mob. The Texas mob. It always came back to them and it always ended there. Jane thought back to her father's comment of "follow the protection money." The Texas mob's side ventures of offering "protection" to foreign businesses against drug entanglements in exchange for a slice of the store's profit was textbook. It was that protection money that could steer Jane to a viable suspect in the case. It could turn out to be some lackey for the mob or it could hopefully turn out to be a heavy hitter.

The more Jane pondered the possibilities, the more she concluded that it had to involve more than one individual. The Stover house was on 24-hour guard. Except for the time when Stover stupidly took his family for ice cream and was accompanied by two patrol cars along the way, there was a fortress of protection around his house. The precise timing it took for the individual to come out of the shadows and plant the crude, C-4 bomb in the drive-way—right in sight of Jane and Chris in their parked car—and then disappear into the night was nothing short of amazing.

"Fucking ice cream," she mumbled under her breath. It was so typical of a druggie when he started "tweaking." They always craved sugar and would do whatever it took to get their dose of the sweet stuff. "Screw the rules," Jane could almost hear Stover saying to the cops as they tried to dissuade him from leaving the house. But Stover had been house-bound and in a forced state of detox for more than two weeks. It was insane to expect him to maintain any sense of mental stability. Jane knew that meth detox could take anywhere from three to six months. After just two weeks off the drug, Stover was most likely hearing voices and hallucinating, two common side effects of withdrawal. He was busting at the seams and would have probably offered to cut off his daughter's big toe for a chance to get out of the house and taste sugar. Jane sur-mised he was still licking that ice cream cone when he drove his SUV into his driveway and tripped the wires that led to the C-4 explosive.

Her dad's "follow the protection money" advice was sounding more plausible. In Jane's mind, whoever organized the Stover hit was either desperate or cunning. Maybe, she thought, a little bit of both. With Stover set to testify the next morning against the mob, it was a last-ditch effort that had to go down without failing. Someone in their inner circle had to be persuaded to act fast, either to prove himself or save himself from the mob's wrath.

The sound of the nightly coal train rumbled loudly through town, tooting its horn several times. As the train rattled and roared along the tracks, Jane heard the quickly approaching footsteps of Emily running down the hallway toward her closed door. With one large sweeping motion, Jane threw all the documents and newspapers into a pile and shoved them into her leather satchel. Emily pounded on Jane's door.

"Come in!" Jane said.

Emily flew into the room and jumped onto Jane's bed. "What's that noise?"

"That's just the damn coal train I told you about. Remember?"

"The house was shaking so hard. I thought someone was trying to break in!" Emily curled her body closer to Jane.

"No one's gonna break into the house, Emily. I've got my pistol right here. Any asshole stupid enough to break in is gonna get a chest full of lead." The train chugged into the night and all was silent once again.

Emily pressed her body against Jane's side. "I want to stay here with you."

"You've got a great room up there with a picture window."

Emily wrapped her arms around Jane's waist and buried her head against Jane's belly. "I want to stay with you."

Jane knew it was no use. "Get under the covers," she said to Emily. After settling in, Jane reached over and turned off the light. Outside the window, the half moon shone brilliantly in the clear sky. "Look at that," Jane said in awe.

Emily pulled away from Jane just enough to look at the glimmering orb. "Wow," she said, truly impressed. Emily sunk back, her head cuddled up against Jane's chest. "What kind of a kid were you?" Emily asked in a quiet voice.

Jane took a drag on her cigarette. The lit orange tip of

the cigarette briefly illuminated the darkness. "Just like any other kid. Nothing special."

"Were you a good kid?"

"That would depend on who you talked to. If you asked my mom, she'd tell you I was good. If you asked my dad, he'd swear I was bad."

"Were you really bad?"

"I guess I was bad when I had to be."

"What do you mean?"

"I was always looking out for my little brother, Mike. I had to make sure that nobody picked on him. If they did, I'd fight them."

"Did you always win the fights?"

Jane hesitated briefly. "It depended who I was fighting. Some fights were lost before they started."

"Why would you fight someone if you knew you were going to lose?"

"Because I had to. I made a promise." Jane took a long drag.

Emily felt herself floating peacefully toward slumber. "Like you promised me," her voice trailed off in a sleepy timbre. She let out a deep breath and mumbled.

"What was that?" Jane asked.

"When I saw you the first time . . ." Emily whispered, half-asleep, "I couldn't believe it . . . but it came true . . ."

"How do you like your eggs?" Jane asked Emily the following morning.

"Cooked," Emily replied with a straight face.

"You're a regular little comedienne," Jane countered as she broke four eggs into a bowl and, after picking out pieces of shell, did her best to beat them with a fork. After heating the pan and plopping in far too much butter, Jane added the eggs and began stirring.

Emily found the "Howdy" coupon book that Kathy gave Jane. "How about this: 'Buy one breakfast or lunch special at The Harvest Café and get another meal *absolutely free!*'" She looked up at the frying pan. "Hey!

The eggs are burning!"

"They're not burned!" Jane said, dragging the pan off the stove. She took a spatula and tried to wedge it underneath what was left of the eggs. Once she was able to lift a portion onto Emily's plate, it was obvious that the bottom was charred.

Emily poked at the eggs with her fork and lifted the whole slab in one section. "You don't call that burned?"

"Pretend they're Cajun."

Emily looked at the blackened eggs and then looked at Jane. "Caged in? Where were they caged in that made them come out like this?"

Within ten minutes, Jane and Emily were headed to The Harvest Café with "Howdy" coupon in hand. Inside the restaurant, they were greeted with the doleful voice of Garth Brooks singing, "The Dance." The Harvest Café was obviously *the* happening spot. To prove that point, there wasn't one empty table or counter seat available. The place had a cramped, greasy, diner-style setup with four booths against the wall and eight tables shoved tightly in the center of the lime green linoleum floor. There were eight additional red stools lined around the Formica counter. Behind that was the kitchen, which could be partially seen through the opening of the pick-up area where waiting plates sat roasting underneath crimson hot lamps. The walls were papered in a floral and vine print that curled at the edges and looked as though years of smoke and grease had taken their toll. A handmade sign taped to the wall summed up The Harvest Café dining experience: "We proudly serve DiGiorno Pizza!"

A waitress dressed in what Jane thought looked more like a candy striper outfit approached the two newcomers. She was loaded down with six steaming breakfast plates that aroused an almost Pavlovian reaction in Emily.

"Just the two of ya?" the waitress asked Jane. Jane nodded.

Emily raised the coupon for the waitress to see. "And we have a coupon!"

"We've got a guy just about to leave at the counter. You could sit there with your daughter on your lap—"

"Excuse me?" said a man seated at a nearby table. The waitress moved to reveal Dan the maintenance man seated at a table for two all by himself. Dan picked up his plate of food. "How's about if I just move on over to that empty counter spot and let these two folks have my table?" When he stood up, Jane figured he was a good six foot three inches. Dan was muscular but not in a way that looked like he worked out at a gym; it came more from sweat and blue-collar work. He wore a denim shirt and clean jeans with roughout cowboy boots. His face was wide and his jaw well defined. The only unkempt part was his light brown hair that looked as if he'd just rolled out of bed.

Jane was uncomfortable with Dan's offer. "Please don't move!" she said.

"Oh, come on!" Dan said in a warm southern drawl. "You got yourselves a coupon. That means you're newcomers. We gotta make a good first impression!"

The waitress walked away as Jane and Emily situated themselves at the table. "Thank you," Jane said, recognizing Dan's face. With Dan's back turned, Emily mouthed, "*Is that the guy in the truck?*" Jane nodded.

The waitress swung by and slid two greasy menus on the table. She took the coupon and slid it under her order pad. "Okay, folks! With the 'Howdy' newcomer coupon you get two eggs any way you want 'em, two slices of bacon or sausage, toast and a big ol' servin' of Uncle Al's famous hash browns!" Jane started to light up a cigarette. "Honey, you can't smoke in here!" the waitress said curtly.

"Right," Jane said, putting away her cigarette. "I'll have my eggs scrambled and the bacon," Jane said, pushing the menu away. "And coffee. *Lots* of coffee."

"What about you, sweetie?" the waitress asked Emily.

"I'd like my eggs scrambled, but not too soft that they're runny and that yellow stuff oozes out. Please cook them really well but not so well that they become caged in."

"Caged in?" the waitress said confused.

"Black," Emily said seriously. "And the sausage and a hot chocolate, please."

The waitress swept up the menus and walked to the kitchen. Jane leaned across the table. "People don't appreciate smart-ass nine-year-olds. Take it down a notch."

"What did I say?" Emily said truly innocently.

"It's Cajun. C-A-J-U-N. Not a *cage*. Cajuns are people and a description of a kind of food that is blackened."

"They burn their food?"

"No, it's blackened," Jane said, feeling more uptight.

"Blackened is burned."

"Cajun is different."

"At the house, you said 'Pretend they're Cajun' and the *house* eggs were burned."

"God, we're like Abbott and Costello!"

"Who's on first," Dan said with his back turned at the counter. Jane looked at Dan, unaware that he was listening to the conversation. Dan spun around in his seat. "You ever heard of Abbott and Costello?"

"No," Emily said, drawn in by Dan's warm smile and dancing blue eyes.

"Aw, I figured a smart girl like you would know them two." Emily shook her head, blushing. "Hey, where are my manners?" Dan held his hand out to Jane. "My name's Dan. Dan Lindsey."

Jane shook his hand. "Anne," she said, checking him out very carefully.

"And I'm Patty!" Emily said, standing up and holding out her hand. She was obviously enthralled with Dan.

"How do you do, Patty?"

"I'm doing just fine, Dan," Emily replied with a dreamy look in her eye.

The waitress arrived with the food. "Two specials!" the waitress said as she set the plates onto the table and placed the receipt under the saltshaker.

"Patty, food's here," Jane said, happy to break the child's fascination with Dan.

"I'll let you folks get to eatin'," Dan said, moving back to the counter as his cell phone rang.

Emily leaned forward to Jane and whispered, "He's handsome."

"Okey-doke! I'm leavin' right now!" Dan hung up, paid his tab and took a final swig of coffee. "You two have yourselves a beautiful day!" he said, swiveling out of his seat. "I gotta go and make the world a safer place for Peachville's residents."

"Just call Dan!" Emily sung out, recalling his truck sign. "*Twenty-four*-hour man!"

Jane cringed. "She means *24-hour maintenance*. We saw your truck."

Dan let out a guffaw that lit up his face. "Well, I'm partial to 24-hour man! That's what I am: on call, 24/7. Say, you all being new in town, if you ever have any electrical, plumbin' or any such thing go wrong, you give ol' Dan a call." He reached into his back pocket and pulled out a business card, handing it to Jane. "I mean it," Dan said to Jane. "You got any problem in that ol' Cooper house, you give me a jingle."

Jane's cop radar went up. "You already know our address?"

"Don't look so shocked. This is a small town. If we don't know where the newcomers live and what they eat for breakfast inside of 24 hours of them showin' up, we're shirkin' our duties!" Jane eyed Dan very carefully, wondering what other lovely tidbits of information he knew, thanks to Kathy, the town crier.

Emily watched Dan walk out of the Café and get into his truck before returning to her meal with a silly grin. The front door of the Café opened and in walked Sheriff George, his belly protruding a good three inches over his belt.

"Shit," Jane mumbled under her breath. "It's like old home week in here."

"How ya doin', Sheriff?" the waitress hollered out from behind the counter.

"Ask me after my third cup of coffee!" the sheriff quipped, heading to the open seat at the counter that Dan just vacated. He spun around in his seat, facing Jane and Emily. "You still brakin' for butterflies?" he asked Jane before quickly turning to Emily. "And how was your first night sleepin' in Peachville? Did the train keep you up?"

"We slept fine!" Jane responded, trying to put on a cheerful face.

"You know, we're the only town in Western Colorado with a coal train that rumbles through it!"

Jane took a sip of coffee. "Is that in your Chamber of Commerce brochure?" The minute the words rolled off her lips, she regretted the sarcasm.

"You know what?" the sheriff replied. "I think it just might be!"

The waitress set a cup of coffee on the counter for the sheriff. He took a hearty gulp and continued to stare at Jane and Emily. Jane ate a few bites of food amidst the awkward silence. The sheriff's radio beeped and a deputy's voice could be heard. "We got it wrapped up over here," the voice on the radio announced.

"Well, that's good news!" Sheriff George said to Jane. "We had ourselves a cow loose this morning and wanderin' up on the road."

"Wow," Jane said, tiring of the prosaic chitchat.

"Yeah. That's about as exciting as it gets 'round here. Oh, we have our occasional car wreck on the highway when folks take the turn too quick. But, that's all that really happens 'round here. And you know what? We like it that way."

Jane realized the sheriff was speaking circuitously to her. Behind his cheerful, good ol' boy exterior, he was sending her a message. "Well, that's good to hear," Jane countered. "With my husband's recent death, we could do with some peace and quiet."

"I'm sorry for your loss," the sheriff said. "I'm sure it's

been difficult for you and your daughter." He pursed his fat lips. "Like I said, we like it peaceful. Peaceful Peachville. Everybody gets along and those that can't stay away from each other."

Jane eyed the sheriff. She was getting tired of his innuendo. The static voice came back over his radio. "Okay, I'll be 10–7 at the park. 10–4."

"Gotta shove off," the sheriff said. He got up and lingered closer to Emily. "You take care of yourself, sweetiepie. Come on over and visit us at the station. I'll let you sit in my big swivel chair!"

"Really?" Emily exclaimed, in awe. "Mom, can we go there after breakfast?"

"Maybe another time. The Sheriff's got to go on patrol while his deputy is on break." It took Jane less than a second to realize she screwed up. She was so used to hearing and saying the code '10–7'—which means, "I'm going on a break"—that it became normal conversation to her. Emily looked at Jane and realized something was not right by the look on her face.

"Well, I must say," said Sheriff George, obviously taken aback, "you must be a mind reader."

Jane nervously sipped her coffee under the watchful eye of the sheriff and Emily. "Mind reader? No, no. Just a lucky guess."

There was a second of uncomfortable silence and then Emily spoke up. "Mom! I think the car is out of gas."

"What?" Jane asked, not catching Emily's attempt to get them out of there.

"Our car is out of gas," Emily repeated, this time more pointedly. "Shouldn't we go fill it up?"

Jane caught the drift. "Right. We need to take care of that."

"If you've got your 'Howdy' coupon book, you can fill up your tank at The Apple Cart and get ten percent off!" the sheriff proudly stated, buying their ruse.

To be on the safe side, Jane visited The Apple Cart and filled up the tank. It was a wise decision since Sheriff

George did indeed drive by the establishment, waving at the two of them. Inside the store, Emily spotted an extra large fanny pack that would safely accommodate Jane's pistol without drawing attention to it. In the car, Jane debated how much she should tell Emily about the back-handed innuendos from Sheriff George and Kathy. But she determined the whole subject would be too complex for Emily to digest. "I don't want you going over to see Sheriff George."

"But he said I could sit in his big swivel chair."

"I don't trust him." Jane turned onto Main Street and headed back to the house.

"How come?"

"It's not always what people say. It's what they do. In fact, it's often more important what a person does, than what he says. It's called reading people. Sort of like reading a book, but instead of reading the language in a book, you're reading the language of their body."

Emily was intrigued by the notion. "Like back at the house when I crossed my arms in front of my body? How you said I was cutting you off?"

"Exactly. As a cop, we always look for those signs because perps . . . I mean, criminals, are always lying verbally. However, a criminal can tell a million verbal lies, but his body will always speak the truth."

"How does someone's body tell a lie?"

"Lots of ways. If he looks to the left and down, that's usually a lie."

"So, everybody who looks to the left and down is telling a lie?"

"No. You have to look at the whole picture. Scratching the nose is another indication of lying. Or licking the lips continually. If somebody is telling you something and looking to the left and down while he's scratching his nose and nervously licking his lips, then you've proba-bly got a good lie going. But there's other nuances you look for. You listen to the tone of their voice. Does it sound like the truth?"

"What does the truth sound like?"

"It's pure."

"Pure?"

Jane thought for a second. "Your voice is pure."

"Really?" Emily said, beaming. She looked out the window. "So you don't want me to go sit in Sheriff George's big swivel chair because his voice isn't pure?"

Jane needed to handle this one carefully. "His voice is usually pure. But there are times when he says two different things in one sentence. And one of those things is not pure." Jane focused a block ahead toward the rental house and saw a car with two occupants parked in front. "Who in the hell is that?"

Emily looked up. "It's Kathy and Heather."

"Shit!" Jane mumbled under her breath. She turned into her driveway and parked the car under the shade of the large cottonwood tree. Kathy popped out of her car carrying a covered dish. Heather followed with a large gift basket.

Good morning!" Kathy cheerfully exclaimed as she darted over to Jane. "Happy first full day in Peachville!"

"Thank you, Kathy," Jane said, subdued.

"I've brought you a little welcome casserole."

"You made us a casserole!" Emily exclaimed as she rounded the Subaru.

"Look at her!" Kathy exclaimed. "You'd think she'd never seen a home cooked meal before!" Jane took Kathy's gibe as it was intended and tried to remain calm.

"Thank you!" Emily said ecstatically.

"You are very welcome, sweetheart!" Kathy handed the dish to Jane. "There's enough in there for four meals." Kathy took the big basket from Heather. "And here's a little welcome basket from our family to yours! There's tea, cookies and preserves, some nuts, spices, *fancy* cocoa mix, assorted fruits and lots of other goodies for you two!"

Jane set the casserole on the hood of the Subaru and took the basket. "Do you give every newcomer this kind of attention?"

"Just the special ones," Kathy said, directing her comment to Emily. Kathy bent down to be on eye-level with the child. "How's that head feeling today, sweetie?"

Emily brushed her hand against her bandage. "It's okay, I guess."

"Oh, you poor little thing," Kathy said, softly touching Emily's cheek with her hand. "Heather, why don't you show Patty your snazzy new line dancing outfit?"

"*Why?*" Heather said in a snotty tone.

"Because I'm sure she'd love to see it!"

Emily looked at Jane, not sure what to do. "It's okay. Go on," Jane said.

Emily crossed over to Kathy's car with Heather. "She's a *very* well behaved little girl," Kathy said, observing Emily. "The way she looked up at you for permission before going over to the car. Most kids would just skip away without a thought."

"Most kids are rude, too," Jane said with a forced smile on her face, alluding to Kathy's bratty daughter.

"Oh, pish-tosh! Kids have to express themselves! They need to push the boundaries and find out what's what!"

"That's assuming there's boundaries to begin with," Jane said without flinching.

Kathy caught Jane's drift. Her pasted smile lost a hint of its phony glimmer. "I don't mean to be forward, but I sense lots of stress in your voice."

"Do you?"

"It must be dreadful to lose a husband in such an awful way. It's only normal to feel angry. It's part of the grieving process. You *will* see the light at the end of the tunnel." Jane hated being placated but she hated it even more when the homilies were in response to an undercover ruse. "Oprah did a show on young mothers who tragically lost their spouses. It was *so* eye-opening for me to see these brave women carrying on with such a dreadful burden. I cried at least twice during that show. *Twice!* One of the experts talked about how important it is to feel the anger but to not take out the aggression on the ones who are closest to you. The ones who are so *innocent*."

"Mom!" Heather yelled in a shrieking, bitchy voice. "When are we leaving?"

Kathy turned to her daughter with her jaw clenched. "In a minute, darling!"

"You said we could go to Montrose and buy those country dance CDs!"

"And we will. Mom just needs one more minute with Mrs. Calver!"

"If they're sold out when we get there, it's all your fault!" Heather screamed.

Kathy turned back to Jane. "Anyway, I just wanted to let you know that I understand what you're going through." Kathy grasped Jane's arm. "I feel your pain."

"You feel my pain because you lost a husband or because you watched Oprah?"

Kathy didn't know what to say. "I'll let you go." She turned and then spun back around. "The gals and I are getting together for our Wednesday gab fest two weeks from today. It's going to be at my house and I'd love it if you and Patty would come! That's our *cherry* night. We'll be up to our elbows in pits, making preserves and juice! Patty's should have her stitches out and, that reminds me, did you call Dr. Armstrong?"

"No. It's been a busy twenty-four hours for us."

"I'd be happy to call him for you—"

"I'll take care of it."

Kathy took a step back, sizing up Jane's comment. "Well, okay. See you 'round the campus!" She got in her car, quickly followed by her very impatient daughter. "Oh, by the way!" Kathy yelled across the yard. "I love your 'I Brake For Butterflies' bumper sticker! You simply *must* let me know where you got that sweet thing!"

Jane and Emily watched as Kathy made a wide U-turn on Main Street, beeped her car horn and took off toward the highway.

"Can I take the basket in the house and look inside?" Emily said excitedly.

"Sure. I'll be in right after I scrape that goddamn bumper sticker off our car."

# Chapter 19

Eight uneventful days passed. Jane wondered when the proverbial shoe would drop. Emily had stopped sleeping in her own bed, preferring to stay with Jane. For the entire eight days, Emily hadn't experienced any flash-backs and was peacefully resting through the thunderous passings of the nightly coal train. On the surface, every-thing looked serene, but Jane knew that something boiled under that tenuous facade.

During those eight tedious days, Jane estimated that she saw Kathy at least three times each day. It was as though the woman was on the warpath, following them and keeping mental notes. She let it slip one day about her husband, Kent. "Kent and Kathy!" Kathy proudly exclaimed, continually amused by the fact that she and her husband were a human alliteration. Kent was a land developer who, according to Kathy, had "made super land investments" in the early 1980s and was reaping the benefits with the newcomers to Colorado. When she wasn't bragging about Kent's sale of land to "those nasty Californians," Kathy was forever reminding Jane about her big Wednesday night "Cherry Jubilee" gathering that was only six days away.

Jane and Emily had only seen Dan in fleeting moments when he was racing to an important maintenance call.

It seemed that Dan was a man of many talents. During one conversation with Kathy, she mentioned that Dan had won the county swing and line dancing championship. He was also an expert fly fisherman, a whiz with an ax and could recite the names of all 50 states in less than thirty seconds. When Jane sarcastically remarked that Dan was a true Renaissance man, Kathy insisted that Dan was not familiar with that period of history.

And then there was Sheriff George. Fortunately, Jane had hardly run into the portly fellow. She'd heard through the grapevine that due to summer road repair on the highway, the Sheriff and his deputies were racking up overtime as they kept the traffic moving and the public out of harm's way. Jane prayed each night for rocks to slide and cause further road damage so the sheriff would stay occupied and out of her face.

As the days blended into each other, Jane checked her pager once every hour. She had it set to vibrate so nobody would hear the telltale beep and have more fodder for gossip. But the damn thing didn't vibrate once. Weyler said he would only contact her if absolutely necessary, but she wanted to hear from him, if only to know that everything was status quo. Jane was still not sure if Weyler had nefarious intentions. And yet, she yearned to hear a familiar voice besides Emily's.

She also yearned to hear intelligent conversation and news. *The Peachville Gazette*, which came out weekly and still only printed a miserable 14 pages, was filled to the gills with advertisements and stories that had to do with farm prices, who was sponsoring the weekly "fruit affair" and updates on highway projects. Clearly, the isolation of the town was getting to Jane. However, Emily seemed to truly love the provincial surroundings. She lit up whenever she caught a glimpse of Dan "the 24-hour man," which became more amusing than annoying to Jane. Unlike Jane, Emily liked Kathy and always remarked how pretty she looked. It didn't hurt that Kathy continued to drop off homemade dishes. Emily even tolerated bellicose Heather, although Jane couldn't understand how anyone could suffer the brat's behavior.

When June 10th rolled around, Jane awoke realizing that she would finally have something new to occupy herself with on that day. It was twelve days since Emily fell from her roof. After examining the wound, Jane knew it was time to remove the kid's stitches. After a breakfast of hard-boiled eggs—which was intended to be soft-boiled—and burnt toast, Jane looked at Emily across the breakfast table with eager anticipation.

"You know what?" Jane said, damn near giddy with expectation. "It's time to get your stitches out!" She crossed to the kitchen drawer.

"I think we should wait a couple more days. Maybe five more days. Or ten—"

"If we wait any longer, the stitches are going to be embedded in your skull," Jane said as she brought out a pair of small scissors.

Emily stood up. "Maybe you should sew something for me and then take it apart so you could practice—"

"Sit up here on the counter," Jane said, patting her hand on the counter.

"How come you're so peppy?"

"*Peppy?* I'm not peppy," Jane replied, a tad too eager. Emily looked dubiously at her and Jane realized the kid was scared. "I tell you what. If I hurt you, you can eat a banana split for breakfast for an entire week."

Emily's eyes widened. "*Real* bananas?"

"No. Plastic bananas. Of course, *real* bananas! Is it a deal?" Emily hesitated before giving in. She hoisted herself onto the counter. Jane grabbed a copy of *The Peachville Gazette* and handed it to Emily. "This'll give you something to concentrate on." Jane carefully removed Emily's bandage to reveal the stitches.

"Hey," Emily said, glancing at the front page of the newspaper, "did you know that today is the 72nd

anniversary of the founding of Alcoholics Anonymous."
Jane remained silent, her eyes on Emily's stitches.
However, the kid's leading tone irritated her. "Over
seventy years," *Emily stressed, "of millions of people*
getting sober . . ."

Jane pulled away. "Is this going somewhere?"

"It's just that," Emily stumbled around for the right
words, "that's a lot of years, don't you think? I just think
it's really cool."

"Fair enough," Jane said, resuming her examination of
Emily's head.

After a few more seconds, Emily spoke up. "How
many years is it going to take before my scar stops hurting?"

"It won't take years. Where'd you get that idea?"

"From you."

"I never told you that."

"It's not what you said. It's what you do." Emily
reached up and pulled Jane's hair away from her right
temple to reveal her old scar. "I see you rubbing it a lot,
like you're trying to rub away the pain."

Jane moved Emily's hand away from her head. "I
don't . . . It doesn't hurt."

"Then how come you rub it?"

"It's a nervous habit. Some people bite their nails, some
people crack their knuckles and I, apparently, rub my
scar."

"You didn't know you did it?"

"Not really, no," Jane said defensively. "I'll make a
point of curbing that tendency!" Jane felt totally exposed.
It was one thing for her to be the observant one but quite
another for someone else—especially a child—to be the
one observing her.

"How come you're mad?"

"Do you want your stitches out or not?" Jane's tone
was abrupt. Emily stared at her, not sure what to make of
her pointed response. Jane let out a tired breath. "Close

your eyes and think of a beautiful forest with soft rain falling."

Emily closed her eyes. "A beautiful forest . . . Soft rain . . ."

Jane clipped one side of the stitches. Emily didn't flinch. "Describe it to me."

"It's really green. So green that the leaves look like they're hiding emeralds."

"Hiding emeralds? I like that."

"And the rain . . . It's more like a mist. It's like a big humidifier spewing—"

"Spewing is not poetic. Use another word."

"It's like a big humidifier washing the forest with a thick mist. When are you gonna take the stitches out?" Emily said, her eyes closed.

"Open your eyes."

Emily opened her eyes. Jane held the stitches in the palm of her hand. The kid was shocked. "How'd you do that?"

"Like I said. I've watched people sew," Jane replied with a wry grin.

Emily threw her arms around Jane's neck. "*You're great!*"

Emily hung on to Jane's neck as Jane stood still, not sure what to do. She softly patted Emily's arm and pulled the child off of her. "Thanks for the vote of confidence."

Emily touched the top of her head. "Hey! I just felt a drop of water."

Jane looked up to see a crack in the kitchen ceiling and droplets of water slowly forming across it. She located a bucket under the sink and positioned it under the leak. On her initial examination of the house, she'd discovered a pull-drop ladder in the ceiling of the hallway that led to the attic crawl space. Jane climbed up the wooden ladder, flashlight in hand, and stood in the musty, cobweb-filled attic. "You oughta check this out, Emily," she said, looking down through the large opening at the kid. Emily examined the ladder and the short distance she would have to climb. "You really should come up here." Jane poked her head through the opening and stretched her hand out to Emily. "I'll hold your hand the whole way up." Emily considered the offer and started up the ladder. Without much fear, Emily safely made it into the crawl space. "You'll be climbing that water tower in no time!"

The two scoped out the attic, dimly lit by vertical shafts of light that shot up through a series of ceiling vents. Jane shone her flashlight around the area and illuminated an old metal pipe that issued a slow leak through a disintegrating bond. Emily's eyes lit up like two cherry bombs. "I know *just* the man who can fix this!"

"Maybe we can put some duct tape around the pipe—"

"Duct tape? That's not safe!" Emily said with a dramatic sweep of her arms. As she swept them through the air, she toppled two fishing poles and a well-worn creel.

"After I put duct tape on that pipe, I'm going to teach you how to fish."

Jane wrapped the pipe with several layers of duct tape that she found wedged in one of the kitchen drawers. After securing the Glock pistol in her new fanny pack, the two set off through the tall grass with fishing poles and creel in hand. Situating themselves at the edge of the large lake that held the massive water tower in its reflection, Jane showed Emily the perfect location for digging earthworms. Once they had enough worms, Jane demonstrated the proper technique of scooping the fishhook under the darkened band that encircled the worm. After that came the lesson on proper casting. Emily was captivated by Jane's knowledge and proved to be an excellent student. With their lines in the water, Jane sat back and lit a cigarette.

"That duct tape isn't safe," Emily avowed.

"I told you I don't want people in our house—"

"But this is an emergency!"

Jane smiled at Emily's obvious crush on Dan. The two of them sat quietly on the edge of the lake. After an hour of not even a nibble from the occasional circling trout, they pulled in their lines, returned the remaining earthworms to their dirt homes and started back to the house. The sound of a vehicle drew their attention toward the water tower. A white truck came to a halt by the lake's edge and a man got out, fishing pole in hand.

Emily squinted her eyes against the noonday sun and the glinting reflection off the tower. "Dan!" Emily screamed across the lake.

"Emily!" Jane said quietly, irritated.

Dan looked up and waved. "How ya doin'? Are the fish bitin'?'" he yelled across the lake, his voice echoing for several seconds.

"No!" Emily yelled. "Don't waste your time! Come fix our pipe!"

Jane knelt down toward the child. "Emily, this is not a game we're playing."

"So, you really *are* my mom?"

"You know what I mean. I don't know anything about this guy—"

"He's got good eyes. He doesn't look to the left and down. He doesn't cover his mouth when he talks or lick his lips. Isn't that what you said you look for in a liar?"

"It's more complicated than that—"

"You talk about feeling stuff in your gut. Well, I got a gut, too, and it tells me that Dan is okay." Dan suddenly emerged from thicket of red willows. Jane quickly stood up and held her hand against the Glock pistol in her fanny pack. It was an automatic knee-jerk, cop reaction for her whenever someone suddenly approached. Emily greeted Dan with a big smile. "Dan! How's it goin'?"

Dan tipped his baseball cap up several inches. "Well, it's goin' even better since I get to see you two!" Dan looked over at Jane. "What's this about a pipe?"

"It's leaking through the ceiling in the kitchen!" Emily dramatically insisted. "Mom put duct tape around it but *I* don't think it's safe. You really need to come—"

"Patty, I don't want to bother Dan—"

"Aw, it ain't no bother a'tall!" Dan said. "Like your daughter said, the fish ain't bitin' so I might as well come on over and get to fixin' that leak. Be over in two shakes!"

Emily snatched her fishing pole and took off through the tall grass toward the house. Jane grabbed her pole and the creel and followed the kid, cussing a blue streak under her breath the whole way home. The second she entered the house, Jane did a quick search to make sure everything appeared normal. The only room that held suspicious items was her bedroom and those items were safely tucked away in Jane's leather satchel. Dan called out as he approached the house. Emily raced to the front door and opened it with a flourish.

Jane led Dan to the kitchen, where he set his toolbox on the counter and surveyed the ceiling. He noticed Emily's Starlight Starbright projector on the kitchen table. "You a fan of the stars, Patty?"

"Yes. I can point out the Big Dipper, the Little Dipper and Orion's belt."

"Well, I'm a real star enthusiast myself," Dan said, smiling down at Emily.

"*Really?*" Emily said, ecstatically.

"Yes, ma'am," Dan replied, turning back to his investigation of the ceiling. Jane observed Dan with her cop radar, desperately trying to detect a sign of deception.

Emily pulled the star chart out of her projection case. "You oughta see this, Dan—"

The familial banter was getting to Jane. "Patty, how about if you take that in the backyard and let Dan do his job." Emily looked a bit dejected but did as Jane asked. "Stay in the backyard like we talked about," Jane quietly cautioned.

Dan waited until Emily was outside. "You've got a beautiful daughter."

"Thank you," Jane said, keeping a close eye on Emily.

"She's not going to wander off. And even if she did, it's a small town. She's safe."

"Yeah, right," Jane said tensely, still watching Emily.

"You okay?" Dan said warily.

Jane spun around. "Yes, of course. I'll show you how to get up in the attic and then I've got to attend to some paperwork." Dan followed Jane to the retractable stairway that led to the attic, pointed out the pipe and retired to her bedroom, closing and locking the door behind her.

Jane leaned down to collect the satchel next to her bed and felt the Glock pistol against her belly. She unlatched the fanny pack and set it on the bedside table. Hoisting the leather satchel onto her lap, she proceeded to organize the paperwork, removing several manila folders and stacking them on a nearby chair. Jane withdrew the legal-sized notepad and flipped through the pages until she reached the odd drawings of the wolf face and upturned left handprint with the backward numbers, 10-24-99. Out of curiosity, she placed her left hand upright over the drawing and found it to be a tight match. A cold shudder pricked her skin as she quickly lifted her hand from the page and wedged the notepad back into her satchel. The dust from the files irritated her nose, causing her to sneeze. Searching for a tissue, Jane unzipped the fanny pack and dug around, removing the Glock and setting it on top of the folders.

Upstairs in the attic, Dan found the leaking pipe. Scanning the adjacent pipes with only the light of his flashlight, he took a step to the right and nearly tripped over one of the several air vents scattered across the floor. Continuing on, Dan found several more fragile pipe connections. Pulling a pen from his pocket, it slipped from his hand and landed between two vents just as he heard Jane sneeze. He peered down and realized that one of the floor vents offered a direct view of Jane's bedroom. He reached down for the pen just as Jane got up from the bed to retrieve a tissue.

That's when he saw it. He quietly knelt down on his haunches and looked down. The Glock pistol was clearly displayed atop the manila folders. Looking more closely at the folder he saw the words "POLICE REPORT" in

bold letters, followed by the case number and JANE
PERRY. The butt of the pistol obscured the word
"Detective." Dan watched as Jane returned to the bed and
sat down, blowing her nose. She let out a long sigh as she
pulled out one of the newspaper clippings that featured
Chris and her on the cover. From Dan's point of view, he
could not see what she was looking at initially but he did
note her reaction. As she reread the front page story on the
Stover case, she shook her head in disgust. The paper
dipped enough to reveal just the front page photograph
of Chris. Dan caught a quick glimpse of Chris' mug. Jane
smacked the page with her hand and said, "You pompous
son-of-a-bitch!" before folding the paper into her leather
satchel and replacing the Glock into her fanny pack.

"Hey, Dan!" Emily said quietly, standing midway on
the stairs that led to the attic with her Starlight Starbright
vinyl case in tow.

Dan turned around and carefully moved away from the
air vent so Jane couldn't hear him. "Whatcha doin' there,
honey?" Dan lifted Emily into the attic.

"I don't want Mom to know I'm up here," Emily said
confidentially. "But since you like stars, I brought my
Starlight Starbright for you to see. It's dark enough up
here for it to work."

Dan continued to mark the sections of pipe as Emily
opened the case. The pack of photographs of her parents
fell out and onto the floor. "Dan?" Emily whispered.
"Could you shine the flashlight over here?" Dan obliged
and Emily retrieved the packet. "Thanks. I can't lose
these."

"What is it?" Dan asked, returning to his work.

"Pictures . . ." Emily said, her voice trailing off, "of
happy days." She flicked on the projector and the entire
attic area was illuminated with a million pinpoint stars.

Dan looked around at the impressive spectacle. "Ain't
that cool!"

Emily opened the packet of photographs and flipped
through the pictures. Dan stole a glance back at Emily.

"Happy days, huh?" Dan said sadly.

"You wanna see a picture of my best friend?"

"Sure."

Emily got up and handed Dan a photo of Emily and A.J. sitting cheek to cheek on a picnic blanket. "That's a good picture of you! You oughta put that one in a frame and keep it where you can see it every day."

"No. That would make me sad."

"How come?"

"I don't get to see A.J. anymore. She moved away and then we had to move away." The projected stars inched slowly around the room, covering Dan and Emily's bodies. The hypnotic strains of "Nessun Dorma" played softly in the semi-darkness. Emily turned to the next photograph. It was a picture of her father, looking glum and clutching a beer. The projector cast a pinpoint beam of light onto the photograph that instantly transfixed Emily.

Dan looked over and saw the photograph. "Who's that?"

"My dad," Emily said quietly, almost trancelike.

"He doesn't look too happy in that picture."

"He's not. He's angry. He's *always* angry." Emily slipped further into a daze.

"Why is he angry?" Dan said in a whisper.

"He drinks too much. He makes bad decisions. That's what Mom always says. That's why we went on that camping trip to Moab. And then they fight and it gets so loud that I hide in my closet and close the door and ask God to make them stop yelling." Emily fell deeper into the memory. "I hide in my closet with the big pillows . . . and it gets louder and louder . . . And then . . ." Emily looked up from the photo, her eyes far away. "There's a loud scream." Emily's eyes widened as the sound of a blood-curdling scream wailed through her head. The photo packet hit the floor. Dan gently touched Emily's shoulder. She jumped in fear, letting out a slight yelp. "Oh, no," she said, realizing she'd spaced out.

"Patty?" Jane said, climbing the ladder.

Emily turned to the sound of Jane's voice with a pan-icked look on her face. "Oh, gosh. She didn't want me to say anything—" She quickly collected the photo packet.

"Patty?" Jane poked her head through the square opening and saw the projector's illumined display of constellations. "What's going on up here?"

Dan thought fast. "Patty was showin' me her projec-tion toy."

"Okay," she said tentatively, squinting through the filtered darkness, "why don't you turn off the projector and let Dan finish his job." Emily quickly repacked the projector and, with her back turned to Jane, tossed the photo packet back into the case.

Ninety minutes later, Dan emerged from the attic and walked into the kitchen. Jane stood at the sink, washing dishes. "You all done?" she asked.

"Yes, Mrs. Calver," he answered, his tone almost solemn.

"Please, call me Anne."

Dan moved pensively to the sliding glass door that led out into the backyard. Outside, Emily lay on her back in the grass, obviously in deep thought. Dan stared at Emily, keeping his back to Jane as he spoke. "She's a real special little girl, Anne."

Jane turned to face Dan. Something felt out of place. "Excuse me?"

"Patty," Dan said, still with his back to Jane. "She's real special." Jane automatically drew her hand to her fanny pack and then realized she'd left it in the bedroom. Her body stiffened as she visually searched the kitchen for a weapon. Spying a large knife on the kitchen counter, she quietly moved toward it. "It must be very difficult for her to live a lie."

Jane cupped her palm around the knife handle. "What are you talking about?"

"I know your secret." Dan never turned away from the glass door.

Jane slipped the knife off the counter and held it close

to her side. "What makes you think I have a secret?"

"It's several things. You're real nervous about Patty being out of your sight. And then, Patty basically spilled the beans about her dad and the drinking and the fighting and how she had to hide in her closet. She told me how she had to leave her house and her friends. But the thing that puts it all together is the fact that you've got a gun in your fanny pack and you're carrying around police reports . . ." Jane's head was spinning. Her first thought was Emily's safety. Her second thought was figuring out how she could duck and take cover when Dan turned on her. She would knife him in the belly and grab Emily. If this was the showdown, she was going to prove her mettle. "You've got air vents up in that attic and one of them is right above your bedroom," Dan continued. "I wasn't spying on you. I dropped my pen and looked down and that's when I saw the police report and your pistol. After what Patty told me, all the puzzle pieces fit." Dan turned to face Jane. The kitchen counter obscured his view of the knife. "There's no dead rodeo cowboy. Isn't that right?" Jane stood motionless, saying nothing as she stared at Dan. He took a step forward toward Jane. "Isn't that right?"

Jane felt her blood boil but she maintained composure. "What do you want?" she said in a staccato manner.

"I want to make sure that you and your daughter are safe."

Jane had to replay his words several times in her head. "My daughter?"

"She's obviously traumatized by what's happened. Who can blame her? You gotta be going through a lot yourself. Being on the run from an abusive husband has gotta turn you inside out. I know it was hard for you to leave like you did with whatever you could throw in a suitcase. But trust me, you did the right thing."

Jane loosened up a bit. She nonchalantly slid the knife onto a lower shelf. "Well, thank you, Dan. I appreciate your kind words and concern—"

"I'm not just spoutin' words. I mean it when I say I want to help you."

"Look, Dan, that's very kind of you, but we don't need your help—"

"What's gonna happen if your husband shows up? Maybe he'll be drunk or ragin' out of his mind. What are you gonna do then? Have you ever fired a gun? I don't mean to be disrespectful, ma'am, but your daughter has some real painful memories that she can hardly get out. She's holdin' a lot of fear inside. Whatever she witnessed between you and your husband has affected her deeply. I can only imagine what that SOB did to you. I didn't exactly miss the fact that the two of you showed up in town wearin' bandages. So don't try to tell me he didn't hurt you."

Jane shifted gears. "Okay, you're right. Patty and I have been through a bad time. We came to Peachville to decompress. But my husband is not going to find us—"

"Jane Perry is your real name." Jane froze in disbelief. "I saw it on that police report. The first rule when you're on the run from an abusive husband is to change your name so he can't track you down. I don't need to know your daughter's real name. It'd probably be less confusing for her if I didn't know. But, if your husband is the least bit intelligent—and most of these fellas are in a real sick way—he's gonna figure out where you and she are hidin'. I'm not takin' 'no' for an answer." Dan took several steps toward Jane. "I'm gonna protect you."

Jane couldn't believe what she was hearing. "Dan, I—"

"I'm gonna drive by during the day and if I see anything out of place, I'll check it out. I'll drive by on my way home and first thing in the morning. If things get dicey and you need anything, you call me on my cell and I'll be here in the blink of an eye."

Jane needed to put a stop to this. "Dan, please—"

"Don't worry about your situation gettin' around town. This is just between us. You know, I think we should have some sort of code—something that will alert me if you sense you're in danger. How about this: you could flick on the porch light and the light over the garage together. That'll be our 'trouble' signal—"

"Dan! Listen to me!" She decided to let down her guard part way. "You have to trust me when I say this. I cannot have you involved  in my situation with Patty. It's extremely complicated. Thank you for keeping this whole mess quiet. But I simply can't risk getting you involved."

Dan hung his head, more in thought than rejection. "You've gotta cover yourself for your own safety. Talk to Sheriff George and let him know what's going on—"

"No! And don't you dare do that on my behalf!"

"Jane, he could help you!"

"Oh, Christ!" Jane's patience was wearing thin. "There are a lot of details that I can't go into with you! But, trust me, I *cannot* get anyone in law enforcement involved! Do you understand what I'm saying?"

Dan considered Jane's words. "Your husband's a cop, isn't he? That's why you don't want law enforcement involved. They could tip him off to your location."

Jane needed to think carefully before answering. "Yes. My husband's a cop."

"Oh, Lord," Dan said as if the weight of the world were resting on his shoulders. "You sure got a full plate of trouble."

"You have no idea," Jane replied honestly.

"Okay," Dan said after some thought. "We keep Sheriff George out of this. But I'm still gonna watch out for you and Patty." He grabbed his toolbox.

Jane realized it was useless to argue. "What do I owe you for fixing the pipe?"

"Nothin'. It's on me."

"Dan, I have money."

"I don't want your money—" Dan opened the sliding glass door and yelled out to Emily. "I'm leavin', sweetheart! I'll be checkin' up on you and your momma!"

Emily turned and waved. "See ya around, Dan!"

Jane headed to her wallet. "I'm serious. How much?"

"Two dances at the Peach Pit Days Carnival," Dan replied without missing a beat. "It's two weeks from this Saturday in the park across the street. There's line dancin' and two-steppin'. It's a real fun time. Maybe it'll take your mind off your troubles for a little bit."

"Two dances, eh?" Jane said, not sure what to think. "Okay, it's a deal."

"I'll drive by on my way home tonight, just in case. You take care." Dan lugged his toolbox off the counter and started out the front door. He stopped and checked the lock on the doorknob. "You keep this door locked, you hear?" he hollered at Jane.

Jane let out a long sigh. "I will!" she yelled back.

"And the garage and porch light on for trouble!" Dan no sooner closed the door behind him when Jane's beeper vibrated against her waist. Jumping to attention, she grabbed it and pushed the play button. After a crack of static, she heard Weyler's voice.

"Jane. Call me as soon as you can get to a phone. We may have a problem."

# Chapter 20

Jane grabbed her car keys and fanny pack with pistol safely ensconced in it, beckoned Emily to come inside and together they took off in the Subaru in search of a public telephone. Emily reminded her of the one located outside The Apple Cart. But being conspicuously seen talking on the phone was not something Jane wanted right now. She wound around to the main, two-lane highway that looped around the west side of town and headed south. Jane recalled seeing a liquor store about one mile south of town along the mesa. There had to be a public phone there. Sure enough, The Pit Stop liquor store was just over the crest of the mesa. And, thankfully, outside the front doors was a public telephone. "Stay here," Jane ordered Emily. "I won't be long."

Jane crossed the small parking lot and grabbed the phone. Only then did she realize that her hands were slightly shaking. Nervously, she plunked in the quarters and dialed Weyler's private office number. It only rang once before Weyler picked up.

"Weyler here!"

"Boss! It's me," Jane's voice was slightly shaky. "I got your message. What's up?"

"Hold on a second," Weyler said, cupping his hand over the receiver. Even though it was muted, Jane could hear every word. "Look, we're gonna work this out. I'm on the case." Jane heard his office door closing as Weyler removed his hand from the receiver. Jane wondered why he cupped his hand over the receiver. Was he just being polite or was he trying to hide who was in the room? "Okay, Jane, here's the deal. I don't know if it's relavant to the case or just an odd coincidence, but your brother came over to drop off your mail and said that your neighbor, a woman named Hazel, told him that two nights ago she looked outside her bedroom window and saw a male yelled out the window at the perp and he immediately ducked out of her sight and took off."

Jane ran her fingers through her hair, trying to piece together the information. "What did he look like?"

"Apparently, Hazel said it was too dark to clearly identify him. He was wearing a heavy coat, looked to be older rather than some young punk and was carrying implements used for breaking into windows."

Jane's head spun with various angles. "I've never had a break-in. Why now?"

"It does seem suspicious," Weyler said carefully.

Jane wondered if Weyler was trying to lead her to say something. She wanted to trust him but she still didn't know if he was setting her up. The thought crossed her mind that there was no break-in at all and the call was simply a ruse to check in and get her talking. Since she was forbidden to contact Mike, there was no way to confirm Weyler's information. "Is Mike still there? Can I talk to him?"

"He's gone. I paged you right after he left."

Jane figured she would play it close to the vest. "Well, the perp sounds like a pro. I mean, there aren't a lot of older burglars out there who bring hardware to the scene."

"That's true."

"You're putting a 24-hour watch on my house, right?"

"I don't have the manpower for that. But I did ask patrol to concentrate more of their night watch around your block."

"Uh-huh," Jane said with a dubious tone. "Okay, so let's say just for the hell of it, that this is not some sort of 'odd coincidence' as you put it. Let's say that there is some kind of motive behind the attempted break-in. I got to ask myself two questions: Why me and what's he looking for? As far as I was told, the media doesn't know I'm on this case. The DA's office doesn't know either. In fact, as far as anyone's concerned, the last case with my name on it was the Stover murder. The only people who could drop my name regarding the Lawrence case are you and Chris. That's saying that this burglar has got some tie-in with the Lawrence murder. But we're just flyin' blind through shit, aren't we? So then I ask, what's this asshole looking for? It's gotta be information. Right?" Jane thought she heard a distinct pop on the phone. "What was that?"

"What?"

An indignant flush came over her face. If Weyler was recording this conversation or having it monitored by someone, she was not going to dish out any more information nor was she going to let anyone think she was stupid. "I heard a pop on the phone. A *pop?*" Jane said in a leading tone.

"I didn't hear a pop."

"Yeah, well . . ." Jane felt as though someone hit her square in the jaw. She turned around and looked at Emily sitting in the car. Suddenly, a boiling rage curled along her spine. "Goddamn, you fuckers!" Jane said under her breath.

"Jane? What is it?"

"Hey, I know!" Jane said sarcastically. "Maybe it's that elusive Texas mob we keep talking about. Maybe I've got the fucking mob on my ass!"

"Jane, you're not making sense."

"Really? Well, shit, I'm sorry. I've got people trying to break into my house and I can't do anything about it! How am I supposed to feel?"

"Look, I don't know that it's anything to worry about,"

Weyler said gently. "I just felt I should touch base and tell you what happened."

"Yeah. Thanks," Jane said brusquely.

"Jane, are you okay?"

"What's that supposed to mean?" Jane said, wondering how many people were waiting for her answer on the other end.

"It means what it means. You're not . . . I hope to God you're not drinking."

Jane was blown away by Weyler's comment. "Fuck! I should be so lucky!" Her words poured forth with venom. "I'm not getting drunk and I'm not stupid, either!"

"I never said—"

"Listen to me." Jane turned away from Emily and spoke quietly but directly into the phone. "You've got an innocent little girl involved in this mess. *A little girl.* If that doesn't mean shit to you, then so be it. But it means something to me!"

"Jane! My God! I'm well aware of your situation! I don't want anything to happen to that child! We're doing everything we can on this end."

The voice automated operator broke in on the call. "You have twenty seconds left. Please insert one dollar for another five minutes."

"How's it going with the kid?" Weyler said, ignoring the automated voice.

"It's going," Jane said succinctly, not willing to throw any more information in Weyler's direction. "I'm out of quarters," Jane added, knowing full well she had a pocketful of change. She quickly said good-bye and hung up the phone with a hard slam. Back in the car, she lit a cigarette and rolled down the window.

"Is everything okay?" Emily asked.

"I don't know," Jane replied uneasily.

Emily stared into the distance. She was still silently beating herself up for zoning out in front of Dan. *And the photos.* She knew Jane would go ballistic if she knew Dan saw the photos. "Was that phone call 'cause of me?"

"No." Jane took a drag on her cigarette. "What made you think that?"

"I don't know. Just wondering, that's all."

Over the next few days, Dan kept his promise, driving by their house every morning, afternoon and evening. A few times, he stopped in to make minor improvements on the house. One day he improved the reception of their television by installing a used antenna on the roof. This addition brought in PBS and NBC when the sky was clear and the wind was not blowing.

As the days progressed, Jane sensed the gradual tightening of a noose around her neck. The more she tried to figure it out, the tighter and more mysterious that noose became. There were moments when she wondered if the feeling had to do with the attempted break-in at her house. Other times, she questioned if it was just the daily tedium in Peachville. No matter the source, the unidentifiable stress built exponentially. If the past was any indicator, this anomalous sensation typically heralded a monumental event in Jane's life.

June 16 rolled around—the day of Kathy's "Cherry Jubilee." Jane hoped Emily would forget the invitation, but no such luck. By four o'clock, Emily was begging Jane to take her to Kathy's house. As much as Jane hated the thought of being part of the insipid soirée, she realized that not showing up would generate further gossip and derision by the town hens. Finally, she agreed to bring Emily with her on the condition that they would be out of there in two hours or less.

Kathy and Kent's house was located atop Strong's Mesa, a fertile plateau that stretched several miles north and west. The landscape was dotted with two-level, wood and stone houses, occupied by well-heeled retirees and the newly rich. Kent and Kathy fit into that mold via Kent's real estate sales and Kathy's modest income managing rental properties and the occasional home sale. Their house was situated on ten acres of rolling green pasture. A bank of floor to ceiling picture windows on one side of the house faced the setting sun, reflecting an almost uncomfortable crimson blaze. The circular drive was packed with SUVs and assorted Subaru wagons. Jane wedged her wagon behind a Toyota 4-Runner with bumper stickers that extolled the driver's love of craft shows. "I Luv Being Crafty" elicited a groan from Jane and a roll of the eyes.

Jane and Emily walked across the gravel driveway and up to the large, Mission-style front door. It was several inches ajar—a common practice for small-town folks and an unspoken signal to come in. The humming din of women's voices could be heard, along with the eruption of an occasional grating cackle. Jane let out a tired sigh and entered the house with Emily close by her side.

The tri-level house was duly impressive. Vaulted ceilings led the eye upward to various odd shapes of windows that framed the second story. The home was furnished in a combination of Santa Fe Chic and classic old Mexican style. Burnt orange hues blended with soft terra cotta tones that effortlessly flowed into deep burgundy and chestnut accents. It was a showplace and an obvious source of pride for Kathy. Jane and Emily stood outside a clique of two dozen women who milled around a long wooden dinner table, munching on nachos and salsa.

"Does anybody know how many points a nacho is on the Weight Watchers' menu?" a woman yelled out.

Kathy poked her head through the gaggle of giggling females and caught sight of Jane. She excitedly waved her arm and motioned Jane forward. "Hi! Come on in, girls!" Kathy maneuvered her way around the band of women to meet Jane and Emily. "I am *so* glad you came!" Turning to the cluster of droning voices, Kathy announced Jane and Emily's appearance. "Girls! *Girls!* I want you all to meet Anne and Patty Calver! They're the two new folks in town who I've been telling you all about!" Jane wondered just exactly what she had been telling these women when they turned in unison to Jane with a look of judgment across their faces. Emily's attention was drawn outside through the open French doors to the backyard where Heather and a few other young girls were practicing line dancing steps in front of the family's outdoor trampoline. "Would you like to go out and say hi to Heather?" Kathy asked Emily with a big, toothy grin.

Emily looked up at Jane. "Is that okay with you, Mom?"

"Oh, there she goes again!" Kathy quickly interjected. "Little Miss Manners!"

Jane's jaw clenched. "Yeah, sure. It's okay."

Emily scooted across the wooden floor and into the backyard.

"Her stitches are out," Kathy said, eyes fixed on Emily.

"Yes," Jane said tersely.

Kathy turned to Jane. "That's odd. Dr. Armstrong didn't mention your visit."

"Kathy!" came a voice from around the table. "We're gonna need more mason jars for the cherries!"

Kathy turned to the woman. "I've got plenty stashed away in Kent's workshop! I'll get 'em for ya!" Kathy took Jane by the arm. "But first, I want to introduce you to the gals!" She escorted Jane to the table and proceeded to point and name each and every woman around the table. In between nodding like a robot, Jane stole a glance toward the backyard where Emily was engaged in her own conversation.

"We're practicing our steps!" Heather announced to Emily with a snotty tone.

"Who's she?" one of the girls asked Heather.

"I'm Em—," Emily caught herself. "Patty."

"Don't you even know your own name?" Heather said with a smirk.

Emily let Heather's comment roll off her back. "So, what are you practicing for?"

The girls looked surprised by Emily's question.

"What do you think?" Heather asked. "*The dance?* At

the Peach Pit Days Carnival? I mean, *duh!*"

"Is that a big deal?"

"*A big deal?*" Heather said with a dramatic gesture. "Oh my god! Where are you from? Yes, it's a big hairy deal!"

"Is there a contest?" Emily asked.

"What do you think, Einstein?" Heather repeated in a mocking tone, taking her place at the head of the line. "Come on," she said to the other girls, "let's do it again."

"Can I practice with you?" Emily blurted out.

Heather took a step toward Emily. "Do you know how to line dance?"

"No. But I'm a real fast learner."

Heather spun around and stood back at the head of the line. "Sorry! Only advanced girls are allowed in my group. Besides, you don't have any cowboy boots. Everybody knows you have to have cowboy boots to be a good line dancer!"

"Oh . . ." Emily said, dejected.

The girls continued to practice their steps. Emily turned and walked toward the house, peering through the panes of glass in search of Jane. A hand draped across Emily's shoulder, causing her to jump slightly.

"I didn't mean to startle you!" Kathy said. "You meet Heather's little friends?"

"Yes," Emily replied. "They're practicing for the dance contest."

"Well, that's what it takes to win! Go join them!"

"That's okay. I've never line danced before and I don't have cowboy boots."

Kathy turned her lips into an exaggerated frown. "Oh, you poor little thing!" Kathy quickly perked up. "Hey! I could sure use your help bringing in some canning jars! What do ya say?"

"Sure!"

Emily trailed Kathy around the corner of the house, away from the gathering women, and followed her into an airy, windowed greenhouse that had been masterfully refurbished into a weatherproof workshop.

"Okay, now," Kathy said, plucking her front teeth with her first finger, "where did I put those jars?"

Emily looked over at a small wooden table. A detailed, three dimensional landscape model filled the table, complete with miniature trees, shrubs, cars and houses. Amazed by the detail, Emily leaned closer to the landscape to get a better look. "Did you make this?"

Kathy let out a soft chuckle. "Oh, heavens no! That's one of Kent's little projects." Kathy crossed to the table and knelt down so she was on eye level with Emily. "They don't call him the real estate wizard of Peachville for nothing. He says it's important for clients to see things visually. This is a model for a luxury home site just over the ridge. He made all those little trees, cars and houses by hand. And he says *I'm* the crafty one!"

Emily was totally enthralled. "The trees look real. Like they have leaves and everything—" With that, Emily brushed her finger ever so gently over one of the trees and it toppled over. "I'm sorry!" Emily expressed, genuinely upset.

"We can fix that!" Kathy said, trying to prop up the tree.

"Here, let me do it." Emily did her best to fix the blunder as she poured a drop of glue from a nearby bottle and affixed the tree back onto the board. "I'm real sorry. You can tell your husband I messed it up."

Kathy closely watched Emily's reaction. "I won't tell him a thing," she said, her voice suddenly void of all perkiness and the smile gone. "You can trust me, Patty. It'll be our little secret."

Emily looked at Kathy. "Thanks. That's nice of you." Emily softly tapped her finger on the tree. "There! Good as new!"

Kathy smiled at Emily, her blue eyes twinkling. "He'll never know."

Emily glanced over to Kathy and returned the smile. "You've got the prettiest blue eyes I've ever seen."

"Well, my goodness!" Kathy said, taken aback, "Aren't you *sweet!*"

"*I mean it.* I've never seen anybody with eyes that blue except in Disney movies."

"Well, you have *made my day!*" Kathy said sincerely. Emily pulled her hair behind her ear. Kathy was silent for a few seconds before carefully changing the subject. "How does your head feel?"

"Fine. Mom says it's healing really good."

"Did it hurt when Dr. Armstrong took out those stitches?"

"Oh, ah," Emily hesitated, caught off guard. "I didn't need to go to see him."

"What do you mean? You had to have your stitches out—"

"Yeah, well, we couldn't go."

"Couldn't go?"

"I don't mean 'couldn't go.'" Emily was obviously flustered. "I mean, we couldn't, um . . . we couldn't afford it. Money's been really tight since daddy died."

"So, your mother took the stitches out?"

"Yeah. And the best part is she didn't hurt me at all!" Kathy stiffened as her eyes filled with tears. Emily was confused by the woman's reaction. "What's wrong?"

Kathy reached up and gently stroked Emily's cheek. "You've been through a lot of pain. I can see it in your eyes. You're so young. You don't deserve that kind of hurt." Emily could feel herself slipping away from herself and didn't want to lose it in front of Kathy like she did with Dan. She quickly turned away from Kathy. "It's okay, darling," Kathy said with great compassion.

"I'm sorry, I can't—"

"There's no need to apologize," Kathy said, increasingly concerned.

"It's just that, ah," Emily felt herself falling into the void, "it's . . . I . . ." The more she searched for the right words, the more she stuttered, sounding more suspicious.

"It's okay." Kathy leaned over and hugged Emily with

all her might. Emily resisted before she fell against
Kathy's chest, draping one arm around her shoulder.
"You're so brave," Kathy whispered to Emily, choking
back tears. "You shouldn't have to endure any of this."
Pulling back, she tenderly cupped her palms around
Emily's face. "Listen to me," she said with great urgency,
"you can tell me *anything* and it will stay between us
forever!"

Emily felt her heart racing faster as her head spun. She
desperately wanted to blurt out the truth. "I'm sorry . . .
I—"

"*I can help you!*" Kathy whispered. "You have to trust
me!"

"Patty!" Jane hollered from a distance.

Emily jumped slightly and turned to the sound of Jane's
voice. "I have to go!" Emily said, pulling away from
Kathy.

Kathy grabbed the child's hand. "Patty, I mean what I
said. If you want to talk to me about anything, I'll be there
for you!"

"Thank you. You're a nice lady." Emily turned and
walked out the door. As she rounded the corner, she ran
smack into Jane.

"Christ almighty!" Jane exclaimed. "I've been calling
your name for five fucking minutes! Where have you
been?" Emily looked back at the open door of the
workshop, knowing that Kathy must have heard Jane's
harangue. Not wanting to create more problems, Emily
kept walking to gain distance from the workshop. Jane,
not understanding Emily's behavior, angrily followed
her. "Hey! Don't walk away from me when I'm talking
to you!"

Emily turned to Jane with a "Be careful" look on her
face. "*Mom, don't!*"

At that moment, unbeknownst to Jane, Kathy quietly
appeared outside the workshop door holding a small case
of jars in her arms. Emily motioned with her eyes to get
Jane to realize the intrusion. Jane caught the drift and

turned around to face Kathy. There was a heavy hush between the two of them as Kathy scrutinized Jane with guarded scorn.

"I'll take these jars into the house," Kathy said, her throat choked with apprehension. "It's time to pit those cherries." She quietly closed the workshop door with her elbow and walked across the grass and into her house.

Jane turned to Emily. "What in the hell was that about?"

"I tried to tell you but you weren't watching my eyes!" Emily said under her breath, slightly irritated.

"Where in the fuck were you all this time?"

"I was in the workshop helping Kathy get extra jars for the cherries."

Jane felt her cop radar encircle Emily and sensed that a lie was afoot. "Then where are your jars?"

"What?" Emily replied, feeling Jane's probing eyes.

"Don't 'what,' me!" Jane said angrily. "You're not being truthful! What in the hell was going on in there?"

"Nothing!" Emily said, exasperated. "I know you don't like Kathy, but that's 'cause you don't know her—"

"The hell I don't know her!" Jane said abruptly.

"She's *nice!*"

"Is that so?" Jane replied sarcastically.

"Yeah, that's so! Emily turned away from Jane. "She just . . ." Emily said quietly, "she just wanted to know if I was okay, that's all."

Jane smelled a rat. "That's all, huh?" she responded, not buying one word of Emily's earnest statement.

Without realizing it, Emily looked down and to the left as she nervously licked her lips. "Yeah. That's all."

Jane saw the telltale signs of a lie. As much as she wanted to verbally force the truth out of Emily, she knew she couldn't. Jane suddenly felt like an outsider and hated it. "Fine. Come on! We're getting out of here!"

"We can't leave yet!"

"I said in and out of here in two hours or less!"

"We've been here less than an hour! We can't leave

before we help with the cherries or it'll look weird!"

"I don't give a shit what it looks like!"

Emily approached Jane with a stern look. "Well, *I* do."
She brushed past Jane with a petulant step. Jane reached
out to grab her arm, but Emily moved too quickly.

"Emily!" Jane said irritated, under her breath. "Goddamnit!"

Emily trod with purpose across the grass and into the
house. Jane went after her. However, once Jane rounded
the corner of Kent's workshop, she slowed her pace in
order to not draw attention. She caught up with Emily
inside the house, just as the child was handed a huge bowl
of fresh cherries by one of the women. Jane started to
move toward Emily but stopped the minute she saw
Kathy. She knew that if she pulled Emily away from the
women, Kathy's case against her would be wrapped up.

"Patty, darling," Kathy said, a tinge of nervousness in
her voice. "How 'bout if you hold that bowl while P.J.
scoops out the cherries into the machine."

Emily looked up at P.J., a fleshy woman who was
dressed in an aqua pant suit and jaunty matching baseball
cap. "What does P.J. stand for?" Emily asked quietly.

"Peggy Josephine," P.J. said with a halfhearted smile
on her face as she eagerly dug the cherries out of the bowl
using two hands. "You can just imagine how that name
went over with the kids in school. So, I decided to
become just P.J.!"

Emily held the bowl steady, as P.J. continued to unearth
more cherries and transfer them to the pitting machine.
"I have a friend named A.J.—" Emily offered.

"Take it easy with those cherries, P.J.!" Kathy
instructed with a smile. "There's already a bunch of them
bruised and leaking at the bottom of that bowl!"

Emily stole a glance through the crowd of women at
Jane. Jane, in turn, regarded her with steely eyes, still
smarting from their backyard confrontation. Kathy didn't
miss Emily's glance, nor Jane's irate facial reaction. As
P.J. got down to the bottom of the ceramic bowl, she

shoved her chubby hands into the cherries and screwed her face into a disagreeable expression. "Oh, Kathy! I see what you mean. We got ourselves a passel of bruised cherries at the bottom of this bowl!" P.J. withdrew both her hands from the bowl and revealed them to the group. Her skin was stained red from the cherry juice and dripping with red pulp. "How do you like that, girls?" she said with a chuckle.

The group of women chortled as they continued chatting amongst themselves. Not one of them noticed Emily's reaction. No one, except for Jane.

Emily's eyes fixated on P.J.'s hands. Her eyes followed one drop of scarlet juice as it traveled down P.J.'s wrist and disappeared under her sleeve, leaving a moist stain on the material. Her glance drifted down to the near-empty bowl filled with remnants of bruised cherries, floating in several cups of crimson juice. Everything went into slow motion. The women's voices were muffled; Emily focused on the bloodred cherry juice sloshing against the bottom of the bowl. Without realizing it, she tipped the ceramic bowl, causing a stream of scarlet juice to pour onto the floor. The small puddle encircled her shoes. Her heart pounded wildly, her throat tightened and her eyes filled with sheer terror. Suddenly, a piercing scream cut through Emily's memory. She quickly let go of the bowl as it crashed to the floor, smashing into hundreds of tiny pieces.

The sound of the breaking shards jolted Emily back into reality. For the first time, the dark memory held on just long enough for the sharp scream to linger amidst the din of female voices in the kitchen. The child looked around, not yet certain of where her body began and ended. She gazed down at the shattered bowl and then urgently looked for Jane. Once she spotted her, she pushed through the pack of women and grabbed her as if she were a lifeline. As she clutched Jane's shirt and buried her head against Jane's belly, she half-whispered in a terrified tone, "I'm sorry."

Jane gently held her hand against Emily's trembling head, knowing that every prying eye was pinned on her. It was the epitome of a rock and a hard place and she knew it. Jane looked over at Kathy, who was obviously disturbed by Emily's reaction.

"It's okay, honey," Kathy said, calling over to Emily. "It's just a silly bowl."

Emily kept her head buried against Jane. "Can I help clean it up?" Jane offered.

"No!" Kathy asserted. "It's not a big deal, Anne. These kind of things happen all the time! Kids can't help themselves!" Kathy's voice was bordering on desperate.

"I know, Kathy," Jane said, trying her best to not look upset. She patted Emily's head and bent forward. "Let's go."

Emily kept a tight hold on Jane as the two walked outside and got into their car. The child was still confused and embarrassed as Jane buckled her into the seat belt and stuck the key in the ignition. Jane looked up at the front living room window and found Kathy staring back at her. "Shit," Jane whispered. She put the car in gear and drove onto the county road. Once she was out of sight of the house, she pulled the car over, leaving the motor running. "You okay?" she said quietly.

Emily leaned her head against the passenger window. "I don't know."

"Did you . . ." Jane stopped, hating every second of this. "Did you remember anything back there?"

"Almost." Emily turned to Jane, hoping for an answer. "It was just a bowl of cherries and some juice!"

Jane stared out the front window. She knew exactly why the cherries triggered Emily's memory of the crime scene. But the devil himself could not force her to reveal the blood-soaked connection. Jane felt helpless. Then she glanced into her rear vision mirror. Kathy was standing on the county road, several feet from her circle driveway.

Jane realized that she was waiting for Jane to make a move toward Emily so she could report it to Sheriff George. Jane wanted to bolt from the car and rip her a new one. But, instead, she clenched her jaw, put the car in gear and drove toward home.

Twilight fell over Strong's Mesa as Jane wound the Subaru around the dirt road that eventually emptied into Peachville's Main Street. Not a word was spoken between Jane and Emily as they slowly crept down the main drag. The stores were closed for the day, leaving a seeming ghost town to occupy the darkness. Jane rolled the Subaru to a four-way stop sign and didn't move. That uneasy, choking sensation she'd felt for the last few days was replaced with a disturbing dull ache in her gut.

She looked at Emily. Her head was propped against the window as she half dozed. The child's palm lay flat against the glass, slightly twitching. Jane could see Emily's eyeballs erratically moving side to side, engaged in an obvious dream. "Don't," Emily murmured, under her breath. Jane waited and watched. Emily's hand twitched again before reaching out into the air as if she were trying to grasp at something. "Don't let go," she whispered. Jane looked on helplessly, not sure what to do. Seconds passed and Emily's body relaxed, falling deeper into sleep.

*Don't let go*, Jane thought. Probably a nightmare from when Emily hung off her bedroom roof, Jane determined. But then again, Jane mused, Emily told her she remained silent so the perp wouldn't know she was there. So, whom was Emily talking to? Jane finally shook off the cop suspicion, chalking it up to the destructive power of nightmares.

She turned her attention to the street and rolled down the window. The crickets issued back and forth inflections to each other. In the distance, the coal train stood in place as the chug-chug-chug reverberated throughout the valley. A summer breeze, slightly cool and wet, swept through the car bringing with it the smell of dried grass mixed with engine oil that puddled on the asphalt. The air was heavy, primed to release a hard summer rainstorm.

And Jane waited. Within the silence, there was something both profound and forbidding. She started to tap the accelerator when she felt her beeper vibrate. Jane pressed the play button and heard Weyler's voice. It sounded different. There was a dour intonation.

"Jane. It's me. When you can get to a phone, please give me a call at my house." Weyler said before hanging up.

Jane looked over at Emily. The child had fallen asleep. An acrid odor blew from the east as she drove down Main Street and up onto the highway. Her heart raced. Turning left, she headed south to The Pit Stop and parked in front of the outside telephone. As Jane dialed Weyler's private number, she debated what tone suited her best for the conversation. But before she could decide, he answered.

"Hello?"

"It's me. I got your page." Jane suddenly felt sick. "What's wrong?"

"I'm sorry, Jane," Weyler said, his voice slightly breaking.

"Why are you sorry?" Jane asked, wincing. The coal train chugged closer.

"I don't know any other way to say this. Jane . . . Your father died."

The world hung in suspension for Jane. She gazed into the distance. A rush of heat raced down her spine, followed by an icy chill. The coal train approached on the tracks across the street. Jane stood still as the clamor of steel and metal ground against each other and screamed into the dark, summer sky. Within a couple minutes, the train passed and all fell silent again.

"It happened around three o'clock this afternoon," Weyler continued. "Apparently he'd experienced minor discomfort in his chest and told the nurse about it. By the time she called the doctor and returned it was over. He didn't struggle. No suffering."

"No suffering?" Jane repeated, halfway outside of her body.

"None. Your brother called me. He's already been over there and he saw your dad before they took him to the mortuary—"

Jane came back to life. "Oh, Jesus! Mike can't handle that!"

"He sounded okay on the phone—"

"I should have been there for him," Jane whispered.

"Are you okay?"

"I don't know . . ." Jane said, her mind drifting far away.

"This is a mess. But I can't have you come back here now. I'm sorry—"

"I have to talk to Mike," Jane said urgently.

"I know you do. It goes against policy, but the Department will understand. Please keep the conversation short and do nothing to reveal your location. Has your brother got Caller ID on his phone?"

"No. And even if he did, who the hell is he gonna tell?"

"You never know. There can't be any slips."

Jane buried her head in her hand. "There won't be any slips!"

"I'm not accusing you of being inept. Please don't take it that way. We've just discovered some possible internal problems downstairs—"

"What internal problems? With this case?"

"No. Nothing to do with your case. Don't worry about it. I've just got to try and keep a cap on it. I don't need any slipups in your direction when you talk to your brother that could put the Lawrence case in jeopardy."

"Are we done here?" Jane's patience was wearing thin.

"Yes. You take care, Jane. I'm sorry for your loss."

"Yeah. Bye." Jane hung up the receiver just long

enough to plop another series of quarters into the pay phone and dial Mike's number. The phone rang several times before someone picked up.

"Hello?" It was Lisa's voice on the other end of the line.

Jane was befuddled. "I'm looking for Mike—"

"Jane? It's me. Lisa."

Jane felt a prickle of anger. "*Lisa?*"

"I'm so sorry about your father, Jane. Mike's sitting right here. Hold on."

"Janie?" Mike said, taking the phone.

"Oh, God, Mike. I should have been there for you—"

"No, no. I understand. It's okay." His voice was choked with emotion.

"No, it's not!" Jane buried her head against the cold metal of the pay phone.

"Janie, please. I'm tellin' you. It's really okay. You got a job to do—"

Jane caught an underlying tone in her brother's voice; there was strength in his inflections that she'd never heard before. "Shit. I can't believe he's really dead."

"I know. I figured he'd never die."

"Yeah."

"When I saw him . . . Lisa and I went over there and, ah, we went into his room. He was lying there with no tubes or nothin'. He looked peaceful. For the first time, Janie, I wasn't afraid of him." Mike broke down. "I talked to him. I told him that I forgave him for everything and that I hoped he'd find peace."

Jane couldn't believe what she was hearing. "What the fuck?" Jane's voice rose. Unbeknownst to Jane, Emily woke up and watched her.

"It was an important step for me, Janie," Mike said, gaining control.

"*Step?*"

"We talked about it at the meeting last week. If you can forgive those who hurt you, you can begin to find peace."

Without realizing it, Jane rubbed her finger against her scar. "Jesus Christ, Mike! You can't *forgive* someone like that!"

"*Yes*. You can. You *have* to."

"No! God won't forgive him and neither will I!"

"I don't wanna fight with you, Janie. Look, Lisa's here. I'm gonna be fine." He paused briefly. "You get the message about that guy trying to break into your house?"

"Yes," Jane said subdued.

"Okay. I'm glad we could talk. You be safe wherever you are." Mike hung up.

"*Mike?*" The sound of a dial tone droned. Jane stood stunned and then hung up the receiver. A few drops of fat raindrops fell on her face as she stared at the telephone. Within seconds, the clouds broke open and a torrent of rain poured from the sky. Jane closed her eyes and bent her head backward. Pellets of water bounced off her face and saturated her hair. She felt someone take her hand and rest their head against her body.

"Hey," Jane said, looking down at Emily, "get back in the car."

"You come, too," Emily stated, sensing something was very wrong.

"Get outta the rain, Emily!" Emily didn't move. "*Go on*," Jane said.

Emily reluctantly headed back to the car. Through the rain swept front window, Emily watched as Jane walked into The Pit Stop and stood at the counter, pointing at an object behind the cashier. The cashier placed a bottle of Jack Daniels on the counter. Jane passed him the money. He bagged the liquor, handed it to Jane and she exited the store. Emily cautiously regarded Jane as she got into the car, stuffed the bag between her legs and stuck the key into the ignition.

Emily fastened her seat belt. "What happened on the phone?" she quietly asked.

"My dad died," Jane replied, her eyes fixated on the bag of booze.

Emily was stunned. "I'm sorry."

"Don't be," Jane said brusquely as she backed out of The Pit Stop and sped down the highway away from Peachville.

Emily held tightly onto the chest strap of the seat belt as Jane shifted gears. The two-lane highway was pitch black and blanketed with puddles of rainwater. Jane reached into the bag and brought out the Jack Daniels, tossing the paper sack into the back seat. Emily quietly watched, her heart beating like crazy.

Jane drove another several hundred feet and slammed her hand hard against the dashboard. "Fuck it!" she screamed as she crossed over the center yellow line and brought the Subaru to a skidding stop on the left side of the road between two large trees. She turned off the engine and flung the keys onto the dashboard. With the headlights on, she got out of the car, Jack Daniels in hand, and slammed the door shut. Emily watched as Jane twisted off the top of the bottle and pitched it across the road. "Fuck you, you son-of-a-bitch! *Fuck you!*" Jane screamed into the darkness. Standing in the blinding glare of the headlights, she drank a hefty gulp of whiskey. Shaking off the bitter taste, she winced as the whiskey burned her throat. "You fucking go to hell!" she screamed, thrusting the bottle into the cloud-dappled night sky. She took another significant swig, allowing the booze to drip down her chin and onto her blouse. After another sip, she began to choke and cough. Swallowing hard, Jane fought her body's reaction to the whiskey, drawing the bottle back to her lips. But before she could take another mouthful, her gut cramped and she doubled over onto the hood of the car. The more she struggled to control herself, the more her body kicked back. "God-damnit!" Jane screamed as she hurled the bottle against the nearby tree, sending it into a million glass chards. She fell to her knees, planting herself in the muddy soil and vomited. Once there was nothing left in her stomach, she dry heaved for several minutes.

Emily opened her car door. Sloping her way through the mud, she made her way to the front of the Subaru. She knelt down next to Jane and draped her arm around her shoulder. "Put your arm around me. I'll help you back to the car."

Jane's face was inches from the wet ground. Her head spun as the fight drained out of her. "Just let me be."

"You can't sit here in the mud. Come on. I'll help you up."

"Please, Emily," Jane urged, "just leave me alone."

Emily leaned her head against Jane's shoulder and gazed off toward the road. Suddenly, she saw the high beams of a car flash against the tall trees as it crested over the far hill behind them. She turned and was greeted with a flash of red and blue light spinning atop the car. Emily turned back to Jane. "We're in trouble."

# Chapter 21

"Did you hear me?" Emily said, poking Jane in the shoulder. The red and blue police lights drew closer. "I think it's Sheriff George," Emily said confidentially as the patrol car pulled up behind Jane's Subaru.

Jane's mind was still somewhat far away. Almost in a daze, she caught a whiff of her shirt where she had just dribbled the whiskey. "Shit," she said under her breath.

From the sheriff's point of view, he saw a Subaru wagon that had been obviously pulled to the side of the road at the rapid rate of speed, thanks to the muddy skid marks along the pavement. The passenger side door was wide open and the two individuals—one, who was clearly a child—were bent down in front of the car and not responding to his presence. Sheriff George kept on the patrol car's high beams and adjusted his glaring driver's side spotlight onto Jane and Emily. He got out of the car, checking the license plate of the Subaru. "Hello?" he called out, walking next to the car.

Emily looked down at the muddy ground and the puddle of vomit that Jane pitched from her gut. She heard the sheriff's footsteps come closer through the sloppy trail of mud. In a desperate move, Emily grabbed her stomach and pretended to throw up right over Jane's vomit.

The Sheriff stopped in his tracks. "Patty? What's wrong?"

Emily lifted up her head, wiped her mouth with her sleeve and turned around to acknowledge the sheriff. "Mom," Emily said in an exaggerated voice that had a tinge of overblown drama to it. "It's Sheriff George." With that, Emily turned back around and pretended to hurl more into the mud.

Jane was momentarily speechless by Emily's quick thinking. "Hello, Sheriff," she said, the words falling like gravel from her throat.

"What's wrong?"

"We were at Kathy's house," Emily said, her head still bent over the puddle of vomit. "I think I ate too many cherries . . ." The Sheriff walked closer. Emily realized that he would smell alcohol on Jane. In a bold move, Emily flung her body against Jane's chest, "Oh, Mom!" Emily said, grabbing on to Jane, "please take me home!"

Jane wrapped her arms around Emily and awkwardly worked herself up onto her feet. Emily stuck to her chest, refusing to let a hint of the whiskey aroma waft toward the sheriff. "Okay," Jane said, playing along. "Let's get you back into the car."

Sheriff George reached out. "Let me help you—"

Emily quickly pretended to start vomiting again.

"Try to hold it in!" Jane said, patting Emily's head. "Thanks for your concern, Sheriff." Jane put Emily into the passenger seat, before heading to the driver's side.

He leaned down and knocked on Emily's side window. "You feel better soon!"

Emily looked up at the sheriff with the weakest expression she could muster. Jane slowly turned right and headed back to Peachville.

Jane pulled into their driveway and turned off the ignition. She sat motionless in the car, as did Emily. Realizing the gravity of what just transpired, she buried her head in her hand. "Thank you," she whispered to Emily.

Emily reached over and stroked Jane's shoulder.

"You're welcome."

There was no way Jane was going to sleep that night. So, instead of heading for the bedroom, she propped up a set of pillows on the living room couch and sat watching television. Thanks to Dan, she could choose from the "semi-snowy" NBC channel or the crisp reception of PBS.

Emily started the evening sitting alongside Jane but quickly wound up sleeping with her head on Jane's lap. Jane lit a cigarette and took a deep drag. A truck's headlights slowed in front of their house. Jane leaned forward just enough to see that it was Dan conducting his self-appointed night duty. She noted that he observed the lone porch light on outside. Jane recalled that he suggested a "trouble code" of both the garage and porch lights turned on to signal his help. She shook her head. Jane was always the one protecting the weak and innocent, not the other way around. Sitting there with only the light from the television to illuminate the room, she was overwhelmed by the realization of her present situation. Gone were the nights of playing pool at RooBar, getting loaded with Mike and passing out on the couch. Her father was dead. Mike had moved on to a new life with a girl who seemed halfway decent. Whenshe took a step back and analyzed the situation, Jane concluded that she was totally alone in the world. As for her career, Jane had no clue where that was headed. Her job had become her identity and she worked hard to get where she was, sacrificing relationships in the process. If her career was going to hell, she had no clue where she could fit into the world.

With this self-realization, it was all Jane could do to keep an interest in the television show. It was the popular *Antiques Roadshow*. The series' premise was simple: average people dug through their dusty attics and crowded closets for cherished knickknacks that hopefully had some monetary worth. The individual— usually with a hopeful glint in their eye—stood by while a knowledgeable antique appraiser discussed the historical and sometimes quaint background story of their treasures and whether they were of any great worth. After suffering through four original Norman Rockwell prints and a woman with a vase that she swore belonged to George Washington, Jane was just about to change the channel to the crop report. But the camera suddenly focused on an unusual desk—the same distinctive desk that Jane's mother had owned and that also stood in the Lawrence house. It was the one Jane nicknamed "The Riddle Desk," due to the hidden compartments that were only known to the desk's owners.

The owner of this particular desk, a middle-aged woman, stood on one side of the piece while the antique appraiser stood on the opposite side. "How long has your family owned this desk?" the appraiser asked.

"My mother bought it before I was born at an estate sale. So, thirty plus years, at least," the woman chuckled self-consciously.

"You don't see many of these desks anymore. They are rare and they are all different. What looks like an ordinary desk with various compartments is actually a clever ruse, thanks to the creativity of the artist and builder of the piece. His name was Cornelius James. James was actually a very gifted painter, renowned for his ability to depict still life objects so well that people would try and grab them out of the painting. However, as brilliant as he was, he couldn't make a living from his painting. This angered James, especially when his peers were raking in the money for their drab artwork. Cornelius James decided to make a bold statement against those 'canvas whores,' as he called them. Consider it poetic justice with a dash of vengeance thrown in for good measure! This desk and the others that he designed became his audacious answer to the art world. You see, besides painting, James was also an excellent craftsman. He blended his artistic gifts and built a desk with a hidden message. That message was 'Look behind the exterior of what you think you see, for what appears to your naked eye is but an illusion.' James was frequently quoted. I remember one quote, 'We believe that what we see is all there is. But behind the facade, lies the truth . . . '"

Jane was struck by the appraiser's words. She paid close attention to his information, sensing somehow that the words held importance.

"The subterfuge was carefully woven into the basic design and, later, the painted surfaces," the appraiser continued. "James never made the same desk twice. However, the similarities were as follows: what might look like the knob on a drawer . . ." the appraiser attempted to pull out a "drawer," "was in actuality a beautifully painted replica of a knob. But if you knew where to look . . ." the appraiser fumbled under the desk and along the side of the desk, "you just might be able to open that drawer!" Turning to the owner of the desk, the appraiser asked with a sheepish grin, "I hope you know how to open that drawer!"

The woman confidently ran her finger down the front leg, pushed a hidden button and freed the front drawer. "My six-year-old nephew found that hidden button!" the woman said.

"How many secret compartments are there?" asked a female onlooker.

"To my knowledge," the appraiser replied, "James never had a set number of hidden compartments. I saw a desk in a Virginia farmhouse with fourteen, while another from a collection down in Birmingham had eleven. At least, eleven they knew of!"

The owner of the desk spoke up. "We had the desk twenty years before we learned of this side panel that pops out when you press a button in one of the top mail compartments." The woman slid her hand inside the first mail compartment, pushed a button and the side panel opened like a sloping cereal bin at the supermarket.

Jane leaned forward. It was as though something was tugging at her gut. Emily opened her eyes and sleepily looked at the television screen.

"Yes, I'm glad you brought that point to our attention!" the appraiser excitedly replied. "There was one common denominator in all of the desks. While they were not all located in the same place, James made sure that there was one secret compartment that was the most difficult to find. For him, that compartment represented the worst trickery that the art world had foisted upon society. In his eyes, when you uncovered that top secret compartment, you had successfully opened your eyes to the real villain that lay buried between yourself and the Divine Truth that would set you free! They were deep thoughts from an extraordinary man who was never able to get the recognition he deserved!"

"Any hints on finding that top secret compartment?" a man asked the appraiser.

"Well, James was fond of placing those highly valued compartments in one of three places. The side of the desk, along the front here and finally, back here at the rear of the desk. For those desks that had the ultra secret compartment located at the rear location, it was not unusual for the owner to situate the desk several inches from a wall in order to accommodate the opening of the compartment." The camera pulled in tightly on the desk's secret side compartment as the appraiser showed the depth of space needed to reconcile the opening.

Emily became fixated on the close-up of the secret compartment. The sound of the appraiser's voice dissolved into the background and was loudly replaced by the sound of her parents yelling at each other.

"How could you keep this letter from me?" Emily's mother yelled at her father. "Goddamnit, didn't you think I would eventually find out? All those nights . . . All those goddamn nights of you calling me and telling me you had to work late . . ."

"I *was* working," her father weakly interjected.

"I don't think they call it 'work' after the second or third cocktail!"

"Patty, please! We've got to talk about this rationally."

"Rationally? Oh, that's rich! Suddenly you want to be *rational?* Why wasn't that thought going through your head when the relationship became clear? Why didn't you just walk away?"

Emily heard shafts of distortion cut through her memory, followed once again by the clear voices of her parents.

"*Didn't you read this?*" her mother screamed.

"I don't want to read it again!"

"No, you don't want to see what you've done to us! Let's pretend it doesn't exist and maybe it'll go away! Am I right? Well, *this* is not going to go away! But I am and I'm taking Emily with me!"

Emily heard the reverberation of wood slamming against wood. The sound instantly jerked the child back into herself.

Jane looked down at the kid. "You okay?"

"We had a desk like that. My mom kept all my hand-made birthday cards in it."

"Where did she store them?"

"In the top secret spot that man was talking about. Mommy said she wanted to keep special cards in a special place. She never told me where it was because that's where she kept private stuff that I wasn't supposed to see."

"What weren't you supposed to see?"

"Santa's reply to my letters," Emily said offhandedly, "report cards . . ."

Jane sat back and stared at the TV screen as the scene changed to another antique. Emily rolled off Jane's lap and curled up against the side of the couch. Jane clicked off the TV and sat in the dark. A familiar feeling tugged at her gut—it was the same psychic pull she felt many times before, akin to the sensation of cresting a long, steep hill and finally locating what you've been searching for. But the more Jane tried to structure the impression into something she could touch and understand, the more elusive it became.

Resting her head against the couch, she closed her eyes and tried to succumb to slumber. But, instead, she hovered between the worlds. She opened her eyes and fumbled through the darkness of the living room and toward the radio console. Turning on the radio, she was amazed how much light the front panel emitted. Odd, she surmised, for an old radio. Jane spun the dial from one band of static to another until she heard the crisp voice of Tony Mooney. Amazing, she mused.

"We all think we own our thoughts," Mooney declared in his deep, trademark tenor. "But do we really? What if two people could share the same thought? The same experience? But, perhaps, from a different point of view?" Jane noted how the light on the radio console seemed to glow even brighter. "Would you allow yourself to suspend disbelief for just one second and believe that?" Mooney leaned closer to the microphone. "Would you . . . Jane?"

Jane rocked out of the bizarre dream and back into the pitch-blackness of the living room. Her heart raced and her head spun as the sound of Mooney's voice echoed. Instantly, there was a rapid flash of blinding light, followed by the date, 10-24-99 and, finally a wolf's face. And then darkness. But somewhere in the air, Jane swore she smelled metal burning.

Shafts of the morning sun sliced through the front curtains. Jane and Emily were still on the couch fast asleep. Jane stirred, checking the time. 6:20. Peachville's morning rush hour would soon begin with the steady drone of trucks heading up Main Street to the highway. Five minutes later, it would be over. In the kitchen, Jane sorted through the basket that Kathy had given them. Discovering a tin of gourmet amaretto instant coffee, she decided to give it a try.

Jane lit a cigarette and sat at the kitchen counter amidst the morning silence. The realization suddenly hit her that Dale Perry was really dead. The greatest known evil in Jane's life was gone forever. She looked outside the kitchen window into the backyard where the tall grass swayed with the smooth morning breeze. In the last three and a half weeks, her life had taken so many twists and turns that she felt as if she'd been on a roller coaster ride. But suddenly, something seemed very different. As the morning light traced a path through the kitchen, she sensed that a door was opening. She looked around the kitchen and noticed things she had not seen until that moment—a tarnished cupboard knob, an indentation in the linoleum and a curl of peeling wallpaper by the sliding glass door. They had been right in front of her all this time and yet, somehow, she was just now seeing them. It was as if she'd suddenly been given new eyes to see the world.

She thought back to the night before and that enigmatic desk on the *Antiques Roadshow*. Recalling her visit to the Lawrence house, she was almost positive that the desk was standing slightly away from the stairway wall. Jane clenched her cigarette between her lips and carried her coffee cup into her bedroom, taking care to walk quietly so as not to wake up Emily. She slipped the Lawrence case file from her leather satchel, set her coffee on the side table next to her pistol and sat down on the edge of the bed. Finding the photos, she pulled them out of the folder. She breezed past the grisly close-ups of David and Patricia Lawrence's butchered bodies until she glimpsed a photo that included the desk. The first photo of the desk was taken from an angle that made it difficult to decipher its placement. The second photo that featured the desk was better but still not adequate. After shuffling through several more photos, she came upon one that precisely showed the entry area and the desk. Clearly, it *was* standing several inches from the stairway wall.

Jane flicked on the table lamp and held the color glossy

photo underneath it so she could really examine the unusual piece of furniture. She canvassed the area inch by inch, noting what looked like a hairline scratch on the photo at the rear section of the desk. However, looking closer, Jane realized it was in the photo. She rummaged in her leather satchel until she found her trusty deluxe Swiss army knife. Pulling out the coin-sized magnifying glass from the side of the knife, she leaned closer to the light and investigated the mysterious scratch. From the angle of the photo, it looked like the edge of a piece of paper that had been stuffed in one of those secret compartments or a shadowy trick of light that bounced off the overhead hallway light fixture.

She pulled the photo away from the light when something caught her eye. In the same photo, in the far corner, was a glimmering square object. The powerful flash on the camera had attracted this silvery box, illuminating it like a bright star. Jane held the photo under the light and steadied her magnifying glass over the object. It looked like a silver cigarette case. She checked the date on the coding strip. May 24—the day after the murders. While she could not be sure, it looked exactly like the engraved silver cigarette case that the homeless lunatic had in his possession when Chris questioned him at Denver Head-quarters. That interview occurred five days *after* this photo was taken. But that was impossible. Jane looked at the object more closely. It had to be a duplicate of the cigarette case that the homeless man had with him. Perhaps a sort of his and hers wedding gift. Yet, the more Jane mulled over that possibility, the less likely it seemed. Who gives his and hers silver cigarette cases these days as wedding gifts?

Jane considered the options. If that was indeed the same cigarette case that the homeless guy found, it had to have been stolen *after* the crime scene photos were taken. The only problem was that the house was locked and taped off to anyone except for police personnel. The only missing objects that could have possibly been photographed and then removed were pieces of evidence, such as blood covered carpeting swatches, destroyed furniture and, of course, that five ounce mound of cocaine. All of these would have been taken into evidence and recorded on the Property Report Form.

The Property Report Form! Jane realized that form could offer valuable insight into the whereabouts of the cigarette case. Jane quickly searched for the Property Report Form in her files. But after hunting through them, there was no form. It was automatic procedure to hold the original Property Report Form in Evidence and then have a copy sent back upstairs to put in the case file. To Jane, the missing Property Report Form was a glaring error. Then she wondered if it wasn't an error at all. Maybe Weyler had purposely removed the form.

She factored a million possibilities and twisted scenarios. Weyler had 24/7 access to the Lawrence crime scene and was, in fact, directing the entire investigation. He was the only one Jane knew of who could have been alone in that house and able to lift whatever he wanted for whatever purpose. Jane flashed back on the phone call she received from him when he told her about the suspect that Chris was questioning.

*"The perp was arrested for public drunkenness and pissing on the sidewalk,"* Jane remembered Weyler telling her. *"When PD searched him during booking, they found an item on his person that sent up a red flag . . . A silver cigarette case with the inscription 'Wedding Blessings. David & Patricia Lawrence.'"*

Jane recalled her observation when Chris grilled the homeless bum. His tattered clothing could barely hold a pencil, let alone a heavy, silver cigarette case. remembered that Weyler opened a file folder and searched the pages. "The PD report shows that the container was found 'near his person.' " Weyler read from the report.

Jane looked down at the Lawrence crime scene photo and that glimmering silver box in the corner. If that was

not a duplicate cigarette case, then she was faced with the
enormous possibility that someone planted the silver
cigarette case next to the bum. "Near his person," she said
to herself. It was the sort of vague terminology cops put
into reports that often signaled suspicious police behavior. "Near his person" was a "wink-wink" term that could
translate to: "We planted the evidence, but we couldn't
plant it on the suspect so we tossed it 'near his person.'"

Jane took a nervous drag on her cigarette. She elimi-
nated Chris from her list of suspects right off the bat since
he was playing on his boat in Dillon that night. "Weyler?"
she said to herself, considering the possibility of his
involvement in a cover-up. All he could say is that he was
home that night watching his favorite PBS programs. But
why would Weyler get involved? What's his motive? The
more Jane tossed the idea back and forth, the more it
didn't add up. Weyler had too much to lose; he'd earned
prestige and respect within the Department for his
integrity and professionalism. It didn't seem rational for
him to risk it all on something like this.

The more Jane thought about it, it almost seemed that
the bum was set up. After all, in some eyes, he was dis-
posable—an incoherent, society dropout who could easily be used by PD Brass to take a huge fall. Who cares if
he took the hit for a crime he didn't commit if it meant
protecting those who were really involved? However,
thanks to Jane and her aggressive stance, their easy target
was allowed to walk, thereby possibly screwing up
Weyler's intended plan. "What's missing?" Jane said to
herself, frustrated. She looked at that odd scratch in the
photo near the desk's back panel. "What's the missing
piece?" she said. If she were able to call the evidence
room and talk to Ron Dickson, the evidence technician,
she could possibly convince him to look on the original
copy of the Property Report Form and see if a cigarette
case was listed. Of course, with Ron being the Good
Christian, Jane wondered if he would release that information to her over the phone—especially since word had

to be out that she was incommunicado. But perhaps she could convince him to check downstairs . . .

*Downstairs.* That was the Denver PD term for the evidence room, located in the basement of Headquarters. She heard Weyler's voice again in her head. It resonated from their emotional conversation the night before when he called to tell her about Dale's death. He said something about "possible internal problems downstairs." Exactly what in the hell was going on downstairs? And furthermore, was Jane possibly sitting on the answer and not even aware of it? She glanced back to the photos when she heard the scuff-scuff of Emily's feet along the floor in the living room. Quickly, Jane gathered the photos together and stashed them into her leather satchel. No sooner were they hidden from view than Emily appeared at the hallway entrance.

Jane turned. "Morning!" she said, feeling a twist of tension in her gut.

# Chapter 22

After a breakfast of burnt English Muffins and over-cooked eggs, Emily sat on the living room floor reading the weekly newspaper. Jane wanted to duck into the bedroom and continue her analysis of the photos and the case folder, but she couldn't risk Emily's prying eyes. With nothing else to do, Jane decided to wash the Subaru.

She was hosing down the wagon when Sheriff George pulled his patrol car along the curb. He rolled down his car window and leaned out. "Hello, Mrs. Calver!"

"Hello, Sheriff," Jane replied, not knowing what to expect.

"How's your beautiful daughter feelin' this mornin'?"

"Much better!" Jane replied. The sheriff said nothing, preferring to just stare at her. She was beginning to feel as if she had a scarlet "A" on her shirt that stood for "Abuser" and she was sick of it. "Please pass the information on to Kathy!"

The sheriff, missing Jane's sarcasm, smiled. "I'll do that, Mrs. Calver! You have yourself a good day. Tell Patty 'hello' for me!"

"I will," Jane said, waving at the sheriff as he drove toward the highway. Then quietly, under her breath, she mumbled, "Once I untie her from the bedpost and cover up her bruises with long sleeves and makeup, you son-of-a-bitch!"

Emily sauntered down the front path toward the Subaru as the sound of laughter erupted from across the street in the park. Jane turned to see Heather and a few of her friends setting up their boom box. After selecting a country tune, they practiced their line dancing steps with Heather clearly in charge.

"Can I go over to the park and see Heather?" Emily asked.

"Why do you like that girl?"

"It's just something to do. I'll be across the street. You can see me from here."

"Go ahead," Jane agreed, dragging the bucket of soap and water toward the car.

Jane watched as Emily approached Heather and tried to make conversation. She no sooner turned back to the car than Emily came back across the street with a discouraged, hangdog look. Jane plopped the soapy sponge in the bucket. "Fuck 'em."

"That's easy for you to say."

Jane lit a cigarette. "Not only is she an A-1 class brat, she's one of the worst country line dancers I have ever seen!"

"You're just trying to make me feel better."

"Lift up your depressed little head and look! They're like robots! Look how stiff her back is. Sure, her feet are in rhythm with the beat and she knows the steps, but she's not breathing any personality into the moves. It's like somebody shoved a key up her ass, wound her up and said, 'Dance!'"

"How would you know anything about country line dancing? You're a cop!"

"Yeah, well maybe I spent every Wednesday and Saturday night country dancing before you were a twinkle in your daddy's eye!"

Emily was astonished. "Really?"

"Shit, yes!" Jane took another drag and glanced back across the street. "Idiots!"

"Are you any good?" Emily said, truly impressed by this news.

"Let's just say I stopped counting the awards a few years ago!"

"Awards?" Jane nodded. The wheels started turning in Emily's head. "So, you still remember how it's done?"

"Every single step," Jane said, returning her attention to the car.

"You know, I saw this old CD boom box up in the attic. And The Apple Cart has a bunch of country CDs at the checkout counter. And being that you're an award-winning country line dancer and the fact that we've got nothing better to do here . . . Well, I was just thinking . . ."

Emily looked longingly at Jane. Jane glanced her way and then across the street to Heather. "Oh, what the hell—"

Within minutes, Jane and Emily were standing in line at The Apple Cart with a stack of brand-new country CDs in tow. After dusting off the boom box from the attic and putting in fresh batteries, Jane plopped in the first CD and cranked up the volume. Standing with her back to Emily to demonstrate the various steps, Jane took Emily through the paces in a kind of "Line Dancing 101" intensive. With cigarette bobbing between her lips, Jane proved to be as good a dancer as she said she was. Emily, while slightly stiff in her approach at first, was a fast learner and a natural when it came to memorizing complicated patterns of steps. After four hours of practice, Emily had then mechanics down pat, along with the infectious enthusiasm. The only thing missing to complete her look was a pair of two-toned brown leather cowboy boots, a cream-colored western style shirt with black piping and a stiff pair of dark denim jeans. Jane agreed and spent one hundred forty dollars of the Denver PD's allowance on the outfit. The thrill of owning a genuine pair of line dancing cowboy boots consumed Emily for days, as did her attention to perfecting the various dance steps that Jane taught her. During those few days, it was as though a dark cloud had been lifted from Emily's life. For the first time since her parent's murder, she was free from the gloom and trauma.

Several days before the Peach Pit Days Carnival, Dan unexpectedly showed up at the house. It was late afternoon and Emily was on the front lawn, head focused on her feet as she ran through another set of dance steps.

"Well, look at the new line dancin' queen!" Dan said, pulling his toolbox from the bed of the truck.

"Hi, Dan!" Emily said, a dreamy smile plastered across her face.

"You fixin' to give those other line dancers some competition?"

"Nah. I'm just having fun." Emily looked at his truck. "Is that new?"

"Yup," Dan said patting his adhesive business logo that had just been secured to the side door.

Jane opened the front door and walked outside. "Dan got a new truck!" Emily exclaimed.

Jane had noticed his new acquisition from inside the house. "That must have set you back a bit," Jane said, quickly realizing she sounded like one of those annoying small town hens.

"Actually, it didn't set me back a penny. I do all the electrical maintenance for the Ford dealership over in Montrose. It's one of my many side jobs. Anyway, instead of payin' me, we worked out this agreement where they trade me a new dealer truck every summer. In the long run, I reckon I'm pullin' the better end of the trade."

"Hey, Dan!" Emily said with a grin. "You oughta work for a place that sells fishing equipment. Then you'd get all your stuff for free!"

"Say, I like that idea! And maybe I could convince them to throw in a boat!"

"Forget the boat!" Jane interjected. "I know someone who just got one and last I heard he was already investing in a new motor. It's like they say, 'boats are just big holes in the water into which you throw money.'"

"Okay, you convinced me. Hey, is that slidin' door in the kitchen still stickin'?"

"Yeah. It worked for awhile after you fixed it, but I damn near couldn't open it the other morning."

Dan followed Jane into the kitchen and went to work. Jane observed that his mood was different when they were alone together. He looked down the hallway to make sure Emily was still outside. "You heard from your husband?"

Jane no longer found herself taking umbrage at Dan's desire to protect her. "No."

"You didn't call him or anything?"

"What's all this about?"

He seemed a bit embarrassed. "Look, you know that I'm not a busybody and I only want the best for you. I promised I would never tell a soul about your situation and I haven't—"

"Cut to the chase, Dan," Jane said abruptly.

Dan placed his tools back into the box and snapped it shut. "Aw . . ." he said, ashamed to say any more but knowing he had to. "I was eatin' at The Harvest Café and I overheard Sheriff George talkin' to someone about how he came up on you and Emily on the side of the road last Wednesday night and how Emily was throwin' up 'cause of some fruit she ate at Kathy's shindig—"

"So? Is that the banner headline of this week's *Peachville Gazette?*"

"The conversation got goin' and the other fellow—he's this farmer that has a place down the road a mile from The Pit Stop—anyway, he was sayin' that he's seen you talkin' on the pay phone outside The Pit Stop late at night a couple times."

Jane stiffened. "Is that illegal in Peachville?"

"Of course not. It's just that folks around here take note of who's buyin' bread at 11:00 at night, who's walkin' their dog at three in the mornin' and who's—"

"Talking on the pay phone outside The Pit Stop after

everyone is in bed," Jane said, finishing his sentence.

Dan nodded. "Look, there's a couple things goin' on here. The first one has to do with me. I was just worried that you were callin' your husband and fixin' to meet him or get back with him."

"I was *not* calling my husband and I have no intention of going back to him." Dan looked relieved. "You said there's a couple things?"

"Oh, it's just stupid, that's what it is. The Sheriff seems to be under some false impression that you're . . ." Dan couldn't get the words out.

"That I'm what, Dan?" Jane knew the answer but she wanted to hear it from Dan's lips.

"Somehow he thinks that you've harmed Patty. It's just all twisted! But that's a small town for you!" Jane figured she had Kathy to thank for the call to Sheriff George after their tense visit to her house and abrupt exit. "I can't be sure, but I think the sheriff is gonna do some checkin' on you—"

"Oh, shit," Jane said under her breath and nervously lighting a cigarette.

"I think you oughta bite the bullet and come clean with him!"

"*I can't!*"

"I know your husband's a cop and that talkin' to the sheriff could put out some sort of alert that would tip him off to where you are. But, I think if you talk to Sheriff George and explain the situation, he could protect you and Patty from retribution—"

"No! I absolutely cannot involve the sheriff!" Jane buried her head in her hand. "God, what a mess! Exactly what is he planning on checking?"

"I would imagine arrests for abuse or warrants out on you."

"Well, he won't find any of those," Jane said, taking a drag on her cigarette.

"He'll find your name attached to the abuse report against your husband."

"There is no abuse report."

"You didn't tell the cops what he did to you and Patty?"

"I would have but it was more important that we just throw what we could in the car and get out of town," Jane said, stumbling over her words.

"Look, I know the cops are worthless, but you should have at least reported what he did to you to get it on record in case he finds you."

"Well, I didn't!" Jane said irritated, crossing into the kitchen as she considered her options. "The sheriff can't do much of anything without a driver's license or social security number," Jane mumbled more to herself. "He could run my license plate . . . Oh, shit!" Jane said, realizing that the plate would either trace back to the original owner—a felon for meth trafficking—or to the Denver PD who acquired the vehicle in the drug seizure. Either way, she was screwed. "*Shit!*" Jane said, pissed at Weyler and DH for choosing not to alert the local sheriff and making her job more complicated. "I gotta buy myself some time," Jane said decisively, squashing out her cigarette in the sink.

"What do you mean?"

"I've gotta figure out a way to take the heat off myself for just a little longer. I can't have the sheriff digging around or certain things could get very compromised." She turned to Dan. "Maybe you could talk to him. Vouch for me—"

"I can't just walk up to him cold turkey and start stickin' up for you. He might wonder what I was up to."

"Yeah, you're right." Jane paced back and forth. "Maybe you could make up some story about Patty. Tell him she's sick or has some kind of disease."

"What disease?"

"A blood disease. That's vague enough. Tell him that she's in remission but I'm real clingy around her because I'm afraid she's going to relapse. Tell him I told you the story in confidence but you figured he should know the truth just to stop the rumors."

"What if he doesn't buy it?"

"He'll buy it if you sell it good enough."

"I don't know, Jane."

"Dan, you stood right there and told me not too long ago that you would do *anything* you could to protect Patty and me. Now, I'm just asking you to tell a little white lie to buy me some time. Talk to the sheriff, Dan. I'll take care of the rest."

For the next few days, Jane felt as though a fire was lit underneath her feet. The more she considered her situation, the angrier she became. In her mind, for the past three and a half weeks, she'd become a sitting duck, held hostage to the whims of the Denver PD and, soon, to the microscope of a small-town sheriff. Never in her life had she rolled over so easily and allowed herself to be played like a puppet. As far as Jane was concerned, those days were over. "Fuck 'em," became her mantra. She didn't feel that she could trust Weyler, although her concern regarding his ethics and integrity were murky. Her mind kept going back to his statement about discovering "internal problems downstairs." While Weyler had assured her that those problems had nothing to do with her case, her gut told her differently. And she always listened to her gut.

She had to figure out a way to call Ron Dickson. Then she had to convince him to check the Property Report Form for that elusive silver cigarette case that somehow jumped from the crime scene photo and into the hands of the homeless man. It went against the rules of the game but Jane knew she had to start making her own rules.

At least, that's what she told herself as she stood in front of the pay phone outside The Pit Stop. Jane knew that the evidence room was usually quiet in the late afternoon. Fortunately, she remembered the direct line to Ron's phone. She also remembered that Ron took breaks around 11 a.m. and 3:30 p.m. She figured she could catch him coming back from his break around 4:00 and cut a deal while he was still giddy from the candy bar and bottle of pop. While Emily stood outside the Subaru, practicing her line dancing steps in the parking lot, Jane dialed the number. It rang twice before someone picked up.

"Evidence, Johnson." Johnson? Jane was taken aback. Johnson was a lackey who worked the back room. "Hello?" Johnson said. "Is someone there?"

Jane's first reaction was to hang up the phone but she'd gotten this far and she needed to keep going. She lowered her voice in a weak attempt to alter her voice. "I need to talk to Ron Dickson."

"Ron's not here. Can I help you?" Johnson asked.

"No. I need to talk to Ron. When is he back from his break?"

"Who is this?"

"When is Ron back from his break?" Jane said, undeterred.

"Ron's on suspension."

"*Suspension?*" At that point, Jane heard Chris' voice in the background. She knew it went against policy, but she had to find out what was going on. "Put Detective Crawley on the phone!"

Jane felt her heart race as Johnson handed the phone to Chris.

"Who's this?" Chris asked in his usual gruff tone.

"It's me."

Chris quickly spoke to Johnson. "Hey, I need privacy for a bit. Thanks . . ." Chris waited several seconds, then pressed his lips into the receiver. "Jane, where the fuck are you?" he asked in a thick whisper. "I need to talk to you in private. Give me your phone number and I'll call you back from the pay phone down the street. That way, no one here can trace the call."

"Chris, I can't! I'm not supposed to be talking to anybody!"

"Then why are you calling Ron Dickson? Anything

you can tell Ron, you can certainly tell me! I'm still your partner, for God's sake!"

Jane felt the walls closing in on her. She quickly regretted concocting this wild scheme. "Goddamnit, Chris. Why is Ron suspended?"

"It seems that your sweet little Christian pal has a pesky cocaine habit!"

"*What?*" Jane was floored.

"And guess where he was scoring his coke?"

"From evidence?" Jane said, skeptically.

"You got it!"

"Has everyone down there lost their mind? Ron is not a coke addict. He wears a D.A.R.E. button on his collar—"

"When did you become so fucking ignorant?" Chris said. "I don't give a shit if he drives around in a mother-fuckin' van with big D.A.R.E. letters plastered across the side! He's been pinching the evidence to the accumulated tune of over five ounces! God only knows what else he's been pocketing. All that time you were talking to him and buying into his Christian do-gooder bullshit, he was a cokehead and you couldn't even see it! I told you that night when we saw him in the hospital after your little ward fell off the roof of her house that something wasn't quite right with him! He was sweating and shaky. Hell, he was probably coming down and jonesin' for some powder!"

Jane thought back to that awful night nearly one month ago. Ron approached Chris and her in the hospital with his finger bandaged—the result of nearly cutting off his left finger while chopping beeswax for his wife's herbal salve. She recalled his pale complexion and shaken appearance. She also remembered Chris jumping to the illogical conclusion that somehow Ron's demeanor was connected to Emily's case. "*It's not true!*"

"Pull your head out of your ass, Jane! I kept an eye on Ron ever since that night and I did my own little investigation. I know drug addicts. I know how they think. Ron stands in that cage every day knowing that literally pounds of coke are sitting right behind him in little plastic K-Pak bags. 'Who the hell's gonna miss it?' he thinks. And he would have gotten away with it if I hadn't convinced Brass about my suspicions. They agreed to do a surprise audit of the property room and what do you know, Joe, but the blow was missing! I'm a fuckin' hero around here, Jane! *A fucking hero!* With the amount of coke Ron took, Brass figures he's been dipping into the powder since May!"

Jane factored the information. "May? How would they know that?"

"They just do, Jane."

"They just do? What kind of answer is that?"

"I don't have to explain anything to you! Shit is going down here, Jane!"

"What about Johnson? Did you question him? Maybe he pinched the coke!"

"Ron had blow in his pocket! He was caught red handed! Deal with it!"

"You're enjoying this. What is it about Ron that you hate so much?"

"What is it about him that you *like?*" Jane turned toward the sound of the chugging coal train as it inched up the mountain to pick up the day's black harvest. "What in the hell is that?" Chris asked.

"The coal train." With that, the train rumbled past The Pit Stop. Once it cleared the area, Jane continued. "Ron didn't do it, Chris. I don't care how much you try to convince me. He's innocent of that and of whatever else you think he did."

"Whatever else? What exactly do you mean by that?"

"You know exactly what I mean."

"You sure are one cocky little bitch!"

"There are some things that you don't know. And this is one of them."

"Don't hold out on me, Jane! You called here for a

reason. What do you know? Has that kid been talking?" Chris' tone was slightly intimidating.

"Maybe. But, if you think I'm telling you, you're more fucked up than I thought."

Chris lowered his voice. "Let me pass on some friendly advice. Whatever you do, don't even think about sharing your information with Weyler."

Jane's ears perked up. It was completely against Chris' character to suddenly become so forthcoming after puffing himself up and dishing out the insults. "Why?"

"You talk to Weyler about anything you know . . . *anything* . . . and you'll have another dead kid on your hands. I'm not bullshitting you, Jane. *You can't trust him.*" Jane felt her heart skip a beat. "Someone's coming," Chris whispered. "I gotta go."

And with that, he hung up.

# Chapter 23

For the rest of that day and most of the night, Jane could not shake Chris' voice in her head. "You'll have another dead kid on your hands" played repeatedly in her mind. Of course, Chris was referring to Amy Joan Stover. Jane knew if she thought of Amy too much, the nightmares would start again.

By eleven o'clock that evening, Jane was still wired. Emily had fallen asleep in Jane's bed an hour earlier, leaving Jane alone to sort out the "what ifs." She paced back and forth in the living room, chain smoking with renewed vengeance. Occasionally, she stopped to look out the front window as the huge trucks pulled up across the street by the park to set up for the Peach Pit Days Carnival. By morning, the park would be transformed into a raucous kaleidoscope of colorful tents, food booths and carnival rides. She needed peace and quiet so she could think clearly. Something was very wrong at Denver Headquarters.

As much as she hated to admit it, she was grateful that Chris was able to squeeze out the warning about Weyler. Soon, though, that gratitude was replaced with anger— anger that she was, once again, a sitting duck waiting to be picked off. The anger passed and a sense of intense vulnerability overwhelmed her. It occurred to Jane that it was the same feeling that blanketed her that night sitting in the patrol car with Chris while they awaited the return of the Stovers in their SUV.

She thought back to those fateful moments before all hell broke loose. Why did she feel vulnerable, Jane wondered. Maybe it was because Chris was so edgy and pissed off at Bill Stover when he was told to stay put in his house. As they both watched Stover drive down the street accompanied by two unmarked police vehicles for protection, Jane suddenly recalled how Chris shook his head and said, "What an asshole! He really wants to sign his own death certificate!" Up until that moment, Jane had forgotten Chris' comment. His voice had that same cocky cadence when he picked up his cell phone and called one of the flank vehicles.

"Yeah, it's me," Jane remembered Chris saying to the driver on his phone. "I can't believe Stover was so stupid! He drives off with his family for ice cream so he can get thirty minutes in the outside world! Thirty fucking minutes! It looks all clear from here but hurry up!"

Whatever it was that triggered Jane's feeling of impending doom and vulnerability on that tragic evening just over six weeks ago, she found herself right back in the middle of the same anxious tension. There was too much going on—too many lies that she had to remember so she wouldn't blow her cover. It was enough pressure to pretend to be someone's mother. But now, she had to lie to the sheriff, and pretend that her "daughter" had a severe blood disease. At least, that hinged on whether Dan was able to successfully deliver the bogus message to the sheriff. It was beginning to feel like a bad soap opera.

By the following Saturday morning, the park across the street teemed with carnival visitors. Jane awoke to the discordant sound of pipe organ music against the steady drone of the strident carnies. Emily was not in bed with

Jane, a fact that was unusual since she spent every night there. "Emily?" Jane called out.

No response.

Jane dashed out of bed and sprinted down the hallway toward the living room. There she saw Emily perched in a chair, eagerly looking out the large front window at all the action across the street. "I called your name!" Jane said, irritated. "Why didn't you answer me?"

"I didn't hear you," Emily replied as the blaring sound of carnival activities grew more noticeable in the living room.

While she had always taken her job of protecting Emily very seriously, Jane felt a heightened sense of duty ever since Chris' disturbing comment. Jane sat on the couch, feeling the weight of the world press down on her.

Emily sensed that something wasn't right. "What's going on?"

"Nothing . . . Just the usual bullshit."

"We're still gonna go to the carnival, aren't we?"

"It's just a small-town deal. Convicts put these rides together. *Drunken* convicts!"

"So we don't go on the rides. We can eat popcorn and, maybe go to the dance. I mean, *I* don't have to go, but *you* do." Jane regarded her questionably. "Remember? You owe Dan two dances for fixing the water pipe."

Jane leaned her head against the couch, in no mood to kick up her cowboy boots. "Fine! But we'll just go for the dance and maybe some popcorn and then back to the house. Deal?"

"Deal!" Emily said excitedly.

Emily had been dressed in her western attire a full two hours before leaving. Jane emerged from the bedroom dressed in a crisp black western shirt, blue jeans and her weather beaten, scuffed cowboy boots.

"You fixed your hair!" Emily said with a big smile.

Jane self-consciously tousled her hair. "I just washed it and fluffed it up."

"You look *really* good." Jane shrugged her shoulders

and slid her pistol into her fanny pack. "Do you have to bring your gun?"

"What do you think?"

Emily stood up, smoothing her jeans. "Just make sure you don't bump into Dan too hard when you're dancing with him. The gun might leave a dent on him!"

The two of them strode through the park just as the sun set behind Strong's Mesa. Jane kept Emily close at hand as they wound around the throngs of people and made their way toward the sound of the country band that was playing "We're From the Country" inside the large center tent. After paying the entry fee, Jane lead Emily through the crowd until they found two folding chairs near the side of the makeshift, wooden dance floor. Couples of all ages two-stepped and scuffed their boots across the floor. In the far corner, Emily saw Heather and her friends doing their robotic line dancing turns and shuffles to the music. Kathy hovered nearby the girls, taking nonstop flash photographs.

Jane and Emily walked over to a long table filled with homemade brownies, cookies and tubs of red punch. The band wound up their song with a striking fiddle chord as the crowd hooted and applauded. Jane bought two glasses of punch and a brownie and retreated to a pair of folding chairs against the wall.

A road weary, middle-aged cowboy crossed over to Jane, holding out his hand. "May I have the next dance?" he asked, a wad of tobacco wedged firmly in his cheek.

"I'm not in the mood right now, thanks!" Jane replied.

"I'm the best two-stepper in town!" he said, licking his lips and blinking rapidly.

Jane was quickly tiring of the guy's incessant advances. *"No, thank you!"*

The guy reluctantly moved on to his next conquest. Emily, who hadn't missed one word or flicker of an eye, leaned over to Jane and spoke into her ear. "I don't think he can dance as well as he said he could. Did you notice his face?"

"I certainly did!" Jane regarded Emily with a sense of pride, realizing that her protégé was quickly catching on to the veiled signs of deceit.

The band swelled into another toe-tapping country tune as Dan approached them. "Glad you two girls could make it!" he said, a broad smile filling his face. "We got ourselves a good band this year!" Dan turned to Emily. "Hey, darlin', would you mind gettin' me a punch?" He passed her a five dollar bill. "You keep the change!"

Emily's eyes lit up as she raced toward the food table.

Dan turned to Jane, his voice becoming serious. "I did what you asked regardin' Sheriff George."

"How'd it go?"

"Okay, I guess. At least for now, I think some of the heat's off."

"Thank you."

"I can't guarantee how much time I bought you."

"That's okay, Dan. We're not gonna be here forever."

Dan's face fell somber. "I thought you were gonna try and make a home here."

Jane suddenly realized that Dan had feelings for her. "No. I'm sorry if I gave you that impression."

"Where are you headed after this?"

"I don't know." Jane looked over at Emily standing at the beverage table. "We have family in Cheyenne," she said, thinking quickly. "That's probably the next stop."

"Cheyenne, Wyoming? Aw, we got lots more to offer you right here! We got a good climate, excellent schools, small town livin' and we're just thirty minutes from a Super Wal-Mart!"

"You oughta work for the Peachville Chamber."

There was an awkward moment between the two of them that was broken when Emily reappeared with the punch. "There you go!" Emily handed the cup to Dan.

"Thank you, ma'am!"

Emily looked over to the dance floor where Heather and her friends were pounding out their moves. Emily yelled above the loud music. "It's just not right!"

"What's not right?" Jane asked.

"You and I are ten times better than they are!"

"We're a couple, Patty. Not a line!"

"How many does it take to make a line?" Emily asked.

"More than two!" Jane announced.

Emily looked up at Dan and tugged on his shirtsleeve. "Are you a fast learner on the dance floor?"

"Well, yes, ma'am!" Dan said proudly.

The band brought the song to a pounding end. Without missing a beat, they launched into a cover of the Dixie Chicks' "Some Days You Gotta Dance." Sensing the moment was right, Emily grabbed Jane by the arm and yanked her toward the dance floor. "Come on! Let's show them how it's really done!"

Jane unwillingly lurched forward. But once she was on the floor, she knew that turning back would only attract more attention. Emily shouted "Cowboy Hustle," and Jane nodded in agreement. They kicked off a series of synchronized steps that drew the attention of Dan and almost every other male in the place. Heather and her friends continued their tired dance steps, unaware that directly behind them, Jane and Emily were boot scootin' to a different drummer. After carefully watching the dance pattern, Dan sidled up along Jane and matched her step for step. He proved to be as good a dancer as Jane, shuffling and sliding in perfect rhythm. Kathy stopped taking photos of her daughter long enough to observe the trio that had taken over center stage. A look of dismay mixed with indignation fell over her.

An admiring group of onlookers circled around the trio, cutting off Heather and her friends. The crowd cheered on the impromptu troupe as Heather was forced onto the sidelines. The hooting and hollering reached a fever pitch as the singer belted out the last line of the song. In perfect sync, Jane and Emily along with Dan stomped on cue to the last beat of the music. The crowd erupted. Both Jane and Emily looked around, a bit overwhelmed by the out-pouring of appreciation. Emily caught Heather's jealous eye and smiled broadly toward the brooding brat.

One of the Festival organizers walked onto the stage and took the microphone. "I think everyone will agree," he said to the crowd, "that we have a brand-new winner of the line dancing contest this year! Come on up here, gals! You, too, Dan!"

Jane and Emily were shocked by the announcement. Dan backed off, wanting Jane and Emily to take the spotlight, but Jane urged him on the dance floor. The last thing she wanted was to be featured in front of all those people. Emily climbed onstage as the announcer brought out a twelve inch, gold plated statue that depicted a single line dancer in a distinctive pose. He handed the statue to Emily. "What's your name, darlin'?" the announcer asked, poking the microphone in her face.

"Patty," she said nervously.

"And who's this?" the announcer asked, pointing toward Jane.

Emily looked at Jane and smiled. "She's my mom. She taught me how to dance." The crowd let out a chorus of whoops and hollers. Emily looked out at the jovial crowd and saw Heather. If looks could kill, Emily would have been shot dead.

"Come over here, Mom!" the announcer said, beckoning Jane toward the stage. Jane waved him off, preferring to stay as far back as possible, but Dan nudged her forward. "You turn a mighty fine step out there!" the announcer proclaimed. "How 'bout if we give the floor to you and Dan for the next number?"

Jane wanted to decline the offer, but the crowd wouldn't have it. Dan leaned over to her. "You do owe me two dances!"

Jane took his hand as the drummer laid out an opening riff, followed by the guitarist and piano player as the singer jumped into "Watching My Baby Not Coming Back." Jane looked around the room for Emily. Once she caught sight of her on the side of the dance floor clutching her trophy, Jane mouthed "Stay there." Emily nodded.

Dan twirled Jane around the hardwood floor. In between synchronized two-steps, several complicated foot changes and a dizzying array of whirling, Dan and Jane looked as if they had been trading dance moves for years. The drummer skimmed his stick on the crash cymbal and suddenly the song was over. The surrounding crowd burst into a frenzy, chanting "One more time!"

"Let's stop while we're ahead!" Jane yelled above the din. Spotting Emily, she made a beeline toward her.

Emily glanced over to see Kathy closing in on the trio with Heather close at hand. Heather never took her eyes off Emily, shooting daggers of hatred toward her.

Kathy tapped Jane on the shoulder. "Well, my, my!" Kathy exclaimed, her plastic smile firmly embedded on her face. "That was quite the display of fancy footwork! Kathy turned to Emily. "And look at you! Little Miss Trophy Winner!" Kathy turned to Heather. "Heather, darling. Isn't there something you'd like to say to Emily?"

The wheels of revenge spun in Heather's head. Her pouty mouth twisted into a phony grin. "Congratulations! You've got moves I've never seen before. Maybe we can get together and you can show me what you know! I've got the new Tim McGraw CD."

"Really?" Emily said, enthusiastically.

"Well, girls, you'll have to make a play date with each other!" Kathy said.

"How about a sleepover?" Heather asked Emily, ignoring Kathy.

Emily could hardly contain herself. "Yeah! Sure!"

Jane bristled, dubious of Heather's intentions. "We should discuss that—"

"*Mom!*" Emily whined to Jane. "She's inviting me to a sleep over!"

Jane felt backed into a corner. "You know what happened the last time you went to a sleepover. You couldn't sleep. I had to come get you—"

"That's okay, Mrs. Calver!" Heather said, her evil mind running marathons. "We can have the sleep over at your house. That way, Emily won't be afraid!"

"Sure!" Emily said, overwhelmed.

Jane knew something was fishy. As much as she wanted to grab Heather by the throat and choke the truth out of her, Jane could only fumble her way through a poor excuse. "Let's table this discussion for now. We still want to catch a few rides and eat some popcorn. If you'll excuse us . . ." Jane lit a cigarette the second they cleared the tent. The bright, colorful lights of the carnival and accompanying pipe organ music washed over the trio as they walked toward the center of the festivities.

"Isn't that cool about the sleepover, Mom?" Emily said joyfully to Jane.

"We need to talk about that later," Jane said, effectively ending the subject.

Emily noticed a woman perched atop a stage, swallowing fire and spitting it out into waves of red and blue flames. "Can I stand over there and watch her?"

"Sure." Jane took Emily's trophy and watched her skip toward the group of onlookers.

"Look at her," Dan said with a smile. "She's ten feet tall and bulletproof! Where'd you learn how to dance like that?"

"Oh, it's just one of the better habits I picked up along the way."

"Better habits?"

"Yeah, you know. Before life got real."

Dan wasn't sure he understood but nodded just the same. "The way you dance, you need a full-time partner. Someone to blow off steam on Saturday night?" Jane realized the hidden message Dan was sending. But she figured if she ignored his comments, he'd give up his pursuit. She was wrong. "What you gotta do," Dan continued, "is find somebody who's got a honest heart and who would never beat on you and Patty. I don't mean to pry but I know that when you're used to gettin' beat on, you tend to pick those kind of men. You may not even know you're doin' it. But I bet a dime to a donut that that's the kind of fellow you lean toward. I know you probably think I'm totally out of line sayin' that but—"

"No, actually," Jane paused, thinking about what Dan said. "you're right." Her mind briefly focused on Chris and his verbally abusive tactics, not to mention his fondness for rough sex. "You're absolutely right."

"It's understandable if you couldn't see that. It'd be like if you were an alcoholic. You can't tell a drunk they're a drunk. They just tell you to 'screw off' and then they take another drink."

Jane shook her head, chuckling at the irony. "I feel like I'm in therapy."

"I shouldn't have opened my big mouth. It's just that . . ." Dan struggled with his words. "I have some personal experience in what you've been through. My sister, Becky, married a guy who looked like Prince Charming on the outside but inside he was more like that Marquis de Sade. I can't tell you how many times I had to go over to her house and pull him off of her."

"Why didn't you guys call the cops?"

"The cops," Dan snickered. "What the hell good are cops? You should know! You've been dealin' with the cops regardin' your husband and you're still on the run! Cops just write a report and walk away."

"Not all cops do that, Dan."

"Well, the ones I knew sure did. And maybe they're right. In the end, it's up to you and you alone to get away and not make that same mistake again."

"What happened to your sister?"

"She stuck with him until she got pregnant again. She was fourteen weeks along when he got worked up because there was a dirty cup in the sink. He started kicking her in her stomach—"

"That son-of-a-bitch—"

"He damn near killed her. If I hadn't gotten over there, she'd probably would have bled to death."

"What happened to her baby?"

"She lost it and she probably won't be havin' any more kids."

Jane couldn't help but feel empathy for Dan's sister. "What did she do?"

"She got smart. She got the guts to grab the kids, file for divorce, get a restrainin' order and move to another state. She also got some therapy. It helped straighten out all those backward thoughts in her head about what love really is. After about two years, she wrote her ex one of those letters that you don't mail. You know, they're just meant for yourself so you can get the words on paper and get them out of your head."

"I bet that was one letter that would make a sailor blush!"

"No, not at all. She read it to me over the phone. She talked about how she was finally aware that she was responsible for allowing him to treat her the way he did. How she should have gotten help or gotten out of the relationship early on to save herself so much grief. At the end, she said she forgave him for all he'd done to her. Then she burned the letter and she was finally free."

"Mom?" Emily called out.

Jane didn't respond. Dan's words were still filtering through her head.

Dan looked over at Emily. "Hey, your kid's callin' you."

Jane turned to find Emily. "What is it?"

"Can I get a bag of popcorn?"

"Yeah, sure!" Jane hollered as Emily stood in the concession line.

"You got family you can talk to?" Dan asked.

Jane really thought about his question and then realized the answer. "No."

"No mother? No dad?"

"My mother died when I was ten. And my dad," Jane turned away, looking off into the flickering carnival lights. "He just recently died." The words sounded new, as if they did not belong to her yet. "So, I guess I'm an orphan." The appreciation of her new reality struck an emotional chord. Although Jane tried to fight it, she felt her guard coming down.

"Any brothers and sisters?"

"A brother," Jane replied. She looked over at Emily, who was five people away from the front of the line. "His name is Mike. But, he's not exactly available."

"Why not?"

"He's got this new girlfriend. *Lisa.*" Jane said, sounding like a catty female.

"You don't sound as if you like her."

"She's . . ."

"She's what?"

"She's . . ." Jane searched for the end of the sentence and kept coming up short. "She's there!" Jane felt the need to explain. "My brother's track record with women is lousy. Half of them look like they crawled out of the sewer. The other half can't put three intelligent words together."

"Which half does Lisa fall into?"

"Not sure. I've only met her once and talked to her on the phone—"

"You must have an idea. I was able to pin my ex brother-in-law from the get-go."

"Well, okay, so far she hasn't fallen into either category. But, you know, she's this clean-cut, Martha Stewart looking, reformed drunk who's dragging my brother to weekly AA meetings. She's got a brother who's a PI and apparently, he used to be some bounty hunter. Big deal! She makes some kind of jewelry for a living and sells it at outdoor art shows." Jane rolled her eyes.

"Maybe I'm missin' somethin' here. So far, none of that sounds bad!"

"Oh, come on, Dan!" Jane said in a cajoling manner. "*AA! Jewelry?*"

"Unless she's sellin' crack at AA meetings and makin' her jewelry out of stolen diamonds, this girl ain't bad! I think you need to dig a little deeper and figure out what's really holdin' you back from likin' her."

"What in the hell does that mean?" Jane was sitting tall on her high horse.

"Look, let's just drop the subject, okay?" Jane was not used to losing arguments. However, she wasn't going to start a scene and be the lead topic of conversation at The Harvest Café. Dan moved closer.

"You know, I meant it when I said that you could call me day or night if there was a problem."

Jane's eyes were pinned on Emily. "Yeah. I know."

"If you need to talk or somethin' . . ." Jane turned back to Dan. He leaned closer and was just about to kiss her lips when she backed off. "I'm sorry!" he said, nervously. "I don't know what I was thinkin'."

"No, it's not you. *Honestly.* Take my word for it, you don't want me."

"Why would you say something like that about yourself?"

"Because it's true." Jane painfully searched for the right words. "You don't know anything about me, no matter how much you think you do."

Dan lovingly touched Jane's hand. "That's what conversation is for."

Jane let out a deep sigh. "Dan, you're a good person. I wish I could tell you the truth. But I can't. You just have to accept it. Okay?"

Dan patted Jane's hand. "Will I get to know the truth one day?"

"Maybe."

Dan lifted her hand and gently kissed it. "Maybe is good enough for now."

They crossed over to Emily who was finally at the front of the line and getting change for her popcorn. Dan leaned down, wrapping his arm around Emily's shoulder. "How'd you feel about a ride on the Whirlwind Roller Coaster?"

"I'd love to!"

Emily looked at her greasy hands from the popcorn.

"Wait up! I'm gonna get a napkin!" She darted off toward the popcorn stand and started to pull a napkin from the dispenser when she was drawn into the shiny, reflective surface. The carnival sounds rapidly melted into the background and were replaced by the pounding beat of her heart. Staring into the dispenser's mirrored side, she saw the reflection of a male figure. Her heart beat faster. She turned toward the figure. Standing about ten feet away was a man with his back to her. A woman stood across from him. He wore a black leather coat, black jeans and dark cowboy boots. Emily's eyes moved down his body to his right hand. In it, there looked to be a shiny, sharp object concealed between his sleeve and the palm of his hand. For a millisecond, another image flashed across her view. That image was a gloved hand, holding a knife dripping with blood. As quickly as the knife appeared, the image disappeared. She jerked backward in shock.

The woman who was with the man leaned toward him and said, "Isn't that thing hot against your face? Why don't you take it off?"

Emily looked up at the back of the man's head, just in time to see him turn to the left. A rubber mask in the shape of a pig's head concealed his face. He brought his left hand up to his face and began to peel off the mask. At that point, a rush of flickering images alternated in front of Emily. As he pulled off the pig's mask, a new image of another male dominated Emily's vision. That man pulled off a dark nylon face mask. Quickly, the pig mask flashed into view. A second later, the nylon face mask burst in front of it. The images rotated at rapid speed until finally the man with the nylon mask ripped it off just as Emily turned away, covering her eyes. "No!" she shrieked, stumbling backward into the crowd.

Turning quickly, Jane saw Emily's disoriented behavior and her obvious terror toward the man with the mask. Instinctively, Jane went for her gun. "Who's that guy?" she yelled at Dan.

Dan squinted toward the man. "That's just Bernie. He's cool. What's wrong?"

Jane took her hand off her gun. "Hey!" Jane yelled toward Emily.

Just as she heard Jane's voice, Emily saw Bernie turn toward her and take a step. Like a thoroughbred bolting from the gate, Emily fled from the scene, racing through the crowd.

Jane jumped to attention. "Oh, Christ!" she yelled at Dan. The two of them took off after the kid. Dan ran to the left around the crowd while Jane took the right-hand flank. Emily broke through the streams of carnival visitors.

"Patty! Sweetheart!" Dan yelled out. "It's okay!"

"Patty!" Jane called out to her, desperately trying to keep up with Emily.

Jane's voice caught the attention of Sheriff George who happened to be patrolling the park on foot. He spun around just in time to see Emily frantically run by him, followed by Jane. He took off after the two of them, loping as fast as he could.

Emily rounded a corner near the edge of the park.

*Boom!*

An explosion of fireworks burst into the night sky. Emily screamed and dropped to the ground.

Boom! *Boom!*

Another set of red fireworks painted the skyline, illuminating the park with an eerie scarlet glow.

Emily looked up as the crimson blossoms floated downward. She looked at her hands, reflected against the scarlet sky. In her mind, they were covered in blood. Buffered by the applause and roar of the crowd, Emily let out a terrified scream as she took refuge in the narrow hollow of a nearby tree.

Jane heard Emily's scream. Pushing her way through the crowds, she made her way to the perimeter of the park, looking around helplessly for any sign of Emily.

*Boom!*

A riveting set of red and blue fireworks pounded into

the air, eliciting another shriek of terror from Emily. Jane spun around and saw the kid crunched into the cavity of the tree. "It's okay!" Jane yelled as she lunged forward, knelt down and attempted to wrap her arms around the kid.

"No!" Emily screamed, in mortal fear for her life. Everything was a blur to the child as she pushed and punched Jane's body away from her.

Sheriff George arrived on the scene in time to see Emily's frantic reaction to Jane's presence. He held back, hiding in the shadows of an outlying game booth.

"Stop it! It's me! You're okay!" Jane pleaded. Emily stopped screaming at the sound of Jane's voice. She blinked hard. Gradually, Jane's face came into her view. One chaotic eruption of fireworks after another blasted into the air, sending Emily into Jane's arms. The sheriff remained fixated on Jane, waiting for her to make a violent move toward Emily. Emily held on to Jane for dear life. The child was hysterical, almost to the point of hyperventilating. "It's okay!" Jane said quietly, stroking Emily's head. But Emily's hysteria reached a fever pitch until she passed out in Jane's arms.

Dan arrived on the scene, quickly assessing the situation. Sheriff George pulled away against the wooden backing of the booth. "Come on, Jane," Dan said, out of breath. "We gotta get her outta here before somebody starts askin' questions!" He knelt down and picked up Emily's limp body.

Back at the house, Jane directed Dan to Emily's front bedroom. "I'll get her some water!" Jane said, rushing off to the bathroom down the hall. Dan knelt by Emily's bed, gently stroking her moist brow. Jane quickly returned with a glass of water and took Dan's place by Emily's bedside. "Wake up," Jane urged Emily.

"Patty, darlin', it's okay," Dan added with an encouraging voice.

Jane considered her words before she spoke. "Her name is Emily."

Dan brushed his hand against Emily's forehead. "What

triggered this?" Dan asked Jane in a half-whisper.

Jane didn't think before she spoke. "She probably thought she saw him."

"Her father? She fears him that much?"

Jane couldn't believe she slipped up. "He's a dangerous son-of-a-bitch."

Emily stirred. She opened her eyes, not quite knowing where she was right away. "What happened?" she said in a weak voice.

"Here," Jane said, tipping the glass of water to Emily's lips.

Emily took a sip and looked at Dan. The realization of what occurred hit her, as did the consequence of Dan observing everything. "Oh, no." She looked at Jane with apologetic eyes.

Jane patted Emily on the shoulder. "Don't worry. Dan understands that you thought you saw your dad." She gave Emily a look of "Please play along."

"Your dad's not gonna hurt you again, Emily," Dan said sympathetically.

Emily looked questioningly at Jane. "I told him your real name," Jane assured her. "I also told him how we had to leave Denver because of Dad."

Emily glanced at Dan then back to Jane. "Dad. Right."

"You rest, okay? I'm gonna walk Dan to the door."

Dan leaned down, cupping his hand across Emily's forehead. "Don't you worry, sweetheart. Ol' Dan's gonna make sure nothin' bad ever happens to you again." He planted a kiss on her cheek and followed Jane outside the front door.

The cacophony of carnival noises echoed from across the street. "I can stay if you want me to," Dan stated in earnest.

"Thank you but I think I need to be alone with her."

"Will you call me if you need me?"

"Yeah. I will."

Dan took a step off the porch. "You remember our 'trouble signal,' right? Garage and front porch lights on?"

"Got it," Jane said nodding. She walked back into Emily's bedroom and sat on the edge of her bed. Tears began flowing down the child's cheeks. "Hey, come on," Jane said in a reassuring tone. "I did some fast talking. He doesn't know the truth."

"I don't know why," Emily said through her tears, "but that man at the fair. He looked . . ." Emily couldn't put words to what she felt.

Jane didn't want to pursue it but she had no choice. "He looked like what?"

"He had something shiny in his right hand. Then it was like cherry juice was on the shiny thing. Cherry juice . . ." Emily tried to reconcile the idea of cherry juice, not wanting to even consider the alternative. "Then suddenly, I had cherry juice all over my hands . . . Why would there be cherry juice?"

"I don't know," Jane said quietly.

Emily traced what she could of the memory against the experience at the carnival. "When I was in the closet at my house, I think I saw the man who . . . the man who . . ." The memory ceased. However, the terror drove Emily into Jane's arms. "When is it going to stop?" Emily said through her sobs.

"When you see it, I suppose."

"I don't want to see it! *I don't want to see it!*" Emily pulled back. "I want things to be the way they were. I want my mommy and daddy back. I want to go to the park with A.J. I want everything right again!" Emily fell back into Jane's arms.

"I wish I could make it so, kiddo. You've just gotta remember those happier days. Let's talk about something else. Let's talk about . . . ah, you mentioned going to the park with—"

"With A.J." Emily said sniffling.

"Who's A.J.?"

"My best friend. I told you? Don't you remember? She moved away with her family and never said good-bye!"

"Right. I remember. Tell me about her."

"She was the best friend ever! Her mommy and daddy and my mommy and daddy all went to park together for a picnic. I have pictures from that day. Remember?"

"Sure."

Emily slipped off the bed and located her Starlight Starbright navy blue vinyl case on a nearby chair. She unzipped the case and handed the photo packet to Jane who turned on the bedside lamp. The first photo featured Emily's parents and herself sitting on the picnic blanket. Emily tenderly stroked her mother's face in the photo with the tip of her finger. "Dad ate two big servings of Mom's potato salad that day," Emily said lovingly.

"So, who took this picture?" Jane asked, trying to pull Emily out of her funk.

"A.J.'s daddy. There's a picture of him in there." Emily sifted through the photos. "Here he is with A.J.'s mommy."

Jane politely took the photo, glancing down at it. At first, the full effect of what she saw didn't hit her. But her mouth went dry as she held the photo closer to the lamp. It was Bill and Yvonne Stover staring back at her.

"And here's me and A.J.!" Emily said, revealing the final photo.

It was Amy Joan Stover.

# Chapter 24

Jane felt as though someone had kicked the crap out of her. The realization that the Stover and Lawrence families were best friends was a frightening turn of events. When Jane saw the photo of Emily and Amy Joan Stover sitting together, an ominous sensation came over her. The photos—the answer to part of the massive puzzle—were at Jane's fingertips for over a month and she never thought to look at them.

Once Emily fell asleep, Jane gathered the photos and walked into the living room, closing Emily's door behind her. She placed the twenty-four photos in sequence on the coffee table and sat on the couch. The impact and implications of a Stover/Lawrence association suddenly came full circle. As far as Jane was concerned, this changed everything. She checked the imprint date on the back of the photographs. May 2. Jane thought back to specific dates in May and, after counting backward, realized May 2 was a Sunday. It was also exactly one week to the day—Sunday, May 9—before Stover and his family was granted around the clock protective custody along with twenty-four hour house arrest. Jane retrieved her leather satchel from her bedroom and carried it back into the living room. She pulled out the Stover file, along with the various newspaper clippings regarding the case.

Jane poured over the fine print in search of dates. Buried within the police report, Jane came up with several insights. By late April, Bill Stover had agreed to testify against the Texas mob in exchange for keeping his cocaine and meth addiction out of the papers. While Stover never disclosed how much he was planning to reveal, there was a notation in the police file that he had "agreed to reveal judicial corruption and drug connections that went to the core of Denver's influential residents." Jane had read that sentence ten times and always assumed that Stover was going to spill his guts about fellow entrepreneurs and businessmen who provided laundering fronts for the Texas mob and who possibly lied in court about their actions. That was still a viable possibility. However, Jane ruminated on the possibility that the nefarious trail of corruption started where crimes are supposed to be solved—the Denver Police Department.

Immediately, Ron Dickson's name popped into Jane's head. Here was a guy who had constant access to evidence—everything from pounds of cocaine to hundreds of thousands of dollars in cash and jewelry. Jane knew that tampering with that evidence was somewhat easy if you knew the ropes. As thorough as the booking process was, there were always the inevitable loopholes that a smart and often desperate evidence tech could use to their advantage.

The process was fairly straightforward. Once detectives logged evidence on the Property Report Form, certain items were then transferred into plastic K-Pak bags. These are thick, heavy-duty, heat-sealable bags that offer the ultimate protection in preserving the integrity of crime scene evidence. When drugs are placed into the K-Pak bag, the bag is weighed. That weight is then notated on the outside of the bag, along with the item number of the evidence, the case number, the date and the detective's initials. From this point, crime scene items are transported downstairs to evidence where the K-Paks are sealed and stored on one of the many metal shelves that house hundreds of thousands of pieces of evidence. Due to the overwhelming amount and the inherent confusion that can cause, it was not out of the realm of possibility that evidence techs could tamper with items and not get caught.

However, there were two ways their criminal actions could be discovered. First, to get inside the K-Pak bag, the heat seal on the packet must be broken. Resealing the packet and making it look as if nothing was touched is almost impossible. If the K-Pak had to be opened for official business such as court trials, the action was always noted on the outside of the packet, along with the date. It was not worth it for the evidence tech to forge a fake "official purpose" on the K-Pak since that could be easily tracked. Due to the sheer number of items and backlog of evidence from years ago, it was easier for the evidence tech to take the risk, open the K-Pak, reseal it as best he could and cross his fingers that no one would notice.

The second way to discover criminal negligence in the property room was via an audit. Audits could not be done on a whim—there had to be verifiable suspicion for such an undertaking. It had been more than one year since the last audit of the evidence room. The fact that Chris—who was low on the proverbial influential totem pole— was able to convince Brass to audit the property room was a testament to his persuasion. His forthright, choir- boy looks didn't hurt when it came to influencing a department to embark on what could turn out to be a massive internal and media embarrassment.

So, Jane thought, if this was the corruption that Bill Stover was prepared to reveal in court, where did it lead? Planting evidence, perhaps? Unfortunately, Jane knew that was nothing new for big city cops. Her mind went back to that silver cigarette case that mysteriously jumped from the Lawrence crime scene photo and into the sup- posed possession of the street bum. That was certainly a case of tampering with evidence and, possibly, planting of evidence. Or maybe it was all about losing key evidence so a criminal would walk. Sure, that was a consideration. However, if key pieces of evidence went missing on a regular basis, it would be too much of a red flag. The more Jane considered the possibilities, the more she crossed off the latter idea. Her gut told her that whoever did this would pick and choose the evidence very carefully so he or she would not draw attention to omission.

Weyler's comment about trouble "downstairs" was an obvious tip-off to the results from the property room audit that Chris demanded. And when Weyler mentioned it, Jane remembered his voice becoming tense and evasive. Was he feeling the heat because it looked bad for his Department or was he feeling the screws tighten because he was part of the deceit? Jane tried to play the process through from beginning to end. Somebody was obviously screwing around with evidence and doing God knows what for God only knows what reason. This brought it all back to Ron Dickson, the "good Christian." The soccer dad. The guy who collected money for D.A.R.E. The fellow who appeared naive but genuine to Jane. Could she have been wrong all along about this man? Or, perhaps, was someone using him higher up on the Department's food chain? Jane knew that Ron would be an easy target to deceive. Between the massive confusion downstairs when large amounts of evidence poured in and Ron's naturally trusting nature, someone he respected higher up in the Department could have slipped behind the counter and stolen key case evidence.

But for what bigger purpose? And, if that was the big corruption revelation that Bill Stover was prepared to disclose, how did the Texas mob fit into this theory? While no one was quite sure, the mob appeared to be pursuing the same old schemes: drugs and fronts for laundering money. They also seemed to have the finances to back them up as well as the power to put mortal fear into those who stood in their way. From the little Jane knew about them, they had to have a tightly-knit infrastructure, built upon blackmail and death threats. And when the Texas mob made a death threat against you, there was almost nothing you could do to prevent it.

They didn't choose Bill Stover out of thin air. He was an easy blackmail target. You can't be Denver's "Entrepreneur of the Year" and also have a secret lust for coke and meth. You might as well walk around with a big "Blackmail Me!" sign on your chest. He willingly allowed his Denver convenience stores to be used as fronts for laundering money. Along the way, he befriended a few drugged out mob lackeys who carelessly bragged about who knew who protected what in Denver. It was a sweet deal for all concerned until law enforcement got wind of the shady dealings and made Stover a "lose-lose" offer he couldn't refuse.

Jane considered the old "Follow the protection money" lament her dad mentioned. Stuck in Peachville, there was no way to do that. Even if she could research the trail via the telephone, it would take hours standing at The Pit Stop pay phone.

She looked back at the picnic photographs. Jane figured that by May 2 when the photos were snapped, Bill Stover knew he was headed for court and imminent house arrest. Staring at the faces of Bill and Yvonne, Jane noticed a stressed demeanor in their appearance. It was the same troubled look she caught on the faces of David and Patricia Lawrence when she saw their photo displayed on their refrigerator. Jane chalked that up to a bad day. But perhaps, there was more to it.

Given the fact that the two families were obviously very close friends, Jane wondered if it was possible that Bill shared information with David. After all, Bill Stover knew he was going to testify against the mob. He was also a struggling drug addict who may have not been able to keep his mouth shut. Jane knew that pattern all too well. Whenever she needed to get information about a perp, her first stop was to the street junkies who were more than happy to trade good information for a few bucks to buy their next hit. Addicts had no code of integrity; addicts just wanted to cover their ass and get a fix. They'd sell out their mother if someone promised them an eight ball.

Jane scrutinized the photos more closely, trying to form a story from them. But the more she stared at Bill's tense expression and David's equally preoccupied countenance, the more questions she had. The only one who might be able to shed light on any of it was lying in her bed and in no shape to answer questions.

The following day, Jane desperately wanted to quiz Emily but the child was still smarting from her gory flash-back at the carnival. By the end of that Sunday, Emily had spent most of the day sitting in the backyard, staring vacantly into space. Her mood shifted from apprehension and embarrassment in the morning to a sullen, angry disposition as evening fell. Jane noticed that even an unexpected visit from Dan that evening didn't alter Emily's brooding temperament. It was as if a resentful shift had taken hold. Gone was the innocent, inquisitive kid. Instead, a confused, frustrated child emerged who felt manipulated by everyone around her.

Jane tolerated the sullen mood change. But on Monday morning, she was determined to pump Emily for information about the relationship between the Stovers and Lawrences. Emily was still asleep in her own bed that morning when there was a knock on the front door. Jane peeked out the narrow glass panels on the front door and groaned before opening the door. "Hello, Heather."

"Hello," she responded with a self-important air. "They're putting up the decorations for the fourth!"

"The fourth?"

"July fourth?" Heather said with a snotty, "you-certainly-are-stupid" tone. "It's this Sunday! We have a huge parade. Anyway, I wanted to know if Patty could come and hang out with us while we watch them put up the decorations."

"Not today." Jane started to close the door when Heather slammed her hand against it.

"Wait!" she demanded.

Jane felt a strong ire building for this brat. "What?"

"We won't go far. Just like a block up on Main!"

Jane wanted to scream. "What part of the word 'no' don't you understand?"

Heather stared defiantly at Jane, her left eyebrow arching slightly. An evil grin crept across her face. "Have a nice day!" she said, turning on her heels.

Jane shut the front door and turned to see Emily standing in her bedroom doorway. "I want to watch them put up the decorations!" Emily said emphatically.

"No," Jane said, lighting a cigarette and walking down the hall to the kitchen to grab her morning coffee.

"Why!" Emily yelled, quickly following Jane down the hall.

"Because I want to talk to you!"

"All we ever do is talk. You and me! I want to be with people my own age!"

"Goddamnit, Emily! I said I need to talk to you!"

"Aw, shit!" Emily said, angrily shoving the kitchen chair under the table. "It's always about you! It's never about me!"

"Hey, what in the hell do you think we're doing in this fucking town?" Jane took her coffee cup and headed back down the hall to the living room.

"I don't know. You don't tell me anything!" Emily said, following Jane. "I just figured we're sitting around waiting for me to remember whatever it is I'm supposed to remember so you can solve your case and leave this 'fucking town?'"

"*Okay, stop!*" Jane realized the conversation was going nowhere. "Sit down," she said with less fire in her voice. Emily remained standing. "*Emily?*" Reluctantly, Emily complied, stoically crossing her arms across her chest. "You want to cut me off?" Jane asked, noting Emily's body language. "Fine! But we're going to sit here and

have a rational conversation whether you like it or not."
Jane set down her coffee cup and took a drag on her
cigarette as she plopped into the chair across from Emily.
"You may not believe this," Jane said calmly, "but I know
exactly what you're feeling right now."

"No, you don't," Emily said, resentment pouring out
of each word.

"Yes, I do. I've been on this earth, breathing in and out,
longer than you. And I've had to endure a lot of shit. I'm
not trying to make out like I've suffered more than you.
I'm just telling you that I know what you're feeling.
You're pissed off because you want to be in control but
the powers that be aren't letting that happen. I'm yanking
your chain every single day, telling you what you can and
can't do. Meanwhile, your memory is serving up little
pieces of disjointed crap that doesn't make sense, but
scares the hell out of you nonetheless." Jane couldn't help
but think of her own chaotic visions of blinding light,
Glocks, bizarre wolf faces and backwards dates on hand-
prints. "Trust me, kid, *I do know* what it feels like to see
things that disturb you and make no sense." Emily considered Jane's statement. "So, you feel like you're being
used. And you know what? You're absolutely right."
Emily looked surprised. "What? You thought I was going
to tell you that you're not being used? That'd be a lie and
I don't lie to you. The Denver PD used you and *I'm* using
you to try and solve your parents' murder. If you want to
know the God's truth, I didn't want this case. Not because
of you, but because of what I know you must have gone
through." Jane leaned forward. "I've seen what you can't
see. I've seen what you don't want to see. I've felt the
same fear that you feel . . . And I've heard the voices,
Emily."

Emily couldn't believe what she was hearing. Was it
possible, she wondered? Could she risk telling Jane
everything or would Jane think she was crazy? Would she
even believe her? "Jane, I—"

"I've never asked you the tough questions," Jane

interrupted. "I've never forced you to tell me every last detail of what you can remember. I didn't want to be the person responsible for destroying you."

Emily realized it was all about what she saw at the house. She quickly reasoned that to reveal anything else to Jane at that moment would complicate everything.

Jane took a long drag on her cigarette. "Some things have changed in the last couple days. You and me are up against the wall. So, I've got to ask you the hard questions in order to connect the dots." Emily slowly nodded. "You've told me that your parents fought a lot and that they fought more frequently in the weeks leading up to their murder. Can you remember anything that was said during those fights?"

"I tried not to listen. I'd go in my closet and close the door and turn on my Starlight Starbright."

"You weren't sitting in your closet all the time. You *had* to hear something."

"Daddy came home later and later. He said he was helping A.J.'s daddy with his computer at his office—"

"Your dad's office?"

"No. At A.J.'s dad's office. A.J.'s dad got confused a lot. A.J. told me he acted crazy sometimes. He didn't know anything about computers and so my dad said he would help him. My dad was a computer whiz." Jane tried to put things together. She pictured David sitting in the back office of one of Bill Stover's convenience stores—the same back office where the Texas Mob was thought to have set up shop. "I heard Daddy say to Mommy once that he felt important 'cause he could help out A.J.'s daddy."

"Did that mean a lot to your dad? Feeling important?"

"Sure. Everybody wants to feel important." Emily's mind drifted momentarily. "But Mommy didn't like that Daddy felt important helping out A.J.'s daddy."

"Really?"

"It scared her. They fought a lot about that before Mommy and me went to Moab for our camping trip.

I asked her when we were away why she was so scared, but all she'd say is that Daddy makes bad decisions because he's a drunk and he wants to be a big man and he's really just a little man. I didn't get what she meant by that."

Jane recalled the conversation she had with Weyler at the Lawrence house. One of David's coworkers said that he displayed a cocksure attitude around the office that was unusual for him. Perhaps, Jane surmised, David's strut was because he felt important when he hung out with Bill Stover. That strut, however, vanished within weeks, according to Weyler's information, and was replaced by muffled telephone calls and erratic behavior. "What kind of bad decisions was your mother referring to?"

"Don't know. Daddy just wanted to be his friend. But Mommy said he was hurting us."

"How was he hurting you?"

Emily's eyes drifted into the distance, as fragments of conversation filtered through her mind. "That's what my daddy said to Mommy that night." The memory gradually unfolded. "I was standing at the top of the stairs. They couldn't see me. 'You're hurting us,' Mommy said . . . She kept shoving the letter in his face."

Jane abruptly came to attention. "What letter?"

Emily was faraway. "The letter in her hand. It made her real angry and scared—"

"What was in the letter?"

"I don't know . . . she put it away . . ."

"*Where?*" Jane asked emphatically.

"She hid it in that secret compartment at the back of the desk in the hallway."

Jane nearly fell off her chair. She thought back to the crime scene photo and that "white scratch" coming from the back of the desk. "You have no idea what was in that letter?" Jane said urgently.

"No," Emily replied coming back into herself. "She just told Daddy that we should never have come back from our camping trip."

"The camping trip," Jane said, feeling a puzzle piece falling into place. "You were gone for nine days?" Emily nodded. Jane did the math and figured out an approximate scenario. Counting back nine days from May 22—the date that Emily and her mother returned from Moab—was May 14, the day after the late night SUV explosion that killed the Stover family. Jane reasoned that Patricia was terrified by the event, felt a need to protect Emily from the tragedy and made a quick decision to pull her out of school and flee to Moab, Utah. There she and Emily would be far away from the fallout and nowhere near a newspaper or TV. Jane surmised it was Patricia's MO to always hide the truth from Emily. Tucked away in the middle of the Utah desert, Patricia made sure that Emily heard and saw nothing about the graphic murder. Jane surmised that Patricia returned to their home on May 22, hoping that nine days was enough time for things to shake out. But instead, it all hit the fan when David disclosed the secret letter to his wife. Whatever was in that letter was pure dynamite and enough to put the fear of God into Patricia. Jane turned to Emily. "What happened next?"

"Mommy said we were going to leave and move to my aunt and uncle's house in Cheyenne. Then they saw me at the top of the stairs and stopped fighting. Mommy told me to go back to my room and that she was gonna talk to me later. I told Mommy I loved her and I told Daddy, too. And he said, 'I love you, sweat pea.' I went back into my room. A few minutes after that, I thought I heard A.J.'s daddy yelling downstairs."

Jane knew that Emily did not hear A.J.'s daddy—Bill Stover—because he was killed ten days prior to that night. "Describe the voice you heard."

"It sounded like A.J.'s daddy." Emily mimicked the sound as best she could. "'How you doin', Emily?'" she said in a semi-gruff, punctuated cadence.

"That's the exact sound you heard?" Jane said. "You sure?"

"Yeah. Why?"

Jane knew that was nowhere near the sound of Weyler's smooth and more articulate voice. "Do you remember anything specific he said that night?"

"Just something about an accident," Emily's memory kicked in again. "It's ten o' clock . . . I can't hear what they're saying . . . Then he goes into the kitchen and everything's quiet until he comes back out . . . Then my daddy's voice . . . he's the first to yell . . . then my mommy yells out . . . I don't want to hear it so I grab my pillows off my bed and go to the closet . . . The clock says 10:04 when I go back to get the last pillow . . ."

Jane constructed a series of possible events. The Lawrences fought over a mysterious letter that terrified Patricia. In anger and fear, Patricia stashed the letter in the desk's secret compartment. Emily interrupted the fight, she was told to go back to bed and all remains quiet until, perhaps under the ruse of there being an accident down the street, either Patricia or David Lawrence let an unknown male into their house at 10:00 at night. It's someone they don't know but someone who is savvy enough to convince them that his plea is legitimate. He then walks alone into their kitchen, supposedly to use the phone. Jane visualized the scene. Knowing that the perp took precautions and covered his feet, hands and face, Jane deduced that he must have quickly done so behind the kitchen door. It all occurred in less than four minutes, which, for Jane, certainly indicated someone who knew exactly what he was doing. Charm yourself into the house, analyze the situation and then get down to the business of killing. Disable the strongest victim with your knife, then start on the second victim. In this case, Jane was now almost positive it was one perp and two knives. *That* fact spoke volumes as well. To her, it demonstrated that the killer was cunning and knew exactly how to throw off investigators. It also told her that whoever did this had to have the strength to wield two separate knives without cross contamination.

Jane started to put the pieces together. "Two nights ago at the carnival, you were doing okay until you saw the guy with that pig mask over his face."

"Yeah," Emily said, still humiliated by the experience.

"I want you to go back to that moment—"

"I don't want to!"

"Emily, it's just you and me sitting here. You're safe. The guy with the pig mask, it obviously triggered something inside you. Something important maybe."

"It wasn't the mask, at first. He was wearing all black. That's what started it. And he had gloves on. Black gloves." Emily focused on the man at the carnival. "And there was something shiny in his hand. His right hand. I couldn't see what it was, but my heart started beating really hard. I had to hold my breath."

"Why hold your breath?"

Emily tried to fight it, but she felt herself drifting back in time. "I have to be quiet," she whispered as her breathing became more shallow.

"Why?" Jane asked, hating every second of it.

Emily closed her eyes. "So he doesn't hear me," she whispered.

"Where are you?"

There was a long pause before she spoke. "Hiding . . . in my closet. I turned off my Starlight Starbright . . . I have to be quiet . . ."

"How can you see him if you're in your closet?"

"Because . . . he opened the door and looked in . . ."

"Why doesn't he see you?"

"I'm hiding under all the pillows . . ."

"He's dressed in black?"

"Uh-huh."

"What's in his hand?"

"I don't know." Emily was fully engaged in the memory, hypnotized by Jane's voice. "I have to be so quiet . . ."

Jane nervously took several puffs on her cigarette, waiting for Emily to make the next move. Suddenly, the child took in a gulp of air, as if she were startled. "What is it?"

"His head's covered with a black sock . . ." Emily drew her hand to her head, unaware that she was now mimicking the individual instead of witnessing the event. "He's pulling at the sock. . . ." Emily began to yank at an imaginary sock around her head. "He doesn't like the sock . . . He's scratching his face through the sock . . ." Emily scratched helplessly at the imaginary sock on her head and face. "He wants to take it off . . ." Emily grabs the edge of the imaginary sock around her neck and begins to struggle with it. "Get it off!" The child neared hysteria when she got a strong grip on the illusory sock and yanked it off her head. As her head jerked backward, she opened her eyes, slamming back into reality. "Make it stop!" she screamed, standing up on the couch completely disoriented and heading backward over the edge.

Jane lunged toward Emily, pulling her back on to the couch. Emily shook violently as she held onto Jane. When Emily calmed down, Jane gently spoke up. "Did you see his face?"

"No," Emily said, burying her head in Jane's chest. "You think it's A.J.'s daddy?"

"No, it's not A.J.'s daddy."

Emily lifted her head and looked at Jane. "How do you know for sure?"

Jane purposely looked straight ahead. "I'm a detective. My gut tells me things. And I know that wasn't Amy's dad."

Emily pulled back from Jane. "How'd you know A.J.'s first name?"

Jane felt the floor fall out from underneath her feet. She kept staring straight ahead, poker-faced, but bumbling inside like a lost child. "Lots of kids are named Amy. Like I said, I've got that detective gut."

Emily stared at Jane in stone cold silence. "What's your detective gut say the 'J' stands for?"

Jane craned her neck as if she were searching for the answer. "Juliet," she said, confidently turning to Emily.

"No. It stands for 'Joan.'"

Jane shrugged her shoulder, desperately trying to act nonchalant under Emily's prying eyes. "Well, one out of two, eh? So, how did you and A.J. meet?"

"I met her last year at my private school. We were in the same class."

The pieces were fitting together very quickly. Did David see incriminating activity or someone important at Bill's office? Possibly. Did Bill confide sensitive information to David? Probably. Drug addicts like Bill can't keep their damn mouths shut. And from what Jane could decipher from the limited contact she had with Stover, he was like all meth addicts: talkative and out of control. "Did you ever hear your dad tell your mom anything that he and A.J.'s dad talked about? You know, any names you can remember?"

"How come you're asking me these questions?"

Jane realized her desperation was too obvious. Reluctantly, she pulled back. "I just thought that—"

"You said your gut told you that the voice I heard downstairs that night wasn't A.J.'s daddy. So, if he wasn't there that night, why do you care what kind of things he and my daddy talked about?"

Jane knew it was pointless to prod further. "Sorry. My detective mind never stops."

Emily sat back against the couch, fiddling with the buttons on her pajama top. "I wonder what A.J.'s doing right now."

Jane turned away, feeling the tug of the moment pull hard on her. "Oh, I imagine she's thinking about you and wanting you to be happy and not worry about her."

"Is that what your detective gut says?"

"Yes. Exactly." Jane stood up, took a drag on her dying cigarette and snuffed it out in the ashtray. She walked across the living room and stared out the front picture window at Peachville's city trucks unloading red, white and blue street decorations. She didn't realize she was nervously rubbing the old scar across her right temple.

"What are you thinking about?" Emily said carefully.

"There's something I've got to do," Jane replied, locked in deep thought.

Emily analyzed Jane's posture and nervous behavior. "Why are you so scared?"

Jane turned to Emily. "Huh?"

"You only rub your scar when you're scared. What is it you have to do?"

Jane pulled her hand away from the scar. "I have to make an important phone call."

Jane checked her Glock before slipping it into her fanny pack. She started to walk out of her bedroom when she returned to her leather satchel and drew an extra clip from the side pocket. Placing the clip into the inside pocket of the fanny pack, she zipped it up and headed down the hallway. "Ready?"

Emily was seated on the couch. "You know, we never talked about the sleepover with Heather and her friends."

"We'll talk about it later. Come on."

"No," Emily stated, not moving an inch. "The sleep-over means a lot to me."

Jane sat on the couch, doing her best to act diplomatic. "Look, you and I are up against the wall right now. I think we should keep the house off-limits to other people."

"*It's one night.* We can lock all the doors and you can sit up in your bedroom with your gun. I just want to feel normal again . . . even if it's just for a little bit."

Jane studied Emily's face. Her gut told her "no," but the kid's candid petition was hard to argue with. "Okay," Jane replied reluctantly.

They drove off in the Subaru, Jane's heart beating hard the whole time. Pulling into the parking lot of The Pit Stop, she checked the time. It was Monday around noon. He should be home for lunch. This phone call was a long shot and risky as hell. She would also have to check her pride at the door for the whole thing to work.

She got out of the car and dialed the number. The phone rang three times and then, "Hello?"

# Chapter 25

"Hello?" the voice repeated. It wasn't the voice Jane was expecting.

She hesitated, not sure what to do. Her knee-jerk reaction was to hang up, but she stayed on the line. "Hello? Is someone there?"

"Yeah," Jane nervously said. "It's . . . it's Jane."

"Well, hi, Jane. This is a surprise."

Jane felt her stomach churning. "Yeah . . ."

"Listen, your brother's not here. But I'll certainly tell him you called."

"Well, the thing is Lisa . . . I was actually calling to ask Mike if he could ask *you* something." Jane realized she sounded like some tiresome high school kid.

"Ask me what?" Lisa replied with an ease to her voice.

Jane snapped into her cop mode. "Here's the drill, Lisa. I don't know you. I've only met you once and you seemed okay." Jane waited for Lisa to say anything but heard only silence. "Do you love Mike? Or is this some sort of cut and run deal?"

"Cut and run? I'm not following you. Are you okay, Jane?"

"*Do you love my brother?*" Jane asked pointedly.

"Yes, I do," Lisa said without hesitation.

"So, am I hearing that you want to be part of our

family?" The words seemed foreign to Jane as they came out of her mouth.

"I'd like that very much, Jane. And I'd also like to get to know you better when you're comfortable with that."

"I'm going to be straight with you, Lisa. I don't usually do this sort of thing."

"What sort of thing?"

"I get to know people very well. At least, I like to think I do. I listen to the change in their voice to see if I can hear a lie . . . Oh, fuck." Jane knew she was rambling. "What I'm trying to say is that I get to know someone extremely well before I *ever* ask anything of them. Especially anything that could be dangerous."

"Jane, I—"

"You have to understand that I would never ask this of you unless I was as fucking desperate as I am right now."

"Jane," Lisa said kindly, "whatever you need to ask me, it's okay. Just ask."

Jane took a deep breath. "You said your brother used to be a bounty hunter?"

"Yeah, right. My older brother, Jeff."

"And now, he's a private investigator."

"Yes."

"I remember that you said that he does fraud and adultery cases."

"That's right."

"So, tell me. Does he have the balls for a case that carries more weight?"

"What kind of weight are you talking about?"

"The mafia. The Texas mafia, to be exact. And the Denver PD. And perhaps how those two may be in bed together?"

There was a long, thoughtful pause on the other end of the line. Jane waited. "Gosh, Jane. I don't know. Are you in some sort of danger?"

"I don't give a shit what happens to me, Lisa. It's someone else I'm worried about." Jane stole a glance toward the Subaru and acknowledged Emily.

"The little girl?" Lisa said with deep concern in her voice.

Jane turned around. "Yes. Look, calling you like this, getting you involved, this is all totally against policy and procedure. But the thing is, I need your help. I need your brother's help. I need you to talk to him and convince him to check out some downtown businesses for me. Specifically, foreign downtown businesses. Asian businesses. They're used to paying protection money back in their home country. They're always the first targets for the mob. He needs to ask around about who's getting paid and who's getting favors. He's gotta work it so he finds a trail and he's gotta follow that trail to wherever it leads. I'm telling you right now that I think that trail leads to Denver PD and possibly to a man named Weyler. I have to know the truth and I have to know it damn fast. I can't . . ." Jane choked up. "I can't lose another kid to those assholes. You understand me? If I have to, I will ditch the car and we will take a bus to another state and we will disappear forever. They will not get their fucking hands on her!" Jane knew she had gone too far.

"How can he contact you?" Lisa asked confidentially.

"Is that a 'yes'?"

"I have a way with my brother. Just like you and Mike, we're real tight. If I tell him I need a favor for a good friend, he'll do it. So, how are we going to contact you?"

Jane was dumbstruck. After all the awful things she had said about Lisa—out loud, under her breath and in her head—after all that, this girl was willing to play the middle-man in a dangerous game. "My pager," Jane said quietly, before giving her the number. "It's a voice pager. So, if he can cut to the chase in sixty seconds or less, have him leave a message. Otherwise, tell him to give me his number and I'll call him right back."

"I'll take care of it, Jane."

"I don't want you involved in this any more than just contacting your brother!"

"Hey, don't worry about it. Like you said, I'd like to

be part of your family one day. And family does this kind of stuff for each other."

Jane was completely floored by Lisa's words. She closed her eyes, listening intently to Lisa's voice echo in her head. She heard neither a lie nor the whisper of betrayal in the timbre. "Thank you."

Monday turned into Tuesday and there was no word from Lisa. Jane noticed that Dan increased his self-appointed, drive-by patrols each day and evening. Late Tuesday afternoon, he stopped by to share news with Jane. While Emily played in the backyard, Dan and Jane stood at the front door, talking in confidential tones.

"I don't know exactly what's goin' on," Dan revealed, a worried look etched into his face, "but I think Sheriff George is fixin' to investigate you."

"I thought he bought the whole story about Emily being sick."

"I thought he did, too. But that's the word I'm gettin'."

Jane let out a tired sigh. "What in the hell made him change his mind?"

"I don't know. Unless . . ."

"What?"

"Unless he heard or saw what happened with Emily at the carnival . . ."

Jane thought it through and realized Dan was probably right. "Shit! If he starts poking around on his computer, he's bound to figure the whole thing out—"

"If I catch wind that he's found out about your ex, I'll let you know."

"Dan, if he finds out the truth about me—"

"I guess all we can pray for right now is water seepin' into the underground lines. It breaks the Internet connection around here."

"Then I suggest you go break a water main."

Tuesday melted into Wednesday and Jane's voice pager remained silent. Knowing that she now had the added stress of Sheriff George searching on his computer for information on her, Jane's tension was growing exponentially. Thanks to her constant paranoia, the two had not left the house since returning home from making the phone call at The Pit Stop on Monday afternoon.

By Wednesday afternoon, Emily was stir crazy. With Kathy's "welcome basket" nearly drained of its contents and the refrigerator and freezer almost empty, Emily begged Jane for a trip to The Mountain Melon Market. Jane acquiesced with the caveat that Emily stay within eyesight of her the entire time.

Main Street was alive with red, white and blue banners, American flags and countless signs and posters heralding Sunday's Independence Day Parade. Jane parked the Subaru. "Stay next to me in there. Understood?"

"Understood," Emily said, feeling like a trapped animal.

The market was empty, save for the cashier whose head was buried in the *National Enquirer*. Jane grabbed a cart and headed to the frozen food section at the rear of the market. No sooner were she and Emily hidden from view when the bell attached to the market's front door chimed.

"Hey there, Sheriff!" the cashier called out. "How's it goin'?"

Jane suddenly felt cornered.

Emily perked up. "Can I go—"

"Shh!" Jane cautioned her.

"Say, is your lotto machine working?" Sheriff George asked the cashier.

"Nah. It's havin' one of them days. Why? Is your computer down again?"

"Yeah. That damn water in the lines is causing it to crash constantly."

Jane half wondered if Dan had taken her seriously when she told him to "break a water main" to prevent smooth transmissions on the sheriff's computer.

"It'll dry out soon," the cashier said.

"Not soon enough," the sheriff said curtly.

"You got yourself a big case?" the cashier said with great interest.

"I might. I don't know just yet. But I might . . ."

Jane stood still, the freezer door propped open against her hip. She heard the sound of the sheriff's boots scuffing across the floor toward a nearby bank of shelves. She knew he wasn't crossing to the shelves to get something as much as he was moving in that direction to see who was in the market. Since he probably spied Jane's Subaru parked in front of the market, Jane figured he suspected that she and Emily were inside. She kept her head forward, appearing as if she were examining a frozen food entree. Her eyes moved slightly to the left where the glass door cast a reflection on the shelving. There was the sheriff, reflected back in the icy glass. He waited for her to turn around but Jane refused to acknowledge his presence. After what felt like an eternity, Sheriff George moved back to the front of the store.

"You have a good day," the sheriff said to the cashier before leaving the market.

Jane dumped an armful of frozen food into the cart. "Come on, let's grab what we need and get the hell out of here."

"Sheriff George is nice," Emily said, confused. "How come you didn't want to talk to him?"

"Not now," she whispered.

"I want chips and salsa," Emily said as she marched down the aisle. "Hurry up," Jane said impatiently.

Emily wound around the far aisle to grab the chips. The front door opened again and the cheerful bell rang out.

"Well, hey Kathy! Hey, Heather!" The cashier said.

"All ready for the fourth?"

Jane let the door to the frozen food section slam shut. "Shit!" she said, turning to get Emily's attention. But it was too late.

Emily skipped to the front of the store. "Heather! How you doing?"

"Hi, Patty! Long time no see!" Heather said in a disingenuous tone.

"Are you here all by yourself, darling?" Kathy

inquired. "No. My mom's in the back. By the frozen food section."

"Frozen food." Kathy said in a catty tone. "Well, *of course* she is!"

Jane shook her head in disgust.

"Hey, Heather! Guess what?" Emily said. "Mom says that I can have the sleep over at our house!"

Jane spun the cart around and headed down the aisle to get to Emily.

"Great!" Heather said. "When do you want to do it?"

"How about this Saturday? The third? Then the next day, we can all go and watch the Independence Day Parade!"

Jane reached the front of the store. "Patty, we need to discuss this."

"No we don't," Emily said succinctly. "We made a deal. *Remember?*"

Jane caught Kathy's prying eyes staring at her. It was as though Kathy was laying in wait until Jane said or did something that warranted a call to the Sheriff. Jane opted for a different approach. "Well, we don't know what Kathy's mom has to say about the idea. She may have other plans with her family for the holiday weekend."

"We don't have any plans, Mrs. Calver," Heather said, looking at Jane with the same hateful appearance Jane had noticed on other occasions.

"Well, Heather," Jane said, regarding the brat with equal hostility, "it's really up to your mother to make that decision. Not you."

"Perhaps we should talk about it, Heather—" Kathy said.

"There's nothing to talk about!" Heather snapped back at Kathy. "Emily invited me and my friends to a sleep over and we're going to go!" Turning to Emily, Heather smiled a sugary grin. "Do you want me to bring CDs so we can dance?"

"Yeah!" Emily said, totally blown away by Heather's offer.

"Hey, you wanna see the cutest new lipstick I found?" Heather asked Emily. The two girls ran down the center aisle, leaving Kathy and Jane in an awkward moment.

"If you can't handle this," Kathy said with a snippy sound in her voice, "we can just forget about the whole thing."

Jane regarded Kathy's comment as almost a street dare. "Oh, I can handle it."

Emily floated ten feet above the carpet for the next three days in excited expectation of Saturday night. By contrast, Jane was emotionally hugging the ground, waiting day and night for any word from Lisa.

Emily dug through the attic and came up with a halfway decent sleeping bag. By Friday night, Emily was wired and unable to sleep. She dragged herself out of the bedroom and stood at the threshold of the living room. The television was on mute. Jane sat on the couch in the semi-darkness pensively looking through the various newspaper clippings that featured Chris and Jane's photos on the front page.

"I can't sleep," Emily said, her back wedged against the living room doorway. Jane nonchalantly stashed the clippings back into the files and replaced them into her leather satchel. "Can I watch TV with you for a while?" Emily asked.

"PBS is the only station that's coming in right now. And it's begging time!"

"Begging time?"

"They're doing their annual pledge drive. So it's not too entertaining."

Emily sauntered over to the couch. She glanced at the clock. "Hey, you know what? Tomorrow at this time, I'm going to be sitting in this living room with Heather and her friends. We're gonna be dancing, telling ghost stories and having fun!"

"Uh-huh," Jane said in a dubious tone.

"How come you can't be happy for me?"

"I don't trust Heather," Jane stated.

"You don't trust anyone."

"That's true. You know why? Because most people have motives."

"I don't and you don't either."

Jane couldn't argue with that. "So you and I are exceptions to the rule, but—"

"Maybe Heather is too!"

"Emily, I don't know what she wants from you, but it's very obvious to me that her intentions are not pure. I can't understand why you don't see it! I mean, she's staring you right in the face and serving you a line of bullshit."

Emily shrugged her shoulders. "Maybe I don't want to see it. Is that so bad?" She plopped onto the couch and motioned to the TV. "They've gone back to the show."

Jane looked at the screen. "Hey, that's the Three Tenors!" She clicked on the sound. "See that heavyset guy to the right? That's Pavarotti." Jane was drawn into the moment, a fact that didn't escape Emily's watchful eye. The orchestra swelled into the heartfelt strains of "Nessun Dorma." For a painful second, Jane was transported back to her mother's bedside on the day of her death. The camera zoomed in on Pavarotti as he sung with heartfelt emotion.

Emily was equally drawn into the aria. She quickly recognized the evocative melody as the same one that played on her Starlight Starbright projector. "Do you know what the words mean?" Emily asked.

"Yeah," Jane said, her eyes still fixated on the screen. "He's talking about a princess, alone in her room. She's watching the stars, trembling with love and hope." She waited until Pavarotti began the second verse. "He's saying, 'But my secret lies hidden within me . . . no one shall discover my name . . . Oh, no . . . I will reveal it only on your lips when daylight shines forth! . . . And my kiss shall break the silence that makes you mine!' " The orchestra performed the interlude as Pavarotti took a step back from the microphone. Jane leaned forward. "Watch him. Watch his eyes."

Emily stared at the screen, completely transfixed by the moment. Pavarotti moved back to the microphone. "What's he saying?" Emily urgently asked.

"Depart, oh night! . . . Set you stars! . . . At dawn, I shall win! . . . I shall win!"

Pavarotti sang out the final dramatic words, his face etched with frightening passion. "*Vincero! . . . Vincero!*" Jane's eyes welled with tears as the audience let out a thundering ovation. "I shall win," she whispered to herself.

Emily finally drifted off to sleep and Jane carried the sleeping child to her bed. But the niggling disquiet inside Jane's mind kept her awake long into the early morning hours. Nothing but test patterns filled the TV screen and she had a throbbing headache from going over the case files. She lit a cigarette and paced between the kitchen and living room, checking the locks on the doors with an obsessive fervor. Jane took another hard drag. *Paranoia.* Chris' mantra echoed, "Just because people call you paranoid does not erase the fact that certain other people aren't out to get you!" She was beginning to see the truth of that statement.

She looked across the living room to the old radio console. It was late enough, she told herself as she walked over and turned on the dial. Sure, it was a long shot but Jane spun the dial across the waves of static in search of Tony Mooney's soothing voice.

"Welcome back . . ."

Jane couldn't believe she found the show and pinched herself to make sure she wasn't dreaming again. She twisted the knob to get the best possible reception. Even so, it was like listening to someone talk amidst a sandstorm.

"Hello again to all you denizens of the predawn madness," Mooney said in his characteristic cadence, albeit buried beneath a blanket of poor reception. Jane settled down on the carpet and pressed her ear to the speaker. Mooney's voice briefly broke through the incessant whirring and static. "In honor of the upcoming Independence Day celebration, we're continuing our discussion tonight on that elusive thing we all crave . . . freedom. Ah, *sweet freedom*. What really *is* freedom? They write anthems to it in notes no one can sing. They tease us with the notion as religion, politics and society chain us to the status quo. So where does freedom really live, my friends? Does it lie outside ourselves or is it born from within?" Mooney's voice faded into a cloud of dissonance, reemerging only briefly. "The reality, my friends, is that most do not taste freedom until the moment of death. But it is the fortunate who can savor the sweetness of true freedom while living." His baritone voice gradually drowned in a wave of static, "Are you free? Or are you waiting for death to give you wings?"

Jane stared at the radio as her blood turned cold.

"Wake up!" Emily said excitedly, poking Jane in the chest.

Jane awakened with a sudden jerk. "What?"

"It's Saturday!" Emily exclaimed, jumping up and down with glee.

Emily's manic joy continued throughout the day as she counted down the hours until seven o'clock when Heather and her friends would arrive. She busied herself by cleaning her room several times, rearranging the living room to accommodate the girls' sleeping bags and getting all the junk food ready for the group.

"Where are you gonna be tonight?" Emily asked Jane in an insistent tone.

"Oh, I thought I'd sit in the living room with all of you—my Glock in one hand and the remote control in the other," Jane replied, dripping with sarcasm. Emily wasn't quite sure what to make of her statement. "I'll either be in the kitchen or my bedroom. And I promise I won't listen to one word you say to each other."

By the time seven o' clock rolled around, Emily was

about ready to collapse in anticipation of her guests' arrival. She sat perched in the chair near the front living room window, watching the road for Kathy's car. "They're here!" Emily yelled, almost falling over as she leapt out of the chair.

Jane moved toward the front door. "For God's sake, calm down! Listen to me," Jane tried to corral her. "You're really wired but you have to remember not to let anything slip out of your mouth by mistake."

"Yeah, yeah! I know! I know! They're getting out of the car!"

"Emily, did you hear what I said?"

"*Yes!*"

"Don't let Heather talk you into doing anything you don't want to do!"

"I won't! Can I please open the door?" Jane stood back as Emily flung open the front door. "Hi!" she exclaimed, her enthusiasm pouring out onto the front porch.

Four girls filed into the living room, followed by Kathy and Heather.

"Hello, Patty, sweetheart!" Kathy said, softly touching Emily's chin. Turning to Jane, Kathy's voice took on a more distant tone. "Hello, Anne."

"Hello, Kathy," Jane replied with a sugary sweet flavor to her voice.

"Girls! Girls!" Kathy said. "Make sure you've got everything you need out of the car! Mary, do you have your eyeglasses?"

Mary, a freckled-faced, red-haired kid, turned to Kathy. "They're in my bag."

Kathy sidled up to Jane and spoke quietly. "It's not easy keeping track of all the girls' personal possessions, not to mention their likes and dislikes. But I do! I know every single one of these girls inside out."

Jane glanced over to Emily, who was showing one of the children where the bathroom was located. "Every girl in this room?" Jane asked, alluding to Emily.

Kathy kept her face forward with a phony smile pasted

across it. "Every single one. I know what they love . . . I know what they fear."

Jane turned to Kathy, contempt shooting from her eyes. "Is that right?"

Kathy faced Jane, matching her contemptible glare. "Yes. And every girl here has been taught to tell her parents anything she sees that scares her or makes her sad."

"How ironic," Jane said with a smirk. "I've taught Patty the same thing."

Kathy observed the girls as they chatted amongst themselves and arranged their sleeping bags. "Perhaps I should stay for a little bit until the girls get settled."

Jane opened the front door. "Oh, now Kathy, if I'm not allowed to hang with them, you sure as hell aren't. See you in the morning!"

Kathy addressed the girls. "Girls, listen up!" The chatter gradually ceased. "I'm leaving now. Mrs. Calver will be available if you need anything. Since she doesn't have a telephone, I'm going to leave my cell phone right here." Kathy pulled out her phone and set it on the side table by the couch. "Now, that's not for play. That's only for emergencies. You dial 9-1-1 and then you call me, okay?" Jane bristled as Kathy held court, obviously sending out a loaded message. The girls nodded their heads. "And remember, girls!" Kathy continued. "What are the rules when someone knocks at the front door? We only let them in if they are someone we know or . . . ?"

All the girls, except for Emily, chimed in. "Someone we trust."

Kathy let out a breath of air and turned to leave. "Happy sleepover!"

The girls plotted out their various sleeping locations across the living room carpet. Jane closed the front door, locking both the handle and the dead bolt.

Emily looked up at Jane. "Mom? Haven't you got someplace to go right now?" Her eyes urged Jane out of the room.

"Why, yes, Patty. I do. I'll be in the kitchen if anyone

needs anything." Jane pulled out a cigarette from the packet in her shirt pocket, lit it and sauntered down the hall to the kitchen.

"Mrs. Calver?"

Jane turned to find Heather standing behind her. "What is it, Heather?"

"Are you going to smoke in the house?"

"Yes," Jane said, her irritation level rising. "Why do you ask?"

"I have smoke allergies. So do Mary and Virginia. Mary even has *asthma*."

Jane regarded Heather as she would a suspect back at DH. "Is that a fact?"

"Yes," Heather said, her steely eyes sharpened on Jane. "*That's a fact!*"

"I'll crack a window," Jane turned and walked into the kitchen. Behind her, she heard the overly dramatic sound of Heather coughing in her direction. Jane kept her back to Heather, as she opened up a bag of chips.

Heather stood in the kitchen entryway for several more seconds, shooting daggers at Jane with her eyes. Without Jane noticing, Heather glanced over to the sliding glass door. She spotted a three-foot long wooden dowel propped up against the wall. She recognized the dowel as a tool to place in the floor tracks against a closed sliding glass door to make it difficult for intruders to break in.

Jane turned around. Heather quickly took her eyes off the dowel and stared back at Jane. "Is there anything else I can do for you, Heather?"

"No, Mrs. Calver," Heather said as she spun around on her heels and crossed back into the living room. "Hey, Patty. If you look in my bag, you'll find all the CDs!"

Emily eagerly opened Heather's bag and brought out a stack of country CDs. "Let's put on Shania Twain!"

Heather smiled the same pasty grin her mother perfected. "That's my favorite!"

Emily plopped the CD in the boom box and hit the play button. Shania blared forth with "Man! I Feel Like A

Woman!" The girls began bopping their bodies back and forth to the beat of the song and shouting out the chorus with Shania.

Jane took a deep drag on her cigarette and realized it was going to be a long night. She grabbed a plate of chips and dip, crossed back into the living room, dodging the dancing girls and headed down the hallway to her bedroom.

Heather danced along to the music but never took her eyes off Jane. She twirled her body in circles until she stood near the front door. From there, she had a clear view of the long hallway that dead ended with Jane's bedroom. Jane closed her bedroom door, never once seeing Heather's inquisitive eyes. "I'm going to the bathroom," Heather yelled to the girls above the music as she sashayed down the hallway. Poking her head in one door, she found the bathroom. Moving a few steps farther down, she discovered the hall closet. She bopped back toward the living room, stopping in front of Emily's bedroom door. The rest of the girls were so into the song that none of them noticed as Heather disappeared into Emily's bedroom.

Heather quietly closed the door behind her. She surveyed the room with a nasty glare. Everything was exceptionally tidy, thanks to Emily's rabid cleaning that day. She spotted Emily's Starlight Starbright vinyl case sitting on a chair and walked over to it. Lifting the cover, she poked around in the case, examining the projector. To get a better look at it, Heather pulled it from the case, uncovering the photo packet. She set the Starlight Starbright on the bed and brought out the photos. The first one featured Emily and her parents. Heather screwed her face into a confused look as she sifted through the photos. After sorting through the stack, she started to put them back into the packet when several of them fell from her hands, landing on the floor upside down. One of the photos had writing on the back. Heather collected the pictures and read the words.

In Emily's writing, it said: "Mommy and Daddy. I LOVE You!"

Heather flipped the photo over to see the Lawrence trio. "Mommy and Daddy?" she said to herself. Suddenly, she heard footsteps outside the door. She quickly stashed the photos back into the packet, tossed them into the case and replaced the Starlight Starbright, slamming the cover shut.

Spinning around, she started for the door when she turned around to check for the one thing she really wanted. Heather scanned the room and spied it propped up on the bedside table. Satisfied, she pressed her ear to the door, waited until she heard no sound, opened the door carefully and walked back into the living room.

The girls were still dancing to Shania's CD. Emily skipped over to Heather. "Come on! You're missing all the fun!" Emily said loudly over the music.

"Hey, I've got an idea for a great game," Heather said, joining the group.

Meanwhile in the back bedroom, Jane tried to view the pages of information on the Stover and Lawrence case with a new eye. Nothing in the Lawrence crime folder alluded to any connection with organized crime. Emily made it clear to Jane that the friendship between Amy and her was strictly of their own making and the subsequent alliance between Bill Stover and David Lawrence was born from Bill's need for computer assistance at his office. After more than two hours of pouring over the documents, Jane concluded that the single link between these two families was that each couple had a daughter and that the husband of each wife had some level of substance abuse that served to cloud their better judgment.

Jane turned her thoughts to Emily's cryptic memory of the man she saw in her bedroom through the crack in the closet door. It had always bothered Jane that the perp butchered two people and then quickly gave up the pursuit of anyone else in the house. In all of the cases that fit the rage-filled kill pattern, the perp was driven to complete his task, leaving no room untouched. The only exception to that rule was if the perp risked being discovered by an unexpected person arriving on the scene. In that case, they would always flee the scene. But as far as Jane could deduce, that didn't happen in the Lawrence case. Jane recalled that Emily mentioned how the perp grabbed at his mask in an agitated way. Why? If there was any chance of someone else hiding in the house, why would a smart criminal like this one expose himself to a witness?

Jane remembered the exact way Emily mimicked the perp's irritation to his mask. It was as though he was clawing at his face. *Clawing.* Jane thought about that image. She'd seen it before many times. But the individuals had no mask on their face. They were clawing at their flesh thanks to the physical and mental effects of methamphetamine on their system. Meth addicts were prone to developing often agonizing rashes that were made more irritating by anything that touched their skin. And so, it came back to meth. Lately, it *always* seemed to come back to meth.

Okay, Jane considered, maybe the perp was a meth freak. It certainly was not outside the realm of possibility these days. The grisly way in which the perp murdered David and Patricia Lawrence could easily be attributed to a meth-induced rage—either coming up on the high or, more likely, *tweaking* and needing more of the drug to maintain their high. Jane pulled out the crime scene photos and referred to the close-up of Patricia Lawrence. Her left eye was partially popped out of its socket. It wasn't the first time Jane saw a direct stab wound to an eye, but it wasn't common. From a profiling angle, a perp who stabs someone in the eye is typically sending a message. It could be "Don't look at me" or "I don't want you to see." It was primitive but some perps retained a certain base animal instinct, especially if they were jacked up on drugs.

For whatever reason, this particular perp was determined to send similar messages through his brutal slayings. Jane assumed that whoever killed the Lawrences also returned and killed Martha Durrett since she was found with a knife plunged into her face. And there was that note attached to the knife that said "PAY-BACK." So much about this case confused Jane and that note was no exception. Was it directed at Martha? If so, what had she done to deserve payback? Martha always played it by the book. Martha simply wasn't capable of doing anything that warranted payback. But still, the perp felt a need to attach that note to the knife.

This time, Jane was certain that the perp had to know Emily was in the house that night because he no sooner thrust the knife into Martha's face than he booked it upstairs to finish the grisly job. Jane surmised that he knew the cops were covering the house and that he had a slender window of time. It was a ballsy move fueled by desperation and a compulsion to kill the one person who could identify him as the perpetrator of the Lawrence double murder. But from what Jane gathered from Emily later that fateful night, the sight of the circling patrol car down the alley possibly deterred the killer from nailing his target.

The intense scrutiny of documentation provoked another headache. Jane looked at the clock. 10:00 p.m. She collected the paperwork, replaced it in the files and stashed it into her leather satchel. Feeling like a mouse trapped in a cage, she decided to venture into the kitchen to grab a soda and a fresh perspective. When she opened her door, she was greeted with near total darkness. She could hear the hushed tones and giggling voices coming from the living room. Jane found the girls in their paja-mas, sitting cross-legged on top of their sleeping bags that were arranged in a circle. The only light in the room came from a single lamp in the corner and two flashlights that were positioned facing upward toward the ceiling in the center of the circle.

"Mom!" Emily said, slightly irritated. "You're not supposed to be in here!"

Heather stiffened when she heard Emily calling Jane
"Mom."

"Just passing through," Jane replied, heading toward
the kitchen.

"Are you going to smoke a cigarette in there?" Heather
asked in a catty tone.

Jane turned around. "Yes, Heather. That's the plan."

"Well, then if you don't mind, I'll open the front door
to clear the smoke." Heather jumped to her feet.

"We're keeping that door closed and locked, Heather."

"I'm just thinking of Mary's asthma," Heather replied,
putting on a very good act as the concerned friend.

"Yeah, Mom," Emily chimed in, "we have to think of
our guests!"

Jane shook her head at Heather's obvious manipulation. "I'll blow it out an open window." She turned to
walk into the kitchen.

"Or, you could just go outside and smoke," Heather
proclaimed.

"Mom?" Emily cautiously suggested, knowing she was
pushing Jane's buttons. "Maybe you should go outside to
smoke. I don't want anyone to get sick."

Jane let out a deep sigh and walked into the kitchen.

Heather waited until Jane was out of eyesight and heard
the kitchen sink faucet turn on before launching into her
devious plan. "Are we gonna play 'Truth or Dare'?"

"Let's do it!" Mary exclaimed.

"Heather," Emily said. "Turn off that corner lamp. Flip
the switch on the wall by the door." Heather fumbled in
the near darkness and flicked up two light switches—one
that illuminated the front porch light and the other that
turned on the bright beam over the garage. "Try the other
switch to your right," Emily instructed.

Heather slapped that switch and the lamp clicked off.
She looked around the room. "Hmmm. The room needs
something more. Something *different*. If we only had one

of those Starlight Starbrights, we could—"

"I've got one!" Emily said, jumping to her feet.

"*No way!*" Heather said.

"I'll get it!" Emily raced into her bedroom and returned with only the projector.

"Where's the case?" Heather said pointedly.

"I left it in the bedroom," Emily replied, plugging in the projector and adjusting the knobs. She propped the projector onto a pillow, casting a starry carpet of pinpoint lights across the living room ceiling. Turning another knob, the soft, melodic tones of Puccini's "Nessun Dorma," interwoven with the sounds of crashing waves and a gentle wind, drifted into the air. The girls sat in awe as the constellation of stars floated above their heads. For a moment, Emily was drawn into the familiar sound.

"Okay!" Heather announced, plopping her body onto her sleeping bag that was in direct line with the kitchen. She glanced toward the kitchen and noticed that Jane was still standing at the sink, running the water. "I'll go first. Mary! Truth or dare?"

# Chapter 26

Mary was surprised to be called first. "I'm first? I'm never first."

"Well, you are now!" Heather said in an aggravated tone. "Truth or dare?"

Mary looked a tad nervous. "Truth," she said haltingly. "No! Dare!"

"Alright," Heather said, the wheels turning in her head. "I dare you to kiss your arm in a real sexy way . . . the very same way you'll kiss your first boyfriend."

Mary looked shocked. "Heather. I can't—"

"*Do it!*" Heather ordered. Mary reluctantly brought her arm to her lips. "Wait!" Heather interrupted. "Instead of using your own arm, you have to use Patty's." The girls, save for Emily and Mary, nervously giggled. Emily looked over at Mary, not quite knowing what to think. The whole thing seemed odd to Emily and yet she tried her best to block out the feeling. She held out her arm to Mary who reluctantly held it between her hands. Pausing briefly, Mary leaned down and kissed Emily's arm as best she could. After a few seconds, she quickly let go of Emily's arm. The girls let out a cacophony of laughter. Heather shook her head in dissatisfaction. "Gosh, Mary. I feel sorry for your first boyfriend!" Mary shrunk down in embarrassment as the other girls laughed even louder.

"You know, Mary," Heather said, "if you now agree to a double dare, you can sit out the next round *and* give out two truth or dares."

"Do it, Mary," one of the girls urged.

Mary looked helplessly around the room. Emily was drawn toward the ceiling as the lilting melody of "Nessun Dorma" from the Starlight Starbright pulled her away from the group. Mary tugged on Emily's pajama sleeve, bringing Emily back into the moment.

"What should I do?" Mary whispered to Emily.

"Um, it sounds like a good deal, I guess" Emily said, not quite sure.

Mary hesitated. "Double dare it is."

Heather leaned forward, speaking in a confidential tone. "You have to kiss Patty on the lips."

Emily's eyes widened in surprise. Mary matched Emily's reaction. The rest of the girls broke into fits of giddy laughter.

"*Heather!*" Mary said in shock.

"You agreed to a double dare, Mary!" Heather haughtily said over the cackle of giggles. "Are you going to take back your promise?"

Mary looked at Emily between the eerie shadows that clutched the room. Emily suddenly felt trapped and anxious. "Okay," Mary said. "I'll kiss her but it won't be like a boyfriend." Mary leaned closer to Emily, who directed her attention toward the ceiling of floating stars.

Part of Emily was in that room and part of her was someplace far away. She focused on the star-filled ceiling and the familiar sound of "Nessun Dorma" rising above the sound of the crashing waves and wind. She felt Mary's warm lips touch hers but she didn't react. Her body was lifting out of her physical skin and drifting behind the thin veil of reality.

Heather watched Emily with great interest, not sure what to make of her unusual reaction. She expected something else. She wanted to see a jolting reflex or disgust for the kiss and she wasn't getting it. Mary pulled back as Emily kept focusing on the ceiling. "So, Patty," Heather said, "is Mary a good kisser?" Emily remained faraway, not moving a muscle or blinking an eye. "*Patty!*" Heather said loudly. Emily still didn't react. "My, my!" Heather smugly said. "I think Patty's in love!"

The girls, save for Mary, erupted into a rowdy chorus of laughter. The raucous sound brought Emily partly back into reality.

"Heather!" Mary said. "That's mean!"

"I'm just kidding!" Heather said offhandedly. "She knows I'm kidding! Right, Patty?"

Emily was still not completely back inside her body. "Yeah . . . Sure . . ."

Heather nonchalantly sat back on her sleeping bag and stole a glance toward the kitchen. In the glow of the kitchen night-light, she saw Jane lighting a cigarette and opening the sliding door. Jane stepped outside and closed the door behind her. Heather turned back to the group with a devilish grin. "Okay, Mary. It's your turn. Remember though, that you have to ask the question to the person on your right-hand side."

Mary looked to her right where Emily sat. "Can't I go to the left for a change."

"No! We always go counterclockwise, which is to the right!" Heather said impatiently. "Go!"

Mary turned to Emily and reluctantly asked, "Truth or dare?"

Emily remembered Jane's words regarding not letting anything slip out of her mouth by mistake. As much as she didn't want to kiss another girl, she had only one response for Mary. "Dare?"

Heather looked both relieved and brimming with sinister intent. She snuck another quick glance toward the kitchen and saw that Jane had moved farther into the darkness of the backyard. "Go on, Mary! Make up a dare!"

Mary hemmed and hawed, which irritated Heather. "I don't know. I'm not good at making up dares."

"I'll help you out if you want," Heather quickly said. "Okay."

"How 'bout 'Blind Man's Hide and Seek'?"

"Yeah, that's a good one," Mary agreed.

"What's that?" Emily asked.

"We put a blindfold over your eyes, spin you around and then *we* hide and you try to find us without taking off the blindfold," Heather explained.

The whole thing sounded fine to Emily. "Okay," she said, standing up. "What are we gonna use for a blindfold?"

"How about a dish towel?" Heather forcefully suggested. The girls agreed. "I'll get it!" Heather announced, popping to her feet and creeping into the darkened kitchen. Taking a quick look around the room, she grabbed a dish towel. Heather then hunkered near the floor and saw Jane standing outside in the center of the backyard with her back to the closed sliding door. Reaching to the side of the wall, Heather took the wooden dowel and inconspicuously placed it in the track of the glass door to prevent the door from opening. She slowly backed up out of the kitchen and returned to the living room. "Here's the towel!" she said, tossing it to another girl who affixed the blindfold to Emily. Heather sidled up to Mary. "You know," she said confidentially, "I think she can see through it."

"Naw," Mary said. "Spin her around!" Mary announced to the other girls.

The girls twirled Emily in circles. Emily could see nothing as she felt her head becoming lighter. The mesmerizing "Nessun Dorma," along with the soothing sound of crashing waves and blowing wind joined together to pull Emily into another realm. Gradually, the music and smooth sound effects captured her senses, leaving the girls' voices far in the distance.

Heather turned to Mary, speaking in a hushed, anxious voice. "I'm telling you, she *can* see and it's not fair!"

"Okay, what do you want to do?"

"Let's put her in the hall closet and then go hide."

"Whatever," Mary said, beginning to tire of the game.

Heather crossed over to Emily's side and started to spin her around as she guided her toward the hallway. "You're spinning . . . you're spinning . . ." Heather said in a melodious tone. The other girls followed, with Mary lagging behind the group. Emily didn't say a word. All the girls, except for Mary, were giddy with anticipation as Heather moved Emily closer to the closet door. Heather opened the closet door. "Okay, one more spin and then we go hide." Heather gently spun Emily into the closet before quietly closing the door. "Shh!" she said in a hushed tone to all the girls. "Wait here." Heather disappeared down the hall, returning seconds later with a chair. After securely wedging the chair underneath the door handle, she turned to the girls. "Okay," she whispered, "everybody except for Mary go hide." The girls scattered down the hall and into the living room.

"*What are you doing?*" Mary said uneasily. "How's she gonna get out to find us?"

"Stop worrying about that!" Heather said in an angry hushed tone. "I want you to go into her bedroom over there, get the line dancing trophy sitting next to her bed and hide it in my duffel bag!"

"*What?*"

"Do it!" Heather commanded with angry bile.

"Why?"

"Because! It belongs to *me!* I've won that trophy for three years straight. I should have got it this year but *she* had to go and ruin everything! *Go get it!*"

"Is that why you wanted to come here? To steal her trophy?"

"Mary, I've got to stay here and watch the door. Go get my trophy!"

Mary stood her ground. "No. I won't. She won it fair and square."

Heather moved closer to Mary in an intimidating stance. "If you don't get my trophy, I'm gonna tell everybody here that you're a bed wetter!"

The blood drained from Mary's face. "How . . . how did you know that?"

A wicked grin crept across Heather's face. "I *didn't*. You just told me! Go get my trophy or I'm telling everyone that you're a little baby who still wets her pants. When they find out, you will have no friends and you will be all alone!"

Mary was panic-stricken. She hated the idea of stealing Emily's trophy but couldn't bear to have her dreaded secret revealed. Reluctantly, she walked down the hall and went into Emily's bedroom. Within seconds, she emerged, trophy in hand and dutifully placed it into Heather's bag without any of the girls seeing a thing.

Heather smiled, a sense of victory engulfing her. She turned around and spoke with her lips close to the door. "Hey, Patty? Time to come out."

Emily sat inside the closet in the pitch-black, the blindfold still covering her eyes. For several minutes, all she heard was the sound of her beating heart. Gradually, her heart beat faster. Her respiration increased until she was gasping for breath. In the distance, she could hear the muffled sounds of her father yelling and her mother screaming out into the echoing darkness. Instinctively, she sunk farther back into the closet until her back was flat against the wall. She suddenly heard the distinctive thump of footsteps climbing the stairs to her bedroom. Her heart pounded and her breathing became more frightened. The blindfold irritated her face. She grabbed at it and tore it off her head.

Emily looked up and gasped. She was back in her bedroom closet, buried underneath her pile of pillows. The scene captivated Emily, and, at the same time, she was completely unsure of what was happening. Her Starlight Starbright was aglow and playing the haunting refrain from "Nessun Dorma," along with the crashing waves and gentle wind. Sensing that something wasn't right, she quickly grabbed the switch and shut off the projector, leaving herself in total darkness. Suddenly, she saw the light in her bedroom quickly flash on and reflect underneath the closed closet door. There was the sound of heavy breathing coming from just outside the door. Emily held her breath. With a abrupt jerk, the closet door swung open. A male figure stood less than five feet from where she hid. She was able to make out the individual perfectly. He was dressed all in black, including black gloves. His shoes were tightly protected with sturdy red cloth covers. Emily was drawn to his left, gloved hand. In it, he held a glimmering knife that dripped with fresh blood. She followed a single crimson droplet as it drifted down the metal surface and fell onto the pink carpeting.

Emily looked closely at the masked man. He appeared highly agitated. Emily watched as he peered into the closet, let out an aggravated grunt, spun around and checked under the bed. Realizing no one was hiding there, he struggled to his feet. In doing so, he knocked over a box of colored pencils that sat on the bedside table. Emily watched as the pencils bounced to the ground and spread out on the carpet. The man got to his feet, slammed his gloved hand against the side of the bed and mumbled under his breath, "Goddamn fucking kid! Where the fuck are you?" Emily listened carefully, realizing she had never heard his voice before that moment. "*Shit!*" the man said, pulling at the nylon mask around his face.

Emily, eyes wide open and heart racing, focused on the distorted face underneath the black, nylon disguise.

"Fuck!" the man said tearing at the mask, approaching a panic state. Emily never took her eyes off the man. In one fell swoop, he grabbed at the mask and rapidly peeled it off his head. He turned toward the closet, standing in full view of Emily and rubbing his cheek frantically with his gloved hand. Emily etched every inch of his face into her memory. "Goddamnit!" he said loudly, plunging the bloodstained knife into the sheath on his belt buckle.

At that point, Emily stared at the man's sturdy cloth

shoe coverings. She instantly realized that they were not naturally dyed red. The original beige color could be seen underneath the moist scarlet top layer. She watched as the man's feet turned toward the open bedroom door and walked out of the room. Emily listened intently as his footsteps creaked and then pounded down the stairs toward the front door. She waited to hear the front door slam but heard nothing. So she waited, still silent and not moving a muscle. A branch from the sycamore tree outside her bedroom window tapped against the glass. Another strong gust of wind swooped across the yard. Emily watched as her closet door gradually swung back and forth. She sat silent and motionless. Waiting . . . Waiting. The wind roared outside and her closet door creaked open several more inches. Sitting there between the bright light of her bedroom and the dark recesses of her closet, Emily realized that the front door was wide open and funneling a draft of air up the stairs and into her bedroom.

Gradually, she moved forward, dislodging her body from the massive pillows that surrounded her. She crept along the closet floor on her knees, stopping every few inches to listen for anything that sounded suspicious. She crawled outside the closet and knelt at her open bedroom door, bending her head around the edge. The front door was, indeed, wide open. All the lights in the living room were on, casting an odd shadow across the stairway that led to Emily's bedroom door. The wind howled outside, moaning and whirring like a distant siren. Her eyes glanced down at the carpeting that led from her door down the stairs. Cherry juice, she kept thinking to herself. Somebody spilled cherry juice.

She drew her body to a standing position and craned her head around the door. "Mommy?" she said, in a half-whisper. The wind responded with a punishing gale that slapped the sycamore tree branch hard against her bedroom window. Emily jumped at the sudden crash. The wind died down and she turned back toward the stairs.

"Daddy?" she said, this time a little louder, her voice tightening with fear.

All was silent.

Emily carefully made her way onto the landing and looked down into the brightly lit living room. The staircase and hallway wall obscured her full view of the scene. "Mommy?" she said, her voice shaking. She started down the staircase, purposely walking to the side of the crimson footprints that stained the carpeting. Her right hand cupped the banister. Emily stepped down two more steps and then another three. She grabbed the banister with all her might as she felt the air being sucked from her lungs. The gruesome scene lay in front of her.

At first, she couldn't connect to it. Her father was face-down in a growing pool of his own blood. His head was turned just enough so that Emily could see his throat slashed down to the bone and muscle. Emily watched as pinpoint jets of blood issued forth from where the knife entered his aorta. The scarlet puddle of blood crept across the carpet toward Emily's mother who lay face up within arm's reach of her husband.

Emily noticed that her head was positioned slightly off-center due to the deep cut across her throat that wound its way up to her right ear. Exposed tissue and muscle fused with the blood that poured forth from over seventy stab wounds to her face.

Emily stared at her mother's face. Patricia's right eye stared back at her daughter while the left eye dangled outside of its socket. Her mouth was open and frozen in an awkward, lopsided position. The upper lip had been sliced off completely, opaquely revealing her front teeth and upper gum that were shadowed by the thick veil of plasma and serum draining from her mouth.

A violent burst of wind blew through the front door, upsetting loose papers and a single silk flower that danced in its vase. Emily walked down the stairs until she reached the wooden floor by the entry. Silently, she walked toward her parents, stopping only inches from the expanding vermilion pool. The wind exaggerated the scent of death—an acrid blend of urine, feces and fear. Gradually, the puddle of blood inched toward Emily's toes, encircling her bare skin. It felt warm and strangely comforting at first to the child. She dropped her head and followed the gory trail as the blood from her mother's body curled around her right heel and joined with the blood from her father's body that quickly surrounded her left foot. For one, unexplainable second, Emily felt safe.

But then, the graphic horror of the scene gripped her body. Far in the distance, she heard a bloodcurdling scream—the same scream that had tricked her memory since the murder. The scream loomed closer, growing in intensity and terror. Suddenly, in one shock of energy, the scream was no longer outside of Emily, but inside of her. It plunged into her throat and projected its horrific timbre into the air.

Emily continued screaming, as she turned on her heels in a frenzied attempt to reach the staircase. But the blood against her bare feet caused her to slip. She fell, landing palms down in the red puddle between her two parents. Blood splattered against the front of her nightgown. The shock drilled through her body and she lost control of her bladder. Emily frantically spun around on her knees and crawled toward the staircase, still screaming at the top of her lungs. Once she reached the first step, she struggled to her feet and fled up the stairs to her bedroom. She flung her body into the closet, swinging the door closed behind her. The door didn't quite make it shut, allowing an inch of light to seep through into the safety of the closet. Emily screamed like a wild child as she pressed her body against the back wall of the closet. Her heart raced and her respiration reached hyperventilation as the walls caved in.

Without realizing it, Emily was now back in the hall closet, secured shut by the chair that Heather had wedged under the knob. Her terrified screams filled the house, drawing the visiting girls one by one out of the living room and back into the hallway. Heather turned to the group with a mischievous smile and let out a mocking scream to match Emily's wail. The other girls, save for Mary, quickly joined in as the house shook with their shrill, contemptuous screeching.

Jane, still standing outside in the backyard, darted to the back door. She instinctively grabbed for her gun and came up empty-handed. "Emily!" Jane yelled, as she attempted to open the sliding glass door. However, the wooden dowel that Heather placed along the tracks prevented any movement.

Almost simultaneously, Dan drove by the house, immediately noting the coded warning sign of the porch and garage light turned on together. He screeched his truck to a halt, slammed it into park and bolted from the vehicle. The piercing screams from inside the house spilled onto the street. He reached into the bed of his truck and brought out a baseball bat. His mind raced with the various scenarios as he sprinted toward the front door. The house was pitch dark inside, except for the eerie glow of Emily's Starlight Starbright projector illuminating the living room. Dan threw open the screen door and tried the front door only to find it locked. He slammed his body full force against the door in an attempt to enter the house, but nothing budged. Inside, the shrieking chorus persisted. He slammed the baseball bat against the glass windowpane in the center of the front door. It took only three hard swings of the bat before the front pane completely disintegrated.

Inside, the crashing glass shocked the girls. Their fake screams turned very real as they saw Dan's arm reach through the broken glass to unlock the door. Jane reacted to the piercing sound of breaking glass and tore around the house. Dan successfully unlocked the front door and burst into the house. The girls backed themselves into a tight group and continued their terrified shrieks.

Not knowing what he was about to encounter, Dan slammed his bat against the wall. "Get outta here, you son-of-a-bitch!" Dan yelled into the darkness. Jane was halfway around the house when she heard Dan's chilling words echo into the night air.

Dan slapped his hand across the light switch, flicking it on and then raising the bat above his head in a predatory stance. The burst of light flooded the hallway as the girls' screams escalated. He froze with the baseball bat raised high in the air. In a matter of seconds, he tried to sort out everything. There were the girls packed tightly against the hallway wall. There was the chair propped up against the hall closet and the muffled screams of Emily trapped inside. "What in the hell's goin' on?" he shouted.

The girls' shrieking petered out as Heather yelled, "We're playing a game!"

"Who else is in here?" Dan yelled.

"Nobody!" Heather said with a bratty tone.

Dan looked toward the closet and the muffled screams. "Who's in there?"

"That's Patty!" Mary replied, as Heather shot her a dirty look.

Dan heard rapid footsteps racing toward the front of the house. He turned, baseball bat ready to strike, just as Jane leapt into the house.

"What the fuck happened?" Jane screamed, out of breath and terrified.

"It's okay!" Dan assured her, putting down the bat.

"The fuck it's okay!" Jane yelled back. She quickly scanned the broken glass, the band of girls and immediately reacted to Emily's screams. "Oh, God!" Jane raced down the hallway toward the closet and attempted to pull the chair from underneath the doorknob. Unfortunately, Heather had wedged the chair so tightly, it seemed glued onto the door. "Emily! It's okay!" Jane yelled, not realizing she used the child's real name. Emily's horrific cries continued from inside the closet. "I'm getting you out of there!"

The girls watched the scene, not knowing what to make of Jane's intense reaction. Dan came to Jane's aid and the two of them were able to finally knock the chair from its locked position. Jane threw the chair down the hallway so hard it skidded out the open front door. She started to open the hallway door, but it was stuck shut.

"Goddamnit!" Jane screamed in frustration, pulling on the door.

"Let me try!" Dan offered, doing his best to jerk open the door.

"Emily!" Jane yelled into the door. "It's okay! It's okay!"

Heather whispered "Emily?" to the girl standing next to her.

Dan continued to pull with all his strength but the door was frozen shut. Jane spelled him while Emily's terrified shrieks continued to reverberate inside the closet. "*Fuck this door!*" Jane slammed her hand against the door. "Who put her in here?" No one said a word. "*Who did it?*" Jane yelled, yanking with every last bit of energy.

"It's starting to budge!" Dan announced. He took over and with one final pull, the door swung open.

Jane saw Emily cowering against the back wall of the closet, screaming and holding her hands out to ward off what she thought was an oncoming intruder. "Get away from me!" Emily screamed as Jane moved toward her.

"Emily! It's me! It's alright!" Jane said, trying to grab onto the child.

Emily flailed her arms in the air, several times making contact with Jane's body, in an attempt to keep her away. "No! I saw you!" Emily shrieked. "I saw you what you did! Get away! Get away!!"

Jane was able to gently subdue the terrified child. "Emily! *It's me!* You're safe!"

Emily felt Jane's heart beat against her chest and finally realized where she was and who was holding her. Her screaming stopped, replaced by hyperventilation. Within seconds, Emily's body started to shake uncontrollably as she went into convulsive sobs. Jane held tightly onto the child, all too aware of what was happening.

Dan ducked into the closet, kneeling down next to Jane and Emily. "Sweetheart," Dan said softly, stroking Emily's head, "it's okay. You're alright."

"Hey, look," Heather said quietly in the background. "She peed all over herself." Jane felt her blood boil as she kept a tight grip on Emily. "That is *so* gross!" Heather said in a hushed, mocking tone.

Jane held even tighter onto Emily. Emily lost control of her bladder again.

"Darlin', it's alright," Dan assured Emily in a tender voice. "Your mom's right here, sweetie."

"That's not her mother," Heather said in full voice.

Jane's stomach tightened. Her emotions raced between outrage and fear of being discovered by a boorish ten-year-old girl. She placed Emily into Dan's arms, stood up and turned around to face the girls. Jane stared at Heather. "*You* did this to her, didn't you?" Heather remained silent, staring down Jane like a gunfighter. "Answer me!"

Dan looked up at Jane, sensing an imminent explosion. "Jane?"

"If you're not her mother, who are you?" Heather asked, refusing to be cowed. "If her name is Patty, how come you're calling her *Emily?* And if *your* name is—"

Jane lunged toward Heather. "What the fuck's wrong with you?" The girls spread out down the hallway. Jane was only inches away from grabbing Heather's neck when Dan yanked her backward and away from the kid.

"Jane!" Dan screamed. "Let it go! Let it go!"

"She wanted the dance trophy, Mrs. Calver!" Mary piped up.

"Shut up, Mary!" Heather shrieked.

"She locked Emily in the closet and made me steal the trophy out of Patty's . . . Emily's bedroom!" Mary continued, determined to spill the beans but feeling as confused as the rest of them. "I'm sorry, Mrs. Calver! I didn't want to do it. I put it in Heather's duffel bag, just like she told me to!" Mary turned to Emily. "And don't worry about wetting your pants. Sometimes I do it, too."

Mary looked at Heather. "*So there!*"

Jane was disgusted with everything she was hearing. She turned to Dan. "Get these brats out of here." Jane lifted Emily from the closet and carried her into the bathroom, slamming the door behind her. Emily clung tightly to Jane as she placed her on the closed toilet seat. The child was still shaking and breathing heavily. "It's okay. Come on, we have to change your clothes."

Emily reluctantly released her grip on Jane. Jane removed Emily's pajama top and tossed it aside. Emily pressed her forehead against Jane's head. Tears and raw emotion spilled from the very core of her soul. "I saw him," she said between heaving sobs. "*I saw him!*" Emily collapsed to her knees. "And I saw my mommy and daddy!" Emily buried her head between her arms, screaming out in shock and anguish. Jane knelt close to her, cradling Emily in her arms. She felt useless and yet, at the same time, she knew that all hell was about to break loose.

Half an hour later, Emily finally fell asleep on Jane's lap. Jane gingerly removed the child's soiled pajamas and slipped a nightgown from the clothes hamper over her clammy body. She couldn't help but hear the hushed voices that emanated from down the hall when Kathy arrived to pick up the girls. As she sat there on the cold tile bathroom floor, Jane was well aware that her days of anonymity were over in Peachville. Between Sheriff George's investigation, Heather's inevitable declaration to her mother that Jane was not Emily's mother and the disclosure of their real names, there was sure to be a reaction more explosive than the Fourth of July fireworks.

Finally, Jane heard the front door close and sweet silence descend over the house. Realizing the coast was clear, she stood up and carried Emily from the bathroom and into Jane's bedroom. She placed her into the bed and glanced over to her Glock pistol that lay on the bedside table next to her fanny pack. Closing the bedroom door behind her, she walked down the hallway in search of Dan.

She found him standing in the semi-darkness of the kitchen. He was squinting down at the tracks of the sliding glass door. "One guess how this got put there." He showed the wooden dowel to Jane.

Jane's anger became piqued. She grabbed the dowel and broke it in half over her knee. "That little bitch!" Jane said as she threw the broken pieces across the kitchen.

Dan pointed over to the country dance trophy on the kitchen table. "Mary gave back Emily's trophy."

"All of this over a fucking trophy! Jesus!" Jane let out a tired sigh. "I knew this sleepover was a bad idea. I knew it and I still let it happen."

Dan hesitated, not quite sure how to phrase his next sentence. "Why do you think Heather said what she did about you not being Emily's real mother?"

Jane briefly turned away from Dan. She was tired of lying to him. "Oh, Dan . . ." She turned back, looking him square in the eye. "Probably for the same reason she locked Emily in the closet! Spite!" Jane said, wearily. She pulled a cigarette from her shirt pocket and lit up. "If Heather were my kid, I'd kick her sorry ass into next week."

Dan carefully observed Jane. "Yeah, well, if I hadn't grabbed hold of you, you would have gotten your chance."

Jane took a hard drag on her cigarette. There was an awkward moment of silence between them. "What is it?" Jane asked.

Dan looked apprehensive. "I . . . ah . . . I'm just . . ."

"*What is it?*" Jane said, losing patience.

Dan pulled away from Jane, confused and uneasy. "I should go." He started out of the kitchen.

"Dan?" Jane called after him.

"Look, I cleaned up the broken glass by the door. I'll come by tomorrow morning and replace the front door pane for you . . ."

"Dan, what's wrong?"

"Actually, tomorrow morning is the big Independence Day Parade down Main, so the street will be blocked. I'll come by in the afternoon." Dan walked into the living room, retrieving his baseball bat along the way.

Jane followed closely behind him, suddenly becoming aware of what he was thinking. "Wait a minute!" She reached out and grabbed him by the arm. "I was furious at what Heather did to Emily! How was I supposed to react?"

"Hey, we're both tired and I need to go," Dan said, turning to the front door.

Jane thought quickly, stumbling on her words. "Dan, wait! Emily's father used to lock her in the closet to punish her! It terrifies her! And when I came in here and saw that she was stuck in there and we couldn't open the door, it brought back all the memories of what he used to do to her and to me! And I lost it! I made a mistake! I went for that brat and that was wrong. But you don't have any right to judge me! You have no idea what Emily and I have been through or what we're going through! You picture hell and multiply it by ten and then you might get a glimpse of our life!"

Dan bounced the baseball bat against the tip of his work boot. "When I drove by and saw those lights on, I thought . . ." Dan let out a tired sigh. "I know how this plays out, Jane." Dan stared at Jane with a piercing gaze.

Dan's shift in behavior made Jane feel very uneasy. "What do you mean?"

"Payback," he replied, not taking his eyes off of her. Jane's gut tightened at his response. Dan looked at Jane another few seconds before turning around and heading out the door.

# Chapter 27

Was it possible?

Jane paced back and forth in the living room after Dan left. Of all the words he could have chosen, why did he choose *payback?* Was it some twisted coincidence that he used the same word that the killer wrote on that sheet of paper? Could Dan be the killer? Or was he a hired gun brought in to take care of Jane and Emily? Jane's mind raced with various scenarios, each one becoming more complex and absurd. Dan was obviously a card-carrying member of Peachville's tight-knit community. If Dan was the killer, what were the odds that DH would place Jane and Emily undercover in his hometown? Jane's thoughts turned paranoid as she tossed the idea of the murders being an inside job between the DH and the mob and that Peachville was chosen on purpose because it was where Dan lived. As quickly as that idea filtered through her logical mind, Jane realized how patently ridiculous it was.

She considered Dan's possible involvement with a clearer eye. Perhaps his "payback" reference had to do with Dan's intense involvement with his sister's abusive marital relationship and the possible outcome that he feared would be repeated if Jane didn't seek help. After all, he preceded the payback comment by saying "I know how this plays out, Jane." He knew, Jane supposed, because he had lived through the experience with his sister. As Jane paced, snippets of conversations with Dan filled her head. There was the conversation when Dan showed up at their house a couple week's before with his brand-new truck.

*"It didn't set me back a penny. I do all the electrical maintenance for the Ford dealership over in Montrose. It's one of my many side jobs. Anyway, instead of payin' me, we worked out this agreement where they trade me a new dealer truck every summer. In the long run, I reckon I'm pullin' the better end of the trade."*

Was that just a story, Jane wondered, her mind drifting back to the possibility of a more nefarious link with the mob. Was the truck really part of a payoff from someone else he worked for? Someone like the Texas mob? There was no immediate way to check out his story. It was close to midnight on the Saturday before Independence Day. Jane would have to wait until Monday to call the Ford dealership in Montrose to investigate Dan's story.

Jane lit a cigarette and nervously walked in circles between the kitchen and the living room. Through her thick mental fog and confusion, she began to center on the concept of accepting a payoff in exchange for a job. Suddenly, pay*off* was dominating the importance of pay-*back*. When she focused on the word "payoff," she felt as though the right key was opening the right lock. The more she considered all the logical angles in relationship to Dan's possible involvement, the more she realized that Dan simply didn't have what it took to be a cold-blooded killer. And yet, for whatever reason, he was the echoing reflection that tripped her thought process and the one person who might unknowingly lead her to the real killer.

Jane pressed her cigarette into the ashtray. Maybe, she thought, another review of the Lawrence crime scene documents would trigger a connection. She retrieved a flashlight from the kitchen and started toward her bedroom. Jane quietly opened the bedroom door and stood in the darkness staring at Emily. She waited, making sure that Emily was still asleep. Jane flicked on the flashlight. After locating her leather satchel, she knelt down and pulled out several folders. The stack of newspaper clippings fell to the floor. Emily stirred. Jane froze, turning off the flashlight. Emily drifted back to sleep and Jane resumed her search, holding the flashlight close to the satchel. She finally found the Lawrence folder and sorted through it. Emily stirred again, this time waking up. Jane quickly shoved the documents back into the file.

"Who's there?" Emily asked timidly.

"It's me. It's okay," Jane whispered.

"Why have you got the flashlight?"

"I didn't want to wake you. Go back to sleep."

There was a moment of silence before Emily spoke up again. "I'm scared."

Jane erratically stashed the file back into her satchel and slid it under the chair. She turned off the flashlight and crossed to the bed. "There's nothing to be scared of." Jane touched her Glock pistol on the bedside table. "I've got a gun right here that'll blow a hole the size of Detroit in someone's stomach."

"He's gonna come get me. *I know it,*" Emily said, her voice quaking in fear.

"No one is coming to get you, Emily."

Emily realized it was time to say the one thing that she'd been holding back—the thing that didn't make any sense but had haunted her since she sat in her closet after her parents' murder. "You're gonna think I'm crazy, but—"

"I don't think you're crazy, Emily."

"No, I mean," the child tried to put her thoughts into words, "I saw—"

Jane interrupted. "I know what you saw. And I promise you that whoever did that will never hurt you." Jane's voice shook. "I won't allow it."

Emily turned to Jane. The soft rays of the moon illuminated her face. Jane could see Emily's furrowed brow and a disarming look come over her. "Your voice sounded like a lie when you said that."

Jane knew the child could feel the truth. "When I say that I won't allow it, that's not a lie. I will protect you with my own life."

Emily turned toward the wall. Jane didn't know what to make of her action and moved off the bed, when Emily's timorous voice splintered through the silence. "Don't leave me," she whispered.

Jane wanted to return to the living room and continue hashing out possible scenarios. But Emily's pleading voice won out. Jane removed her shoes and slid under the covers.

Emily wedged her back closer to Jane's body and let out an exhausted sigh. "I love you," Emily whispered.

Jane was all at once paralyzed in the pitchblack of that room. In one sweeping movement, the staggering enormity of her situation punched her hard in the face. Emily wasn't just saying those words as an aside; she meant them from her heart. Jane started to respond, but she couldn't. She closed her eyes and quickly drifted off to sleep.

The first thing she felt was heat—blazing heat that smoldered against her body. She opened her eyes and found herself standing in the center of a pool filled with blinding light. Jane brought her left hand to her face to shield her eyes from the glaring reflection. Seeing her left palm, she noted the backward date of 10-24-99 burned into her flesh. There was the distinct smell of metal . . . hot metal. She felt movement behind her and spun around. Out of nowhere, she suddenly had a Glock clutched in her right hand. The intense light played tricks with Jane as she extended the Glock outward. She waited, her heart racing. All of a sudden, the head of a wolf leapt from the brilliant glare and consumed her. Jane knew she was dying; she could taste death's acrid bite on her tongue. This is what it truly felt like. The heat devoured her as she slid into the void.

Emily awakened to silence—dulcet silence. She turned and saw a magpie perched against the bedroom window. He pecked his beak at the dusty glass. Emily watched as the bird turned to face her. She couldn't help noticing how his penetrating stare seemed so cold and vicious. He let out a loud *caw*, cocked his head and flew out of sight.

She turned to check the time. 8:45 a.m. Looking over at Jane, Emily saw that she was still sound asleep. The child's head felt heavy and numb—an emotional hangover from reliving the gruesome memories the night before. The more she remembered everything, the more she wanted to get out of bed and move around the room. Emily heard the city trucks plodding down Main Street, getting ready for the July fourth Parade. Right now, watching a truck set out orange cones sounded like the perfect distraction.

Moving slowly so as not to awaken Jane, Emily slipped out from under the covers. She looked around the floor for her slippers. Jane stirred, turned her body toward the bedside table and went back to sleep. Emily peered across the room to the corner chair and spotted her pink slippers hidden underneath it. She tiptoed across the floor. In kneeling down to collect her slippers, she brushed her hand against Jane's leather satchel. She looked at the satchel as something caught her eye.

It was one word: *child*. The word was part of a larger headline from one of the many newspaper clippings Jane had shoved into the satchel the previous night. Emily tried to unfold the newspaper to see it more clearly, but it was stuck too tightly into the satchel. Emily slid the satchel toward her. She lifted the article in question out of the satchel and read the headline:

### DENVER NEIGHBORHOOD STILL IN SHOCK OVER FAMILY'S MURDER—TEN-YEAR-OLD CHILD AMONG VICTIMS

Emily first thought the article was about her parents, but realized that the accompanying photo did not match her neighborhood. The photo showed a middle-aged woman standing on a street with the Stover's house diffused in the background. Emily read the caption under the photo:

"This is just tragic," Gilpin Street resident, Ellen Del Alba sadly told reporters. "I didn't know the little girl very well, but she seemed like such an adorable child."

Emily looked at the house in the background. It looked just like . . .

But, it couldn't be. Emily set the clipping aside and pulled out the next one.

## CAR BOMB KILLS FAMILY OF THREE
## IN THEIR DRIVEWAY

This story featured a photograph that showed the scene the morning after the attack. The photo showed Jane standing near the yellow crime scene tape, her left hand freshly bandaged. Nearby was the green and white Gilpin Street sign. Emily stared at the photo of what was left of the charred Range Rover. She studied the driveway with its distinctive manicured cedars. It started to look far too familiar.

Emily pulled out another newspaper clipping. Her eyes filled with terror and she began to shake uncontrollably. She worked her way up to a standing position, never letting go of the newspaper clipping.

The scuffling sound awoke Jane. Still half asleep, all Jane could see was Emily's back and that the child was looking down at something. "Hey . . ." Jane said quietly.

Emily spun around, gasping in fright. She hid the newspaper clipping behind her back and regarded Jane with a look of abject fear mixed with contempt.

Jane quickly surveyed the scene. *The crime scene photos*, she said to herself. "Oh, Jesus. You saw the photos?"

Emily was breathing so hard, she could hardly speak. "Yes."

"You weren't supposed to ever see those," Jane said, flipping back the bed covers. "Here, let me—"

"Get away from me!" Emily shouted, nearly choking on her words.

Jane sat on the bed, perplexed by Emily's behavior. "Emily?"

Emily backed up several steps to the wall, never taking her eyes off of Jane. She inched toward the bedside table, keeping a healthy distance between herself and Jane. "I don't understand! You promised me. But you . . . lied to me," Emily nervously stuttered.

Jane sat frozen on the bed. Something was very wrong. "Emily," Jane said calmly, as though she was talking a sniper down from a tall building, "what is it?"

"I was wrong! You don't want to protect me . . . You want to kill me!"

"Kill you? Emily—"

"Don't lie to me!" Emily screamed. "You knew him all this time!"

"I knew who?"

"The man in my bedroom!" Emily screamed. With that, she revealed the newspaper clipping that was hidden behind her back. "*The man in my bedroom!*"

It was the front page of the *Rocky Mountain News*. It was a photo of Jane. Right next to a photo of Chris.

It didn't immediately register with Jane. "Chris?" She let his name sink into her consciousness. "*Chris* was the man in your bedroom? Are you sure?"

"You knew!" Emily screamed.

"No, I didn't!" Jane uttered in a state of shock, glancing away from Emily. "Oh, my God," was all she could say. "Emily, I—"

Jane turned back, just in time to see the newspaper clipping fall to ground. Emily lunged forward, grabbed Jane's Glock pistol on the bedside table and moved back against the wall. The child pointed the gun, two-handed at Jane.

"You're not gonna kill me like you killed my mommy and daddy."

Jane felt a strange calmness come over her. It was the same, eerie, centered feeling she always got when her life was in danger. "Emily. Put the gun down."

"*No!*"

"I didn't kill your mommy and daddy. You know that."

"It says in the paper that he's your 'partner.' I know what that means! It means you do things together!"

"We didn't—" Jane stopped. "I didn't take part in any of this."

"Liar!" Emily screamed, aiming the gun toward Jane's head.

"Look me in the eye, Emily. I am not lying to you. I did not know Chris was the man in your bedroom until you told me!"

"How could you not know? He's your partner! Partners know everything about each other!"

"No, Emily. That's not always true."

"How could you not see all the bad in his eyes? Didn't you look?"

Jane was asking herself the same question. She shook her head in frustration. "I can't answer that question."

"I trusted you. I *believed* in you."

"You still can, Emily."

"No! I *can't!*" Emily screamed, fighting back tears.

Silence washed over them, interrupted by Emily's gasps of air. "So, this is the way it's gonna end?" Jane carefully asked. "Okay. So be it. You know, Emily, I could tell you that if you kill me, they'll put you in jail. But that's not true. When the police ask why you shot me, tell them you were positive that your life was in danger and that you had no choice. They'll believe you. They'll believe you because you are a good, decent, innocent person and I'm pretty much the opposite. You talk to Sergeant Weyler about Chris, okay?" Jane reasoned that Weyler wasn't involved in the corruption. "He'll take care of it for you. And when all the dust settles, you'll go to your aunt and uncle's house in Cheyenne where you can live happily ever after. At night, you can rest easy, knowing that I'm dead and that Chris is on death row for what he did. Right now, all I ask is that when you shoot me, use only one bullet. I'd rather you didn't have to unload a clip of ammo. You've got enough gruesome memories, you don't need more. Just lower the gun a little bit so it's square with my chest. That's called a 'center punch' and it always works. You've got one shot and if you aim for the head . . . well, even good cops miss that one. So, lower the gun, pull the trigger and then get out of here."

Emily stood paralyzed, her finger dancing across the trigger. Jane's words echoed loudly in her head. "You're trying to confuse me."

"No, I'm not, Emily. I've been dead since I was 14 years old. You'll just make my demise a reality for everyone else. Lower the gun, Emily. Go on," Emily gradually lowered the Glock in line with Jane's chest. She stared back at Jane, who returned her glance, expressionless and with no emotion. "Go on." Jane said quietly.

Emily slid her finger onto the trigger. She looked deep into Jane's eyes. "You really didn't know about him, did you?" Her voice was strangled with emotion.

"It doesn't matter now," Jane whispered. "Pull the trigger, Emily."

Emily brushed her finger against the trigger, tears streaming down her face. "I can't!" She lowered the Glock, letting it drop to the floor. Emily bowed her head, sobbing uncontrollably.

Jane sat on the bed. She didn't say a word or move a muscle as Emily fell to the floor, her chest heaving with each gut-wrenching cry. After several minutes, Emily calmed down. Jane leaned over, retrieved the Glock and set it back on the bedside table. Emily stood up, wiping her tears. Jane handed her a handful of tissues, which she took without acknowledgment.

"What are you gonna do?" Emily asked.

Between learning that Chris was the murderer and

having a gun pointed in her face, Jane was still partially spinning in an altered reality. "I don't know."

"You don't know?" Emily replied, both surprised and angry.

"This is all hitting me at once. I've got to figure out a way to alert Weyler without making him think I'm crazy."

"But I know Chris was the man in my bedroom!" Emily yelled.

"I believe you!"

"So what's the problem?"

"Oh, Emily, it's egos and politics—"

"*What?*"

"Just give me a second." Jane grabbed a cigarette from the bedside table, lit up and began pacing around the room.

"What if you don't figure it out in time? What's gonna happen when he shows up and finds me?"

"Chris doesn't know where we are! I didn't let anything slip when I called him."

Emily's eyes widened in fear. "You talked to him while we've lived here?"

"I wasn't calling him! I was calling another guy. Chris just happened to—"

"I can't believe you did that!"

"He doesn't know where we are!"

Emily began to shake. "Yes, he does!"

"How does he know?"

"I don't know. *But he does!*" Emily began to get hysterical. She tore out of the bedroom and started down the hallway toward the front door.

"Emily! Where are you going?" Jane ran after her.

"I've got to get out of here! He's gonna find me!" Emily was half out of her mind. She started into her bedroom. "No, I can't go in there! He can see me through the window!" Emily shot back up the hallway.

"Emily! Nobody's watching you! Calm down!" Jane tried to grab on to Emily, but she moved too fast.

"He's watching me!" Emily screamed hysterically as

her eyes fearfully scanned Main Street before she retreated back into the hallway.

"Emily!" Jane yelled back, trying to verbally knock the child out of her growing frenzy. "Chris is not here!"

"*Stop lying to me!*" Emily yelled in a state of panic.

"I'm not lying!" Jane shouted back in full voice.

"If you're not lying, then tell me where A.J. is right now!" Jane was taken aback by the sudden subject shift. "Where is she?" Emily yelled, tears welling in her eyes.

Jane looked at Emily. "She's dead. So are her parents."

For several seconds, Emily looked completely calm. "He killed them, too?" Emily whispered. She looked up at Jane, her eyes wild with terror. "He killed them, too!"

Emily beat her fists against the hallway wall with such force that she cut open the skin on the side of her hands. "*No!*" she screamed hysterically, losing control.

Jane clenched her cigarette between her lips. She tried pulling Emily away from the wall in an effort to protect the child from harming herself. But Emily's primal fear was impossible to restrain. "Emily! Stop it! You're bleeding!"

Emily kicked the walls while still beating them with her fists. Bloody imprints from her skin covered the wall. She shook her head violently, screaming at the top of her lungs. "*No! No!*"

Jane grabbed Emily and turned her around so she couldn't injure herself. The child continued to flail her body in a deranged motion. Jane took one look at Emily and did the first thing that came to her mind. She laid a swift, open-handed slap across Emily's cheek. Emily fell to the floor in stunned silence. Gradually, the child touched her left cheek and looked up at Jane in disbelief. Jane felt sick. "Emily . . . You gave me no choice."

Emily started to cry. "You hit me."

Jane leaned toward the child, "Emily, I—"

Emily slapped Jane's arm as she struggled to her feet. "Get away from me!" She smacked Jane's arm again, this time with more force. "I hate you! I hate you!" She ran down the hall into her bedroom, slamming the door behind her.

Jane stood paralyzed in the shadows of the hallway. Every nightmare she ever had was coming true. She took a long drag on her cigarette. As alone as she felt at that moment, she suddenly realized that somebody was watching her. She looked up. There standing at the front door with its front pane smashed out, were Kathy and Heather. It didn't take Jane much time to figure out how long they had been observing her; their incriminating expressions of disgust answered that question.

Jane moved toward the front door. Kathy and Heather took a step backward off the front porch, but still held their ground. Jane flung open the door. "What is it?"

"We wanted to come by and see how Emily was doing," Kathy said, her voice low and modulated.

Jane turned to Heather. "Is that right?"

Heather took another step back, hiding partly behind her mother's body.

"We want to invite her to watch the July fourth parade with us," Kathy said, measuring every word with care.

Jane took a resentful step toward Kathy. "She is no longer allowed to be anywhere near your sick, fucked up daughter. Do I make myself clear?"

Kathy's steely eyes contracted. "Oh, yes. *Very* clear." Kathy turned to Heather. "Let's go."

Jane slammed the door shut. She watched as they walked down the front path. Kathy stopped for a moment, lingering on the sidewalk as she stole a glance toward the right front window. When she saw that Jane was observing her actions, Kathy took Heather by the hand and walked down the street. Jane turned toward Emily's closed bedroom door. "Emily?"

"Go away! Leave me alone!" Emily screamed at Jane from inside the room.

Jane debated whether to pursue a conversation with the kid and apologize for slapping her. But she figured it was best to let Emily calm down. Jane walked into the living room, standing with her back to the front windows. After several minutes, she heard a distinctive *click* from inside of Emily's bedroom. She turned and realized Emily had just locked her door. Jane stared at the doorknob, distressed that Emily felt the need to lock her door.

Jane headed for the kitchen and sat at the table, burying her head in her hands. The full impact of Chris' involvement began to hit her hard. Anger melted into betrayal and then merged into disgust. The enormity of the situation overwhelmed her. The man whom she had called a partner, both on and off the job, was responsible for the murder of two innocent people. The second that thought crossed Jane's mind, she realized that if he killed the Lawrences, he was also the killer of Martha Durrett. Furthermore, it was reasonable to assume that Chris was also involved in the SUV explosion that took out the Stover family.

Jane puffed on her dying cigarette as a fountain of memories flashed in front of her. There was that fateful night outside the Stover's house. She recalled Chris' edgy behavior. Jane had disregarded his attitude that night, chalking it up to his usual surly demeanor. But in retrospect, she realized there was more to it. Within the folds of his words, there was a sense of urgency. A desire to dominate. A need to coordinate a deadly deal and not get caught. She broke the memory down minute by minute and then second by second. Stover and his family took off for ice cream in their SUV, surrounded by two police flank cars.

"*What an asshole! He really wants to sign his own death certificate!*" Chris remarked in a self-satisfied tone as the final flank vehicle drove past their observation car.

Jane remembered looking at Chris and seeing beads of sweat drift across his forehead. At the time, she thought nothing of it. But now it started to fit together.

Chris grabbed his cell phone, speaking in the same cocky cadence. "*Yeah, it's me. I can't believe Stover was so stupid! He drives off with his family for ice cream so he can get thirty minutes in the outside world! Thirty fucking minutes! It looks all clear from here but hurry up!"*

That's when it hit Jane. All this time, she thought he was talking to an officer in one of the flank vehicles. But now the words had a different flavor. Was it possible, Jane wondered, that he was talking to a lackey who was hidden in the darkness near the Stover's house?

A lackey who was in place—C-4 bomb in hand—and waiting for Chris' call and coded language, telling him that he had thirty minutes to set up the explosive.

The more Jane tossed the notion in her head, the more it fell into place. The cops had done a thorough sweep of Stover's residence and come up clean for any explosive devices. The crude, military C-4 bomb that was placed in the darkened recesses of the Stovers' driveway that night was most likely detonated from just outside the Stovers' house. Jane had always struggled with the idea that the perp who set up the bomb in the driveway must have had the guts of a front line soldier to brazenly walk into the shadows when two cops were seated across the street. But perhaps it didn't take a lot of nerve when you had a Denver Police Detective calling you and giving you the green light while he covered your ass. The thirty minute window of time gave the minion enough time to set up the explosive, while Chris engaged Jane in conversation, purposely directing her attention away from the action taking place on the driveway. When Jane could not get the lid off of her coffee thermos, Chris jumped on that unexpected opportunity to further distract Jane from witnessing anything.

The deadly link between the Stover and Lawrence families was still vague to Jane. Was Chris on Bill Stover's list of Denver's influential and powerful? Was he tied in with the Texas mob? Did one of the mob's cronies tip off Chris' tight connection with the mafia to Bill Stover? And then did Bill spill the whole story to David Lawrence?

*The letter.* Did Bill Stover decide to write everything

out in that letter as an informal affidavit of what he knew and then hand it to David? Was that letter an insurance policy that David kept from Patricia until he broke down that evening and showed it to her? When Patricia read the letter and understood the gravity of the situation—of their sideways involvement—that could have fueled her vitriolic outburst, simply from the realization that her family's life was in grave danger.

Jane's mind raced as she recalled Emily's words when the child recalled her mother's frightened appeal to David Lawrence and her resentment over his "bad decisions." Perhaps his worst decision was agreeing to go to bat for Bill Stover just in case anything happened to him. From what Jane could deduce, David was the quintessential, self-conscious technical geek who had a secret longing to live life on the edge. He could feel important because he possessed the pivotal, written proof that law enforcement was desperate to acquire.

Jane considered the possibility that Stover may have mentioned Chris' involvement with the mob in the letter. She realized it was a leap on her part but maybe . . . maybe it was the inked proof. Somehow, the personal relationship between David and Bill became apparent to the Texas mob who were obviously concerned enough about this affiliation to alert their number one gopher, Chris, to the situation. Did Chris make grand assumptions due to his paranoia and conclude that Bill was talking to David about Chris' involvement? It was doubtful that Stover described Chris' physical appearance in his doomed letter since Chris was obviously welcomed into the Lawrence home that fateful evening. Jane figured Chris probably put on his choirboy smile, uttered the words "ma'am" and "sir" in a cordial way to endear himself and then used the ruse of an accident down the street to get into their house.

Once inside, it only took several minutes for Chris to observe the house, discreetly place himself out of eyesight in the kitchen and quickly change into gloves, shoe covers and a mask—all of which, Jane presumed, he stashed in his jacket pocket. It was pure Chris, she surmised: cunning, smart and efficient. Jane could easily picture Chris' subsequent quick attack homicidal maneuvers—all learned and perfected during his stint in the Marines and his subsequent law enforcement training. Jane knew that Chris would leave nothing to chance. She surmised it was for this reason he used two different knives during the murders and was careful to never cross contaminate the blades. His plan, Jane figured, was to make the homicides look as if two different people committed the crime. Jane remembered standing in the Lawrence living room with Sergeant Weyler during her first visit to the house. After Weyler went over everything—from the chaotic living room with its destroyed furniture and pristine pile of undisturbed cocaine to the meticulous way in which each victim met their death— Jane recollected how she called the whole scene "premeditated manipulation." Looking back, Jane realized she was right on target. Who better to know what cops would look for than another highly trained cop? *Brilliant evil,* she thought.

Jane considered the five ounce pile of cocaine at the Lawrence crime scene. Her comment that it was planted amidst the turmoil was dead on. "Cocaine," Jane said out loud. She suddenly realized that the amount of cocaine found at the scene was just under the amount of coke missing from the evidence room. Chris' voice radiated in Jane's head. It was the conversation they shared when she secretly called the lab and got an earful from Chris about Ron Dickson's suspension.

*"With the amount of coke Ron took,"* Chris told Jane, *"Brass figures he's been dipping into the powder since May!"*

That's where Chris slipped up. Chris probably stole the coke from a K-Pak evidence bag in early May in preparation for the Lawrence murder and eventual cover-up. No doubt Chris used his altar boy sweetness to con Ron into leaving him alone in the property room long enough to steal the drugs and reseal the K-Pak bag. But when Chris was telling the story to Jane on the phone, how could he or anyone possibly know that the cocaine went missing around a certain date since there had been no audit of the evidence lab for over one year.

Jane wondered if Chris was planning to set up Ron from the beginning. As a detective, Chris was always projecting five steps in front of the case, factoring the variables and coming up with enough possible scenarios to fill several crime novels. He left nothing to chance; he played on people's character weaknesses and took advantage of every plausible "in" that he could find. Jane flashed onto the scene at the hospital, after Emily fell off the roof. When Chris saw Ron walk into the emergency room with his injured hand and shaken demeanor, he jumped on the opportunity like a cougar on fresh kill. He had to. He was desperate.

Jane rapidly put two and two together regarding that fateful evening. He thought he had killed *Jane* under the blanket on the couch, not Martha Durrett. As far as Chris knew when he went off shift that evening, Jane was still guarding Emily. He was never aware of her fight with Emily and eventual departure from the scene. Suddenly, the cryptic "PAYBACK" note that was plunged into Martha's eye made sense. On some level, Chris felt that Jane knew more about the murders than she was disclosing. That's why Chris bugged the living room to eavesdrop on their conversation. He was convinced that Emily was sharing pertinent information with Jane and so, in his twisted mind, he had no choice but to kill her. No wonder Chris looked so surprised to see Jane when he reached the hospital. Once again, Chris' words echoed in Jane's head. He was speaking to her at the hospital, doing his version of consoling her after learning that Martha Durrett was killed.

"*Shit happens,*" Chris said to Jane. "*At least the son-of-a-bitch couldn't find the kid and had to take off. Don't blame yourself for this huge mistake.*" But in retrospect, Jane realized that Chris misspoke. At that point, Weyler had not debriefed anybody about the crime scene. More importantly, Jane was the only one who had spoken to Emily and knew that the intruder on the roof suddenly left when he couldn't find the kid.

As Jane began to see everything with clearer eyes, she took into account Chris' appearance over the past months. His wardrobe had become increasingly slovenly. His breath had taken on an acrid odor. His eyes looked dark and puffy, as if he had been on a five-day bender. Jane concluded that her own drunken demeanor prevented her from attaching any significance to Chris' disintegrating appearance. And then there was his attitude: restless, anxious, overly talkative, intensely paranoid, an obsessive interest in rough sexual activity, all juxtaposed against a false sense of confidence and raw power. Jane sat back in shock; it was almost exactly like Bill Stover's behavior during his last few months. She felt the floor drop away from her.

"*Meth?*" Jane said out loud.

Could it be? Could meth be one of the fateful connections between Chris and Stover? True, it was difficult to be a high-functioning meth addict and a cop without other cops catching on. Chris' often erratic behavior could easily be chalked up to severe stress and a driving desire to catch the crook and close the case. But it was also true that meth addicts have zero stress tolerance. Then again, Chris had a lot of things going for him, including his keen intelligence and profound understanding of the criminal psyche. Who better understands the way a criminal thinks than another criminal?

Jane recalled a comment she made to Weyler. "*There's a thin line between the mind of a cop and the mind of a criminal. Do you have any idea how often they are one in the same? And how they hide it so well?*" At the time, she was referring to her father. But now, those words were meant for Chris. Just like Dale Perry, Chris walked a tightrope between light and dark, dipping his toe more frequently into the black sludge and emerging a little more sullied each time. Jane understood the seductive call of the darkness—the sultry whispers and tempting promises of power and prestige that it held.

When you cut a deal with demons, you do whatever it takes to execute your contract. You steal evidence, like that silver cigarette case. Jane surmised that was accomplished when Chris was briefly alone at the scene after being sent out to get food for Jane and Emily's stay at the Lawrence house.

You frame homeless bums who you probably know from hanging with the degenerates of society. That would explain why the bum kept looking at Chris and saying that he looked familiar.

You concoct stories of stalkers leaving messages on your voice mail tape at Headquarters that threaten to take out the kid. That was just another back pocket insurance policy so Chris could say "I told you so" when the kid turned up dead.

You attempt to break into the lead detective's house to find out if she left any notes behind that might clue you in to where the Department sent her. Jane briefly took solace in that she never gave Chris a key to her house.

You lie about your whereabouts. The more Jane charted the timing of events, the more she realized that Chris was never anywhere near Lake Dillon with his boat; that was just a ploy to throw off DH. "And what about that damn boat?" Jane thought.

Ultimately, for Jane, the final questions came down to "Who benefits?" and "Why risk your career on a murderous rampage?" Did Chris benefit from their deaths? Or did someone else benefit who Chris feared? Was Chris acting on his own volition or was there more to it? The final connection murky in Jane's mind. But the loose puzzle pieces were joining together to form a psychotic portrait of a man who was hell-bent on destroying everything that was good and decent. A burning rage gripped

Jane. She grabbed a small vase filled with plastic flowers and flung it against the wall, shattering the glass across the kitchen table. "Goddamn you!" she shouted, her voice cracking in pain.

One way or the other, Jane knew she had to alert Weyler and carefully manipulate the situation so that no one was tipped off. Jane walked into the living room. She stopped near Emily's closed bedroom door. Jane started for the door when she suddenly heard her name. She turned in the direction of the voice. It was muffled and anxious. In an instant, Jane raced down the hallway to her bedroom, as the voice grew louder. She stormed into her bedroom just as the male voice clipped off quickly. Jane eyed the blinking red light on her beeper that sat on the bedside table. She grabbed it and nervously hit the play button.

"Jane Perry? This is Jeff. Lisa's brother? Look, I did some digging like you asked. I followed the protection trail. That Weyler guy you mentioned is not involved. But it is clear that a Detective Christopher Crawley has been offering illegal police protection to the immigrant businesses downtown. He gets paid off in goods and services. Something about a boat and other stuff. From what I can sort out, Crawley edged in on businesses that were already paying protection to the Texas mob. They could have killed him and Crawley knows that, but the mob decided to keep him in their back pocket. He does things for them. Jobs . . . Intimidation . . . Whatever they ask. Maybe even murder. The business people downtown are terrified of him. I tried to track him down but he suddenly left town this morning. Mentioned something to one of the shop owners about having to pay back somebody—" With that, the sixty second tape cut off.

*Payback.* Jane's adrenalin hit the roof. She grabbed her shoulder holster, snapped it across her body and shoved in her Glock pistol. Tearing open her fanny pack, she quickly pulled out two extra clips and secured them in her front pockets. She threw on her leather jacket to conceal the gun and started down the hallway when she stopped and quickly ran back into the bedroom. Flinging open the closet door, she grabbed her duffel bag and emptied the contents onto the floor. She rummaged through the assorted items until she located the square, thin, black leather container that held her police badge. Jane hid the badge in her back pocket and ran down the hallway toward Emily's bedroom door.

She tried the door. Still locked. "Emily!" Jane shouted, pounding on the door. "Unlock this door! Let me in!"

An eerie silence fell around Jane. Something was very wrong. She backed up several feet and kicked the door with her cowboy boot, sending splinters of wood flying across the floor. With one final devastating kick, directly onto the doorknob, the door flew open.

Emily was gone. Her pajamas lay in a heap on the floor. Her jeans, boots and shirt were missing from the chair where she'd left them. Jane turned. A gust of wind blew in through the narrow front window. The window screen had been punched through and tossed onto the front lawn.

"Oh, God, don't do this!" Jane shouted as she spun around and ran out the front door.

# Chapter **28**

Jane skidded to a halt outside the house on the front pathway, quickly observing the scene. From what she could tell, it looked as if two separate footprints—one belonging to Emily and one clearly belonging to an adult—left indentations in the dewy grass and tracked away from the house, heading down Main Street toward town. The sidewalk was quickly filling up with parade watchers. Orange cones and wooden barricades lined the periphery, preventing people from walking into the street. Half a block up toward the highway, Jane saw a crowd of parade participants busily getting into line in preparation for their procession down Main.

Jane looked up in a nearby tree and saw a city worker adjusting a patriotic flag. "Hey! Did you just see a little girl being grabbed out of that window over there?"

"Uh-huh," he said, casually.

"Did you notice where the kid and the guy were headed?"

"*Guy?* There was no guy."

"She was alone?"

"No. That woman . . . what's her name? She works at the real estate office . . ."

"*Kathy?*"

"Yeah, Kathy. She walked up there and, I don't know,

I guess asked her if she wanted to watch the parade or something—"

"Oh, shit," Jane muttered under her breath. "Did you notice where they went?"

"They walked under the barricade and across the street, headin' down Main." Jane scanned the growing crowd on the other side of the street. She ran to the Subaru and started to get in when the city worker called out to her. "Hey, you can't drive anywhere until the parade is over! City regulations! The street's blocked!"

"It's an emergency!" Jane shouted back to him.

"Lady, you can't drive anywhere! They can't have gone far. You're better off catching up with them on foot!"

Jane slammed the car door and brusquely fought her way through the throngs of revelers. She slunk underneath the orange wooden barricade and raced across the street, repeating the same maneuver on the other side until she reached the empty sidewalk. Jane ran down the sidewalk, scanning the crowd for any sign of Kathy, Heather or Emily. A block and a half up Main Street she spotted Heather leaning against a metal stair rail. As usual, the child had a petulant look on her face as she stood with her arms tightly folded across her chest. Jane made a mad dash for her.

"Heather!" Jane said, out of breath, "Where's Emily?"

"I don't know any Emily!" Heather said with a nasty tone. "I know a *Patty*—"

"*Where is she, Heather?*" Jane yelled, tiring of the kid's attitude.

"You better stay away from me! If you hurt me, I'm telling the sheriff!"

Jane suddenly looked up at the building behind Heather. "For God's sake!" Jane yelled as she tore up the front stairs of the sheriff's office and ran into the building. She stopped momentarily when she stepped inside the antiquated office. A heavy wooden counter stood ten feet in front of her. There wasn't a soul in sight. She heard two voices speaking in quiet, subdued tones in an adjacent room. Jane lunged toward the counter's latched door and tried to open it, but it was locked. She jumped onto the counter and spun over to the other side. Once her feet hit the marble green flooring, she could see Sheriff George having a serious conversation with Kathy. "Hey!" Jane called out in a clipped shout as she moved toward them. They turned in unison with looks of apprehension on their faces. Jane walked toward Kathy. "You stupid bitch!"

"*There!* You see, Sheriff?" Kathy said, standing closer to Sheriff George's side. "That's the kind of hairpin anger I'm talking about!"

"Now, look," the sheriff warned Jane, "you better just calm yourself down."

"You have no idea what's going on here!"

"I have a very good idea!"

"Where's Emily?" Jane demanded.

"Emily? Right, *Emily*. She's just fine and dandy," the sheriff replied.

"Where is she?" Jane shouted.

"She's safe. She's in the back room with our deputy," Sheriff George said sternly.

Jane started for the back room. "I have to talk to her!"

The sheriff moved his large physique in front of Jane, halting her progress. "You don't need to be talking to her right now—"

Jane stared down the sheriff. "You don't understand—"

"Oh, yes I do. I know you're not who you say you are. I know you are not that child's mother!"

Jane took a step back. "Oh, Christ," Jane mumbled as she ran her fingers through her tangled brown hair. She didn't want to deliver the bombshell in front of Kathy but she realized she was backed into a corner. "Okay, look, before I go into this, I want it known that I have done everything above board and according to procedure."

"Is that right?" Sheriff George retorted, a smug look on his face.

"Yes!" Jane said, taking offense at his tone.

"Is slapping that child across the face part of your 'procedure?'"

Jane was rattled by the sheriff's question. She searched for the right response as Kathy stared at her. "I . . . ah—" Jane stumbled on her words.

"Do you deny assaulting that child?" the sheriff intoned.

"She was hysterical. She was hurting herself. She'd just heard devastating news—"

"So you decided to assault her to make the news more pleasant?"

"Stop saying 'assault'! I did what I had to do!"

"Ah! You *do* admit striking the child?"

"Yes, I hit her! Look, what happened back at the house is between the kid and me! No one else needs to get involved!"

"You mean, like, Social Services?"

Jane regarded the sheriff with a confused stance. "Social Services? This is bullshit! Time is ticking away! I've got to talk to her!"

Jane started for the back room when the sheriff once again stood in front of her. "She is perfectly alright back there!"

Jane knew she had to spill the whole story. The familiar, off-key clamor of the Peachville High School marching band could be heard moving down Main Street. Jane turned to Kathy, "The parade's starting. Go outside and watch it with Heather."

"I'm staying right here," Kathy defiantly replied.

Jane let out an exhausted sigh and faced Sheriff George. "Fine. You know I'm not her mother—"

"And I know your name is not Anne Calver. Your real name is Michelle Mason."

"Michelle Mason? *What?*"

"You were arrested earlier this year for methamphetamine production. Your vehicle was impounded by the Denver Police Department but somehow you managed to get it back—"

Jane realized the sheriff did a license plate check on her Subaru and the data still showed the previous felon who owned the car. "Shit! PD didn't change the plates!"

"How's that?"

"The plates! They didn't change the plates before they gave me the car!"

"Is that right?" Sheriff George rolled his eyes in contempt.

"My name is Jane Perry. *Detective* Jane Perry. I work homicide at the Denver Police Department."

"Sure you do," the sheriff replied in a dubious tone.

Jane was outraged. "That kid in there is Emily Lawrence. In case you were paying attention to Denver news, six weeks ago her mother and father were murdered in their Washington Park house. Certainly you heard about it! It was the top story for weeks! If you don't believe me, get on the goddamn phone, call DH and ask for Sergeant Weyler!"

"Sure. I imagine he'll be in his office on a Sunday, not to mention July fourth!"

"For God's sake! I'm telling you the truth! I was hired to protect her!"

"Is assaulting her part of that protection?"

"Jesus!" Jane reached into her back pocket to pull out her badge but before she could touch it, the sheriff grabbed her arm and swung her over a nearby desk.

"That'll do, Ms. Mason!" Sheriff George said as he forcefully held Jane's left arm across her back and used his other hand to keep her chest flat against the desk. "You're giving me no choice! You're looking at kidnapping, false imprisonment, impersonation, assault—"

"I was reaching for my badge! It's in my back pocket!"

The deputy exited the back room, closing the door behind him. "Hand me my cuffs, Travis!" Sheriff George yelled to the deputy.

The deputy walked over to the sheriff, cuffs in hand, and muttered loud enough so Jane could hear what he was saying. "Man, the guy from Social Services was dead on about how she was gonna react."

"What guy from Social Services?" Jane demanded.

Sheriff George flipped open the cuffs. "The fellow who got here in the nick of time and alerted us about you! He's in the back talking with the child."

Jane's heart began to race. "Oh my God! Chris! No!" The sheriff was just about to slam the cuff across Jane's wrist when she quickly slipped her freed right hand into her jacket and pulled out her Glock. In a high-voltage adrenaline rush, she kicked the sheriff's leg, throwing him off balance. He let go of her left wrist just long enough for Jane to peel herself off the desk, spin around, grab him around the neck in a chokehold and shove her pistol against his temple. Kathy shrieked, backing up against the wall. "Shut up!" Jane yelled at Kathy. "I am not fucking around!" Jane turned to the deputy. "You! Slide your gun across the floor!" The deputy complied. Jane turned to Kathy. "Don't you try anything stupid or I'll fucking shoot you!" Turning back to the deputy, Jane yelled, "Get over here! Reach into my right back pocket and pull out my badge."

The deputy hesitated.

"Do what she says!" Sheriff George bellowed.

The deputy carefully approached Jane and pulled out her badge. He took a look at it and held it up to the sheriff. "It looks real, Sheriff."

"You're goddamn right it's real!" Jane said. Keeping a tight chokehold on the sheriff, Jane spoke in a quieter, yet forceful manner. "That guy in the back room is not from Social Services. His name is Chris Crawley and he's responsible for murdering six people. Emily is next on his list. Now, are you gonna help me or not? Because either way, I'm busting through that door!"

"Alright!" Sheriff George quickly agreed. "Let's do it!"

Jane let go of the sheriff and raced toward the back room and the closed door. Kathy ran outside, calling hysterically for Heather. The deputy retrieved his gun and followed behind the sheriff as they set up point with Jane. The sheriff signaled to Jane that he would go first and then she should follow. Jane nodded. Sheriff George backed up two steps and slammed his foot into the door, sending it open in a chaotic flurry.

The sheriff, gun pointed forward, moved quickly into the room. "Get down!"

Jane entered the room, gun drawn. The deputy followed.

There was no one in the room.

"Shit!" Jane yelled.

"He was only talking to her for a little bit. She seemed in shock, but I chalked it up to your—"

"Where the fuck did they go?"

"Out the back door!" Sheriff George said nervously.

Jane bolted toward the door and flung it open. She walked outside, gun held out in a defensive stance, scanning the immediate area. Nothing. Jane noted two depressions of footprints in the wet grass that lead to the left and around the building. She followed the quickly disappearing wet footprints toward the front of the building. When she reached the sidewalk, Jane had to make a decision. Did Chris turn right or left? It was an accepted fact that when a perp is fleeing a crime scene, most of them turn right. It made even more sense for Chris to go right since all the major parade action was heading to the left down Main Street. If he was trying to take Emily somewhere discreet, chances are he would turn right and head for the park or the highway.

Jane holstered her Glock and took off up the street. But it was nearly impossible to make headway with the packed crowds of people standing on the sidewalk. The discordant sound of trumpets blended with tubas. Each time the drum majorette threw her baton into the air and caught it, the crowd applauded and let out whistles of appreciation. Chris had found the ideal diversion in this Independence Day celebration. Jane tried valiantly to push through the throngs of bodies, but she was losing ground fast. She spotted a graduated brick wall that surrounded one of the houses. At its highest point, Jane figured it stood about ten feet high. If she could crawl on top of the brick wall, she knew she would be able to see far more than from ground level. Taking quick steps up the narrow blocks, Jane reached the top of the narrow wall. She got her balance and canvassed the scene with her eyes. "Emily," Jane whispered, terror gripping at her heart, "where are you?"

Just then, Jane looked about a half block up Main Street toward the park. A girl's head turned around in Jane's direction as if in response to Jane's query. It was Emily. Chris was walking closely alongside her, his right arm tightly gripping her right shoulder. Directly under Chris' jacket, Jane could faintly make out the barrel of a gun wedged into Emily's side. As soon as Emily turned her head, Chris' right hand immediately came up and slapped her face forward. "You son-of-a-bitch!" Jane shouted above the roaring parade noise. Jane scrambled down the side of the brick wall and jumped the rest of the way to the sidewalk. Her adrenaline kicked into high gear as she frantically pushed her way through the crowd. She factored that Chris was about seventy-five feet in front of her. "Emily!" Jane yelled in a futile attempt to get her attention. "Emily! I'm right here!!" Jane continued shoving people aside and plowing through the spectators. The band became louder and the crowd grew more exuberant, creating a tense background of chaos against the chase. "*Emily!*" Jane sprinted within fifty feet of Chris and the kid.

Jane's frantic voice alerted Dan, who was standing on the hood of his parked Ford truck, watching the parade, directly in line with Emily. Dan spotted Jane in the crowd and knew something was very wrong. Noting Emily and Chris, he put two and two together, figuring Chris was Jane's ex-husband. He jumped off the hood of his truck and made a beeline toward Emily.

As Jane closed in on the scene, she saw Dan moving

toward Emily and Chris. "No! Dan! Get away from him! *Get away!*"

But the parade mayhem prevented Dan from hearing her warning. Dan shoved his way through the crowd and grabbed Emily by her left arm. She jumped, startled by Dan's sudden appearance.

"Dan!" Emily shouted in mortal fear. "Help me!"

"You fuckin' get away from her!" Chris ordered Dan.

"You ain't hurtin' her no more!" Dan yelled back, trying to grab Emily.

"I said get away!" Chris shouted. With that, Chris pulled his pistol away from Emily's side and slammed it hard against Dan's forehead.

Dan fell to the ground, sending several parade watchers scattering. Blood poured from a deep gash on Dan's forehead as he fought to stay conscious. "Run, Emily!" Dan yelled, almost incoherently. "*Run!*"

Emily bit down on Chris' arm, causing him to release his grip. She slipped into the crowd and charged across Main Street, nearly knocking down several marchers.

Chris turned, realizing that Emily was gone. He stared at Dan, still struggling on the sidewalk and lowered his pistol, aiming at Dan's head. "You fucking asshole!"

Jane moved within twenty feet of the scene. "*Gun! He's got a gun!*" Jane screamed.

The crowd scattered. Chris holstered his pistol and followed Emily's trail across Main Street, around the parade floats.

Jane reached Dan just as Chris bolted across the street. "Are you alright?"

"Yeah. Get help for her!"

"I am the help!" Jane yelled as she tore across Main Street.

Emily breathlessly darted over backyard fences until she reached the open meadowland that framed their Peachville house. Her youthful, agile build allowed her to stay far ahead of Chris as she tore through the tall grass and slopped through muddy inlets where the nearby lake overflowed. She was making excellent progress when she suddenly plunged waist high into a hidden pool of muck and algae. She struggled to break free, attempting to pull herself onto the slimy embankment. But each time she grabbed for a branch, it splintered and she felt backward. Emily could hear Chris fast approaching. Fighting through the deep sludge, she struggled ten feet to the left where the tall grass grew in dense clusters. She sunk into the muddy water, leaving only her face above water, camouflaged against the thick grass.

Chris rounded the corner, sloshing through the same muck that trapped Emily. He stopped dead in his tracks. His breathing was labored as sweat poured from his brow. Emily held her breath, taking care not to make a move that would send a ripple of water toward Chris. Chris started to move forward when his right foot plunged into the dark recess of the muddy inlet.

"Shit!" he yelled. Dislodging his foot, he grabbed on to a strong branch and pulled himself onto the bank. Looking around the grassy area, he decided to take off to the right, away from the mud pool.

Once he was out of sight, Emily pulled herself out of the muck and took off running in the opposite direction, toward the water tower.

Chris turned, hearing the slipslop of racing feet in the distance. He saw Emily making tracks across the meadow. "Goddamn you!" he yelled as he took off after her.

Jane came to the waterway just in time to see Chris heading toward Emily. To stay hidden from him, she opted to take a dense path that curved around the lake and then sneak around the back of the water tower.

Emily burned tracks into the soggy grass, cheating several glances back at Chris. When she reached the water tower, she stood for a second staring up at the foreboding, olive green metal ladder that led four stories up to the top of the tower. *This was it*, she thought to herself. This is where it all became real.

Breathlessly, she started up, becoming more terrified with each step. Turning, she saw that Chris was closing in on the tower. Panic propelled Emily up the ladder. Once she reached the top of the tower, she stole a look down. Chris was several steps up on the ladder. The hot sun beat against the metal tower, causing a profound glare. Emily pulled away from the edge and, shielding her eyes from the shimmering metal, frantically looked for anything she could throw at Chris. Spotting a small heap of gravel, Emily quickly gathered the pebbles and returned to the ladder.

Chris was halfway up the ladder. "Get away from me!" Emily shrieked, angrily pelting him with the rocks.

"Fuck you!" Chris yelled back to Emily, skillfully dodging the stony barrage and continuing his ascent.

Emily dumped every last pebble she had on his head. She started to turn to retrieve more rocks when Chris' hand clamped down her ankle. Losing her balance, Emily fell forward onto the burning hot metal surface, her scream echoing into the distance. Chris heaved his narrow frame onto the top of the tower, almost doubled over from exhaustion. Emily flipped over on her back, but Chris grabbed hold of her shirt, preventing her from moving another inch. He worked his way back onto his feet, let go of her shirt and pressed the sole of his shoe into Emily's solar plexus.

"You fucking little snitch!" Chris muttered as he drew his pistol from the holster. He lowered the gun toward Emily's left eye. "Say 'good-bye,' Emily."

With tears streaming down her face, she screamed, "No! I won't!"

Chris was so deeply embedded in the moment that he didn't hear the approaching sound of boots charging up the second ladder, directly across from where he stood. He was seconds from pulling the trigger when he caught a glimpse of motion. Chris turned, just in time to see the top of Jane's head cresting the tower. Without missing a beat, he swung his foot off of Emily's and aimed his gun toward Jane's head. He fired a round, narrowly missing Jane's left ear.

"You fucking bitch!" Chris angrily screamed as he jerked Emily up to a standing position, wrapped his arm tightly around her tiny neck in a chokehold and wedged the barrel of the gun against the kid's temple.

Almost simultaneously, Jane rolled onto the top of the tower, pulled out her pistol and aimed it directly at Chris. The searing heat reflected off the tower and onto her prone body, issuing a burnt smell of metal. For a moment, the bright light blinded Jane. Her head spun as she held the Glock outstretched with her right hand and supported herself with her left. The visions were becoming a ghastly reality.

"Well, fuck you, Jane! Fuck you!!" Chris roared.

"Chris! Don't do this!" Jane shouted, frozen on the hot surface of the tower.

"You couldn't just let it be, could you?"

There was a sense of disjointed reality for Jane as if she'd already gone through this hell. She carefully stood up, lifting her left palm from the tower's surface. In shock, she saw a depressed, backward imprint across her flesh. Glancing down, Jane recognized a domed cap with the raised date of 10-24-99. Impossible, she thought, but true. "Put down the gun, Chris," she said, her voice low and restrained.

"Why didn't you just tell me what this little fucker knew from the get-go? I'm your partner! You owed it to me!"

"I didn't know anything, Chris."

"Don't sell me that bullshit! She was talking to you all along! Whispering her little secrets back and forth! She was talking about me! *Me!*"

"She didn't know it was you until this morning!"

"Don't fucking lie to me!" Chris exploded, jamming the barrel of the gun harder against Emily's temple. Emily winced, paralyzed with fear. "All your little whispers. Like that first day when you interviewed her and she whispered her little secrets in your ear. You wouldn't tell me! All you had to do was tell me what she said. Then I could kill her and finish the whole fucking thing. *But no!* You wanted to slowly nail my fucking ass to the cross. Well, I don't sit back and roll over that easy! I won't be taken out because of some brat blabbing to the Department! I've worked too hard to get taken out! Nobody takes me out! *Nobody!*"

"Taken out?" Jane said. "Did the mob threaten to kill you if you didn't do their bidding? Is that it?"

"Fuck you, Jane! Nobody threatens me!"

"But they did, didn't they?" Jane replied solemnly.

"I'm nobody's fucking errand boy! I do my own bidding! I have power over people! *I live well!*"

Jane found herself glancing down to Chris' pant leg—it was stuck on the top of his custom cowboy boots, exposing the shaft of the boot. Staring back at Jane on the shaft was the starkly stitched pattern of a wolf's face. Jane steadied herself. Off to the left, she could see Sheriff George and his deputy plodding through the meadow and heading toward the water tower. Dan was not far behind them. Chris was so out of it, he didn't hear them advancing. Jane looked at Chris' bloodshot eyes. "What are you on right now, Chris?"

"I'm not on fucking anything!" Chris snarled, his voice full of rage.

"Then what are coming down off of?"

"Oh, this is rich! A fucking alcoholic telling me—"

"It's meth, isn't it?" Jane yelled.

"What does it matter? If it's Sunday, it's meth, if it's Monday, it's coke—"

"You're not thinking clearly!"

"Well, I'm thinking more clearly than you! You call me on the phone and that coal train passes while we're talking. The fucking coal train, Jane! There's only a few towns that a coal train still goes through. You gave yourself up and you didn't even know it! So, who's not thinking clearly here?"

"That train covers twenty or thirty miles. Why'd you choose Peachville?"

"I'd already been doing some research with my private consultant who explained the Department's criteria for a good safe town. So I just plugged his info into the equation. It took a couple weeks to figure out but here I am!"

"What private consultant?" Jane asked warily.

Chris smiled broadly and let out a guttural snicker. "Who do you think was keeping company with your ol' man all those weeks when you were incommunicado?" Jane felt as if the wind was knocked out of her. "After you left, Dale and me got even tighter than we were before."

Jane felt sick. "Before? I don't believe you."

"You don't think your own dad would sell you down the river? Think again!"

"I never told him where I was going!"

"Procedure, Jane. The Department has always had the same criteria for a good, safe town. It was the same for him when he was on the job as it is now. He gave you up, Jane. It was like talking to the magic genie. That coal train just sealed the coordinates down to a smaller area. The rest was all *me*. Me knowing you. Me knowing how you act and what to tell the good sheriff. *You're so fucking easy, Jane*. Don't you know that?"

Emily winced as Chris dug his forearm into her neck. "Jane . . ." Emily muttered.

"Shut up!" Chris yelled at Emily, squeezing her even tighter.

Jane saw that the sheriff and his deputy had quietly taken up strategic positions next to the tower. Dan followed suit. "You want to kill somebody?" Jane shouted, trying to divert Chris' attention away from Emily. "Kill me!"

"No!" Emily screamed.

"Oh, fuck! I thought I already did that! I thought that was you under the blanket that night. Not Martha! Christ, I gave you so many chances to look good. I had that bum with the cigarette case I took from the house. Weyler would have gone for it. But you had to throw the wrench in it. Then there was good fuckin' 'Christian Ron!' You know the trouble I went through to set up that asshole? He could have gone down for it and everything would have been sweet! But you stuck your fuckin' nose in that one, too!"

"You would have been found out one way or the other!"

"Do you mean this little bitch here?" Chris tightened his grip around Emily's neck. "Shit! I had all that worked out! I'd wait 'til the smoke cleared and you were away from her. Then I'd track her down in Cheyenne and take care of business!"

"Chris, listen to yourself! You're not rational!"

"You try tweaking off meth and tell me how fucking rational you are!"

Jane had to buy time. "Is that how it all started? Getting high on meth? The Stovers?"

Chris was taken aback by Jane's words. His surprise then quickly turned into hatred for Emily. He pushed the gun barrel with more force into her forehead, leaving a circular imprint in her skin. "I knew it! I knew your dad would open his fucking mouth!" he yelled at Emily.

"*I* figured it out, Chris! Emily didn't know shit! Chris! Look at me!" Jane was desperate to distract Chris. "Why'd you do it?"

"What choice did I have? You think I was gonna let that prick Stover walk into the DA's office and give me and the others up? They thought I was doing it for them! To protect their asses! But I was doing it all for *me!*"

Jane observed his body language. "But they still threatened your life."

"*Fuck you!*"

"Is the meth one of the perks?"

"Don't get righteous with me, bitch! Don't pretend you're not an addict! You know what it feels like when you can't get it! And you know how good it feels when you finally taste it!"

The sweat dripped down Jane's face under the searing solar glare. "I am a drunk! But as fucked up as I am, I'll never be as fucked up as you!"

"Oh, Jane, I look at you and it's like I'm looking in a mirror! We know what hell looks like because we've been there, baby. We love the dark and the shadows and everything that goes with it —"

"Don't shove me in your nightmare, Chris!"

"You know you love it! You just don't want to look bad in front of the kid!" Chris pressed his lips against Emily's ear. "You want to know the truth about your pal?"

"I don't care!" Emily said, choking on her tears.

"Of course you care!" Chris said, jerking Emily closer to him. "She's got a real appetite for brutality. It's amazing she hasn't kicked the shit out of you, 'cause she's into serious pain."

"It's not true!" Emily yelled defiantly.

"It *is* true!" Chris stared at Jane in silence as a twisted grin crept across his face. "Emily, you love little secrets, don't you?" he said with an eerie quiver to his voice. "Wanna know a dirty little secret about your protector? Violence runs in her blood. She likes to punch hard because she likes to be punched. She loves to get the shit kicked out of her." Jane's eyes widened in shock. "Gee, Jane," Chris said with a crazed look. "Now, who do you suppose told me that little gem of family trivia?"

For Jane, it was as if the earth turned on its axis. All that had come before fell away. Every memory that had haunted her faded into the background. There was no apprehension. There was no doubt. There was no fear. There she was, standing there with both hands wrapped around the Glock. And there was Emily and the absolute knowing inside of what she had to do.

"Emily?" Jane said, as an intangible calm washed over her.

"Yes?" Emily quietly responded, fearful of what she knew was to come.

Jane focused on Chris but her innate connection to Emily was palpable. "Look at me, Emily." Emily peered up at Jane through the reflected sunlight. If there truly was any kind of otherworldly link between them, Jane prayed her thoughts would resonate loudly. "Do you understand, Emily?" Jane asked, not quite sure if it was possible.

"What the fuck is going on here?" Chris interjected.

Jane directed every ounce of energy to Emily. "Do you understand, Emily?"

For Emily, the dream fused into the moment. "I do," Emily replied in terror.

"Hey!" Chris yelled out. "Who's in charge here?"

Jane raised her pistol to Chris' forehead. "I am, Chris." There was a whisper of silence between them, before Jane yelled to Emily, "Now!"

Jane pulled the trigger. The bullet hit Chris square between the eyes. Within that second, Emily skillfully ducked just as Chris' finger depressed the trigger on his pistol. The bullet from his gun singed past Emily's scalp. A surge of blood poured from Chris' head wound, splattering across Emily's face and shirt. Chris fell backward, his arm still tightly encircling Emily. Emily reached out toward Jane as she felt herself heading over the edge of the tower with Chris. Jane raced across the tower and grabbed Emily's wrist, just as Chris began his fatal descent. The momentum, however, proved too powerful for Emily. Still grasping onto Jane's wrist, Emily slipped over the rim of the tower, slamming her chest against the metal side.

Jane fell to her stomach, hanging on to Emily's wrist. Chris hit the ground head first, snapping his neck backward with a loud pop. Emily screamed, flailing against the side of the tower.

Emily turned her tear stained face toward Jane, slightly losing her grip on Jane's wrist. "Don't let go!"

"*Hold on to me, Emily!*" Jane ordered Emily as she let go of her Glock and slid her other arm over the side of the tower.

Sheriff George, along with his deputy and Dan, ran toward Chris' body, kicked away his gun and called up to Jane. "I've radioed for help!"

"I'm gonna die!" Emily shrieked.

Jane looked down at the trio standing sixty feet below, realizing it was too risky for them to try to catch Emily. "Emily!" Jane said abruptly. "You want to live?"

"Yes!" Emily said, choking on her tears.

"Then quit thinking you're gonna die!" Jane felt herself losing her grasp on Emily. "Grab my wrist with your other hand!"

Emily complied. The child's weight started to pull Jane over the side. To brace herself, Jane curled the tip of her boot around an eight inch metal rod that jetted out from the tower's surface. "I'm gonna pull you up, but you gotta help me. Come on!" Jane harnessed every last ounce of energy and yanked Emily toward her. Emily tightened her shoulder muscles and wedged her boots flat against the side of the tower. The child struggled against gravity but was finally able to reach the edge of the tower with her hand. Jane grabbed Emily by the belt loop of her jeans and hauling her frail body closer to safety. With one last pull, Jane swung Emily onto the tower's flat surface.

Emily collapsed into Jane's arms. "I'm safe," she sobbed, as if questioning it.

Jane held her tightly. "You're safe."

Emily buried her head in Jane's chest. "It changed," she whispered. "It really changed."

"What changed?"

Emily held on to Jane tightly and then passed out.

# Chapter 29

The Denver police contingent—led by Sergeant Weyler—showed up in Peachville about three o' clock that afternoon. They spent four hours at the water tower, taking crime scene photos and interviewing Sheriff George and his deputy. Emily was driven to a local doctor's office to be examined and then released to her home in Peachville, in the temporary care of a nurse.

By seven p.m., the shooting death of Detective Chris Crawley in Peachville was the top story on every Colorado news station. Likewise, everyone in Peachville knew the true identity of Jane Perry and that she pulled the fatal trigger. Jane paced nervously in the front yard—a cigarette carelessly dangling from her lips—and watched as cars crept in front of the house. The occupants often pointed at her. Some of their faces showed fascination and awe; others looked disgusted and angry.

"How does it feel to be on display?"

Jane spun around and saw Dan standing on the sidewalk, outside the front gate. "Dan!" She quickly crossed to the gate. "How's your head?"

"Oh, it's nothin'. Couple stitches."

Jane noticed that Dan seemed reticent. "Are you sure you're okay?"

"I'm fine. How's Emily?"

"She's in her bedroom with the nurse and Sergeant Weyler. They're talking. I haven't had much of a chance to be with her since it all went down."

Dan looked away. "I keep thinking this is some sort of dream . . . or nightmare. God, what you must think of me—"

"What are you talking about?"

Dan stiffened, keeping his distance. "All the comments I made to you about cops and how worthless they were—"

"Dan, I agree with you! I don't have a lot of respect for most cops—"

"And me tellin' you how I was gonna rescue you! Man, I looked like a fool all these weeks!"

"Dan, you did rescue me . . . and Emily."

"You don't need to patronize me—"

"If you hadn't distracted Chris, God only knows what would have happened!"

"You weren't that far behind them—"

"Every second counted! You *did* make a difference. And that's not me bullshitting you!" Jane let out a deep sigh. "Look, I realize this is awkward. But I want you to know something. I hated having to lie to you all those weeks."

"You were just doin' your job," Dan replied curtly.

"Okay, fine, you're pissed off at me. I can deal with that. But Emily really likes you. Before we leave, you owe her a decent good-bye. So do me a favor and put aside your attitude when you talk to her!" Jane turned toward the house.

"Jane, wait!" Dan called out. She turned around. "I don't want to leave it like this between you and me." Dan gathered his thoughts. "It's my own damn fault. I thought maybe you and me and Emily had a future together. I just gotta get my head straight. And I gotta face the fact that I never really knew you."

"You did know me, Dan. Do you remember when you and I were walking around the carnival after the dance contest? You told me about your sister and that ex-husband of hers that almost killed her."

"Yeah. What about it?"

"You compared your ex brother-in-law to my supposed ex-husband. You told me that when a woman is used to gettin' beat on, she tends to pick that kind of man, and she doesn't even realize that she's doing it. Then you said that you'd bet a dime to a donut that that's the kind of guy I'd fall for. And you were right."

Dan stood dumbfounded. "You're so much better than that, Jane."

"You know, I've said those exact words on the job to hundreds of women. They just ring differently when they're aimed back at you."

Dan teared up. "From this moment on, you deserve the best life that anyone could ask for."

Jane was touched by his words. "Thank you. Now, all I gotta do is convince myself of that."

"Tell Emily I'll come around later to say good-bye." Dan turned and walked down the street.

Jane discarded her dying cigarette and quickly lit a new one. Weyler had been inside talking to Emily for over an hour. Jane felt like she was at the whim of protocol and other people's agendas. She was just about to storm into the house when she caught sight of a familiar car parked across the street. It was Kathy. There she was sitting in the driver's seat with Heather buckled into the passenger seat next to her, gawking at Jane. Jane clipped her cigarette between her lips and barreled across the street toward the car. Kathy started to jam the key into the ignition. Jane rounded the hood of the car, heading toward the passenger door. "Take the key out of the ignition, Kathy!" Jane ordered with every ounce of cop attitude.

Kathy dutifully obliged, scared to death. "What's going on?"

Jane swung open the passenger door. "Get out of the car, Heather!"

Heather turned to her mother, paralyzed in fear. "Mom! Do something!"

Jane quickly reached in, unbuckled Heather's seat belt and dragged the kid out of the car by her arm. "I said get out of the car and I mean it!"

Kathy stormed out of the car and onto the sidewalk. "Where are you taking her?"

"Police business!" Jane said with a serious tone.

"Police?" Kathy said, frightened. "But wha—"

"Stay on the sidewalk, Kathy! This is between your kid and me!" Jane lugged Heather across the park about fifteen yards before jerking the child behind two large bushes that obscured them both from sight. Jane kept a tight grip on Heather's shoulder as she leaned down to get on eye level with the kid. For dramatic effect, Jane pushed back her jacket to reveal her Glock in its holster. Heather shook with fear. Her eyes widened when she spied the gun.

"Well, look at you!" Jane said. "You're really shaking!"

"I . . . I . . ." was all Heather could force out of her mouth.

"How does it feel, Heather?"

The kid couldn't take her terrified eyes off the Glock. "Please, don't—"

"How does it feel to be so terrified and so trapped at the same time? That's exactly how Emily felt when you locked her in that closet!"

"Please . . . I—"

"How does it feel to think you're gonna die?"

"*Die?*" The air caught in her throat. "I don't want to die. Don't shoot me!"

Jane eyed Heather with a sinister glare as she sucked the life out of her cigarette and flung it on the green grass. "Shoot you?" She waited, oozing the kind of intimidation usually set aside for hard-core criminals. "Well, let me think about that." Jane said, as if she were actually contemplating the notion of plugging the brat. "No, I think shooting is too damn good for you. Here's the deal,

Heather. I've always known the truth about you. Now, you know the truth about me. So, here's some advice. Number one, I strongly suggest that you straighten up fast and be kinder to those around you. And number two, you better grow eyes in the back of your head. Because you will never know when I'm gonna be right behind you. You may think that you're all alone, but I'm gonna be watching you. And if I see any sign that you are harming another human being . . ." Jane stopped and sent angry blades of malice toward Heather.

Heather seized up, cringing at what was coming next. "Wha—What?" she stuttered.

A satisfied grin crept across Jane's face. "If I told you, I'd ruin the surprise."

Heather bought Jane's story. Jane matter-of-factly adjusted the kid's collar and glanced down at the moist grass where Heather stood. Jane found another reason to smile. "So, you're gonna remember what I've told you?"

"Yes," Heather replied, still frightened.

"Okay. You're gonna walk back to your mom's car, you're gonna get in and you're gonna keep your mouth shut about everything I just said to you. Because if you don't, this entire town is gonna find out that you just wet your pants. Do I make myself clear?" Heather's mouth dropped open. Jane leaned closer to the kid's face. "Do I make myself clear?" Heather nodded, absolutely terrified. "Go on! Get outta here!"

She watched Heather make a mad dash across the grass toward the car, jump into the vehicle and urge her mother to get in and drive fast. Jane lit another cigarette as Kathy tore up Main Street. Just then, Jane spotted Weyler walk out the front door carrying a briefcase. As usual, he was dressed in his tailored navy blue suit, crisp white shirt and crimson red tie. She made a beeline toward the house and met him on the front steps. "Can I go in and see her now?"

"Not yet. The nurse hasn't finished with her," Weyler replied, sitting down on the porch steps, his long legs awkwardly extended.

Jane anxiously sat next to him. Weyler clicked open his briefcase and pulled out a sealed plastic bag that held a one page, single spaced, typed letter. The notepaper had obviously been crumpled into a ball and then recently flattened. "After I got your call today," Weyler said, "I stopped at the Lawrence house per your instructions. I pushed on that damn desk for fifteen minutes to find the secret button. Finally, I got that back compartment open and I found this." He handed Jane the plastic bag. "You were right."

Jane looked at the paper. "The letter." Reluctantly, she read it to herself.

*David,*

*After we talked the other night at my office, I gave your offer of help a lot of thought. I hope it wasn't the booze talking on your end, because I really need you to back me up in case the shit hits the fan. I got myself painted into a corner and I now I have no choice but to testify and tell the court what I know about the T. mob and all the Denver big shots that front for them. They're going to be putting Yvonne and Amy and I into protective custody until it blows over. But, like I told you, I got a bad feeling about things. I'm pretty much screwed either way you cut it. When I told you the names of the players the other night, I couldn't remember the last name of that homicide cop I mentioned. You know? The one from the Denver Police Department? Well, I remembered it. It's Chris Crawley. He works homicide at the Denver PD. I've never met the guy, but from what I've been told, he's a loose cannon. He works both sides of the fence. From what the boys told me, late last year he cut in on some off-hours 'security' jobs downtown in the immigrant section where the T. mob has a foothold. He was strong-arming the Asians, lying to them, telling them they had to have protection if they wanted to succeed. He got some sweet deals out of it, money, a boat in trade, etc. Anyway, the way I heard it, the T. mob said they were going to blow* his cover to the higher-ups in the police department if he didn't agree to what they said. So Crawley agreed to work with them. But it wasn't like they had to twist his arm to do it. I heard he pretty much got off on the idea. He protects them. He hides evidence for them. Sometimes, he even steals evidence so it goes permanently missing. He'll lie in court for them. But here's the thing, David. The word I got is that he'll partner with them on hits and then work the same case to swing attention away from the mob. He got fucked up on meth like I did so there's no telling what he's capable of. The thing is, I was just shooting the shit with one of the mob guys and I let it slip that I knew about the cop. And I may have mentioned that I told you about Chris. David, I was high and I wasn't thinking straight when I said it. Anyway, I'm not sure but I think it might have gotten back to Chris. It doesn't take a rocket scientist to figure out the rest.

I don't know who to turn to right now and I sure as hell don't know who the fuck to trust. You're the only one I've told this to. You can't tell Patricia. She'd go fucking nuts. I just figured after your offer of help, that if I got it in writing, you'd have proof if anything happens to me. Keep this letter like we talked about. If they kill me, maybe this'll hold up in court and Yvonne and Amy will at least know that I tried to do the right thing. I've done the wrong thing for so long and fucked up my life and the lives of my family. If the mob does take me out, at least I'll die with some integrity.

Please hide this letter in a safe place until everything blows over. And watch out for yourself and your family, okay? Knowing me isn't safe right now.

*Your friend, Bill*

Jane handed the letter back to Weyler. "'Nobody takes me out.' That's what Chris said up on the water tower. They threatened to kill him if he didn't do the murders. Do we know any of the other players that Stover was going to give up?"

"No."

"So, you're telling me that every single one of those victims died for nothing?"

"That's what I'm saying," Weyler said somberly as he placed the plastic bag with the letter into his briefcase.

"How did we miss the connection between the Stovers and the Lawrences?"

"Chris ran some pretty good diversion tactics. Hey, we checked computers, email, interviewed coworkers—"

"There were photos of them together, boss!"

"Yeah, I just saw them inside when I talked to Emily."

"They were stuck way in the back of Emily's bedside table drawer. I had a helluva time prying them loose. But I never once thought to look through them!"

"The ball got dropped on that one, but everything else we did *was* thorough. Look, it's damn difficult to put two and two together when someone on the inside is constantly screwing with the equation."

"You know, every time I sat in this house and tried to piece the case together, I never once considered Chris in the mix. I thought . . . I thought it was you."

Weyler looked at Jane. "How did you reason that one out?"

"You put me in a town with no backup. You make a point not to inform Sheriff George. I can only talk to you and no one else. And you're always talking about your 'connections' and people who owe you favors. I mean, come on, boss. It all added up."

"Well, let's see. I put you in a town with no backup because there was no viable reason to get others involved and we didn't want to attract unnecessary attention. As far as I was concerned, you were just laying low until we caught a break in the case. I chose not to inform the sheriff because I was told that Sheriff George can't keep his mouth shut. I only wanted you to talk to me because, once again, it simplifies everything. As for my 'connections,' well, what can I say? You hang around long enough, you have connections. It doesn't mean they're nefarious in nature. That was just the spin you decided to put on the word."

"Then tell me this: when I was going through the Lawrence file, the Property Report Form from the crime scene was missing. Why did you leave that *one* page out of my pack?"

"One of the evidence techs must have forgotten to copy it and send it upstairs."

Jane wasn't expecting that simple an answer. "They forgot to make a copy?"

"Apparently so." Jane shook her head in stunned silence. "So, Detective, if you don't mind my asking, how are you doing?"

Jane stared off into space. "Oh, shit, boss. I don't know. When I woke up this morning, I thought I knew who I was."

"And now?"

"Now I don't know anything."

"That's not true."

Jane knew she couldn't share her odd, paranormal experiences with Weyler. "It's been a weird six weeks, boss. And it all lead up to me . . ." Jane's voice trailed off.

"Did you think you could actually kill a man—even a man who deserved to die—and not feel something deep down in your gut?" Jane was surprised at Weyler's candor. "Good God, Jane, you're not a damn robot. When did you start thinking you weren't allowed to feel like the rest of us?"

Jane's mind drifted back to that loathsome memory so many years ago. "A long time ago, boss."

Weyler observed Jane. "Because of what your father did to you?"

Jane looked at Weyler in shock. "You know?"

"I don't have to know the details. All I know is that you've walked around your entire adult life talking yourself into a lie."

"You're losing me, boss."

"You've told me that you've been dead for years. But you're very much alive. You walk around with that cocksure swagger because you think you're inadequate. I've told you many times, you're one of the smartest people I've ever met. You believe that evil breeds evil. So, you think you're evil. But your heart tells me differently. Your actions don't equal your perceptions, no matter how hard you try to fit that mold. All these years, you've been living an illusion. You're not dead. You're not stupid. And you're sure as hell not evil. Your father? That's another story. As always, it comes down to that inevitable question of nature versus nurture. Your good nature triumphed over your nurturing. Jane, you've been waking up in someone else's nightmare for a long time. Let it go."

Jane let his words sink in. She took a drag on her cigarette. "All the stories we tell ourselves. All the convictions we serve that don't serve us. It's like falling into the ocean and you're hanging on to the towrope of a boat. And it's dragging you under, and killing you. But you hold on because you think it's your job to drown. We're all just too afraid to let go of that towrope."

"You let go of that towrope, Jane, and you might find freedom."

Jane took another drag on her cigarette. "That's a frightening proposition."

"Fear is a brilliant weapon, my dear." Weyler stood up.

Jane turned away from Weyler. "When you finally come face-to-face with the thing you fear the most, the thing that's been dogging you for your entire life . . . when you really look at it for what it truly is . . . it's not that it's easy . . . but . . ." She looked at Weyler. "I killed a man today in order to save another person's life. And I don't regret it. But there's no satisfaction in it."

Weyler rested his hand on Jane's shoulder. "I want you to take some time off."

Jane nodded. "Yeah. I think I will." She stood up and faced Weyler. "I got to do some thinking. I gotta figure out where I fit in and what I'm good at."

"I already know the answer to that one."

"*I* gotta know it, boss. I've got to be able to picture where I'm supposed to be."

"Well, how about this: Picture yourself sitting at Sergeant Hank Weiting's desk down the hall from me. He retired last week so that office of his is real empty and just begging for a competent individual to occupy that swivel chair."

"Boss, I don't know . . ."

"I hear you." Weyler started off down the front pathway. "Sergeant Jane Perry. That's got a damn good ring to it." Weyler glanced back at Jane, who returned his look with a skeptical expression.

The nurse exited the front door. "She's asking for you," she said to Jane.

Jane tossed her cigarette and jumped to attention. "Good. I need to talk to her."

"She needs to be unconscious for a while. I gave her a sedative five minutes ago." Jane winced at the thought. The nurse handed her a prescription bottle. "When she wakes up, if she's the least bit fretful, give her two more. That should even things out."

"Even things out?" Jane's said in a mocking tone. "That's a tired euphemism, don't you think? Be honest. You want to keep her numb."

"That's the kindest thing you can do for that child right now. I'll check in tomorrow morning." The nurse strode down the path and out the front gate.

Jane stared at the bottle of pills. "And so it begins," she said to herself.

She entered Emily's bedroom, quietly closing the door behind her. Emily lay under the covers with her back toward Jane. Jane set the bottle of pills on the dresser and started out the door when Emily spoke up. "I'm not asleep."

Jane walked to the bed. "You're gonna be out of it in a few minutes."

"No, I won't." Emily turned around to make sure

nobody else was in the room before letting two pills slide out from her pajama sleeve.

Jane smiled at Emily's slight of hand. She sat on the bed. "You know, the nurse wants you to take those so you'll sleep."

Emily rolled on her side facing Jane, resting her head in her hand. "Maybe I don't want to sleep." A sporadic "boom-boom-bang" sound erupted outside the house. Emily turned, startled for a second. "What's that?"

"They're setting off fireworks in the park across the street."

Emily rolled the little white pills between her thumb and first finger. "The nurse said these would help me forget my problems. But I think she was lying."

"Why?"

"She looked down and to the left when she talked to me. She kept covering her mouth with her hand. But it was more than that. It was the sound of her voice when she said, 'Here, take these and you'll feel so much better when you wake up.'" Emily pitched the pills across the room. "I'm never gonna forget it, am I?"

"No. It'll always be with you. Sometimes the memory will stand next to you; sometimes it'll fall into the background. But it'll never completely leave you. You can take all the pills and drink all the booze but it'll always be there when you wake up."

Emily considered Jane's words. "Were you and A.J. good friends?"

"I didn't really know her well enough to be her friend. Our job was to sit in the car and do night watch on the house. I went inside the house once to introduce myself. She smiled at me from across the room. She seemed like a real nice kid."

"You tried to save her life, didn't you? That's how you burned your hand."

"Yeah."

"You know, I knew A.J. better than anybody else. We were like twins. We'd think the same thoughts. We were connected." Emily paused. "Just like you and I?" Jane was taken aback by Emily's statement. "And you know what I know?"

"What's that?"

"She doesn't hate you because you couldn't save her." Jane was silent. "Okay?"

"Okay," Jane whispered.

Emily held Jane's hand. "I'm sorry I ran away from the house. I'm sorry I trusted Heather and her mom. But more than anything, I'm really sorry that you got kicked." Tears welled up in Emily's eyes. "That must have hurt you a whole lot."

Jane felt a tear stream down her cheek. "Yeah. It did."

Outside, several *pop-pop-pop* explosions signaled a gigantic display of color and light. A mushroom of green, blue and red quickly flared into the night sky, followed by a breathtaking gold and silver fountain of cascading fireworks.

Emily took in the glowing spectacle, then turned back to Jane. "Happy Independence Day."

Late Monday morning, July 5, Weyler drove Jane and Emily back to Denver. Once back at Headquarters, paperwork was signed, reports were taken, and logistics were arranged for transporting Emily into the custody of her aunt and uncle in Cheyenne. Weeks earlier, the child's possessions had been collected from her home, packed into boxes and set aside for later shipment until her situation was determined. While it broke department protocol, Jane insisted upon driving Emily to Cheyenne. To expedite matters, Mike had driven Jane's Mustang to DH. The family was expecting Emily at their Wyoming house by 8 p.m. The last official document was signed and sealed at 6:15 p.m., prompting Jane and Emily's frenetic exodus out of DH five minutes later.

The ninety minute drive to Cheyenne was somber and filled with few words. Emily spent most of the trip clutching her Starlight Starbright navy blue vinyl case and tiny travel bag as she stared out the window. A wide, lonely expanse of dusty land lay in front of them as they crossed the Wyoming state line. At 7:45 p.m., Jane rolled her Mustang in front of the narrow, one hundred and fifty foot, dirt and gravel driveway that led to Emily's new country home. The modest one-story, rural house stood against the stark summer sky as the setting sun draped a warm orange glow over the melancholy scene. Jane turned off the engine and looked around the area, noting the stone cold silence that painfully lingered in the air.

"Well," Jane eventually said, "here we are."

Emily stared straight ahead, almost afraid to look at the house. "Can't we drive around some more? It's not eight o'clock yet."

"You'll feel the same way in fifteen minutes. Why stretch it out?"

Emily looked down at the floor mat. "How come I can't live with you?"

"Emily, you know why—"

"No, I don't!" Emily replied, somewhat defiantly.

"There's a lot of reasons. The top one being I'm not a blood relative."

"Blood?"

"People you're related to by blood ties. Like your aunt and uncle."

Emily turned and eyed the long driveway and unpretentious house. A look of scorn came over her. "I only see them once or twice a year. I've slept in that house three times in my entire life. I've spent more time with you in the last month and a half than I've spent with them in my whole life. They don't know how I like my eggs cooked. They don't know what music I like. They don't know my favorite candy. They don't know anything about me." Emily started to softly cry.

"When we first met, I didn't know anything about you."

Emily turned and looked Jane in the eye. "Yes, you did." It felt like a loaded reply to Jane. "You knew everything about me. You knew what I was thinking. And what I felt inside." Emily knew it was time to finally say it. "You knew me before you knew me."

Jane was stunned. She felt her mouth go dry. "What are you talking about?"

Emily stared out the front window. She'd practiced this in her head many times but she still wasn't sure how it would sound. "When I was in my bedroom closet . . . before I remembered what happened to my mom and dad . . . I fell asleep. At least, I think I fell asleep. I had a dream . . . even though it didn't feel like a dream." Jane felt the hair on her arms tingle. "I saw you." Emily's breathing became more rapid. "You were standing across from me on this . . . hot . . . metal . . . round thing. I didn't know what it was then. But the light was blinding. And I was scared because you were pointing a gun toward me. And I could feel . . . his arm around my neck and I could smell the heat off the metal. I looked down . . . and I saw the face of a wolf staring back at me." The fear of that moment gripped Emily. "And then I looked back up at you and I . . . I heard your voice in your head and it was saying that you didn't think you could save me. But I *knew* you could! I knew you were the only one who could do it." Tears welled in Emily's eyes as she turned to Jane. "It wasn't a dream because it came true." Jane's heart raced. She kept telling herself that this couldn't be happening—that it was too bizarre. Emily reached out to Jane. "When I saw you in the stairwell that day, I couldn't believe it. You were in my dream and now you are real. I'd found you. Just like you found me, but you didn't know it yet." She turned to the house. "They'll never know me like that. They'll never feel what I feel or think what I think. They'll never know what I've seen. You're the only person in the whole world who will ever really know me."

Jane swallowed hard and tried to get hold of herself. "There's no way you could live with me. I don't know what my future holds. But whatever I decide to do, there's always going to be a lot of grit in my life. That's no environment for a kid to grow up in. Anyway, I'm nobody's mother."

"You were mine for awhile and you were good at it!"

Jane looked outside the window, desperately trying not to lose it. "The last six weeks were like a controlled game. Living the real, day-to-day with me is completely different."

"Is what we had been broken?" Emily asked, tears streaming down her cheeks.

"I don't know. Maybe it was a moment in time that opened up . . . Maybe it was . . ." Jane realized that intellectualizing was futile. Jane reached out and stroked Emily's long brown hair. "Emily, all I know for sure is this: there will not be a day that goes by when I don't think about you."

"For true?"

"For true."

"I want to know how to picture you so I can feel like you're still with me."

"Why don't you just picture me standing beside you."

"How are you gonna picture me?"

Jane thought about it. "Growing up. Going to school. Laughing with your friends. Being happy.

"I don't know how I'm ever going to feel happy again. How can I be happy when I saw them on the floor?"

"Emily," Jane said with a serious tone, "look at me." The child turned to Jane, her eyes sad and lost. "You might not be able to understand these words, but I want you to say them every single day for the rest of your life. I want you to say, 'I had this experience, but it didn't have me.'"

"I had this experience, but it didn't have me."

"That may not make any sense to you right now, but one day, it's gonna click and you'll feel . . . a sense of freedom. It would be so easy for you to blame Chris for ruining your life. But, take my word, it'll just end up destroying you. Don't feed the memory. You do that and you give him so much power—power he doesn't deserve. If you do that, his memory will take over your life until you can't figure out where he ends and you begin. Don't let him live inside your head and tell you lies about who you are. Don't let him define who you become. And no matter how much you want to, don't picture him as some kind of towering monster. Think of him as if he were a small, dry leaf that's easily crushed when you walk over it. If you can do that, he will *never* have power over you."

Emily really thought about Jane's advice. "You know what?"

"What?"

"When I grow up, I don't want to be what I want to be. I want to be who I am."

Jane smiled. "Well said."

"When I talked to my aunt on the phone today, she told me that I'm supposed to go see a therapist."

"I think that's a good idea."

"You do?" Emily said, seeking Jane's approval. "I thought you didn't like therapists."

Jane shifted in her seat. "Perhaps I spoke too quickly. There's nothing wrong with sitting down and talking to someone about what happened to you."

"Are you going to sit down and talk to someone about what happened?"

Jane smiled. "Have you and Sergeant Weyler been communicating?"

"No. I just thought—" Emily reached over and brushed her finger across Jane's scar. "I just thought that maybe if you could talk to someone who knows things, maybe they could make this not hurt so much."

Jane clasped her hand around Emily's palm as her emotions got the better of her. "Do you think that's possible?"

"I think pretty much anything is possible. Even the things that don't make sense are possible."

Jane's attention was drawn toward the house as Emily's aunt and uncle exited their front door and peered down the long driveway at Jane's car. Emily turned, looking more irritated than happy to see them. "Come in with me," Emily said.

"No," Jane replied, wiping away her tears. "You need to walk up that driveway alone." Emily threw her arms around Jane's neck, holding on to her tightly. Jane, in turn, wrapped her arms around Emily. "You have my home phone number and my work number," Jane whispered into Emily's ear. Emily nodded, still holding on to Jane for dear life. "You call me whenever you want. Okay?"

"Uh-huh," Emily said, sobbing on Jane's shoulder.

Jane pulled Emily away from her chest so that they were eye-to-eye. "They're waiting for you." Emily lowered her head. "You don't have to look back," Jane whispered in Emily's ear. "I'll be right here."

Emily reluctantly let go of Jane and sadly collected her Starlight Starbright vinyl case and small travel bag. She opened the door, hesitated and then turned back to Jane. "I love you."

"And I love you," Jane said, her voice cracking. Emily got out of the car and closed the door. She stared up the gravel driveway, clutching a bag in each hand. "Go on," Jane quietly urged the child.

Emily softly cried as she walked forward. Slowly, she made her way toward the house. Jane got out of her car, never once taking her eyes off of Emily. She peered across the Mustang's shimmering roof as Emily neared the house. The child suddenly stopped walking and bowed her head.

"Don't," Jane whispered. "Keep going, Emily. Don't look back."

Emily lifted her head and continued her journey up the driveway. Her aunt and uncle ran toward the child and cradled her warmly in their arms. Emily's aunt looked toward Jane's car and waved. Jane returned the gesture, taking in the familial scene. Once they were inside the house, she climbed back into her car and lit a cigarette. After several long drags, she turned on the ignition and drove down the road.

Jane could have headed straight home. But thirty miles down the road, she pulled off the rural highway, got out of her car and lay on the hood of her Mustang staring into the night sky. For the first time in her life, she had no clear mission planned—no sense of where she was meant to be. But she felt something close to her—like a heavy page turning. The sounds of the warm night echoed in the distance. The soft hum of trucks in the distance blended with a lone red-tailed hawk circling above her three times before disappearing into the distance. Jane lay there for three hours waiting for an answer that never came.

She got back in the Mustang and drove south toward Denver. Lighting a cigarette, she checked the time and flicked on the radio, turning to the familiar station.

". . . And so it is, my peripatetic voyagers of the unconscious mind," Mooney said with his characteristic warm resonance. "Like all cycles, my time with you has come to an end." Jane felt a twinge of sadness at Mooney's announcement. "Your regular host will be back tomorrow from her time off and I will wander off toward my next uncommon foray into the marvelous unknown." Jane smiled at his atypical tangle of the English language. "To fall into that place and allow the current of synchronicity to sweep me toward my destiny, ah, now that is true bliss. My, my . . . I think I just got a chill. But then again, did you ever have an experience that gave you a chill and then wonder if you were just standing in a draft? How do we connect the dots between what we know from what we can't understand? Do we chalk it up to a strange moment in time? Or do we trust, quietly holding that experience against our heart and protecting it in that sacred space when, for one implausible instant, we saw the face of God in our own reflection?" Jane let Mooney's voice wash over her. "If not now, my friends . . . then when?" There was a long, thoughtful pause. *"When?"*

Jane drove into the night and let the towrope slip gently from her hand.

Here's an excerpt from Laurel Dewey's

next novel featuring Jane Perry.

## REDEMPTION

On sale in hardcover now.

THE
STORY PLANT

"Barmaid!" Jane Perry yelled above the din of the smoke-laced barroom. "Two more whiskeys for me and two tequilas for my friend!" Jane came to an unsteady halt in front of the waitress, her back to Carlos. "You got that?" Jane said, her eyes asking another question.

The waitress cautiously looked at Carlos before quickly locking back on to Jane's iron gaze. "Yeah. I got it." The waitress headed back to the bar.

Jane nervously lit her fifth cigarette of the hour and surveyed the sparse crowd mingling in the center of the bar. The dim lighting painted heavy pockets of darkness across the tables and chairs, making it difficult to discern faces. A dozen beer-splattered Christmas garlands hung carelessly against the nicotine-soaked walls. It was the bar's inept attempt to define the holiday season, but the cheesy decor reminded Jane of topping a dead tree with a broken angel. The Red Tail Hawk Bar was located on East Colfax in Denver, Colorado—a location that supported seedy establishments and attracted drug deals, bloody brawls, and twenty-dollar hookers. The clock with the beer keg image read 4:45. Within thirty minutes, Jane knew the grimy hole would be packed with hard-core drinkers and enthusiastic partiers, all looking to find a warm refuge from Denver's December chill and to extend their stoned post-Christmas revelry. Her jaw tightened, a sign that the stress was taking its toll. The deal had to go down tonight, and it had to go down exactly as Jane planned it. Wearing a mask of bravado, she turned around. "You said 4:30. We're fifteen minutes past that. I'm not used to waiting!"

"Chill out, Tracy," Carlos replied in a lazy tone, his oily, black hair obscuring his pockmarked, swarthy visage. "I told you I'd hook you up. This is a busy time of year. Santa may have stopped sliding down chimneys two days ago, but Camerón and Nico are still in business."

Jane drunkenly moved around the pool table. "Shit, man, I'm jonesin'."

"Have another shot," Carlos suggested, motioning over to the approaching barmaid and her tray of shot glasses.

"Two tequilas," the barmaid said, setting the shot glasses in front of Carlos, "and two whiskeys," she managed to stammer as she slid two shots in front of Jane and surreptitiously tilted her head toward two men who had just entered the bar.

"Is that them?" Jane asked Carlos, dismissing the waitress and angling her pool cue in the direction of the front door.

Carlos squinted against the poor lighting. "See? I wasn't fuckin' with you!" Carlos raised his hand, catching the eye of Camerón and Nico, who made their way through the syrupy darkness.

Jane felt her heart race as the two Columbians moved toward the pool table. They were as imposing as she expected. Both were in their late thirties, but their road-ravaged faces made them appear fifteen years older. They seemed to drag the darkness of the bar behind them as they loomed closer. Camerón was the lead guy, but Nico was clearly an equal partner.

"Hey," Carlos said, proud to be part of this nefarious deal. "How's it goin'?"

"It's goin'," Camerón said, sizing up Jane.

"This is Tracy," Carlos said. "She's *real* happy to see you guys!"

"Are you?" Camerón replied, his black eyes boring holes into Jane's face.

"You got the stuff?" Jane asked, crushing her cigarette into a nearby ashtray.

"You think I'm stupid enough to bring a quarter kilo inside a fuckin' bar?" Camerón quietly replied with a sharp timbre to his voice.

"Where is it?" Jane said, undaunted.

"First things first," Camerón announced. "You check her out, Carlos?"

"Yeah, she's got the fifteen Gs."

"No gun?" Camerón asked Carlos, never taking his eyes off Jane.

"You think *I'm* stupid enough to bring a gun inside a fuckin' bar?" Jane retorted, echoing Camerón's prior statement. She noted a stream of patrons entering the bar and realized if she didn't move things along, the set-up was going to get complicated. "I got your cash." Jane opened her leather jacket to reveal a fat envelope secured in an inside pocket. "Where's my coke?"

"You gotta love these trust-fund snow junkies!" Nico said with a cocky grin.

Camerón stared at Jane for what seemed like an

eternity. Jane matched his steely glare, hoping he couldn't hear the deafening beat of her heart. Finally, Camerón nodded. "Take a shot to kill that edge and then we'll go out to the car," he suggested.

Jane grabbed one of her two shots and quickly knocked it back. "Let's do it," she declared, taking a drunken step away from the pool table.

Camerón eyed the remaining shot of whiskey, shrugged and drank it. Jane turned toward him as the last drops of liquid slid down his throat.

"What the fuck—" Camerón said, checking the aftertaste. He grabbed Jane by the arm. "How do you get drunk on tea?"

Jane started to react, but Camerón moved too quickly. He jerked Jane's body toward him, opened her leather jacket, and pressed his palm against her side. "She's wired! *She's a cop!*" Camerón pulled out his nine-millimeter handgun and aimed it at Carlos. "You dumb motherfucker!"

Jane caught Camerón's hand, moving it just enough off target for Carlos to escape the deafening gunshot. The shockwave sent the bar into a frenzy. Patrons ducked for cover as Jane skillfully punched the butt of her pool cue into Camerón's groin, causing him to drop the gun. She kicked the pistol under the pool table with her boot as Nico drew his gun, aiming it squarely at Jane's head. Jane rapidly swung the cue at Nico's forearm, deflecting the gun before it discharged. A split second later, Carlos leaped onto the pool table and took a forceful dive onto her body. The loosely hung fluorescent light fixture above the pool table crashed down as Jane hit the wooden floor with a hard thud. As the fluorescent tubing exploded around them, Carlos landed a brutal punch to Jane's right cheek.

"Fuckin' bitch!" Carlos screamed, nailing Jane with another savage smack.

Jane managed to roll onto her back and slam the side of the pool cue against Carlos's forehead. The momentary dazing afforded her the opportunity to struggle to her knees, just as a burly male bar patron jumped into the mêlée. Chaos broke loose as the muscle-bound guy pounded Carlos's head against the pool table until he passed out. Jane, slightly woozy from the two punishing blows that Carlos had delivered, ducked under the pool table and swept Nico's handgun under a nearby chair. But as she turned her body, the thick envelope of cash slid out of her jacket and onto the floor, spreading several hundred dollar bills under the pool table. Jane reached for the envelope, but Nico quickly snagged it and disappeared with Camerón into the dark recesses of the bar.

Jane achingly emerged from underneath the pool table just as the beer keg clock came loose and smashed to the floor. A stream of blood spilled from Jane's lip and she stood, disheveled, amidst the chaotic aftermath.

All eyes in the bar focused on her.

But one set of probing eyes was more intensely interested in her than the rest.

*So begins Jane's next adventure. After the events in* Protector, *Jane has resigned from the Denver Police Department. Trying to make her living as a private investigator, she finds her past haunting her at every turn and her old demons rising up to torment her. Seeking some level of comfort at an AA meeting, Jane encounters a woman who knows what Jane does for a living. The woman wants Jane to drive with her from Colorado to Northern California in search of a man who matches the* description of the killer who murdered her granddaughter many years before. She's convinced that the man has started to kill again and she wants to stop him.

Jane thinks the woman is crazy—especially when she discovers that she's a New Age devotee—but Jane is desperate for work. They head out on the road, gathering critical information about the killer, and themselves, along the way. Jane has recently experienced several events in her life that seem to border on the paranormal, though she is a complete skeptic in that regard. Now, those experiences come with greater frequency. And when the trail of the killer leads to a fundamentalist church, the consequences of belief and faith propel her toward a deadly confrontation.

Once again, Laurel Dewey has created a novel as rich in character as it is in suspense. Juxtaposing spirituality and religion, mission and manipulation, revenge and redemption, this is a powerful, taut mystery that will confirm the author as a top-flight storyteller.

You can read a longer excerpt of
**REDEMPTION**
at
www.laureldewey.com
and
www.thestoryplant.com

JUNE 6,
2010